# DEAD HAPPY

## Murder or Mercy?

*Warwick & Fru Jaggard*

*Call no man happy 'til he is dead*
Aeschylus (525 – 456 BC)

DEAD HAPPY
Copyright © Warwick & Fru Jaggard 2010
All rights reserved.

This is a work of fiction and any similarity to
places, events or people, living, dead or unconscious,
is purely coincidental.

No part of this book may be reproduced in any form by
photocopying or any electronic or mechanical means,
including information storage or retrieval systems,
without permission in writing from both the copyright
owner and the publisher of the book.

ISBN 978-0-9565026-5-0

Published by
BEECHWOOD PUBLISHING LTD
First Published 2010
Second Edition 2011

Printed & Bound in Great Britain by CPI Antony Rowe, Chippenham and Eastbourne

# *Acknowledgements*

Thank you to Nola Jaggard, Harold Neville,
Brenda McAuley, Nina Vieira, Thuto Mali, Quentin Reynolds and especially Jeanette Murphy for their help and advice.

We are very grateful to our editors Jacquie Sinclair and
Lorena Goldsmith of Daniel Goldsmith Associates, for
their invaluable guidance and support.

To our children, Ria, David and Peter, thank you for
your  love and encouragement during our incredible
journey  in writing Dead Happy.

*This book is dedicated to our parents:*
*Mick and Alice Jaggard*
*Steve and Maria Lillitos*
*Auntie Stella Loizides... Fru's second mum*

# Chapter 1

## The O'Neill Family Secret

*Making provision for your own funeral is not uncommon.*
*Deciding when it would be most definitely is.*

## County Cork, 1860

Father Eammon O'Malley stood at the window in the vestry, looking out over the church graveyard through the light drizzle. It was a bitterly cold November morning and the thought of this afternoon's funeral made him shiver involuntarily. After the mass, he would have to stand outside in the freezing weather, at the mercy of the elements, to read prayers at the graveside of one of his dearly departed parishioners. As the wind sent a spray of dead leaves into the air, it whistled around the leaded glass window shaking it for good measure, and he longed to stay in the warm vestry, where the log fire crackled and beckoned with its leaping flames.

A man in his sixties, Father O'Malley, a rotund and jolly figure with a round face and a ruddy complexion, had been the parish priest for the past twenty years, ministering to the community and attending to their pastoral needs. He was a man of simple pleasures, enjoying reading and rambling, when the weather was clement. But his great love was food and wine, to which his adequate girth bore testament. The notion of braving the cold turned his thoughts towards medicinal help and his eyes fell on a whisky bottle, standing invitingly on the sideboard. 'Just a sip,' he thought, 'just a sip to keep out the chill.'

With a gentle pop, he withdrew the cork and poured a sizeable measure of whisky into a glass, then held it up in a mock salute.

"Praise the Lord," he said quietly to himself, before swallowing a good mouthful. The fiery liquid had an instant warming effect, which spread from his belly to his fingertips and toes.

"Ahh!"

It felt as though his whole body was being heated from the inside.

Now warmed by the alcohol, the thought of going outside seemed a little less daunting and, in any event, the service wasn't for awhile yet, so there was plenty of time to get prepared.

Pouring a second glass, he thought about the New Testament, and in particular Timothy 1, chapter 5 verse 23, and murmured the quotation, "Take a little wine for thy stomach's sake."

This was followed by another "Ahh!" as he sat down by the fireside in a high backed leather chair, gazing at the dancing flames, both mesmerised and soothed by the heat.

It was a pleasant feeling, sitting by the fire, his back moulding deeper into the comfortable chair, while his feet drew warmth from the fire's glow. As he relaxed, a slight grin and his nose growing redder by the minute showed the tell tale signs of growing intoxication.

An hour had passed before he woke, and for a few seconds, he had no idea of the day or the time. A glance at the mantelpiece clock snapped him back to the here and now – one thirty pm – there was a requiem mass scheduled for two o'clock.

"Mary, mother of God!"

The sudden ascent from the comfortable seat left him feeling unsteady on his feet, as he reached out for the arm of the chair, while outside, the wind now howling like a Banshee sounded even stronger. He turned his attention to his robes. Before putting on his purple cassock, he donned an extra vest, and a pair of long johns.

"There," he said to himself, in front of a full length mirror, "all done."

The clock showed ten minutes to two. The cortege would be arriving shortly. He scanned the table next to the fireside chair for his bible, but instead his eyes again fell on the bottle of whisky. Picking it up, he moved towards the library shelf, and withdrew a leather bound volume. Taking one large, final, warming swig, he placed the bottle in the space behind the book.

It had begun to rain as the hearse, drawn by two horses with black head-pieces, pulled up in front of the old stone church, and the undertaker stepped down from the transom. The glass windowed carriage was easily recognis-able as O'Neill & Co's, not by any signage, but by the simple motif of leaves and flowers etched on the glass panels. The elegant design formed a rectangle, with the name O'Neill's Funeral Directors, in the centre, and below that 'Dignitas in morte', the O'Neill family motto, the leaves in the art work, holding the only real clue to the true ethos of their business.

As the fallen leaves swirled through the gravestones in the churchyard, O'Malley stood somberly at the church door, waiting to receive the coffin bearing the last mortal remains of Rosie Fitzpatrick. In the freezing air, the priest's nose shone like a beacon.

Patrick O'Neill, undertaker and senior pallbearer, moved in a solemn and dignified manner to the rear of the carriage to supervise his four assistants, as they slid the coffin from the horse-drawn hearse, and in a manner well practiced, lifted the oak casket, with one fluid movement, onto strong shoulders. Stepping to the head of the casket, O'Neill removed his stovepipe hat and bowed respectfully, holding the position for a few seconds, before straightening up and replacing the hat back on his head. The solemn procession moved from the hearse to the church steps, and, when the pallbearers were almost at door, Father O'Malley turned and walked slowly through, leading the deceased into the house of God. The pallbearers followed at a dignified pace, before finally placing the casket on two stands immediately in front of the altar, and opening the lid. The mourners seated inside, waited patiently for the priest to mount the pulpit and commence the Requiem Mass.

It was almost as cold inside the small village church as it was outside. While not directly exposed to the elements, the gale blew under cracks in the door and through window frames that long ago had seen better days, while the congregation of sixty or so people huddled into their coats, arms tightly folded and hands thrust deep into their pockets. Most shivered at the sound of the wind outside, even the bank of brightly burning candles at the altar failed to create any sense of warmth. At length, the shuffling died down, as Father O'Malley moved from his position by the now opened coffin toward the steps to the pulpit, the *clack-clack* of his heels on the grey stone floor reverberating sharply throughout the church. Slowly, he mounted the steps, stumbling on the final one, before miraculously regaining both his balance and composure. Two women in the front pew and closest to him exchanged knowing looks, pursed their lips and slowly shook their heads. Father O'Malley opened a large and dusty service book and began the mass.

"Let us pray."

Bridie Gallagher, a thin, small woman with a weather-beaten face and a large nose, was seated towards the rear of the church. She had known Rosie

Fitzpatrick very well. They went back many years, first meeting as young wives, after the bad years following the famine and before the children, when times seemed full of promise and life was good. Now here, in this cold, cold church, all she could think about were her feet, freezing, despite the two layers of stockings and stout leather shoes. Kneeling to pray was excruciating and returning to the seated position on the hard wooden pew even more so. But at seventy years of age, what could one expect? Down, then up, down then up again, before finally standing to sing some ancient hymn… it all seemed to take an age. Finally, Father O'Malley closed the service book and began the eulogy.

"Rosie Fitzpatrick was a woman of strong personal beliefs and great character," he began with a slight slur, followed by a small hiccough.

Steadying himself against the lectern, he leaned forward, right elbow positioned on the closed service book, left arm and hand raised to heaven.

"She was a regular worshipper here in this very church for many years and held in high regard by a great number of people in the community."

A sweeping movement of his heaven-facing arm caused his elbow to slip off the lectern and he stumbled forward. The congregation gave an audible gasp.

He paused, gathering his balance and thoughts and continued in a sonorous voice thick with alcohol, slurring his words.

"Her life's work was in the shervice of others, a practice she maintained until illness dishcontunued that work."

The effects of the whisky were embarrassingly apparent to all as he gripped the lectern with both hands. But there was no stopping him now.

"As one of a small band of dedicated worshipers, she regularly helped with the upkeep of the church, attending every Wednesday, no matter how inclement the weather, cleaning the altar, polishing the pews and lighting the candles. She was a blessed sight, to be sure."

There was a long pause as he searched for more virtues to extol. The seconds ticked agonisingly past, but nothing came forth. The priest's mind had reached a dead end, yet still he searched for the next elusive attribute.

"Rosie was a, was a…"

As one, the congregation leaned forward in expectant anticipation of the concluding part of the statement.

Lost in the alcoholic soliloquy, Father O'Malley released his grip on the lectern, and spread both arms in mock crucifixion, eyes raised to heaven, as he opened his mouth to speak. His lips moved, still searching for the words with which to end the eulogy, yet no sound came from his mouth.

"Rosie was a... Rosie..." there was an excruciatingly long pause followed by a flamboyant wave of his arms, "Rosie was a wunnerful woman!"

Mercifully, it was over, a stifled belch signalling the end of the eulogy.

Steadying himself against the pulpit, he looked down upon the small gathering, all of whom had sunk back into their pews. It had been a moment of high anxiety.

"Let us pray."

Throughout the service, the undertaker, Patrick O'Neill, remained at the rear of the small church flanked by his four attendants, all five like statues, hats removed, hands overlapped in front and heads slightly bowed in respect. A large, gaunt man with narrow features and a sallow complexion, his clean shaven face and slick, jet black hair enhanced his dark intense eyes. The effect was striking. In many ways, he resembled Abraham Lincoln without the beard and, despite his proffession he was someone with whom most people felt instantly at ease.

With the priest's monotone echoing throughout the building, Patrick's mind began to drift back to the early days, when he was just a boy and before any of this was even contemplated. He had begun his working life as a carpenter, apprenticed at the age of fourteen – first to a barrel maker and then a general builder, before striking out on his own at the age of eighteen, full of confidence and skill, ready to tackle what ever the world had to offer. What he was not prepared for was a chance meeting with a funeral director at a local tavern.

A hundred and sixty kilometres from home, and seeking accommodation for the night, he chanced upon an inn, secured an evening's lodgings and was drinking ale, when the conversation on the next table made his ears prick up. James McCafferty, the local undertaker was talking to another man and discussing a serious problem – the coffin maker in the village had fallen ill with fever and was confined to his bed and now, with a double funeral coming up in just two days, there were no coffins available.

Opportunity presents itself in many ways. During a lull in the conversation, Patrick leaned across and introduced himself to McCafferty as a carpenter, new to the district and travelling through. The undertaker, a kind old man, had insisted Patrick join his table, bought him another beer and ordered them both a dinner of roast beef and potatoes. The talk flowed easily and, at the conclusion of the meal, their stomachs full and mouths wet with the lingering taste of ale, a bond had been formed.

McCafferty placed his hand over Patrick's.

"What are your plans, young man?"

Patrick was slightly confused by the question.

"I'm not sure what you mean. Plans for now, tomorrow, next year?"

A wave of his hand to the landlord signalled two more drinks.

"You probably overheard me talking to Martin – he's the landlord of this fine establishment."

Martin arrived at the table with two clay pots of the local brew, breaking into a wide smile as the drinks were placed on the table.

"A fine establishment this most certainly is," agreed the owner.

"Thank you, Martin, but now I have important business to discuss with young Patrick here, and it's not for your ears, my friend."

It was a friendly rebuke, devoid of malice and part of the banter between two long standing friends.

With the landlord gone, the old man's tone became more serious.

"If you overheard me talking to Martin earlier, you'll have gathered I'm in a bit of a spot. I need some urgent work done, and, depending on what your immediate plans are, maybe we could come to an arrangement that suited us both?"

Patrick sipped at his beer, as he considered the question, before responding,

"I'll be honest with you, James, I like you. You seem like a decent man and I'd like to help. I've no immediate plans and I don't have to be anywhere tomorrow, or the next number of tomorrows, for that matter. I've set out to see a bit of the country and maybe find my fortune. Exactly, what is it you need?"

"I've two people to bury the day after tomorrow and O'Leary, who's the coffin maker around these parts, is ill and confined to bed. He never keeps any spare caskets. They're all made to order. Have you ever made a coffin before?"

"No, but I can't imagine it's all that difficult. I've been making cabinets and other furniture since I first began my apprenticeship. I'm sure I could make a coffin."

"That'd be grand, young Patrick".

"There's just one problem."

A worried look spread across James' face.

"Problem?"

"Well, for a start, I've no tools, and secondly, no materials."

"That's not a problem. You can use O'Leary's tools and the wood I can get from Burns' wood yard. Do you think you can make the two caskets in time?"

Patrick looked into his ale, deep in thought.

"Providing the wood and tools are available, then yes."

McCafferty looked squarely at Patrick with pleading eyes.

"Then you'll help me?"

Patrick held the look and with a phrase that would one day become the family's trademark, nodded his head and smiled.

"Yes, I will help you."

The wood and tools had arrived by noon the following day and the young O'Neill started the job, working throughout the day and well into the night. True to his word, two coffins were ready on time the following morning, buffed to a fine shine and complete with brass furniture. So professional were the finished articles that he was offered a job to stay and produce not only for this local man, but others in the region as well.

During his three-year stay with the undertaker, living in a workshop on the premises and eating with the other staff, his outgoings were meagre and enabled him to save a modest sum. Those years were also highly instructive, as he frequently assisted with the embalming process and also at funerals, as aide to the chief pallbearer. His quick intelligence, easy charm and natural empathy with those who were suffering, made the transition from carpentry to funeral director a natural move and O'Neill's was born. That was forty years ago. Today, with sons of his own to carry on the tradition he had started, Patrick O'Neill, felt proud to have created something that not only provided a good living for him and his family, but also brought him great satisfaction. It was a true calling, with his sons, showing the same vocational devotion.

A loud bang reverberated throughout the church, as the priest closed the leather bound book, signalling the end of the eulogy and snapping O'Neill back to the present. Father O'Malley commenced the Lord's Prayer, intoning the famous words in a soft Irish brogue.

"Amen," he said finally before moving unsteadily down to the coffin.

Standing next to the open lid, revealing Rosie's upper body, he addressed the congregation, arms outstretched in a welcoming gesture.

"You may now pay your final respects to our dearly departed…"

He began, turning slowly to face the open casket.

'Jesus, Mary and Joseph!'

Quickly composing himself, he continued in a faltering voice, "…to our dearly departed sister *Rosie*."

Making the sign of the cross over the coffin, he stepped to one side, withdrew a handkerchief from inside the priestly garments and mopped the sweat from his brow.

For Bridie Gallagher the service had been a mixture of comfort and sadness – comfort, in the knowledge a mass and a warm if slightly intoxicated eulogy had been said for her friend, but sad, knowing she would never see her again, after today.

A movement to her left broke her concentration on the rosary beads in her hand, as one of the ushers gestured for her to move to the aisle. A queue had formed, slowly moving its way to the open casket in front of the altar, where mourners were paying their last respects. Shuffling forward, while holding the rosary and looking at the stone floor, she was lost in thoughts of the woman she had known for over fifty years and what it must have been like at the end for her.

Barely audible, muffled exclamations of 'My god!', 'Jayysus!' and 'Mary and Joseph!' drifted up from the head of the queue. However, these hardly registered in her brain.

Instead, she was thinking of the time when she had visited Rosie a week before her death and how painful it had been to see the woman suffering so, the life literally being drawn out of her, as she wasted away. She remembered the shock of seeing her that last afternoon and how poorly her friend had become, a far cry from how she had been, just a few short weeks before.

Without realising it, Bridie found herself at the first of three marble steps, leading to the casket, which lay dark and polished, on its stand some two metres away. A short woman, slight and frail, she grasped the wooden rail and proceeded, with some difficulty, up the three steps leading to the coffin. Moving slowly to the body and gazing into the coffin, she was totally unprepared for what she now saw.

Rosie Fitzpatrick, dressed in her best clothes, grinned back at her with a look of indescribable joy, as though she had seen her maker at the moment of death.

The church suddenly felt very warm, as a heady mist enveloped Bridie. Her eyes opened and closed several times in quick succession, before finally rolling back in their sockets. Her knees buckled and the last thing she remembered was Rosie Fitzpatrick's face rushing up to meet her as she collapsed over the open coffin, a loud crack reverberating throughout the church as her forehead hit that of the deceased's. Like a rag doll, her arms draped themselves over the casket, before following her limp body, which slid slowly off the open coffin and onto the floor, where she lay motionless.

Aghast, Father O'Malley watched the whole scene unfold, just a few metres in front of him, but remained rooted to the spot until the woman hit the floor. Then, and only then, did he leap into action, joining the man who had been standing in the queue immediately behind Bridie, and, who was now kneeling at her side. A third mourner quickly appeared and, with an arm wrapped around each of their necks, she was raised up from the floor and dragged unceremoniously to the vestry, where smelling salts were administered.

Some time later, as they gathered in the village hall, Bridie remained both shaken and stirred. The four stiff brandies she had consumed in quick succession had done little to remove the vision from her mind, of her once dear friend Rosie, now a grinning corpse.

"I never expected to see Rosie like that," she confided to one of her women friends. "She looked like she had seen the Virgin Mary – her face was ecstatic and full of joy. Do you suppose the Virgin came to her at the end?"

"Perhaps," her friend whispered confidentially, "but Amy Flynn told me that Rosie had talked to her a while ago, about going out in style. I never really gave it much thought at the time, you know, but now…" the sentence trailed off leaving a void in its wake.

Bridie looked up from the remainder of the fifth brandy she was about to drink, the glass a couple of centimetres from her lip.

She had stopped in mid-flow.

"What do you mean 'now'?"

Her friend paused.

"What do you mean '*now*'?" she repeated, as she drained the small glass.

The friend poured herself another brandy, took a sip of the fiery liquid, looking around to check if anyone else was within earshot.

"Well?" prompted Bridie.

Leaning closer and within whispering distance, the friend quietly said, "There is talk of a *special arrangement*, one can make with Patrick O'Neill."

"Patrick O'Neill?" replied Bridie with a thick tongue, loosened by the alcohol.

"You know, Patrick O'Neill… the undertaker."

The friend gulped down the remnants of the spirit, and refilled both glasses.

"What kind of *special arrangement*?"

"There is talk of being out of it all, when one's time is near and being happy at the end. Some say O'Neill can speed things up, if you want it to be that way."

The two ladies' eyes locked and Bridie gasped at the enormity of what had just been said.

Bridie quickly crossed herself several times.

"Jayyyysus! Mary, mother of God!"

Turning her head to see if anyone else had overheard the conversation, she stopped in mid-rotation at the sight of Patrick O'Neill, standing just a few metres away.

Like a rabbit mesmerised by a snake, Bridie found it impossible to look away. Her stomach turned and her lower jaw gradually fell open as the intense eyes of Patrick O'Neill held her captive. Slowly and imperceptibly, a wry, knowing smile, formed on the undertaker's face. Without warning, he promptly turned on his heel and left the room as the noisy wake continued. She was glad to see him go.

## Chapter 2

## Mrs Papadopoulos' Own Hitman

## Sydney, 2006

The results from the tests had not been unexpected, but hearing them from her doctor had caused her heart to sink... Alzheimer's!

So it ran in the family. She had the same degenerative brain condition as her late mother. However, the one thing which Maria Papadopoulos was determined to ensure was that her own end would *not* be the same. She had other plans for herself, plans that were going to take her from this world into the next in a better and happier way. She left the doctor's office, keen not to waste time, for time was no longer her friend.

Heading immediately for the bus station, she boarded the Number 69. The steely determination that had been the essence of her character throughout her life was about to be applied now, to plan her own death.

She knew *exactly* what to do and who to see.

Fifteen minutes later, she disembarked outside the offices of O'Neill's Funeral Directors. The bus pulled away, leaving just Maria standing there, dressed in black, with a matching black scarf covering her silver hair and clutching a black handbag.

It was the customary attire of a Mediterranean widow who had never remarried. She was small and bird-like, with high cheek bones and pointed features. The lines etched on her thin face, and her hands, misshapen by arthritis, bore testament to the life she had lived, a life of sacrifice and hard work, which had brought her out of the poverty of her early years, to a comfortable retirement in old age.

Supported by a walking stick and squinting in the bright sunlight, she made her way past the adjacent solicitor's office to the front door of the funeral director's premises.

Boldly and without a hint of hesitation, she pushed against the handle and opened the door. The blast of cold air on her face from the air conditioner was a welcome relief from the oppressive heat of the hot January day.

The receptionist, a young woman in her twenties, slightly overweight and wearing thick framed glasses, looked up from her keyboard.

"Good afternoon. How may I help you?"

The voice was friendly and polite.

"I'm Maria Papadopoulos – I am here to see Mr O'Neill."

After all these years, the trace of a Greek accent still remained.

"Do you have an appointment, Mrs Papa, Papa…?"

"… dopoulos, Papadopoulos."

Maria had experienced a lifetime of repeating her name to people who struggled to pronounce it.

"No, I don't have an appointment, but I *do* need to speak to him urgently, so if he's busy, I'll wait until he's free."

Despite her frailty, she still had a commanding presence and a no-nonsense approach which left no room for negotiation.

"Won't you take a seat, Mrs Papadopoulos? I'll let him know you're here."

The old lady lowered herself into the settee, the soft brown leather cradling her bony frame. The young woman knocked on the door, adjacent to her desk and, without waiting for a reply, went straight in, closing the door behind her.

She could hear muffled sounds of the receptionist and a man talking, the tone was urgent, the visit completely unexpected. Maria smiled to herself. The older she got, the better these tactics worked and so far as she was concerned, this was not the time to be making appointments and waiting around. She wanted to see O'Neill immediately.

The spacious reception area was decorated with a sand coloured carpet and pale cream walls. A display of exotic flowers in the corner caught her eye as sunlight poured into the office from the large windows, muted by the wooden blinds opened at a careful angle.

Her thoughts were broken when the door opened and the receptionist came out of the office followed by Michael O'Neill.

He entered the room and extending his hand said, "Good afternoon, Mrs Papadopoulos, I'm Michael O'Neill. I believe you wish to see me, won't you come this way?"

O'Neill's posture was straight and erect in marked contrast to the old lady in front of him. A tall and imposing man, his long narrow face, straight nose, high cheekbones and greying moustache gave him an aristocratic presence. The great grandson of the founder, Patrick O'Neill, he was an empathic, kind man with old school values.

Ushering the old lady into his office, he drew back a chair for her, making sure she was comfortably seated before asking, "Would you like some refreshments? Tea, coffee, a soft drink perhaps?"

"Thank you, a glass of water would be nice."

"How may I be of assistance?" he asked as he poured a glass of iced water from a carafe.

The old lady took a long sip and paused. She faced the undertaker and looking him squarely in the eyes, she began.

"I have come here to make my funeral arrangements, Mr O'Neill. I am eighty years of age and I know that I don't have much time left, so, while I'm still capable of making my own decisions, I want to be sure that the burden of these arrangements don't fall on my family."

"I understand," he said. His tone was measured and sincere.

"We have a long tradition ensuring our clients' wishes are carried out and I can assure you, I have met many people who feel as you do, Mrs Papadopoulos. This is a perfectly reasonable and sensible approach for what we all must face one day."

"I'm glad you understand me, Mr O'Neill."

She paused, searching for the next part of her story. Michael sat silently, letting the old lady speak in her own time, not wishing to prompt or urge in any way.

"I was at the doctor's this morning and he gave me some rather bad news."

"I'm very sorry to hear that, Mrs Papadopoulos," replied the undertaker, genuine compassion in his voice.

"I have been diagnosed with dementia," she faltered, before quickly regaining her composure.

There was a protracted pause as O'Neill listened intently with the fingertips of both hands meeting in a prayer-like gesture.

Touching his lips he spoke gently, "That must be very difficult for you to hear. Do your family know?"

"Apart from myself and my doctor, you are the first person I have told."

"I see. May I enquire of your immediate family?"

Years of experience had taught him how to listen and get to the heart of the matter.

"I have a son who lives here, in Sydney, with his wife and two children and two daughters who both live in America. They're all married to wonderful people and I've been blessed with seven grandchildren."

"You must be very proud of them."

"Yes, I am."

"Do you live alone, Mrs Papadopoulos?"

"I did, but I felt I was getting too old to manage on my own, so I decided to sell my house and move in with my son and his family. They've been wonderful and welcomed me into their home. They even built a small extension for me with my own facilities. That way I felt I wouldn't be under anyone's feet but I'd still have the benefit of being close to my son and grandchildren. Now, of course, in the light of what the doctor has told me this morning, everything has changed."

O'Neill studied her face, sensing that she had still not come to the point of her visit.

"My mother died over twenty years ago when she was eighty two. She was a strong woman, resolute and sharp as a razor and she helped me raise my family after my husband, Stavros, suddenly died, leaving me with three young children and a restaurant to run. When she was about eighty, I started to notice that she was becoming very forgetful. She couldn't remember little things like where the bread was kept or where she'd put the cutlery and she started to repeat herself, telling me the same thing over and over again. At first, it was annoying, but I soon realised there was something wrong and then I became frightened. When the doctor gave us the test results and confirmed she had dementia, my worst fears were realised."

The old lady, her throat dry, extended her bony arm and picked up the glass of water to take a drink.

O'Neill studied her, before speaking.

"So your mother had dementia too – dementia is a very difficult disease to deal with. Your own diagnosis must be very upsetting for you."

The old lady took another sip of water.

"Yes, it is, because I know what's coming. My mother's decline was in many ways as bad for me as losing my husband. During the last year of her life she didn't recognise me or her grandchildren, a woman so strong and independent had ended up in nappies and needed to be fed like a baby. But the worst thing for the family was seeing that somewhere behind the fog, she seemed on occasions to glimpse the real world and we'd have her back for a short while only to have her snatched away again."

Michael nodded.

"I never want to go through that, Mr O'Neill, and I don't want my family to face that either. I refuse to exist like a vegetable or be a shadow of what I was. That's definitely *not* for me!"

The atmosphere was close and charged.

O'Neill broke the silence, "Are you afraid of dying with dementia?"

"I have no intention of dying with dementia!"

Her voice was suddenly forceful and the tone unambiguous.

"I don't want to end up like my mother and that is why I have come straight from the doctor's surgery to see *you*, Mr O Neill."

The undertaker was taken aback.

"I'm not certain I understand, Mrs Papadopoulos?" he questioned, unsure where this was going.

"I am not accustomed to asking for help, Mr O'Neill, but on this occasion, destiny has forced my hand. I need your help to make sure that my life will not end in the same way as my mother's did and that my family will not have to go through what I went through with her. I have to know now, while I'm capable of making a rational, informed decision and having weighed up all the circumstances that I have put in place a plan of action to ensure my wishes are carried out."

The undertaker remained still, his eyes locked on the old lady's as he shifted uneasily in his seat, wondering what was coming next.

"Mr O'Neill, I have heard that you are a man who can be trusted in delicate situations. I want to retain my dignity for as long as I am able, but when I become incapacitated, either physically or mentally, I don't want to linger and I need to know there are people of integrity I can trust who will carry out my instructions."

"I'm not sure I understand what you're asking of me."

"I think you do, Mr O'Neill. I'm asking for your help to die when I'm past knowing or caring. When that day does come, I want to know I've prepared for it and I can only do that with your assistance. I believe, in certain circumstances, O'Neill's offer a *special service*?"

O'Neill coughed. Her candour had shifted the dynamics of the meeting. He no longer held control.

"You talk about a special service, what exactly do you mean?"

There was a long pause.

"You know what I mean, Mr O'Neill. I've seen your work before."

Silence filled the room.

"Do you remember Caroline Hutchinson? She was my neighbour for nearly thirty years. We were very close and before she passed away last year, she told me of an arrangement she'd made with you, God rest her soul. At the end, her face had none of the pain and suffering that had been there in the last few days. That's what I want. If the end is near or I'm not the same person because my mind has gone, then I want to go quickly and I want you to help me. That way I'll go smiling. I'm not afraid of death, Mr O'Neill. It is just a gateway to another world. I will see my husband, my mother and father and all my friends again, of that I have no doubt. No, I'm not afraid of going, but I want to travel first class. When the time comes, I want to check out quickly and I want *you* to check me out. I'll get to the other side with a smile on my face. It's how I want to greet my friends and family and the way I want those I leave behind to remember me. I want to die… happy and, before I go anywhere, I need to have your assurance now, here in this office, that you will agree to carry out my request."

"Mrs Papadopoulos, I don't know what to say – I think you may be asking for something the law expressly prohibits and I'm a law abiding man."

He leaned forward attentively, the palms of his hands open and upwards, searching for the best words in the silent room save for the clock which continued to mark the passage of each second with its relentless *tick-tock, tick-tock…*

"Perhaps…" the dialogue was cut in mid sentence by the old lady.

"There *is* no perhaps! I need to know I can count on you when the time comes. Now *promise* me!"

Caught off guard by her insistence, O'Neill's mind was racing. The special arrangement was normally only used to hasten a painful and inevitable death at the very end of life. His great grandfather, a keen botanist, had created the family remedy to alleviate the distress of people who had no effective pain relief and who would have died in agony. But, in the case of Caroline Hutchinson, a Multiple Sclerosis sufferer, he had administered the family remedy at her request because she wanted to avoid the final ravages of the disease.

Michael was torn. This was an unusual situation, because Maria was asking him to make the decision on her behalf about the right time to administer the fatal drink… 'when she was past knowing or caring,' she said. When the quality of her life was so poor, that she had no dignity. She didn't want to linger and reach the awful end stage of the disease, when she couldn't eat or drink. He'd seen that happen before, when, as a young man, his neighbour, George, who'd been like a grandfather to him, died in that way. The old man was left without food or water by the staff in the nursing home, because he could no longer eat or swallow. There were some long, agonising five days, before he succumbed. George's wife was there each day and there was nothing Michael could do, but watch the terrible end. He couldn't have administered the remedy even if he'd wanted to, because George wouldn't open his mouth. As the nurses were going to let the old fellow die anyway, he'd always wondered, what the point was of letting him endure those last few days. Wouldn't it have been kinder to give him something to end his suffering sooner? He'd heard many similar stories from relatives who'd come to him to arrange funerals for their loved ones.

More than a few had told him that if they could have hastened the end, they would have done so.

He looked at the old lady in front of him. She was genuine, he sensed it, and she was determined to die in her own way, just as he would want to. He had made exactly the same arrangement she was asking for, with his own daughter, should he become debilitated by a stroke or dementia, yet, on this occasion, he wasn't sure what to say or do. Legally, what she was asking was dangerous, but morally, he didn't believe it would be wrong to help her end her days with dignity even if it meant her life would be shortened.

"I'll need some time to think about it. This is not a situation where one can make an immediate..."

Her bony hand shot out and grabbed his forearm in a vice-like grip.

"*Promise* me!"

Her eyes held his as a smile crept onto her face and she winked at him.

"Dead happy... OK?"

The pendulum on the grandfather clock stopped.

There was silence in the room as their eyes remained locked.

She showed no sign of letting go and he relented, "So – you're determined to die happy?"

"Yes, and I'm hiring you to do the job!"

Slowly Michael nodded.

The pendulum resumed its slow to and fro motion; tick-tock, tick-tock...

"Very well, if that's what you want, I will help you, but this is not a matter to be taken lightly. What we are about to discuss must never leave this room."

"Of course."

The old lady relaxed visibly and sank back into the leather chair.

"Circumstances such as this require an agreement and it is important you know the terms of that agreement. Are you comfortable with this?"

"Yes, yes I am."

"Mrs Papadopoulos, my family and I carry on a proud tradition of service, going back one hundred and fifty years. For the O'Neills, this is a true calling in the best sense of the word, but there are occasions when the wishes of the client, in this case yourself, are in conflict with the laws of the land."

Clasping his hand behind his back, he moved slowly from behind the desk to a position adjacent to the old lady.

Drawing up another chair and now sitting to her left he continued, "While what you are asking is illegal, we believe there is a higher moral dimension to be considered. However, this moral dimension usually takes second place to the law. Suffering has many forms, from physical pain to the loss of one's dignity and for some people both are equally intolerable. Are you familiar with Latin?"

"No, I'm afraid I'm not."

"Dignitas in morte, Mrs Papadopoulos… dignity in death. It's the family's motto," he said, pointing to the wall behind his chair at the framed tapestry bearing the O'Neill family crest.

"Dignity in death," and then, in a soft and barely audible voice asked, "is that what you want, when the time comes?"

"Yes, yes it is."

"Then I would be honoured to be of service. Would you like me to explain the procedure now or would you prefer to think about the arrangement at your leisure and finalise matters later?"

The old lady shrugged her shoulders and spread her hands, palms upward, and a smile on her face.

"You think I should wait? Time is not on my side, Mr O'Neill. I've thought about this and I want to finalise the arrangements now."

"Very well. At regular intervals from this day onwards, I or a member of my family will make periodic checks as to your well-being. We are very discrete. If you become infirm or are transferred to a nursing or residential care establishment, we will maintain a vigil. Is this clear so far?"

"Yes, quite clear."

"In the event your health or mental faculties deteriorate to a point we feel you would consider," he searched for the most appropriate word, "undesirable, we would move to the next stage."

His voice was sincere and calming, almost hypnotic.

After a short pause he continued, "The next stage involves more regular monitoring and it is during this stage we would check very closely to discern whether you are indicating in any way that you wish to change your mind. If there is no indication you feel differently about what we have discussed, we would move to the third and final stage."

The word *final* had an added impact in the context and was not lost on the old lady, who swallowed deeply.

Now at the crux of the issue he went on, "Once satisfied that you are in a position you expressly wished to avoid, we will administer a drink. We like to think of it as our family remedy, a sweet drink, which at first will make you very happy and will then put you into a deep and peaceful sleep. Passing occurs within a very short period of time. The liquid leaves no trace in the body. It goes without saying your funeral arrangements would then be carried out according to your wishes."

Michael sat back in his chair, folding his hands in his lap.

"Do you have any questions?"

The enormity of what had been confided rendered the old lady temporarily speechless. It had been said and couldn't be unsaid.

Turning to O'Neill she asked, "Will there be any pain?"

O'Neill leaned forward, gently taking her hand in both of his and looked her directly in the eyes.

"Mrs Papadopoulos, I can assure you that it is painless. You will feel nothing but a sense of complete happiness. My family have used this remedy for generations and, before you ask me how I know the process is painless, let me tell you that, after fifty years in this profession, I know the difference between a passing that is peaceful and one that is not."

"I believe you, Mr O'Neill," she replied, a grateful smile spreading over her face, "do I need to sign anything?"

"We would never think of charging for administering your wishes, that is a sacred trust. However, we do make a small annual fee to cover the cost of monitoring your situation – this is common practice as clients often wish to check on their funerary arrangements and modify or update them from time to time. My daughter Kathleen handles this."

There was another long silence.

"Do you have any more questions, Mrs Papadopoulos?"

"No, you've been very candid and reassuring. Thank you, Mr O'Neill. May I finalise the arrangements now?"

"Consider the important part done. Would you mind if my daughter, Kathleen, joined us to complete the visitation paperwork?"

"Of course not."

The undertaker pressed an intercom button and spoke to his daughter.

"Kathleen, would you join Mrs Papadopoulos and me in my office, please?"

"I'll be right in."

A few moments later there was a gentle knock at the door and Kathleen entered the room.

The family resemblance was immediately recognisable. A tall, slim woman of thirty two with long, jet black hair, Kathleen had a small straight nose, high cheek bones, wide lips and dark, intelligent eyes. Her smile was warm and Maria instinctively liked the young woman.

"Would you be kind enough to prepare some visitation papers for Mrs Papadopoulos, to sign?" prompted Michael to his daughter.

A look passed between them and then Kathleen eyed the old lady. Her father nodded, communicating with his eyes what he required her to do. Saying nothing, she moved to a cabinet and withdrew a series of papers before handing them to O'Neill.

"Mrs Papadopoulos," he said, "this is a contract between yourself and this firm to visit you on a regular basis to ascertain if you require any amendments to your funerary arrangements. Take your time, read through it and, if you are happy, sign where I've placed the pencilled cross."

Mrs Papadopoulos skimmed through the document. She had achieved what she had set out to do. By signing the document, she was agreeing to her own assassination. She would die before her time.

The realisation hit her as she held the contract. She hesitated for only a moment. Casting her thoughts back to her mother's last months and the pressure and strain of caring for her, she remembered how unhappy her mother had been at the end, though she could not express it. Maria recalled how she'd longed for her mother's suffering to be over. Death, when it came, was a welcome relief and Maria knew she didn't want to die like that. Picking up the pen and looking straight at Michael, she nodded and signed the paper.

He faced the old lady and addressed her directly.

"Mrs Papadopoulos, I want you to know that you can cancel this contract at any time. Whatever you decide, we will honour your request."

"No, Mr O'Neill, I won't change my mind. I thank you for taking a great worry from my shoulders."

"If there is anything else I can do for you," he said, handing her a card, "my direct telephone number is on the back."

"Thank you, Mr O'Neill," she replied, rising from her chair and taking his hand, a feeling of relief now spreading through her, "you have been very thorough."

She tapped the side of her nose with an index finger.

"Until we meet again," she grinned, before turning to Kathleen. "It has been a pleasure to meet you, my dear."

Kathleen gently placed her hand under the old lady's elbow while she walked to the door.

"Let me take you out, Mrs Papadopoulos."

It would not be long before those words took on an altogether different meaning.

# Chapter 3

## The Business of Undertaking

## Sydney, 2008

Jerome T Spitz, a fifty eight year old American entrepreneur was loud, colourful and brash and, although he did not have the profile normally associated with the funeral business, the man had taken to it like a duck to water. Driven by an insatiable appetite for success, negotiating and completing a deal was his drug of choice and when it came to strategy, few could hold a candle to him. His crude social morays belied a fox-like guile, where every action was instigated with a specific purpose in mind and each formed a piece of the strategic jigsaw necessary to fulfil the venture's objectives.

Most people saw him as ostentatious and frequently vulgar, but when circumstance dictated, he could be charming and the essence of tact. Everything he did was aimed at achieving a specific goal. Recreation and relaxation were not words in his vocabulary and he had no time for non-work related pastimes. Tall and lean, with a long face, thin lips, a shock of white hair and penetrating grey eyes, he ought to have cut a dashing figure, were it not for his outrageous dress code. Loud, often clashing colours, large check jackets with brightly coloured shoes were no strangers to his wardrobe. In a different occupation, he would have made the perfectly dressed game show host, but the strategy worked on two levels.

First, his persona and appearance gained him notoriety. An unsubtle disposition mirrored by the garish attire made people talk, and talk he courted mercilessly.

Spitz worked on Mae West's premise of it doesn't matter what they are saying, as long as they are saying it.

There had already been several newspaper articles about him, all with pictures and this free publicity helped promote his new business.

Secondly, his outward idiosyncratic appearance masked the true man, cunning and calculating. His agenda was to use any and all means at his disposal to become the largest funeral director on Australia's east coast and thereafter the whole nation. That the plan was ambitious and well publicised was laudable, however no one, except for Angelo Radic, the brawn behind the plan, knew the true extent to which he was prepared to go to realise his dream.

By comparison, Radic was his antithesis. Short and stocky, blunt and with little education, he had a Neanderthal-like appearance and the intelligence of a tadpole. Radic was devoid of all but the most basic social skills, yet somehow he bumbled through life, shunned by one group after another, his inability to blend with those around him equalled only by the ease he found in his own company. Born in 1973, his family had migrated to Australia from Croatia in the former Yugoslavia in 1986 and settled in one of the poorer suburbs of Sydney.

Both parents were unskilled and found jobs in nearby factories, working long hours to make ends meet. This left young Angelo 'home alone' on many occasions, and, without friends in school, he settled into a life of isolation. Yet, even at the age of thirteen, he quickly gained a reputation of someone not to cross. When a much larger schoolboy was teasing him about his name, calling him 'Radish the Vegetable', the joke backfired badly when the former suffered a broken jaw. The irony was that, after this event, the schoolchildren began calling him Angel, and the name had stuck. He rather liked the nickname and was dimly aware of the humour of it, as he looked nothing like the perceived image of an angel. A succession of dead end factory jobs ended abruptly one evening some months ago when he happened upon Spitz at a local pub.

In truth Spitz, ever the opportunist, had sought him out. He had heard of Radic through the grapevine and wanted to meet him, casually of course and in an indirect manner. His plans called for a loyal enforcer, one who was not too bright and who wouldn't question the whys and wherefores of a particular job and Spitz had a feeling Radic might be just that man.

Radic was standing alone at the bar of a local pub drinking a beer and eating small savouries from a bag when Spitz entered. It was immediately obvious to him who Radic was. Short and stocky with a powerful build, there was a respectful distance between him and other patrons. Spitz took advantage of the space, stood next to the Croat and ordered a large beer. Taking a gulp, he belched loudly.

"Goddamn marvellous, I needed that," he said to no one in particular, and then looking at the beer as though it was a precious antique, "almost as good as Krenna."

Radic turned his head at the mention of the word.

"Krenna?" he said in a dismissive voice, "vot vould you know ov Krenna?"

Despite the years living in Australia, the accent was still thick from the old country and he reeked of garlic.

Spitz turned and faced him directly, one elbow on the bar, the other hand holding the glass.

"Krenna, my friend, is the best goddamn beer in the world and the only place you could taste it was in Miranovich."

Radic beamed, "Miranovich – I vos born in Miranovich: my farzer used to drink Krenna all za time."

Spitz's eyes widened and his mouth fell open.

"Well, I'll be a son of a bitch. I was there from '71 to '73, most beautiful place on earth, wonderful people, the most amazing food, and of course... Krenna!"

By now Radic was positively ecstatic. In this brief moment, all the childhood recollections of his home town flooded back – his mother and father in their prime, the simplicity of childhood and a thousand happy memories. Spitz had done his homework well. It was proving much easier to engage this man than he had originally thought. Pressing the advantage he too smiled broadly, stood erect and extended his hand.

"Jerome T Spitz, my friend" he warmly announced, "it's a pleasure to meet someone from so special a place."

Radic was still grinning from ear to ear and there was a touch of moisture in his eyes.

"Angelo Radic," he replied, taking the American's hand in his and shaking it profusely, "but everyone calls me Angel."

The pain was immediate and Spitz winced as they exchanged greetings. With fingers the size of bananas, Radic's hand enveloped his in a vice-like grip and pumped it vigorously. With difficulty, Spitz managed to extract his hand from Radic's and signalled to the barmaid.

"Two beers, honey!"

It was possible the little finger was broken and still Radic was beaming at his new-found friend. He had no idea of his strength. People usually shied away from him, yet this man was different. He picked up a small bag of garlic cloves and offered it to Spitz.

"Try zome. Iz nice. I make myself in vinegar. Keep you strong."

Spitz' stomach made an involuntary spasm at the thought of eating pickled garlic and it was all he could do to raise a weak smile and slowly shake his head.

From nowhere two beers arrived. Grateful to be rescued, Spitz paid and pushed one of the large glasses to Radic.

"Cheers," he offered, as the two glasses touched. "So, Angel, what do you do?"

"I vurk in za paint factory, five years now. I'm azzizdant to za paint tin supervisor. I check za lids and za cans for leaks."

His chest expanded, flushed with pride at the elevated position he had managed to achieve in so short a time.

"An zere is a good chance I vill take over my bozz's job when he retires next year."

Spitz clapped the man on the shoulder. It was solid rock. Now his other hand hurt.

"That's fantastic, you must be pretty important in the factory."

This was going to be much easier that he had thought.

"Yez," replied Radic with a nod of his head. "Zink vot would happen if za lids on za paint tins came off," tapping his index finger against the side of his head. " Zat's vere I come in. I make sure zay don't!"

"What about your parents, Angel? What do they do?"

"Ahh!"

A long pause.

"Zay dead. Five years now, accident on highway – drunk driver." It was clear this was a topic he didn't want to discuss in any great detail.

"Goddamn drunks behind the wheel," snorted Spitz. "They should lock those bastards up and throw away the key."

"No," said Radic in complete innocence, "my farzer was drunk and he had za accident driving home from za pub wiz my muzzer."

Spitz froze in horror. Surely, the man would now proceed to beat him to a pulp for the insult. Instead, nothing happened. Radic had not taken offence and hadn't made the connection between drunks behind the wheel and his own father.

After a short silence, Radic asked, "Zo, Jerome, vot do you do?"

Grateful that the topic of drunk drivers was now behind them, Spitz answered, "Well, Angel my friend, I am in the business of making people happy by fulfilling their last wishes."

Like a dog encountering a new phenomenon, Radic cocked his head to one side. His face mirrored the workings of a pea brain struggling to understand what this could possibly mean.

"Making people happy..." Radic echoed, as though repeating the kernel of the sentence would somehow make it all clear.

"Yes," repeated Spitz, "making people happy. You see, Angelo, I am an undertaker extraordinaire, and my mission in this life is fulfilling my clients' final wishes."

Radic remained motionless, head still cocked to one side with the same perplexed look and his mouth now slightly agape. If his brain was a gearbox, it had just moved from first to second gear and that was as high as it went. This was a limited gearbox.

"I bury people," offered Spitz.

Suddenly all was clear, the mist lifted from Angelo's mind and he understood – at least sufficient for his capacity. He smiled and nodded sagaciously.

"But I have a problem."

"A problem?" mimicked Radic.

"Yes, a problem. You see, Angel, I need a partner. Not just anyone, but a partner in whom I can confide and trust. Someone who will work with me shoulder to shoulder, to establish the greatest funeral home chain in all of Australia!"

The mini-speech rose in timbre and volume, climaxing at the 'all of Australia'. One or two of the motley patrons turned around then resumed their drinking, the moment had passed as quickly as it had arrived and was instantly forgotten in an alcoholic haze.

But not for Radic. For him, his new-found friend stirred something deep inside, a purpose, perhaps even a calling. He was of course unaware of exactly what it was, but he felt stirred nonetheless.

For Spitz, this was like fishing. He knew he had a nibble from the off and now it was obvious his fish had taken the bait. All he had to do was secure the hook and reel in the catch. Next was the barbed hook.

"But where to find such a man?"

The question hung in the air, as he turned to face Radic.

"I want someone with old-school values, someone from the old country, someone who shares my dream."

"I vould be very happy to join in your dream," offered Angel, "if... if you zink I vould be zuitable."

"Suitable... suitable?" gasped Spitz. "I am an astute judge of character, Angel, and I can tell you without fear of criticism that you are one of the most adroit, perspicacious and insightful people I have ever met."

A blank face stared back at him. The gearbox had blown up.

"You would be perfect!" Spitz translated.

"I vould?"

"Yes, you vould, I mean would. But, Angel, my friend," continued Spitz, lightly touching him on a granite-like shoulder, "I couldn't pay you much."

The granite-like shoulders sagged slightly at this news. The prospect of being involved in something exciting, with someone from the old country, someone who really liked him, only to be told the job didn't pay much money.

"I could only afford, say, two thousand a month to start with, but, if things go the way I think they should, we would be talking about more, much more."

The shoulders straightened and the head lifted. In a flash, he grabbed Spitz's right hand and shook it vigorously. If not from the previous assault, the little finger was now definitely broken.

"Tvoo zauzand! Ven do I start?"

"Why not come and see me tomorrow?"

The bear hug came from nowhere and Spitz thought he felt a lower vertebrae dislodge.

When Radic finally let him go, the air rushed into his lungs as the Croat announced, "I am za happiest man in za vorld. Zank you, zank you, Jerome," he blurted out as he pumped the American's hand.

There were tears in his eyes.

Spitz tried to speak, but his lungs were on fire, his back felt as though it had been broken and he had lost the feeling in all the fingers of his right hand.

There were tears in his eyes.

Seeing this, Radic once more embraced his new partner in a constrictor-like grip, mumbling, "I am zo happy, zo happy."

When the bonding had finished, it was all Spitz could do to remain vertical on the bar stool and sip his beer. He had gone out hunting, but had been savaged by his prey. However, despite the injuries, it had been a stunning result and he was sure Radic could be directed ruthlessly without the man having the faintest inclination he was being used. Passing his business card to Angel and slipping off the bar stool he rose gingerly to his feet and bade the now ebullient Radic a fond farewell, being careful to wave from a safe distance, thereby avoiding further digit and spinal injuries.

"See you tomorrow about one o'clock," he uttered in a voice still recovering from the lung damage.

"Zee you tomorrow," came the reply.

And with that, Spitz was out of the door and gone.

Although his hand and back ached, the evening had been a spectacular success. He had found the brawn to go with his brain and the first business acquisition was already in his sights – another firm of undertakers – Robertson & Co. Yes, with Radic at his command, the middle aged couple who owned Robertson's would be easy meat. After that, he would take on Gordon Humphries, another sole proprietor of a funeral firm. Excellent! He smiled contentedly to himself. Shouldn't take more than a few months to have both of those businesses in the bag, and after that? Well, O'Neill's looked like a promising candidate.

The smile widened. Finding a faithful heavy like Radic had been so easy there should be a law against it. With Radic as a loyal enforcer, the master plan could now begin and woe betide anyone who stood in his way.

# Chapter 4

## Jerome T Spitz, Funeral Director Extraordinaire

James Robertson was a respectable man. He ran a respectable business and liked to think of himself as someone to whom people naturally warmed. His soft round face had a gentle demeanour and with a patch of thinning hair, greying at the temples and doe-like eyes, he looked more like your average grandfather than an undertaker.

Together with Betty, his rosy-faced, short and buxom wife of over thirty years, they had formed Robertson & Co, Funeral Directors, soon after their marriage. Their union had not been blessed with children and, as a result, both had had more time to devote to the business. Rightly or not, Robertson considered himself an arbiter of good taste and ethical corporate conduct, which is why he was so captivated by "Focuspoint", a current affairs programme about the funeral trade, now being shown on the television. His wife sat in an armchair next to his, idly leafing through a Home & Garden magazine, oblivious to the drama now unfolding on the small screen.

A panel of informed guests on the television program was discussing the conduct of the funeral trade in front of a studio audience. The talk was largely about Jerome T Spitz, an undertaker new to the area – Spitz, the brash American specialising in outlandish funerals, who had offended many people in the process. Some of his more notable examples included the scattering of ashes by skyrocket, vertical burials and above ground life-like entombments with the deceased encased in polycarbonate resin and then later bronzed. This last type of funeral involved a local wealthy eccentric being so encased to resemble Rodin's *The Thinker* and being placed on an two-and-a-half metre high pedestal in the centre of the Garden of Peace.

Church groups had been particularly vocal in their condemnation of such practices and a strong evangelical group in the television audience was making their presence felt.

Spitz had acquired several acres of land on the suburban border and been granted planning permission to use the land as a private cemetery by Jack Sullivan, the then mayor of Sydney. The speed with which the permission had been granted had caused considerable talk and rumours of back-handers to Sullivan persisted.

A woman from the audience spoke into an extended microphone and asked the panel, "What's wrong with having a funeral service that suits me?"

Turning to one of the panel, the chairman directed his question, "Canon Johnson, that's a fair question, isn't it? What *is* wrong with having the right to choose?"

"There's nothing wrong with the right to choose as long as the choice isn't offensive and, frankly, what we're talking about is not only hugely offensive to decent, ordinary people, but an abomination before God."

The woman was on her feet in an instant.

"An abomination? You belong back in the dark ages, Canon Johnson! It's that kind of blinkered, pig-ignorant philistine outlook that is an impediment to true social progress and enlightened thought!"

It was as if a match had been thrown into a drum containing pure petrol vapour as the studio audience erupted with their opposing and supporting views. The mayhem continued unchecked for several seconds, oblivious to the chairman's persistent pleas.

"Ladies and gentlemen, ladies and gentlemen, order please, order!"

Finally the studio audience settled down and the chairman had control once again. This was great television and made for riveting viewing. The camera moved to close focus on the chairman again and, speaking directly into the camera, he began.

"Well, as you can see, this type of alternative approach to the treatment of the dead evokes very strong feelings. But is the same true for the 'My Way' range of current television advertisements? We've selected one of five such advertisements for discussion here tonight. Let's have a look and then we'll ask the studio audience what they think."

The advertisement opens with a close shot of a white middle-aged man, perfect hair and teeth, smartly dressed and, by all appearances, reasonably well off. In the background is a beautiful scene of yachts on a sparkling river. The day is bright and sunny.

The narrator begins, "When my father died, we wanted to give him the send-off that he would have truly loved. The only problem was that most funeral homes only offered a traditional service and we wanted something that would be special for him. We looked everywhere and were at the point of giving up when we found 'My Way'."

Gentle strains of the Frank Sinatra song begin, providing the perfect audio backdrop and with old blue eyes singing as the camera draws back, the rest of the family are revealed: an attractive well-dressed wife and two children, a boy aged about twelve and his sister, a year or so younger. Dad has one arm around his wife and the other draped across the shoulder of his son. The wife, in mirror image fashion, is doing the same – one arm around the waist of her husband, the other similarly draped across the shoulder of the girl. In the huddle, it is a scene of the perfect family – all radiantly healthy and impeccably turned out, dad at the helm and in charge, his wife with the 'little lady at home' look and in complete deference to her husband's authority.

With the camera in tight focus on the four of them, the narrator continues, "My Way understood our wishes completely. There was no fuss or bother, in fact, they offered us the choice of a large number of exiting options, so many in fact, that our only trouble was choosing the one which was exactly right for dad. They even have their special final resting area just out of town. Who would want to go economy when first class doesn't cost any more?"

The advertisement switches to a new scene in front of ''My Way' Funeral Home', the husband shaking hands with Spitz, both smiling broadly.

Turning to the camera, Spitz says, "I'm Jerome T Spitz and I've been serving the needs of the bereaved and the deceased for over twenty years. I'm passionate about providing the *right* funeral, whatever the circumstances. Having established a chain of funeral homes across America, based on core values of service, reliability and value, I'm now doing the same thing right here, in Australia."

The volume of the background song increases slightly and is nearing the end as the scene changes to a night-time one with dad, mum and the two children standing around a large skyrocket in their back yard. Dad turns to the camera while holding up a small white cylindrical container.

"We're so glad we found 'My Way'. Dad would have been really happy knowing he went off like this."

Turning to face the white cardboard canister and addressing it directly he says, "We all love you, dad."

Kissing the canister, he places it in the body of the skyrocket, screws the pointed top back on, lights the fuse and then returns to join his family standing a few metres away. In a blistering explosion of heat and light, followed by a great 'whoosh', the skyrocket takes off. The Frank Sinatra song reaches its climax as the rocket explodes some three hundred metres in the air in a huge multi-coloured sphere, sending the dusty remains of granddad in a thousand directions. The camera returns to the family huddle. They are all smiling sadly, a job well done as the voice of Spitz concludes, "Come and see us at 'My Way'. You'll be glad you did. And don't forget, we won't be beaten on price! Ask about our special Rainy Day and Senior Citizen plans."

Robertson could stomach no more. The discussion of the rights and wrongs of what is pure circus was bad enough and discussing this theatre gave it a measure of credibility, but the television advertisement was simply a bridge too far. This was one of a series of such advertisements, all equally in poor taste.

Rising out of his chair, he turned the television set off.

"Do you really think people can't see through this clown?" he asked angrily.

"It may work in America where the entire population is composed of idiots, but it certainly won't work over here!"

"Now dear," his wife replied, "remember what the doctor said about your blood pressure and getting worked up."

Robertson sighed deeply in exasperation and shook his head.

"He's nothing, but a cheap hustler, the kind of person that gives the rest of us a bad name," he paused to drink from a glass of water and continued, "he's ruthless about expanding his tacky business and doesn't care who or what gets in his way, of that I'm sure!"

His wife looked up from the magazine, a slightly puzzled look on her face.

"Ruthless – that's a bit strong, isn't it, James? Whatever makes you think he's ruthless?"

He didn't want to frighten his wife by telling her more than he had to.

"Trust me, Betty. I'm not wrong about this. This Spitz fellow is deadly serious about being the biggest operator in Australia and he just happens to be located in our back yard!"

"Oh, James," his wife chuckled out loud, "you do make mountains out of molehills. I don't know why you let this chap get under your skin so, I really don't."

She put down the magazine she was reading.

"Now, why don't you sit down and forget all about this ridiculous American? I'll make you a nice cup of tea. No sense getting worked up about nothing."

'Nothing… that was a joke. If only she knew the half of it.'

His mind drifted back to the time last week when Spitz had called unannounced at the office with his "associate", Angelo Radic, a stocky Croatian with no neck and dressed in an ill-fitting suit. They had arrived after the staff had left, while he was alone and closing up for the evening. As he opened the front door, Spitz and Radic walked in.

Taken aback, Robertson had been the first to speak.

"I'm terribly sorry, gentlemen, but we are now closed."

Spitz looked him coolly in the eye.

"I don't think so."

Both men were now between Robertson and the door. Radic locked the door from the inside, drew the blinds and stood guard over the exit like some immovable statue, while Spitz calmly addressed the now visibly shaken Robertson.

"We're here to have a little chat."

Both flustered and angered, Robertson challenged the relaxed Spitz.

"What is the meaning of all this? What do you think you are playing at? Who on earth do you think…?"

The diatribe was halted in mid-flow, as Spitz held up an index finger in a 'stop' gesture.

"Mr Robertson, allow me to introduce myself. Jerome T Spitz, Funeral Director extraordinaire. I run a chain of funeral homes in the States. I'm the biggest operator there, on the West Coast and have interests in many of the businesses on the East Coast."

Clearly in control of the situation, he paused to sniff the carnation pinned to his lapel before indicating with an open palm, the stocky figure standing at the door.

"My associate, Mr Radic."

At the mention of his name, Radic reached into his jacket pocket and withdrew a flick knife. The razor sharp blade shot open, catching the light from the overhead halogen bulb. The sight of the stiletto caused Robertson to utter a small yet audible gasp. He now gave the man his full attention.

"I'm good at what I do, Mr Robertson, and currently my business is in, how shall we say… a phase of rapid expansion? The opportunities here in Australia are immense, and if I may be candid, the competition …" he paused, as if searching for the phrase, "with no disrespect, the competition isn't really much of a problem."

In the background, Radic had taken a small cellophane bag out of his pocket containing pickled garlic cloves, the delicacy from his homeland, and opened the bag with the knife. Robertson was mesmerised as the Croat stabbed a number of cloves with the point of the knife and transferred them into his mouth. The slow munching sound formed a strange backdrop to the main conversation.

"You see, Mr Robertson, I am interested in purchasing your business and I can move quickly. I am prepared to discuss terms of sale in my office. Shall we say... Friday? Today being Monday gives you ample time to think carefully about your price. I, on the other hand, already have a figure in mind. You won't need an estate agent and I will take care of all the legal fees, so, all in all, you would be getting a good deal."

Robertson's face was reddening by the moment, galled by the bare-faced arrogance of the man.

"Look, Spitz, I'm really not interested in selling to you or anybody else at this point in time, so I'd like you both to leave – now!"

Spitz's tone instantly changed. There was menace in his voice as he moved close to Robertson, so close, their noses were almost touching.

"I want to acquire your business, Robertson, and acquire it I will, by whatever means it takes and I *always* get what I want. I trust we understand each other," he smiled menacingly, darting a look in the Croat's direction.

Radic, who had been standing quietly by the door and had almost consumed the entire contents of the plastic bag, was instantly at Spitz's side. Placing his head next to Robertson so that all three noses were touching, he added in a thick Croatian accent, "Alffays!"

The '*alffays*' emphasised the 'ffffff' sound and, with it, a mouthful of garlic breath. Robertson blinked several times in rapid succession before stifling a couple of coughs and stumbling backwards in a series of short, drunken steps. Like a boxer who had just received a stinging left hook, he shook his head to clear his brain. The garlic had come from out of nowhere and taken him completely by surprise.

By contrast, Spitz rotated his head very slowly to face Radic and, as if talking to a child, spoke with emphasis on each word, "Angelo, you moron – don't... ever... do... that... again."

Taking one step back to be out of range of the garlic breath, he removed a handkerchief from his lapel pocket and wiped his brow which was now covered in a light film of moisture.

Addressing the henchman, he spoke again, with added emphasis.

"Repeat – ever."

Radic began to speak, but was quickly silenced by Spitz holding up his index finger as a warning.

"Don't say anything. Don't say anything at all."

Turning to the still stunned Robertson he continued, "I believe our little chat is over, Mr Robertson. I shall have the sale papers delivered to you in the next few days and I expect the deal to be concluded by close of play next Friday, which should give you ample time to put your affairs in order. Now be a good chap and don't mess me around. People who mess me around have to face the consequences and the consequences are always severe. Always!"

At the sound of the word 'always', Radic came to life and, like a parrot, performed on cue, "Alffays!" again with the strong 'ffff' sound and again the garlic blast.

Already pre-weakened by the first garlic punch, Robertson crumbled backwards into a waiting chair. He sat down with an inelegant flop and did not move.

Spitz exhaled and slowly shook his head. Instructing Radic was like speaking to a very dim child.

"Come, Angelo," he called to Radic, "our business here is done. Let us leave Mr Robertson to his thoughts."

They moved to the door, which Radic unlocked and held open for Spitz to exit. Immediately, in front of the door and adjacent to Radic, Spitz paused and faced the seated Robertson.

"Don't forget, I always get what I want."

Both men had left as quickly as they had arrived. Robertson got up, opened the drinks cabinet and, with trembling hands, he poured himself a large whisky. He drank deeply and sat down, his heart racing.

'What the hell happened there?' he asked himself.

If the aim of the visit had been intimidation, it had certainly worked, because he was definitely shaken. His mind was racing.

'What should he do now? The police... yes, that was it. He would go to the police and tell them everything, how he had been threatened and intimidated by that awful American with his Rottweiler companion and how he didn't want to sell...'

The line of thought died in mid-flow. Sure, go to the police and tell them what? The first thing they would ask for would be evidence. Was there anything on tape, or in writing? Were there any witnesses? Was there evidence of any injury he could attribute to Spitz or his sidekick? Clearly, the answer to all these questions was 'no' and the brutal reality of the situation was that he was on his own. If the police drew a blank in their investigations, then that would be more dangerous – the cat would be out of the bag and he would have to face an angered Spitz. He was scared, that much he knew, and the more he thought about it, the only conclusion he kept arriving at was that he would have to deal directly with Spitz and his thug.

His thoughts were interrupted when he heard, "James."

His wife was calling him from the kitchen.

"James."

"Yes, dear?"

"Would you prefer a camomile tea, I'm making one for myself?"

'Tea!' He could do with more than tea right now. Tea wouldn't solve his problems, wouldn't change anything, hardly the panacea for his predicament, not that his wife knew anything about it. There was no point in sharing the problem with Betty, she'd be terrified and that would only make things worse.'

"James?"

He sighed resignedly.

"Yes, thanks. A cup of camomile would be nice."

\* \* \*

Unbeknown to Robertson, Spitz had also turned his attention to another funeral parlour, Humphries & Co, located in one of the town's most affluent areas.

Sited on a large and valuable plot, the freehold was owned by the sole proprietor, Gordon Humphries.

It was an open secret that Humphries, a man in his late sixties, was gay, his effeminate mannerisms, carefully manicured hands and soft features leaving little room for doubt regarding his sexual orientation. Prissy and pernickety with his staff, he had however, a great rapport with elderly women in times of bereavement and exploited this to the full.

As James Robertson was drinking his tea and getting ready for bed, a few kilometres away Gordon Humphries was still at his office, immersed in paperwork. Looking at his watch, he shook his head.

'Ten thirty! Where had the time gone? Well, at least one thing was for certain, the paperwork is now completely up to date. Enough for one day! Time to lock up, go home and have a light bite to eat before turning in for what was left of the evening.'

Switching off the office lights, he opened the main door. Two men walked briskly out of the shadows, the first man moving into the office area, while the second man pushed him roughly inside and closed the door. The sound of the lock turning meant he was trapped inside the building with two strangers. His heart was beating like a drum. It had all happened so fast. Suddenly, a small side light was turned on, clearly illuminating the first man.

"Ah, Mr Humphries I presume," announced Spitz with an effusive smile. "I hope I haven't called at an inopportune time, but there is something I wish to discuss with you."

Humphries was furious at the intrusion and livid at being pushed out of the way.

"What the bloody hell do you think you're doing?" he roared. "Get out of here immediately. Get out now before I call the police!"

Spitz remained where he stood, calm and relaxed.

"There's no need to be like that, Mr Humphries, we'll only take a few moments of your time."

"Damn right you will," fumed Humphries, walking to the telephone on the reception desk just a few metres away and picking up the handset, he began to dial the emergency number.

Spitz looked at Radic and made a short sideways gesture with his head towards Humphries. In four rapid steps, Radic was next to the undertaker. Reaching down, he snatched the telephone off the desk, the handset still at Humphries' ear and, in one fluid motion, flung the unit over his shoulder with such force, that it dragged the attached answering- machine with it. The elastic connection propelled it with lightning speed from the desk, striking both Spitz and Radic a glancing blow on each forehead, as it passed them in its trajectory to the nearby fish tank.

There was a loud 'splash' as the machine entered the water, followed by several electric popping sounds. The fish in the tank stopped swimming as the electricity coursed through the water. Humphries looked on aghast at the spectacle unfolding in front of his eyes. A loud bang from the three pin socket on the wall signalled the end of the incident. Silence and an acrid electrical smell hung over the room. Nobody moved.

Slowly Spitz turned to his associate, the swelling on his forehead clearly evident, and spoke slowly and unambiguously.

"Angel." A long pause ensuring the latter's full attention. "The next time you stop a call you don't have to assault me, injure yourself, destroy someone else's property or even kill several dozen fish."

The Croat's eyes glazed over, the message wasn't getting through. Spitz retrieved the dangling telephone from the outside of the fish tank and held it up in front of him.

"To stop a call, you just have to put your finger here," he said, pointing to the receiver cradle and the two plastic contact buttons.

"Here," he repeated, holding the telephone under the man's nose.

Radic grunted, his only acknowledgement that telephone calls could be terminated by two little white buttons. Humphries remained rooted to the spot. Although the whole incident had lasted only a few seconds, it had taken him completely off guard and any sense of control he may have had was now lost.

Spitz addressed him gently.

"Mr Humphries, I must apologise for Mr Radic's behaviour. He has a tendency to be somewhat... energetic on occasions. Shall we begin again?"

He leaned against the reception counter, quietly examining his fingernails, removing a bit of dirt here and there.

"You see, Mr Humphries, I want your business and I'm going to get it. You will sell it to me – it's that simple."

"You're mad! What makes you think I would ever sell my business to...?"

Radic took a step towards Humphries, glowering like a guard dog. The words froze in his mouth.

Spitz continued, "You see, it really *would* be in your best interests to listen very carefully to what I have to say. Am I making myself perfectly clear?"

Humphries nodded vigorously.

"You have had, as you Australians say, a good run. But now it is my turn. Your business is not as profitable as it once was. Anyone can see that your custom has declined and you must be well past retirement age. On the other hand, I aim to offer a much greater range of funeral options, giving people what they want, letting them choose what's right for *them*, and in the process I intend to create the largest undertakers' chain on Australia's east coast and then across the continent. People like you just get in my way."

He paused for effect and to reinforce the previous statement. There was an eerie silence in the room, the only audible sound being Humphries' shallow breathing.

"So, once again, I want to acquire your business and you will sell it to me. Here is my card. Take your time and think things over for a couple of days, then give me a ring to discuss the terms of the sale. However, if you don't, there will be consequences, *serious* consequences, and I'm not talking about a few dead fish and an answering-machine."

Removing a small piece of lint from the shoulder of his suit, he held it up for inspection before blowing it away and slowly walked to the door. Like a faithful dog, Radic followed. With one hand on the door handle, he turned to face Humphries, who had not moved or said anything for a minute or so.

"I'll be expecting your call and please don't do anything stupid like going to the police or you'll make my associate here very angry, very angry indeed."

He smiled menacingly and then looked at Radic, who, on cue, snarled like a demented animal. The undertaker took a faltering step backwards.

Spitz smiled.

"Don't bother, we'll see ourselves out."

Recovering from the shock of Spitz and Radic's visit, Humphries caught sight of himself in a mirror on the wall. He looked dreadful. Sweat ran down his face and his hair was a mess. Taking out his handkerchief, he mopped away the perspiration and reached for his comb, as he tried to gather his composure.

For Gordon Humphries, appearance was everything, no matter what the situation, and the mirror never lied.

Except sometimes it did. Sometimes, it lied with devastating consequences.

## Chapter 5

## Red Light District of Sydney, 3am

M aria sat in front of a dressing table mirror, brushing her long grey hair. A young woman with flowing brown locks stared back. Dressed to go dancing in a sequined red evening dress which had seen better days, she was going to meet Stavros, her fiancé, at the Hippodrome later that night in the heart of Sydney. Like a naughty child, she chuckled at the thought of the illicit rendezvous. The only problem she could think of was how to leave the house without waking up her mother and father. There were however a number of other problems of which Maria was unaware. Both her fiancé and her parents had long since died and the Hippodrome was now a super-market car park in the red light district of Kings Cross.

Every city has a sleazy underbelly. In London, it's Soho, Paris, the Pigalle, Hamburg, the Reeperbahn and for Sydney – Kings Cross. At two thirty, on a Friday morning it was living up to its image as dealers and junkies, whores and clients conducted their business.

PC Tony Brown and his partner, PC Jim Clarke, cruised slowly around the red light district in an unmarked police car surveying the night life. Neither especially liked working vice. It was dirty work dealing with unpleasant characters and at the most anti-social of times, but, when your Chief Inspector marked you down for a stint like this, there was little to be said.

Tonight had been especially tedious and in the four hours they had been on duty, all they'd managed to do was caution a couple of women for solic-iting and move them on.

After fifteen minutes of silence, Clarke spoke,

"Let's get a coffee, what d'ya say?"

"Good idea," replied Brown, glad of something to break the monotony.

Clarke swung the car off the minor road and onto the main street and, even though it was nearly three o'clock, there were still plenty of people milling about as the late licence bars closed. He stopped the car next to a trailer selling burgers and hotdogs. The two policemen got out and approached the proprietor of the café on wheels.

"Evening, Mario," announced Brown to the short Italian man with the grease-stained apron.

Mario turned around from the sink where he had been washing coffee cups and plates.

"Ahh, Constable Tony, how nice-a to see you," he said in a thick Italian accent, "and Constable Jim too, what a nice-a surprise."

PC Clarke nodded to the vendor, "G'day Mario."

"You, boys, wanna some-a nice-a burger?" he offered enthusiastically, "maybe a 'ot dog? Best in Sydney!"

The thought of a grease-laden burger or hot dog made both men feel ill.

"Just a couple of coffees, please, Mario," Clarke quickly replied, anxious not to get anywhere near the offer of free food.

"Okey, dokey – but you donna know what you missing! Best in Sydney!"

The coffee appeared in an instant, the proprietor refusing to take any money and they returned to their car with the two polystyrene cups.

Both men sat silently, sipping the hot liquid and watching the passers by.

Brown was the first to speak, "How much longer do you think we'll be doing this for Jim?"

"Hard to say, mate, as long as the old man wants us to, I guess."

Though it was true, it wasn't the answer Brown had wanted to hear.

"Sitting in this car, every night, moving slappers on and not making waves is a complete waste of our time," he grumbled. "I joined the police because I wanted to do something useful, something that would make a real difference," sighed Brown, looking glumly out of the window.

Jim, the older of the two men, understood Brown's frustration but he knew these stints came with the territory, and it was important not to let them get to you. He'd seen many a promising policeman burnt out over too many shifts like these.

"Yeah, I feel the same, but unless we win the lottery or get promoted, we're stuck with this for now. We follow orders, do the job and go home. That's the lot of an honest policeman, my friend, but with a bit of luck maybe next week we'll be with Robbery or Narcotics or perhaps even Homicide. You never know what's around the corner in this job", Clarke said reassuringly.

Brown gave a resigned sigh, "Mmm, you're right, but I hate being bored. Nothing exciting has ever happened on this shift… it's the same crap night after ni…"

A late model Mercedes car had pulled up some twenty metres in front of them and an old lady, dressed in a flowing red evening dress, got out of the passenger's side and closed the door. The car drove off into the night while the old lady waited by the kerb.

As the two policemen got out of the car, a smirk spread across Clarke's face and quickly mushroomed into a full-blown toothy grin followed by an uncontrollable chuckle.

"She has to be eighty... *minimum,*" spluttered Clarke between laughs.

"Shit... I thought I'd seen it all," mused Brown, "but this is something else! Come on Jim my friend, let's check it out."

Both police officers walked up to the old lady and stood at her side.

Brown coughed loudly.

"Good morning, madam," he offered.

"I'm PC Brown from Parramatta police station and this is PC Clarke."

Both men produced their warrant cards.

"May I ask you what you are doing here at this hour?"

The old lady smiled broadly at the two policemen, the bright red lipstick and rouge on both cheeks giving her a clown-like appearance.

"I'm meeting my fiancé," she replied coyly, "he's taking me dancing at the Hippodrome."

The smile became larger and she fluttered her eyelashes in quick succession before the look changed to one of suspicion.

"But I'm not allowed to speak to strangers."

Both men looked at each other, searching for an appropriate response to this situation.

Clarke broke the silence, "What's your name, dear?" he asked.

"Maria," she replied, her previous answer already forgotten. "Maria Christou."

"Maria, whose car was that you just got out of?" he continued.

"What car?"

The officers looked at each other again and Clarke rolled his eyes upwards, grinning at his mate.

"Where do you live, Maria?" he probed gently.

"I live in Cambourne Street," she replied jauntily.

"But Cambourne Street's only got offices, Jim, there used to be houses there but they were knocked down years ago," said Brown, who was now highly amused by the unexpected events.

Clarke nodded in acknowledgement and winked at his colleague, then turning to Maria, he asked, "Have you got any ID on you Maria?"

He was met with a blank stare.

"It's very late for you to be out. I think we should take you back home, don't you? Let's see if you have anything in your hand bag with your address on it."

The old lady offered no resistance, as Clarke lifted the bag from her arm.

"Jesus Christ!"

The policeman's mouth was agape.

"Take a look at this, Tone," he spluttered.

Tony Brown stepped forward and looked inside the bag.

"God, that must be at least three or four hundred dollars," he exclaimed.

"Maria, my dear, where did you get this money?" probed Clarke.

Maria looked confused.

"Did somebody give you any money this evening?"

"Yes, yes. I met a very kind gentleman and he…"

The memory faded again and she drifted away into a world of her own, looking at the two officers without recognition. The two officers stared at each other in disbelief. Brown could barely contain himself.

Gently, taking the old lady by the elbow and trying to suppress his laughter, he spluttered, "I think you'd better come with us to the station, where we can get to the bottom of this."

"Station! Are we going on a train?"

Brown could no longer help himself and laughed out loud. The evening had suddenly and unexpectedly changed from a dull routine. Clarke however, was more concerned for the old lady's welfare. He was already contemplating how to tell some unfortunate relative that he'd found their mother or grandmother in the red light district in the early hours of the morning with a lot more money in her handbag than her weekly pension.

"No, Maria, not the train station, the police station, we're going to let you ride in a police car," added Clarke, in a tone used when speaking to a child about to be given a special treat.

"But what about Stavros?" she asked.

"Stavros?" he questioned, "who is Stavros?"

"Stavros Papadopoulos – my fiancé. He's taking me dancing at the Hippodrome! I do love to dance."

Clarke smiled warmly.

"And I suspect you're an excellent dancer too, but, Maria, you must come with us now. We want to make sure you are safe, and standing on a street corner at three am in Kings Cross is probably not the safest place for a lady to be. We'll get to the station and have a nice cup of tea and then you can tell us all about yourself."

He opened the rear door while Brown gently guided the old lady to the back seat of the car, helping her into the vehicle and doing up her seat belt.

"How will Stavros know where I am?" she asked, "he might be worried."

"Don't worry, we'll contact him for you ," assured Clarke, "then he can come to the police station and have a nice cup of tea too."

"How kind of you," she replied, "how very kind."

The car drew away from the kerb, both men in the front and the old lady, rescued from the street, sitting comfortably in the back as the question, "You won't tell mum, will you? I'm not supposed to speak to strangers," floated out of the window and into the night.

As the old lady was driven to safety, sixteen kilometres away, her son, his wife and their two children were soundly asleep, oblivious to what was happening and what was to follow. Their world would never be the same again.

\* \* \*

Several hours later, Nick Papadopoulos, Maria's son, was sitting opposite Michael Hammond, his best friend since childhood. They had found a quiet corner in a noisy pub, the conversation was heavy and intense.

"It's not your fault, Nick, you were asleep. Christ, that's normal, you have to sleep sometime. You've always looked out for your mum, but she obviously sneaked out."

He held up the stump of his index finger in admonishment, "Don't let this get to you, mate."

Mick Hammond had rapidly acquired the nickname 'Stumpy' in primary school after a game of chicken involving his brother, a chopping block and an axe had gone badly wrong.

"Ah… shit, Stump, I just don't know what to do for the best, she's getting worse."

"I know, mate, but you have to think of yourself as well, you've got a wife and kids."

Nick cradled a beer in his hands and continued to stare at the table, considering his friend's comments. His mother's cognitive faculties had been steadily declining since she sold her house and moved in with him and his family two years ago. They had used part of the sale proceeds to extend the house, adding a bathroom on to the spare room, and his mother had settled in well with the family. Maria Papadopoulos was an independent woman and living with her son and his family had at first been relaxed and easy. However, over the last eighteen months things had changed. There were frequent gaps in her short term memory – she often didn't recognise her family or friends and on occasions she even went missing with no recollection of where she had been or what she had been doing.

Nick reached for the beer jug and poured himself half a glass.

"It never ends, man, it's crisis after crisis. I never know what's going to happen next. We've only just got over the fish thing, though my neighbour doesn't talk to us at all anymore."

"Sod the neighbour," replied Stump indignantly, "what did that old bastard ever do for you or your mum anyway, except maybe complain about foreigners to the rest of the street?"

He paused to take a sip from his beer.

"Anyway, Nick, you have to admit, that whole thing was fuckin' funny."

A wry smile spread across Nick's face as he recalled the evening his mother had called him to say she had prepared a lovely fish dinner for the whole family. He, his wife and two children then aged eight and ten, had been presented with the neighbour's prize Koi carp wrapped in silver foil, steaming in a beautiful aromatic juice made from almonds and Ouzo. She told them she had 'gone fishing in a beautiful lake' and was serving up the meal when the police knocked at the front door. In Maria's mind she was back in her restaurant, preparing her well-known dish. In reality, the old man next door was furious at the theft of his beloved fish by this senile old woman who still thought she was a famous chef. Thankfully, the police hadn't pressed charges and they had managed to persuade the neighbour to back off as well.

"Yeah, it was funny," he said with a chuckle, "but it still cost me three thousand dollars to stop it going to court. I must admit though, it was worth it just to see that old Nazi so pissed off! But now mum's getting worse, it's causing real problems between Dianne and me."

He sighed deeply while shaking his head and reached for his beer, downing the contents in one gulp.

Stump refilled both glasses, emptying the jug.

"Cheers mate."

Nick rubbed his forehead with the fingers of his right hand, the elbow resting on the table with his head downcast, looking at the stained beer mat.

"This whole thing is a nightmare."

Silence hung over the table while both men toyed with their drinks. There was a long pause.

Nick was the first to speak, "Diane says she and the kids can't take much more. My mum doesn't even know them sometimes, she thinks they're her sister's two kids and they're both in their fifties and living overseas. My own two get really freaked out by that kind of thing, it's not the grandma they knew. I've been helping mum out on the money side of things for a while now, but keeping two kids is expensive and we've already gone through a lot of the money from her house sale. After paying for the bloody Carp I had to pay to get a steel net to cover the old boy's pond, which meant I had to choose between buying Diane another car, which she really needed, or send the kids on the school trip to Canberra. Diane insisted on letting the kids go, but she was furious. I tell you, Stump, it's causing real problems."

"It's a real bastard, this dementia thing," observed Stump philosophically.

"Dianne says the best thing for everyone is for mum to go into a home where she can be looked after properly. A *home*... this is my *mum* we're talking about. I don't want to put her into a home like some old piece of furniture. I feel guilty even *thinking* about it, I reckon she should stay with us, with her family who know and love her. The problem is she's on another planet most of the time. Honestly, Stump, I don't know what to do."

"Mmm, yeah, that's an awful situation to be in. You're caught in the middle between your wife and kids and your mum. I wouldn't know what to do in a situation like that either. There's no easy answer, is there?"

"You said it mate, but last night really took the biscuit."

"Last night?"

"Diane got up because she heard the dog barking, he was outside when he should have been in. Anyway, in the process she noticed mum's door was open but she wasn't there and the bed hadn't been slept in."

"Bloody hell!"

"That's when Diane woke me up. I was dead to the world, it was nearly three o'clock. We had a good look in all the rooms – nothing. Then I got a torch and had a look outside, but there was no sign of her."

Stumpy was listening intently.

"So, when your mum's gone AWOL at three in the morning, there's only one thing to do, call the police, which is what I did."

"And...?"

Nick picked up his beer and swallowed some of the cold amber liquid.

"They were really good. The copper said they'd report her description to all the mobile units in the area to look out for her but I didn't know what she was wearing or anything. They suggested I take my own car as well and drive around to see if I could spot her. The police operator told me that she would send an officer around to my house as soon as possible and she was trying to reassure me, telling me she couldn't have got too far if she was eighty two. I was driving around for almost an hour and covered all the local streets and parks with no luck, before I went back home. Diane was frantic because the kids were up and crying, and she was exhausted and didn't know what to tell them. Then, just after four this morning, a squad car turned up and a couple of coppers knocked on the front door and asked if I had reported a Maria Papadopoulos missing an hour ago. I thought maybe something had happened to her, you know, like a heart attack. Maybe she had been taken to hospital and they were here with the bad news."

"Your mum had a heart attack?"

He took another drink and smiled ruefully.

"Part of me was hoping that's what they were going to tell me and that it was now finally going to be over… the torture, 'cause that's what it is, torture for all of us. For a moment there I was looking at the coppers and a part of me was actually praying they were going to tell me that my mother was dead. I still feel guilty thinking about it, but I couldn't help myself. I'm too much of a coward to make a decision to send her away, but she's not my mum anymore. It's like she's already dead and someone else is in her body. Living like this, no one's got a life anymore, not her, not us. If she'd died I wouldn't have to decide about a nursing home."

"So she didn't have a heart attack?"

"No, Stump, no heart attack. She hadn't died or been taken to hospital or anything like that. Do you know why the police were at my home at four o'clock this morning, waking my kids up and half the street too?"

His friend looked at him quizzically.

"Because my mother went walkabout last night, out of her room and down to the red light area in Kings Cross looking for my dad, who incidentally has been dead for over forty five years. She went there to meet him because she thought he was going to take her dancing at the Hippodrome, which was pulled down years ago. She'd gone out dressed up to the nines, in a red evening dress, gloves and slippers and a ton of makeup. She was picked by the vice squad who thought she was soliciting!"

"What?"

"Yeah, you heard me. Luckily she had her pension card in her handbag with the next of kin's details, my details."

Nick shook his head in despair. A wry smile crept across his lips. Stump was speechless.

"That's when they brought her back home. She didn't remember any of it – thought she'd just been out for a little walk."

"Nothing?"

Stump was trying hard to suppress a growing smile.

"Nothing. We just put her to bed. But, the main question is where the four hundred bucks she had on her came from."

Stumpy cocked his head.

"Four hundred bucks?"

"Four hundred bucks. The cops saw mum getting out of a Mercedes and she had four hundred dollars in her purse when they found her. She didn't remember getting out of the car and she couldn't explain to them where the money came from."

The latent smile now erupted into a full-blown laugh, complete with tears. Nick was unmoved, a resigned look on his face.

"Go on, Stump. Laugh it up. I know it sounds hilarious, but it's not funny. My mum has to have an AIDS test because none of us know what happened last night, not even her. We don't know where she went, who she was with or what she did."

The laughter died immediately and a look of disbelief spread across Stumpy's face.

"Ohh, fuck!"

"It was the last straw for Diane and we had a hell of a blue this morning. She's insisting I put my mum in an old people's home. She says it's best for everyone and that we can't go on like this. She says I have to choose. I love my mum, but I love my wife and kids too and a lot of what Dianne is saying is true. The kids get upset every time their grandmother blanks them, which happens a lot these days. So, for the sake of my family, I have to throw my own mum out. Part of me feels like a traitor for even thinking about putting her in a home and part of me can't bear all of us living like this, because it just goes on and on and it's not going to get better, it's only going to get worse. I can't keep tabs on her 24/7 and neither can Diane but I don't know how they'd treat her if she went into a nursing home and you hear real horror stories. She'd hate it. She always said she'd rather die than go into a home."

His friend remained silent throughout. There was little he could say.

"You know, Stump, if she died tomorrow, we'd all be sad, but we'd be relieved too."

He shook his head in despair and reached for his drink.

"I don't know what to do for the best, I really don't. The police want me to go to the West Sydney station later to make a statement. They want to know if mum mentioned anything after they brought her back home. I've got to meet a DI Thompson. I hope he's not some stupid copper who's going to give me a hard time. I've had enough for one day."

In fact, that was the least of his worries, or should have been. Ian Thompson could be incredibly kind and unbelievably dangerous.

Accidents followed him as sure as night follows day. He ought to have come with a health warning.

# Chapter 6

## DI Thompson

An austere turn of the century building, West Sydney police station was the headquarters for all suburban police stations from just outside the city centre to within thirty-two kilometres of the Blue Mountain range. Its three storeys contained twenty cells in the basement, were home to several hundred police officers and administrative staff and had an entire floor set aside for the State Forensic Service. The ground floor was the only area open to the public, who were there every working day in their hundreds, applying for clearance licences, reporting instances of crime and a dozen other matters. Like a living, breathing entity, the building's population swelled at nine in the morning and contracted at five in the evening.

Nick Papadopoulos' interview that evening was less traumatic than he had feared. DI Thompson, gentle and compassionate, had only been interested in finding out about anybody who might have tried to exploit a vulnerable pensioner. By the time Nick met with the policeman, he'd acquired an explanation for the money his mother had in her bag when the police picked her up. He and his wife had looked at the old lady's bank book which showed a four hundred dollar withdrawal the previous morning, although she'd completely forgotten she'd been to the bank. It was a miracle she hadn't been robbed or worse, but neither her son nor the policeman had any idea how Maria Papadopoulos had found her way to Kings Cross and probably never would. By pure good fortune, Brown and Clarke had found her before anybody else.

The discussion with Thompson had gone well, but as Nick was leaving, something continued to nag at the back of his mind. During the interview, he couldn't help but notice how the police officer, who came in with coffee, having left both cups on the desk had virtually run from the room. Then later when Thompson, cup in hand, was leading him out of the building, staff stood well back to let him pass, almost as though he had some kind of communicable disease. He seemed like a nice fellow, so approachable, but his colleagues were avoiding him. Nick didn't get it.

Thompson had only spent about half an hour with him, before concluding their interview. As he left the police station and walked out of the door to the street, Nick had no idea that DI Thompson, accompanied by PC Selby on their way to interrogate a suspect, was about to create the mayhem for which he had become infamous.

In fact, DI Thompson was a popular detective and often assumed a paternal management style to some of the younger officers. Universally liked, he was nonetheless treated with caution by his underlings, due to his propensity for causing chaos from the most innocuous of situations. During his three years at West Sydney headquarters, disasters seemed to follow him. Thus far, he had set fire to the men's toilet after throwing a discarded cigarette into the waste paper bin, crashed the computer network after spilling a cup of coffee over a main frame computer and, in his most recent catastrophe, he'd dropped a tray full of drinks over fellow officers at the Christmas party. After the last episode, it was now generally held to be true that, because Thompson was so clumsy, anybody with a modicum of a survival instinct should keep well away from him if there was anything remotely sharp, hot, or wet within his reach.

And so PC Selby, a tall, slim man in his late twenties, who would have made a good look alike for a young Paul Hogan, ought to have known better than to accompany his Inspector to the drinks vending machine.

"Drink?"

"Orange juice, thanks, sir."

Putting a few coins into the slot, DI Thompson pressed a few buttons before retrieving a plastic cup from the machine. As he offered it to his young colleague, he took a pre-emptive step towards him, juice in hand, unaware of the trapped shoelace which would instantly halt his forward movement. Selby's reflexes were good and the young policeman would have managed to avoid the sticky juice as it left the cup and headed towards his body, were it not for the woman police sergeant immediately behind him waiting to use the machine. Trapped and with no place to turn, he was directly in the line of fire. Like a wave breaking on the shore the liquid hit Selby full on, soaking his shirt and trousers.

Thompson remained rooted to the spot, partly from shock and partly because of the errant shoelace, which, following the movement of his right foot now lay innocently on the floor. Selby also appeared to be in a state of mild shock, standing like a wet statue and saying nothing, the only sound at the scene being the slow drip, drip, drip of the juice from his clothes onto the floor.

Thompson was the first to speak:

"I'm so sorry, young fella. I don't know what happened there. Look, you'd better go and get changed."

"I don't have a spare uniform with me, Sir. I'll have to go home to change."

"Yes, of course. You scoot along now and get back as soon as you can. I'll get someone else to sit in for the remainder of the interview. Go on, off you go, I'll be fine, don't worry about me."

The young policeman suppressed a wry smile – '*I'll be fine*' – that was choice. He certainly wasn't. Slowly shaking his head he walked down the corridor leaving wet yellow footprints on the white linoleum and shaking his leg from time to time in a futile effort to remove the sticky juice from his trousers. He was relieved to get away.

"How on earth do you do it, Ian?"

WPS Shirley Hall had appeared next to him.

A Sergeant with over twenty years experience on the job, she had seen a couple of incidents involving Thompson and generally kept herself at a safe distance when he was around.

"I dunno, Shirl, it just seems to happen. We were on our way to interrogate a suspect and young Selby and I stopped to get a drink. The next thing I know, he's covered in orange juice!"

"Well, no real damage done, eh, Ian?"

"I guess not, but it puts me in a bit of a spot. I really need another officer to come to the interview with me. Can you spare anyone for an hour or so?"

"Sure, Ian... no problem. I'll send someone down."

The section office was just a few metres away and picking up the telephone, she dialled an internal number and spoke into the handset, "June, this is Sergeant Hall. I need you to be present at an interview. Drop whatever you're doing and report to my office straight away, will you?"

A few minutes later, a young and newly qualified WPC knocked on the open door and stepped into the office.

She was tall, slightly overweight, with a round plain face and short blonde hair.

"Sarge?"

Shirley Hall looked up from an accident report.

"DI Thompson is waiting for you by the vending machine. He's about to conduct an interview with a suspect and his brief and needs a replacement officer to sit in on the session."

"I thought PC Selby was doing that one?"

"He was, but he had to leave unexpectedly."

"Yes, Sarge."

The young officer looked apprehensive.

Her sergeant studied her and offered, "There's nothing to worry about. DI Thompson is an old hand at these things; all you have to do is sit and listen."

WPS Hall put her glasses back on and resumed filling in some paperwork. A few seconds had passed before she realised the young policewoman was still standing in her office.

"Was there anything else, June?"

"Would that be DI *Ian* Thompson, Sarge, the one they all talk about?"

"Is there a problem, Constable?" There was a touch of annoyance in her voice.

"No, Sarge."

"Then get along, he's waiting."

"Yes, Sarge," she replied hesitantly.

A sharp "Now!" propelled the WPC into an about-face position and out of the door.

Ian Thompson had taken a cup of coffee from the vending machine as the cleaner mopped up the last of the orange juice. He was still trying to piece together what had happened to Selby when he heard a voice behind him.

"Excuse me sir, I'm June Taylor. Sergeant Hall told me to report to you. You need another police officer to sit in on your interview?"

"Oh, yes, wonderful, wonderful!" he enthused, turning toward her.

Instinctively she took a step back, wary of the hot coffee in his hand.

He tried to put her at her ease.

"You're new here, aren't you?"

"Yes, Inspector."

"Well, don't worry, I just need you to sit in with me while I interrogate the suspect, you'll be fine."

As the two police officers walked side by side to the Interview Room, June left as much distance between her and the accident prone detective as she possibly could.

\* \* \*

Three floors above, Peter Wilson, a gifted young forensic scientist, continued his work on another case for DI Thompson. Sitting hunched over a microscope, he was scouring a small piece of fabric for the tell-tale signs of a flammable accelerant. A tall, thirty five year old man with an athletic physique and thick brown hair, Peter had worked as a forensic scientist for the State Forensic Services since leaving a dull teaching post at The Australian National University five years ago. Good looking, intelligent and gentle, he was liked and respected by his colleagues and, although possessed of a friendly demeanour, he was often reserved, preferring his own company to that of a crowd. His passive nature was often mistaken for weakness, an error made by many barristers who had discovered to their cost in cross examination, that Peter Wilson was no push-over.

Whilst his career was flourishing, Peter's love life was a disaster, and he had given up on women since his last catastrophic date and had thrown himself into his work. There had not been anyone to whom he had felt drawn for a long time, until recently that is, when he noticed an attractive young woman at a local club event. Although his expertise was forensic science, his passion had always been botany and in particular plant toxins and their uses, so joining the horticultural club had been a natural move for him. The club regularly hosted guest speakers with specialised knowledge and not just in the contemporary management and care of plants, but in their historical uses as well.

As Peter sat and stared through the microscope at the small fabric sample he was supposed to be examining, his mind drifted back to the time he had first noticed Kathleen O'Neill, a local undertaker. 'Better get your act together, sunshine, if you want to make any kind of favourable impression on her,' he told himself. He was looking, but no longer seeing anything through the high-powered lens. There was something rather nice, something strong, appealing and disarming about this woman. Her long black hair and sharp eyes he had noticed immediately and when she had taken her coat off it was obvious she had an amazing figure.

'The next time, the very next time I see her, I'm going to introduce myself. No backing out, I'm just going to do it!'

A voice behind him broke the daydream.

"Hello, Peter."

He turned around found himself looking into the face of DI Thompson.

"Ian, how are you?"

"Never better!"

Peter smiled and touched the policeman's shoulder. He couldn't help but warm to the man and, despite his clumsiness, he found him winsome whenever they met. Peter had worked on a number of forensic investigations related to Thompson's cases over the past three years and the two men enjoyed an excellent rapport. Thompson had been widowed for over ten years and had no children. In a strange way, the gap seemed to have been filled by Peter and the two men enjoyed a kind of father-son relationship.

"Mind if I sit down?"

"Of course not. Here, pull up a stool, let me show you something. You know the suspected arson case you're working on?"

Thompson drew up lab stool and perched precariously on it. He hated anything so high off the ground.

"The Fish & Chip shop one?"

Yep... one and the same. Well, take a look at this."

He moved the microscope towards the policeman. Peering into the eyepieces, Thompson could make out nothing.

"What am I supposed to be looking for, Peter?" he asked.

"Can you see those blue stains there?"

"Yesss?", came the uncertain reply.

"Those blue stains are unmistakable evidence of accelerant use."

The Inspector straightened up and turned to the young scientist.

"What is it?"

"Kerosene. This is a fabric sample taken from what was left of one of the seats in the Fish & Chips shop. It's been doused with Kerosene. This was not a fire caused by hot oil catching alight. It was deliberately set!"

Peter eyed the policeman.

"It's arson, Ian, and I'd bet money on the fact there's a hefty insurance claim involved somewhere. Would I be right?"

"Very clever, young man. I found out the insurance premium had been increased just before the fire."

He paused to rub his chin.

"I think after what you've just told me, I'd better have a chat to Mr Fish & Chips shop man."

Thompson touched Peter's arm.

"How long will it take you to write up a report of the findings?"

"I just need to do a couple of extra tests to exclude any wild cards, but after that, I guess I could have it ready by, say, tomorrow afternoon."

"Excellent! I'll come back in tomorrow. See you then."

Peter suspected that the results were wanted quickly, more because Ian liked to come and see him than because of any urgency in the investigation.

As Thompson left, Peter tried to get back to work, but he found it hard to concentrate. He just couldn't get Kathleen O'Neill out of his mind.

It was an attraction that was to change the course of his life and turn his world upside down.

# Chapter 7

## Kathleen O'Neill

It had been a long day at O'Neill's. Four funerals. Four very *large* funerals had kept Michael, Kathleen and their small team busy before and after each event. Scheduling was vital on these occasions – making sure one funeral didn't overrun and cause a cascade effect on subsequent bookings while at the same time preserving a sense of control and calm. Both father and daughter were now glad to be home and, even though home was an apartment above the premises, it was sufficiently removed from the work environment to create the necessary psychological distance where one could switch off and relax. Michael had lived here for over thirty years and, for Kathleen, it was the only home she had ever known. The apartment itself was surprisingly spacious. Three large bedrooms, two bathrooms, a good sized sitting room, a dining room and a well appointed kitchen.

Michael sat at the dinner table nursing a small sherry while Kathleen busied herself in the kitchen mashing the potatoes. The simmering saucepan of thick gravy coupled with grilled sausages and steamed carrots produced a wonderful aroma which wafted into the adjacent dining room.

"I visited Mrs Papadopoulos again, Kath, she isn't doing at all well."

"Mrs Papadopoulos – the Greek lady who came to see us about two years ago?"

"Yes, a sweet old dear. I really felt for her."

"What do you mean 'she isn't doing at all well'?"

"Yesterday was the third visit I've made since she went to the Deepdene nursing home. She was already quite bad when she went in, worse on my second visit, but this time the decline has been dramatic. She doesn't recognise anybody anymore, just sits there staring out of the window and dribbling. This is exactly the situation she most feared."

He gently placed the glass on the table.

"It's time," he said quietly. "Do we have any of the mixture prepared?"

Kathleen stopped in the kitchen and looked directly at her father. Even though they had faced this situation many times before, it was never an easy moment.

"Yes, dad, we have some outside in the greenhouse. It'll be enough. When do you propose completing the arrangement?" she asked.

"There's no point delaying the inevitable. She isn't getting any better and we have a duty to carry out her wishes. I'll go tomorrow morning."

Kathleen applied the finishing touches to the meal and brought both plates to the table. Even though O'Neill's had a long tradition of providing this special service, each time an agreement was due for completion, a certain sadness crept in, like some unwelcome visitor. The hastening of death to spare the misery of life was something generations of O'Neills had treated with reverence and compassion and it always evoked the same ambivalent feelings, comfort in the knowledge that suffering was at an end and sadness at another's passing. Father and daughter ate in silence, aware of what tomorrow would bring. At last the conversation, like a rekindled fire, began again. It was perfunctory and light, but conversation none the less. They both needed to move past this point in time and deal with tomorrow's events tomorrow, not tonight.

Fifteen minutes later Michael placed his knife and fork on a now empty plate, uttered a large sigh and exclaimed, "Kath, my love, that was absolutely delicious!"

Kathleen smiled, she loved the way in which her father enjoyed his food. "Some ice cream?"

Michael held up hand in the universal 'halt' sign and turned his head away.

"No, no… I couldn't eat another morsel, not another thing. I'm absolutely full to the brim."

"A whisper of chocolate cake? I only made it yesterday."

"You could sweet talk the devil himself," smirked her father. "A hint, and I do mean a small suggestion, not a slab… OK?"

"A small suggestion it is!"

The remainder of the evening passed in front of the television. Channel Nine was showing the epic Doctor Zhivago, but, by ten thirty, Michael was clearly asleep and snoring intermittently.

"Dad… dad… *dad!*"

Kathleen was shaking his shoulder. Michael half opened his eyes and turned his head slowly to face his daughter.

"What?"

"You were snoring, why don't you go to bed? Tomorrow's going to be a big day and you need to be on the ball."

"I suppose you're right. Tomorrow *is* going to be a big day."

Michael rose stiffly from the settee and stooped to kiss his daughter's forehead. "Goodnight, love."

"Goodnight, dad," she answered without looking away from the television. The movie had reached a crucial part.

Michael shuffled out of the living room and into his bedroom, closing the door behind him with a loud 'click'.

\* \* \*

Morning at the Deepdene Nursing Home was a busy time, residents to be woken and fed, linen to be changed and a hundred and one other chores to be tackled by a small staff of dedicated and overworked men and women. At the very top of the hierarchy, all seeing and all controlling, was Matron Stephanie Banks, a large woman of forty six years with an ample bosom and a backside to match, her hair pulled back tightly into a bun on which sat a small white nurse's cap. Her features were heavy and her leathery skin bore testament to a face that had never been pampered with cream or makeup. Thick rimmed glasses and a starched white uniform completed the ensemble. There was nothing remotely warm or feminine about the woman. Were she a lorry, she would surely be displaying an "oversize load" notice. Her twenty six years as a nurse and then a sister in the Royal Australian Army Medical Corps had left their mark.

Matron Banks commenced her daily inspection at 06.25am. Striding into the kitchen as though storming an enemy position, she scanned the surroundings with radar like precision, her eyes taking in the state of cleanliness, and, at what point the breakfast preparations had reached.

The cook was the first person to receive a tongue lashing.

"Mr Burnell!" she boomed, "your apron is filthy! I will not tolerate anything but total hygiene control in my establishment."

Ken, the sixteen year old kitchen porter with an IQ of 86, stopped peeling the potato in his hand and looked up.

Burnell faced the large frame standing in the doorway and with an appeasing smile countered.

"Matron, this *is* a clean apron, it was laundered yesterday and what you can see is a tiny burn mark which will not come out."

A well-read man, Burnell was able to cut to the heart of the matter with perfect grammar. She had always felt slightly uncomfortable by the way this man failed to cower under her tirade, a part of her was intimidated by his casual self-assuredness and quiet confidence.

"I don't care, the apron is not white and I do *not* approve."

Burnell, swore under his breath. '*Her*' establishment – that was a joke. She might be in charge, employed by the corporate owners, but it was most definitely not *her* establishment.

Ken the dim porter smiled idiotically at the woman and received a rebuke for his troubles.

"What are you grinning about? Get on with your work!"

And with that she was gone, looking for another unfortunate individual on which to vent her spleen.

Maria Papadopoulos rose from a deep sleep as the curtains were pulled back, causing the morning light to come flooding into the small room.

"Good morning, Maria."

Evelyn Moore, a nursing assistant, stood by the bed and gently stroked the old lady's cheek.

"How are you this morning?"

A middle aged woman, kind and caring to those in her charge, she was in complete contrast to the thunderous Banks. The old lady stared dully through the window to the park outside. The sun had risen, the birds were cawing noisily and joggers were already out and about, but none of this registered on her face.

Unperturbed, Evelyn continued with the light banter, "It's going to be a beautiful day, that's for sure. After breakfast, why don't I take you out on the sun terrace? All kinds of birds come there to eat the crumbs left out for them, it's lovely to watch the parrots and cockatoos."

Still no response.

Undaunted and having dressed the old lady, she continued brushing her hair.

"What are your favourite birds, Maria?"

The blank look remained.

"What are you doing, Evelyn?" boomed the Matron, sneaking up behind her like an enemy soldier, startling both the old lady and her carer in equal measure.

The nursing assistant turned to face her but before Evelyn could respond, Matron's voice went up a decibel, "You know you haven't got time to chat, you have three more residents to dress and have them in the dining room by 7am sharp. Anybody not there on time must eat in their room. You know the rules, and we can't make any exceptions."

"I was only talking to Maria, while I was brushing her hair, Matron."

"Don't be ridiculous, girl. She doesn't understand anything you say, I don't know why you bother. You may as well talk to yourself. Now hurry up. You've got work to do, and I don't want my schedules messed up by your pathetic sentimentality. Just get her dressed and out of her room as quickly as you can."

"Yes matron," replied Evelyn.

'The woman is soulless,' she thought to herself as she waited for Banks to leave, and after a few seconds continued with the light, one-sided chit-chat.

"Matron still thinks she's in the army, Maria. What do you think of that? You understand what I'm saying, don't you, Maria?" she nodded, looking at her knowingly.

Maria had good days and bad days, but the urine infection had taken its toll and she had become more confused and withdrawn of late. Still, that was no reason to behave as though she wasn't there, she could be quite responsive sometimes.

Maria looked back at Evelyn, an enigmatic smile on her face, as they made their way to the dining room.

"Now, I wonder what cook's prepared for our breakfast."

It was the same happy tone and the same non-response.

Halfway down the corridor leading to the dining room, they were joined by Burnell, pushing a covered trolley of delicious smelling food.

"Morning, ladies," came the salutation. "How are we this fine morning?"

"Good morning, Derek," replied Evelyn. "What ever is under that cover smells incredible? Tell me how you make such wonderful food and I'll marry you and have your babies," she offered in a mock theatrical voice.

Burnell smiled broadly and continued pushing the trolley.

Moving so that her lips were close to the old lady's ear Evelyn continued, "Perhaps Mr Burnell has made pancakes, thick golden brown-pancakes, dripping with maple syrup. How does that sound, eh?"

Maria Papadopoulos remained still and quiet. It was impossible to tell how much of the last few minutes banter she had taken in.

Ever kind and compassionate, Evelyn patted her gently on the shoulder.

"Come on Maria" she said, "let's go and get some breakfast."

Burnell smiled compassionately yet said nothing.

\* \* \*

Back at the O'Neill residence, Kathleen was invariably the first to rise, setting the table, making coffee and turning on the radio to catch the domestic and international news. Some light music playing on the radio was interrupted by a series of pips and then a resonant male voice.

"This is the Australian Broadcasting Commission. Good morning, it's six o'clock... the news with Peter Donaldson."

The kettle competed with the radio as the water neared boiling. Kathleen found two cups and a jar of coffee before walking out of the kitchen and rapping gently on her father's door.

"Dad, coffee's ready, it's time to get up."

Normally Michael needed no such encouragement, in fact he usually awoke before the six o'clock news on the radio. Kathleen went back to the kitchen where the kettle had boiled, and proceeded to make two cups of coffee. Despite losing her mother from a heart attack five years ago, they had remained a closely-knit family, although both she and her father missed sharing this part of the day with her. Since her death, Kathleen had taken her mother's place in this regard, generally getting things off to a start each morning, and even though it had been many years since her mother had passed away, she sometimes still found herself looking at the place where she had sat each morning, desperately wishing her back.

The news from the radio babbled on in the background as the toaster ejected two slices of golden brown toast.

"Dad," called Kathleen in a loud voice. "Dad!" she said, louder this time. "Breakfast is on the table... Dad!" she called again, and then, with a touch of frustration, walked out of the kitchen and down the corridor to the nearby bedroom door.

Knocking loudly, Kathleen called out again, "Dad, get up, breakfast is on the table!" before striding away in the direction of the kitchen.

A few paces down the passageway, she caught herself and stopped, head cocked to one side, ears straining to hear movement from her father's room. There was none. Slowly, she returned to the door and knocked again, this time with less urgency, her voice registering a note of concern for the first time.

"Dad? Are you alright?"

Nothing.

Pensively turning the handle and opening the door a few centimetres, she called again in a quiet voice.

"Dad? Is everything OK?"

Her father was sitting up in bed still wearing his glasses, the book he had been reading now on his lap and the table lamp still lit. As restful as any scene one might imagine, Michael O'Neill had died peacefully in his sleep, a slight smile on his lips.

# Chapter 8

## A Pill That Gets You As High As Smack

Life continues despite death's dark despair, and, while Kathleen was still grappling with her father's unexpected passing, James Strapp, a man who would have a profound effect on her future, was preparing for the customary Saturday afternoon at his favourite watering hole, the Railway. Situated in the small town of Jackson, the Railway hotel was built in 1925 at a time when the only link with Sydney, some sixty-four kilometres away, was the Sydney and Country Railway line. The line had long since been consigned to history as the sprawling city eventually engulfed the town, which was now an outer suburb. However, in truth, little had changed in eighty years. Jackson was still a backwater, where the pace of life was slow and monotonous and little ever happened.

This particular Saturday afternoon was hot and dry and ten or fifteen motley patrons – mostly men in their sixties with nothing better to do than get drunk, were propped up on stools in the public bar or seated at cheap Formica tables. The wall-mounted television was showing the afternoon's racing from Sandown, as a nasal commentator reported form and weight, on and off course odds and previous history of the horses and their riders. The atmosphere was banal and uninspiring as the front door swung open and two younger men wearing torn, oily jeans, vests and motorcycle boots, walked in and approached the bar.

The shorter of the two, slim with short cropped red hair and a large fake diamond stud in his misshapen ear, wore an expression like a gnarled dog, his arms covered in tattoos.

"Hello, darling," he slurred, as the barmaid, a woman in her forties with large breasts, stood in front of him at the bar, "give us a couple of middies."

His friend, tall and very skinny with narrow shoulders and bad acne, stared lewdly at her cleavage and grinning stupidly remarked to his friend, "A bloke could suffocate between tits like that."

Both men laughed loudly as the beer was being poured. The barmaid, not unaccustomed to dealing with this kind of behaviour, ignored the comment and placed the two beers before the men.

"$9.80."

It was a command, not a request.

The shorter man, Kevin Cosgrove feigned deafness, "I'm sorry, sweetheart," he replied sarcastically, "I don't think I heard you correctly. $9.80 w*hat*?"

The atmosphere had changed. It had suddenly become hostile.

"$9.80, *please*."

"That's fuckin' better."

Cosgrove threw a crumpled and stained ten dollar bill on the bar. The sneer which went with it was almost a permanent feature of his long thin face. Together with the acne scars and greasy hair, his appearance was unkempt and scruffy. The friend, Stephen Pickersgill, was created from the same mould. His torn shirt and jeans in a strange way complemented his rotten teeth and a body that hadn't felt soap and running water for weeks.

Leering at the barmaid he added, "Show us your tits and you can keep the change."

Both men broke into laughter again, Pickersgill choking on his beer at his own joke.

"A twenty-cent flash."

More hilarious laughter.

The barmaid left the change and busied herself at the other end of the counter, while the two men leaned against the wooden bar top, surveying the rest of the public bar area.

Cosgrove was the first to speak.

"Fuck me, Steve, this is a real shit hole, I don't know why he wanted to meet us here, what a dick!"

"Who exactly is this guy, Kev? You still haven't told me anything."

"That's because it's on a need to know basis, and you don't need to know! But I will tell you this… he's brilliant and what he's working on now is gonna make me rich."

"Yeah, yeah. How many times have I heard you say that before?"

"No, Steve, this one is the big one… my contact is working on an upper that will get you as high as smack and he's gonna give me the exclusive rights to sell the stuff. No one will be able to get these pills except through me. He's even making them in the shape of mini-torpedoes… great marketing, eh… that was my idea."

"When are you gonna get them?"

"That's why we're here, mate. Mr X is sending someone over to arrange a meeting between me and him to let me know when I'll get my first delivery. He doesn't want anyone else to know who he is."

"Well, your contact is late and I reckon he sounds dodgy. How do you know he isn't a cop?"

"Steve, I'd know a scam like that a mile away. This dude's on the level, mate... I spoke to him on the phone – sounds posh – like a bit of a geek if you ask me, but he owes a lot of money to guys who are going to give him a real hard time if he doesn't pay up. He's got a bit of a gambling problem, so he's working round the clock to get the merchandise ready for me. The sooner I get it, the sooner he gets paid. I told him that I could distribute a good product all over Australia, which made him very happy, so I'm gonna have my very own designer uppers that are cheaper than coke and home-made by my very own chemist. I'm gonna hit the big time, Steve, you wait and see!"

"You've got delusions of grandeur, mate."

"You'll be eating your words, Pickersgill, I'm telling you."

Cosgrove picked up his beer and poured the contents down his throat.

He belched and put down the glass.

"Your round," he snorted to Pickersgill, "and now I'm going to thrash you at pool, you poor sad bastard."

He walked over to put a dollar in the pool table, the balls crashing loudly as they were released.

The table now set up, Cosgrove flipped a coin in the air and caught it before smacking it loudly on the back of his hand.

He signalled his friend at the bar, "Heads or tails?"

"Heads."

"You lose – you break."

Pickersgill came over to the table, placing the drinks on the side and spilling some on the green pool table surface.

"Sorry about your beer," he chuckled.

"You little prick. I *was* going to give you a two ball start, but you can stick that up your arse now."

The game was loud and animated, expletives filling the air throughout and when finally Cosgrove had won convincingly, Pickersgill immediately pressed for a rematch.

"No problem, my friend." Cosgrove was self-assured and preening, "why don't we make it interesting and put a few bucks on the outcome?"

"Can you afford to lose ten bucks?" replied his friend, inserting another dollar coin in the machine.

Again the balls dropped noisily, as Cosgrove called from the bar where he was getting another round.

"Can you afford to lose twenty? I don't play for small change."

The publican approached the two men.

"Same again for you, blokes?" he asked.

"Yeah, mate, fill 'em up."

Trevor Edwards was a big man in his sixties, he'd been the governor of the Railway Hotel for over twenty years and had dealt with young men like Cosgrove and Pickersgill many times. In his younger days they would have been out at the first insult, but he'd slowed up a lot since the heart attack a year ago and now adopted a more tolerant line in the interests of his own health. He needed the income from the pub and dealings with guys like these were thankfully rare, they usually had a few beers and then went their way. There wasn't much in the Railway Hotel to interest anyone under sixty.

He poured two beers, took the money and while handing back the twenty cents change said, "Keep the language down, fellas – I don't really want that kind of behaviour in front of the ladies."

Cosgrove laughed and looked around. The four women present were seasoned drinkers and didn't exactly fit the term 'ladies'.

"Sure," he answered contemptuously, "whatever you say, we wouldn't want to upset the *ladies*."

Returning to the table, Pickersgill was about to break as his friend aped, "Whatever you do, mate, don't fuckin' swear 'cos it might upset the fuckin' *ladies*!"

His friend stifled an explosive laugh, then miscued, ripping the table cloth and knocking the cue ball half way across the room.

Hearing the rip, the landlord came storming across to the table, his face like thunder. He was a seasoned veteran of many an incident such as this and was now in no mood to tolerate any more of this behaviour in his establishment.

"OK, that's it," he said in a menacing voice, barely keeping his temper in check, and pointing to the door, "Out! Now!"

He could feel his blood pressure rising, as his hands clenched into two hammers, ready to strike in the next few seconds. Cosgrove sided up to the man, clearly not intimidated by his size and placing his face close to the publican's.

Edwards was on the verge of completely losing his temper and from the way the situation was rapidly deteriorating, it was going to be at any moment.

In no mood for compromise he continued, "And that table cover will cost you as well. Don't think you're going to get away without paying for the cover you've managed to destr…"

The sentence ceased in mid flow as the switch blade knife magically appeared under his thick throat. Feeling the needle-like point of the blade against his skin, the landlord froze.

Cosgrove spoke slowly in a cold and menacing tone, "Pay for what? That table was fucked before we got here. What you got here is normal wear and tear and we ain't paying for *nothing*."

"Alright, boys, easy now. Don't make it any worse, easy, easy."

"Yeah," replied Cosgrove, clearly sensing the advantage. "Easy, that's all we want, easy, mate, just an easy time."

The tip of the blade remained touching the loose skin between the point of the jaw and the Adam's apple where a small drop of blood had appeared. After what seemed an age, Cosgrove slowly withdrew the stiletto from his throat, moving it directly in front of the burly publican's face and, waving it precariously from eye to eye, the tell-tale red droplet unmistakeable to both at such a close distance.

This was not the time to play John Wayne and Edwards knew it. This was the time to back off and regroup.

Swallowing deeply and conscious of the weapon in his face he managed, "Alright, no one wants any trouble here, so why don't you, boys, just leave and we'll call it quits, fair enough?"

"Yeah, old man," sniped Pickersgill, silent until now, "we'll just leave when we've finished our business meeting."

It was an unfair game of one-upmanship and, despite the sarcasm, the publican was prepared to concede at this point. He'd get these two clowns later somehow when he'd evened the odds – right now the knife was his biggest concern.

"Good," he managed with cold defiance.

The metallic snap of the blade as it sprang back into the knife shaft broke the silence and immediately the tension lowered a notch. Pickersgill and Cosgrove followed Edwards back to the bar where they stood finishing their drinks at a leisurely pace. The landlord, on the verge of a licence renewal application, had decided not to call the police. They had had their fun and would, he was sure, be gone soon.

\* \* \*

Five kilometres away, roaring down a side road on his Harley Davidson motorbike, James Strapp, an ageing Hell's Angel, was in his element. Loud music from his Sony Walkman filled his helmet as Steppenwolf belted out 'Born to be Wild', the Harley twisting and snaking along the dangerously narrow roads. A cat, quietly crossing the quiet suburban road was in the bike's path. It screeched and leapt for its life to the kerb and then straight up the nearest tree where it stopped on a branch, petrified and panting as the machine thundered by.

At sixty three, Jock, as he was known, was as hard as they come. Born and raised in the Gorbals of Glasgow, Jock narrowly escaped trouble with the police on several occasions, and at the tender age of twelve had stolen his first motorbike. That was when his passion for motorbikes took seed and, from that moment on, all he could do was think about owning a Harley. His parents had migrated to Australia when Jock was fourteen and, two years later, he left school to take up an apprenticeship as a bricklayer. The apprenticeship kept him out of trouble and taught him a valuable trade at the same time, but the love of Harleys and his rebellious nature stayed with him. When he was twenty two, he was introduced to the West Sydney chapter of the Hell's Angels and his love affair with the American motorcycle was sealed. He had stayed with the West Sydney Angels for over forty years, being tagged with the nick-name 'Jock', a no-nonsense Scot who was always up for a drink and a rumble, anytime, anyplace, anywhere.

Steppenwolf finished and ZZ Top started. 'Tush' took over where 'Born to be Wild' left off. At ninety-six kilometres an hour he was winding down a suburban street, man and machine in complete harmony. A terrified pigeon abandoned the small piece of bread on the road it was pecking and hastily took to the air. Jock ducked his head and felt the bird's tail feathers brush his temple, its wide staring eyes centimetres from his own for a split second before it was gone. Saturday was the man's favourite day: sleep in until 10am, generally ponce around until early afternoon then off to the pub. He had never married, preferring the life of a single man and although there had been no shortage of women in his early days, they were less available now. All of that didn't bother Jock however, he still had his beloved Harley and riding it at speed on a sunny afternoon was pleasure enough. A further two hundred metres down the road, the Railway Hotel came into view. Lowering his speed to a respectful 60 kph he continued to slow down until, a hundred metres from the main entrance, the motorcycle was travelling at walking speed. The unmistakeable sound of the Harley Davison filled the small area and reverberated inside the pub.

Jock liked the Railway – the patrons were older, the company easy and the barmaid friendly. His hell raising days were behind him and he preferred a quiet beer, a game of pool and some unhurried conversation. Stepping inside, the first thing he noticed were two young men, quite drunk and very loud, standing at the bar. He had never seen these boys here before and wondered why they had chosen this pub – they looked out of place. Most of the clientele were on the wrong side of fifty.

Walking up to the bar, he greeted the barmaid and the publican.

"G'day Joanie, g'day Trev," he said with a smile.

"Hello, Jock," replied Joan the barmaid.

"Jock," nodded Trevor in a constrained voice.

"Large middy?" prompted Joan.

"Yeah, ta. I'm really thirsty. It's pretty hot 'oot there."

Standing nearby, Cosgrove picked up on the comment. Parodying the Scotsman, he turned to Pickersgill and referring to the televised cricket where Pakistan was playing Australia, said in a thick Scott's accent:

"Looks like the fookin' pakis are all *'oot* for a hundred and twenty."

Pickersgill laughed wildly at the lame joke. Strapp ignored the jibe. It seemed guys like these were everywhere now, real punks, with no respect for anyone, not even themselves. Taking his drink from the bar, he walked over to the pool table and was about to put a dollar in the machine, when he abruptly stopped, noticing the torn table-cloth, the dark grey slate clearly visible.

Pickersgill noticed the arrested movement and called across the bar, "Hey, mate! Sorry about the table, but my mate made me laugh and the fuckin' cue just went right through the skin."

There was a small snigger.

"Shouldn't be a problem for an old bloke like you though, you probably only need half the table!"

Both Cosgrove and Pickersgill laughed loudly.

The Scotsman turned around and walked back to the bar. This was an insult too far. He decided to do something about it.

Squaring up to Pickersgill, he began, "I don't think I like your tone, pal. You need some manners when you speak and, if you're not careful, you'll be learning them from me."

In an act of defiance, Pickersgill shrugged his shoulders, smirked and pushed past the older man, his shoulder catching Jock's and knocking the full glass from his hand. It fell to the ground, smashing into a thousand pieces and throwing beer into the air.

The fury in Jock's face was instantaneous.

"What the f...?" the curse drifted into the air. "Hey, sonny!" he snapped, "you owe me a beer *and* an apology."

"Fuck you! You can stick it up your ar...."

A lightning right hand came from nowhere and hit Pickersgill on the left side of his head just in front of the ear, bone against bone. He dropped like a stone, the sentence dying in his mouth. The Scotsman turned to the publican, Cosgrove looked stunned.

"Sorry about that, Trev, but he was really pissing me off, just asking for a slap and he got one."

"Little prick," replied the landlord, showing little sympathy for the now unconscious Pickersgill. "Is he OK, Jock?" he asked.

"Yeah," replied Jock, leaning over the prostrate figure, "he's OK, but he'll have a pretty good headache for a while."

"Lookout, Jock," was all the Scotsman heard, before a bright light flashed in front of his eyes and the darkness enveloped him.

\* \* \*

Jock was vaguely aware of a distant voice calling his name. It seemed far away, yet something in his brain was telling him it was nearby and he couldn't quite reconcile the two.

"Mr Strapp, can you hear me? Mr Strapp, Mr Strapp."

One eye opened tentatively, revealing a man dressed in green, surrounded by bright lights. There was a slow recognition of pain in his head.

"Mr Strapp, I want you to squeeze my hand," said the voice.

He felt a hand clasp his, but it was all he could do to respond. There was absolutely no strength in his fingers and all he could manage was a feeble touch.

"Good," said the voice.

"He's OK. Nurse, move him into the ICU, and give him a saline drip and an injection for the pain. I've written it up in the notes. If his BP moves significantly in either direction, call me instantly, otherwise I'll be back to check on him when I've grabbed a couple of hours kip. Bleep me if you have any cause for concern."

"Yes, doctor," the nurse replied and signalling an orderly, moved the gurney from casualty into the Intensive Care ward.

Several hours later, Jock was fully conscious. The nurse told him that he had sustained a nasty blow to the head and had been rushed here, to the West Sydney

Memorial Hospital for emergency treatment. It had taken a while for Jock to piece together the last sequence of events, but slowly, like a picture coming into focus, he remembered. The Railway pub, a couple of young punks, having the glass knocked from his hand, the insult, hitting one of the guys and then nothing.

The nurse who was checking his blood pressure was quick to notice the confused look.

"You were involved in some kind of fight at the Railway Hotel, Mr Strapp," she began. "It appears someone hit you over the head from behind. Do you remember any of that?"

Jock tentatively raised a hand to his head. It was heavily bandaged.

"I remember decking one guy, that's all. Jeeze, it hurts," he said.

"You're very fortunate you don't have a fractured skull," continued the nurse, "I gather from the police you were hit with a heavy bar stool, you must have a very hard head!"

She smiled sweetly, putting a positive spin on the whole matter.

Jock was concerned.

"Police?" he asked, "how did they get into all this?"

"All in good time, Mr Strapp. Right now we just want you to rest. Is there anything I can get you?"

"Ma heed feels like someone's used it for a punching bag and I'm as dry as a bone," he replied slowly rubbing his throat. "Stop the pain, get me a cold beer and I'll feel better," he replied somewhat sarcastically.

The nurse suppressed a blossoming smile.

"We can't give you anymore painkillers at the moment, you're up to your limit, but in a short while we'll see how you're feeling and we can sort something out. As for the beer, I'm afraid that's out of the question."

She reached for a small plastic cup of water and held the straw to his lips.

"Here, drink some of this."

Gratefully he drew on the plastic straw.

The nurse was sympathetic, "You'll feel better soon, don't worry."

She replaced the cup on the bedside cabinet and straightened the bed linen before addressing her patient, "Now, why don't you try and get some rest? You've been through a lot and I think you could do with a little sleep. Are you comfortable?"

"Yeah," he replied, "I'm OK. I do feel pretty tired though. I might close my eyes for a couple of minutes."

"Good, I'll be just over there at the nurses' station, so I can keep a close eye on you. Close your eyes and rest."

Jock slowly closed his eyes and immediately fell asleep. He dreamed of his beloved Harley, racing down the road, the wide, terrified eye of the pigeon next to his for an instant and then the two young men at the pub, laughing.

\* \* \*

It was morning when he awoke. Gone were the drips and tubes, the steady beep-beep of the cardiac monitor was absent too. He was alone in a small room, although he could hear activity outside and smelled food, the pain in his head had subsided considerably and was no more than a dull ache. Turning slowly to his side, he located a cable with a red button on it, which he pushed. In a few seconds the door opened and a middle aged nurse entered.

"Good morning, Mr Strapp," she said cheerily, "how are we feeling?"

It was almost cant, like some kind of 'have a nice day'. Jock wondered why she had used the plural pronoun.

"*We* are hungry if you want to know the truth," he retorted. "Where am I?"

He struggled to sit up, but felt desperately weak.

Her strong arms encircled his torso and helped him into a more upright position. Extra pillows were placed behind his back and head.

"You were transferred from Intensive Care down here to the general ward last night. I'm Nurse Phillips."

She took a thermometer from a nearby cradle on the wall and shook it vigorously before taking Jock's temperature.

"I'm just going to check your pulse and blood pressure."

After taking his wrist and finding the pulse, there were several seconds silence as she counted off the beats while looking at a watch pinned to her lapel, she then produced a sphygmomanometer, wrapped the black material around his upper arm, and began pumping the bulb. The reading was a little high, but not dangerous.

Jock felt too tired to make a fuss and just let the woman get on with whatever she had to do. He was feeling like a battery hen and didn't want to be in this place. Nurse Phillips retrieved his chart from the clipboard at the end of the bed and noted all the vital data, before replacing it and returning to the bedside.

"Good. Everything is normal. Would you like some breakfast?"

"Yes, please. I'm starving."

"Fine, I'll send someone in."

And with that she was gone.

Jock's recollection of what had happened and why he was here was now clearer. One of the arseholes at the pub must have decked him with a barstool after he had dropped his friend. He was partly angry at himself for turning his back, but furious at the cowardly attack from behind.

'I must be slipping,' he thought to himself. 'In the old days I would have taken them both 'oot.'

The door opened and a male orderly, pushing a trolley, entered the room.

"Morning," he said in a pleasant voice, "nurse says you're up for breakfast. Would you like porridge and omelette or toast and poached eggs?"

He swung the ironing-board like table over the bed and drew it closer to Jock's chest. The variety was bleak and Jock felt his appetite fading.

"Toast and eggs," he replied sullenly.

The orderly produced a plate with a metal cover from a shelf on the trolley and placed it on the table.

"There you go," he announced, removing the aluminium cover and revealing a tiny slice of anaemic white toast graced with two lifeless poached eggs.

"Tea or coffee?"

"Coffee."

A weak cup of coffee magically appeared to complement the meal.

"Eat up now and I'll be back later for the empties!" called the orderly over his shoulder as he pushed the rattling trolley to the door. In an instant he was gone, leaving the Scotsman staring at the food placed before him.

A mouthful of the toast and eggs confirmed his original suspicion, bland and tasteless, the coffee too. It seemed as though all the jokes he'd heard about hospital food were true. Jock felt a desperate urge to get out, and the sooner the better, but there were lots of unanswered questions. How quickly would the head injury heal and how soon could he ride his bike again? In fact… where was his bike?

That's when he felt a rush of confusion and helplessness as a wave of nausea swept over him and his vision blurred. Disorientated and weak, he grabbed at the breakfast table and swung his legs out of bed in a desperate attempt to get up. The breakfast tray slid off the table and fell to the floor with a loud crash, shattering the plate and spattering coffee and eggs on the nearby wall. The crash was heard at the nurses' station and Nurse Philips was quickly in the room, a worried look on her face.

"Is everything alright, Mr Strapp?" she asked urgently.

He had managed to swing one leg out of bed and was half sitting, half lying, propped up on one elbow.

"Nay, everything is *not* alright," he replied angrily. "I wanna' go home. Now! I need to get 'oot of this place *now*! I need to check my bike."

The outburst made him feel faint-headed and he fell back against the pillows.

"Jesus," he gasped.

Strong hands were on his shoulders.

"Just relax, Mr Strapp." Nurse Phillips was very much in charge. "You've been through a lot and you need time to recover. You'll be allowed to go home in a couple of days, but first you must rest."

He was starting to breathe more evenly, as the shock of his frailty began to sink in.

"Now, relax and rest. I'll see what else I can get for you and I'm sure your bike is perfectly safe." She leaned closer to his faced and prompted, "Deal?"

Jock sighed and nodded weakly, a look of resignation washing over his face.

"Good. Now I'm going to get you some food. How does vegetable soup and a ham sandwich sound?"

When there was no reaction, she added, pointing to the uneaten breakfast, "It won't be like that, I promise you."

The Scotsman, still coming to grips with his sudden relapse, stared blankly at the bed covers.

"Deal?" she urged gently, needing some feedback from her patient.

He nodded a couple of times in acknowledgement.

"Alright," she said soothingly, "just rest and I'll be back in a jiffy."

Jock's day had not got off to a good start. Frustrated and weak, his spirits were low and breakfast was the last thing on his mind. A sense of unease crept over him.

\* \* \*

Kathleen O'Neill, sitting alone in her kitchen, was experiencing similar feelings. Since the death of her father, her life had also taken an unexpected turn. The cosiness of their shared meals had disappeared and his absence was all the more stark when the day was just beginning and she was eating breakfast alone. She sat quietly sipping coffee and pushing a piece of toast around a small plate, thinking of where her life was going, as the newsreader droned on. She missed her father almost more than she could bear.

Since Michael O'Neill's passing, she had become his natural successor throwing herself into work to help ease her pain. It hadn't really worked, even though she'd volunteered to do hospital visiting and called in at a local nursing home at weekends, to look in on old people with no close relatives. Though it gave her company on the evenings and weekends, when she had nothing else to do and the work was rewarding, she still felt a deep void in her life. She had been so close to her father and, despite her strength, she thought nothing would ever really fill the aching loneliness she was experiencing now that he was gone. The people she visited felt the same kind of emptiness, she sensed it, and she was able to connect to their pain. But she also knew that she had to pull herself together. It's what her father would have expected.

'Come on, Kath, you need to get on with your life, it's time to move forward,' she told herself as she rose from the chair and moved to look at the calendar on the wall. She had circled today's date and made a short note which read, 'Hort Club, 8pm.'

It referred to a meeting at the local Horticultural Club where a guest speaker was to give an address on the healing properties of St John's Wort.

Kathleen had maintained an interest in plants and their uses for as long as she could remember, well before using that knowledge as an integral part of the family business. The cultivation and preparation of the plant which was used to conclude those 'special arrangements' had been managed by Kathleen for some time now, as it had been by generations of O'Neills before her and so this evening's address at the Horticultural Club held a unique fascination. Her friend, Sally, had been trying to persuade her to go along to one of these meetings for weeks.

'This is a good starting point, I'll go along,' she promised herself.

It was to be the most important decision she would ever make.

## *Chapter 9*

## Five Weeks Left To Live

Back at West Sydney police station, DI Thompson sat in the cafeteria chatting to a colleague about the case of attempted murder at the Railway hotel. He'd tried to nail Cosgrove and Pickersgill many times and was now convinced that the thugs were in his sights.

"This time, Frank, I think we've got those two bang to rights," he said, sipping a cup of coffee. "The barmaid and the guv'nor have given detailed statements and I'm sure that, at the very least, a charge of GBH will stick on this occasion. What do you think?"

Sergeant Frank Pierce nodded in agreement.

Thompson was dipping a chocolate biscuit in his coffee. Raising it to his mouth, it fell away, streaking chocolate and crumbs down his tie. The rest of the biscuit made it safely to his mouth, the small accident unnoticed by Thompson as he waxed lyrical. Pierce slowly shook his head.

"You know, Frank," he continued, "I can sort of understand how someone might want to steal, perhaps if he or she was hungry. No money, that kind of thing."

Another biscuit was being dunked. Pierce watched intently, contemplating saying something about another potential accident.

"But physical violence, well, that's another matter. I've never been able to reconcile how one person can do so much harm to another, especially over such small things."

He lifted the biscuit to his mouth. Pierce raised his hand, a warning about the loose structure of the soggy wafer, but it fell away, centimetres from Thompson's mouth and landed back in the coffee with an audible "plop!" A small spout of coffee was ejected from the cup, landing on Pierce's white shirt. Thompson, looking at some distant object and deeply immersed in the philosophy of human behaviour went on with his monologue.

Pierce continued to wonder why, knowing Thompson as he did, and despite the man's reputation for clumsiness, he continued to put himself in the line of fire. He pulled a handkerchief from his pocket and dabbed at the coffee stain on his chest. They had been friends for some time and it was impossible to be angry with him. Even though he was a walking disaster, you couldn't help but like the man. People warmed to him – but at a safe distance. Thompson usually got to the bottom of things more by accident than design. His bumbling exterior had its uses and often caused villains to let down their guard, resulting in a few notable breakthroughs.

Thompson reached for a third biscuit. Pierce moved his chair a couple of metres away from the table.

"How is the victim?" he asked from a safe distance.

"Took a pretty bad knock on the head. The barmaid told me that Cosgrove used a bar stool and then put in the boot a couple of times for good measure when the guy was unconscious on the floor."

The biscuit separated and the wet part fell to the floor. It was becoming a mini war zone.

"I spoke to the surgical resident yesterday and it looks as though our Scottish friend will be OK to be interviewed tomorrow. He's out of intensive care and in a general ward, so I'll go and pay the fellow a visit this afternoon."

Pierce rose from his chair.

"Well, Ian, nice talking to you, but I'd better get back. Duty calls."

"Yep," replied Thompson, "me too."

And draining the last of the coffee stood up and walked away from the table, narrowly missing soggy chocolate biscuit number three which had fallen to the floor.

A uniformed policeman, however, carrying a lunch tray of pasta was not so fortunate. His right heel found the slippery chocolate remnant, causing him to ice-skate into a nearby table of diners, showering them with tagliatelle and a rich red sauce. Thompson and Pierce, now at the door and several metres away turned at the sound of the commotion.

Pierce was fairly sure it had something to do with his companion – it usually did, but Thompson, clicking his tongue and shaking his head simply said, "Young kids, always in a rush. You can't run around in a place like this. It's an accident just waiting to happen!"

\* \* \*

Ben Adams had been Chief Surgical Resident at West Sydney Memorial

Hospital for five years, and, in that time, he had encountered most types of hospital situations… everything from minor injuries to trauma and chronic illness. A man of many years experience, he had been on duty the day Strapp was admitted to the Emergency Department and was present throughout. A routine X-ray examination had revealed bruising of the skull and on this occasion surgery had not been necessary. It was however the slight shading on the X-ray film which had aroused his suspicions and prompted him to order an MRI scan. The results confirmed his worst fears. There was a large tumour towards the rear of the brain. This type of growth was inoperable and signified an almost certain terminal condition. He had called for a second opinion from the hospital's senior neurosurgeon and together they had poured over the MRI images. The colleague's opinion concurred with his own, an inoperable brain tumour giving the patient, at most, a few weeks to live.

The conference with the neurosurgeon had taken place last night, and now, the following afternoon, he had to tell his patient the awful diagnosis. In all the years he had been a doctor, he hated these moments the most. There was no easy way to break this kind of news. It was a sad fact of life. He had requested Jock Strapp be located in a small private room, adjacent to the nurses' station, after being moved from intensive care.

He approached the duty Sister.

"How's he doing, Sister?" he asked, inclining his head in the direction of the private room.

"He's made a good recovery, doctor. Blood pressure and pulse are normal, he had his first real breakfast and lunch today and wants to go home already."

"Good. Look, Sister, there is something you don't know and you need to be aware of."

"Yes, doctor," she replied, a bemused look on her face.

"When Mr Strapp was admitted, we did a scan and the results show a large tumour on the brain. I asked John Simons, the chief neurosurgeon to look at the images and he confirmed the diagnosis."

He paused wanting to be quite certain what he was saying was registering.

"The prognosis is not good. I'm afraid the tumour is inoperable and we aren't able to offer any suitable chemo or radiotherapy treatment, only palliative care, this man has just weeks to live, a few months if he's lucky and, at this point, he has no idea."

The gravity of the situation registered on the Sister's face.

"I see," she said solemnly.

Adams continued, "So I am now going to give this patient the news. I suspect he's going to feel confused, angry and frightened and probably a hundred other things. It's important you and your staff are there and that you are all fully in the picture. We'll need to keep a very close eye on him for a while, so don't leave him alone for long periods without checking he's OK."

"Yes, doctor, I understand. You can rely on me and my staff to be there and do our job."

"Thank you, it's important."

The conversation over, he moved towards the nearby room and knocked gently on the door before entering. Jock Strapp was watching television, a re-run sitcom was playing, canned laughter punctuating each dismally unfunny line.

"Mr Strapp, I'm Ben Adams, Chief Surgical Resident here, how are you feeling?"

Jock pointed to his bandaged head.

"Thank God it's tough. I've been in worse scrapes. I'll be OK in a day or so."

"Any headaches?"

"Just the usual ones. But the girls here are great. They keep me topped up with the good stuff!"

He gave a wry smile.

Adams gave him a quizzical look.

"What do you mean by 'just the usual ones'?"

"I've had them on and off for the last couple of months. Real thumpers, at the back here," he said, pointing to his head. "It's probably the booze. I should really cut down, but what the hell, you only live once, eh, doc?"

Adams did not reply, the television droned on in the background. At length, he drew up a chair and in a serious tone addressed his patient.

"Mr Strapp, when you were brought in unconscious, we did some X-rays of your skull. They showed an area of bruising, but nothing that merited surgery, however, I noticed something that worried me and I ordered some more tests."

Adams sighed deeply, this was tougher than he had envisaged.

"The results of the scan show a growth in the back of your head."

Jock looked puzzled.

"A growth? What do you mean, a growth? You mean like something that shouldn't be there?"

"Yes, that's right, something that shouldn't be there."

Strapp was silent for a moment, digesting what the doctor had said. Adams remained still throughout.

At length, the Scotsman asked, "But... you can remove this, this... growth?"

"No, we can't and that's the problem."

"What's the problem, doc?"

Adams gathered himself to unveil the moment of truth.

"Mr Strapp, you have a large, inoperable brain tumour. It has almost certainly been the cause of your severe headaches, which are going to get a lot worse without medication as the tumour grows. I'll not beat around the bush, the future doesn't look promising."

Jock forced a feeble laugh.

"Well, I can cope with the headaches, doc. I mean it's not like it's gonna kill me, is it?"

"I'm afraid the condition is terminal, Mr Strapp. I wish I were able to give you better news, but I can't. You have a tumour which we can't remove and it's going to prevent your brain from working in the way that is necessary to keep you alive."

Jock was stunned as the gravity of what he had just been told sank in. There was silence between the two men, the television sitcom with the canned laughter babbling incongruously in the background.

Blinking his eyes in rapid succession several times, Jock turned to the surgeon.

"How long?"

Adams slowly shook his head.

"Mr Strapp, doctors aren't gods, I can't give absolutes, there are all kinds of factors to consider, including remission, although I'll be honest, that looks extremely unlikely."

A steel-like grip latched onto his wrist.

"How long?" the question came again, this time vehemently.

"Maybe two or three months, four at most." He paused. "I'm sorry."

The grip relaxed and Jock seemed to shrink in size, dealing with the enormity of the situation.

"I see," he said, "you're sure?"

Adams nodded.

"I obtained a second opinion from the senior neurosurgeon. It happens to be his area of expertise and he concurred with my diagnosis. I'm really sorry."

The Scotsman was mute, there was little more to be said at this point.

Adams gently probed, "Is there anyone you would like us to call?"

Jock sat immobile, staring at some point in the distance and oblivious to all around him.

"Would you like to be alone for a while, Mr Strapp?" Adams asked softly.

Jock slowly nodded, a single tear rolling down one cheek. The doctor rose from the chair and pushed it away from the bed.

"I'll ask Sister to look in on you in a while and I'll come back later this evening," he said quietly before leaving the room and closing the door behind him.

Outside, the ward Sister confronted the surgical resident.

"How did he take it, doctor?"

"On the chin, Sister, on the chin. What a bastard of a thing!"

The Sister nodded in agreement.

"Look in on him in a few minutes, but give him a little time to be alone with his thoughts. I'll be back later this evening to talk with him."

"Of course, doctor."

Adams turned on his heel and left the ward, glad to be away from the small side room. It never got any easier, he thought to himself as he strode down the long corridor and out of the building into the bright afternoon sunlight.

* * *

As the doctor was leaving, Ian Thompson was pulling his car into the hospital car park. The afternoon was hot and humid and his shirt was sticking to his back as he opened the car door and stepped out. Ever since he had tinkered with the vehicle's air conditioning unit, it had never worked properly. 'This interview shouldn't take too long,' he thought, locking the car and walking towards the main entrance. The latest report from the charge nurse on the general male ward indicated that James Strapp was recovering well from his injuries, and was able to be interviewed, provided of course he didn't object. Thompson had in mind a few simple questions, before charging Cosgrove. He found the ward without too much difficulty and approached the nurses' station.

A pretty young nurse sitting behind at the reception desk looked up from her paperwork and asked in a melodious voice, "May I help you?"

"Yes," answered Thompson, displaying his warrant card. "I'm Detective Inspector Thompson, CID. I'm here to have a chat with Mr James Strapp. Is he up to that?"

"Well, yes, I suppose so. Perhaps I should call Sister Mason just to be sure."

"That won't be necessary – I just need a few minutes with Mr Strapp, then I'll be on my way. So, if you would be so kind as to direct me to your patient, we'll have a little talk and then I'll be out of your hair."

"Certainly, Inspector. If you'd like to follow me."

Moving to the nearby room, she tapped lightly and entered the room without waiting for a response.

"Mr Strapp, there's a policeman here to see you. I'll be outside if you need anything."

Ushering Thompson into the room, she discreetly stepped aside and then retreated, closing the door gently behind her.

Thompson approached the Scotsman.

"Mr Strapp, I'm Detective Inspector Thompson from West Sydney CID. I'd like to talk to you briefly about Saturday's incident in which you sustained those head injuries."

Strapp lay motionless, completely unaware of the policeman's presence and lost in a world of his own.

"Mr Strapp, did you hear me? I'm here to discuss the assault on you at the Railway Hotel last Saturday."

The Scotsman stared out of the window.

"Piss off," was all he could muster in a half-hearted reply.

"I beg your pardon?" asked Thompson incredulously. "What did you say?"

"You heard what I said. Piss off! I ain't talking to nay copper!" he said, this time much stronger.

Thompson was rooted to the spot, taken completely off guard by the overtly hostile victim.

"I just want to get a few facts straight surrounding the attack at the Railway Ho…" the apologetic response was quickly and decisively cut short.

"Piss *off!* Get out of here *now!*" he shouted.

The door burst open as Sister Mason, followed by the young nurse, entered the room. Mason quickly assumed control, instructing her charge to see to the needs of their patient and gently but firmly taking the detective's arm and guided him out of the room.

Closing the door behind them she turned to face the policeman.

"I'm afraid this isn't a very good time, Inspector, as you can obviously see. I gave strict instructions Mr Strapp was not to be disturbed. He's been through quite a lot and he's not in any state to have visitors."

"But I, I, I asked the…" lost for words and pointing in the direction of the young nurse, "… and she said it was alright to talk to…"

The words trailed off into the ether.

"She has just come on duty and apparently wasn't made aware of my instructions by the outgoing shift." Then, in a soothing voice, "I'm sure it can keep for a little while, can't it, Inspector?"

Thompson was still perplexed by the outburst and the speed and dexterity with which he had been evicted from the room.

"Can't it, Inspector?"

"Well, I suppose I could call back, on say…" raising his eyebrows in a hopeful entreat "… tomorrow?"

"Why don't you leave your details with me? I promise I'll be in touch the *moment* he's ready to see you. It would be far better for all concerned and I can't have my patient agitated now, can I?"

"Well, I suppose under the circumstances that's probably the best option," concluded Thompson.

He handed over his card.

"My contact numbers are all there."

"Thank you, Inspector. I'll ring you when he's well enough." Then, seeing the lost look in the detective's eyes added, "I promise."

"Thank you, Sister," he said in a resigned voice. "I'll wait for your call."

He walked slowly away, down the long corridor to the hospital reception area and then through the main doors to his parked car. It had been a disappointing afternoon and it looked as though Cosgrove might escape justice yet again.

* * *

Four days had passed since Jock had been discharged from hospital. The pub landlord had collected him and taken him back to pick up his Harley, still outside the Railway Hotel. He didn't tell Trevor anything about his diagnosis, that wasn't Jock's style, allowing the man to chatter on about the police enquiry into the assault. The landlord told Jock that he suspected Cosgrove was there to do a drugs deal after a dodgy looking character came into the Railway Hotel looking for Kevin and Steve. Because the landlord knew all his customers, they could only have been the two thugs involved in the altercation with Jock. Both had vanished after the fight, the police and ambulance were called and, on hearing the sirens, so did the third man. The landlord hadn't seen any of them since.

"Thanks for the lift, mate. I was gonna get a cab."

"No problem, Jock, if it hadn't been for you, who knows what those creeps would have done? I'm pretty sure they won't be back. I definitely don't need their kind in my pub. They'd scare away all the regulars. Why don't you have a drink before you go?"

"Nay, thanks, I'd better be on my way. I've got some things to catch up on," smiled Jock, thinly.

The publican waved as his friend got on the bike, started up the engine, and roared off at neck-break speed. He chuckled to himself. 'The man must think he's indestructible,' he thought. How wrong he was.

Jock had done some fairly deep thinking in the past few days. Ben Adams, the doctor who first told him of the tumour and who had visited him every day until Jock left West Sydney Memorial, had been a source of strength and inspiration. Adams was right about one thing however, the headaches. They were definitely more severe and came more frequently, often lasting several hours. Adams had explained the pain relieving tablets would only work for just so long and then there would be a rapid decline with the loss of some of his motor functions. He strongly suggested this was the point to return to hospital, where they would be able to manage the pain and offer a suitable care regime. The thought of returning to hospital appalled Jock. He had always hated being in them, even as a visitor. They smelled, well, smelled like hospitals, a place for the sick and the dying. As he rode his bike slowly down the street, the association made him shudder and he resolved to embrace the inevitable full on and go out with a shout, not a whimper.

The Scotsman had no immediate relatives, no wife, no kids and no brothers or sisters. His parents were long gone. His life was his beloved Harley Davison and the strength that the solitude of a loner brings. He was determined to live life on the edge right to the end and that decision somehow made him feel lighter. Living with the certainty of a looming death brought with it an ironic sort of freedom. Once he'd faced that fact, there was really nothing more to be afraid of. He quit his job the same day and left the decks clear to see a few old friends and do as he pleased. So long as his body remained strong enough, he would live for the moment.

'Who knows,' he thought to himself, 'perhaps I might even go out on a high and cheat this tumour after all'. The thought made him smile.

It was late afternoon as the Harley rounded the corner and travelled the short distance down the street, its unmistakeable sound turning heads. The bike was in concourse condition. Older men shook their heads in disapproval at the apparent arrogance of the ageing Hell's Angel and his machine. Younger men cast envious glances. Strapp cruised down the street, stopping his bike and giving it two short bursts on the throttle before killing the engine. There was nothing shy or timid about his arrival which said, '*I am here and I want you all to know it and I don't care what you think.*'

Jock dismounted from the heavy machine in front of The Diamond café, where members of the Sydney Hell's Angels hung out, pushed the kick stand to the ground and rocked the bike back onto its support. The grey-blue chrome exhaust pipes tinkled as they cooled, the smell of motor cycle and oil pervading the air.

He was going to find the little bastard who'd put him in hospital and for that kind of information, he was definitely at the right place – find him and teach him a lesson he'd never forget – there was a score to settle and, besides, why change the habit of a lifetime? After all, he had nothing left to lose.

Or did he?

# Chapter 10

## Make Them an Offer They Can't Refuse

In the twelve years since she had left college, Kathleen worked in the family business and, despite a few flings over the years, none of the men she dated held her interest long enough for a strong relationship to develop. Her choice of profession appeared to be an impediment, as very few men were comfortable whenever the topic of funerals came up. Because her work took up so much time, if she couldn't talk about it, then there wasn't much to say. Over time, dealing with the harsh reality of death and the pain of the bereaved, had made Kathleen impatient with trivia. Her days were filled doing all she could to ease the distress of the clients who came to see her and she often stayed late, keeping the funeral parlour open, so that bereaved relatives could spend a last few hours with their loved ones, before a burial or cremation. Compassion had become her jailer and she had very little time for herself.

After her mother died, her father did his best to encourage her to get out more, hoping that she would meet somebody, but in reality he was the only real man in her life and, with one less pair of hands, the funeral business took up all of their time.

Kathleen did once take a class in flower arranging, but the course, while fun, was attended mostly by housewives, the only man present being the teacher, and he was gay! Michael O'Neil had teased her mercilessly about it. Since then, she had more or less given up on the prospect of finding 'Mr Right' and she'd resigned herself to life as a single woman, adopting instead a rather fatalistic attitude to romance. If the right person came along, fine, if not, que sera sera. In truth, Kathleen would have loved to meet an intelligent man, with the calm inner strength and dry wit she saw in her father, but she knew men like him were rare, and with her father gone, she was lonely.

With him, she could show her sensitive, gentle side. The nature of her job required her to be strong and the world saw a capable and supportive woman, who seemed to cope with everything. It was only with her father she would show her pain and vulnerability. Losing her mother was awful, but losing her father, even worse.

Kathleen had abandoned all social life during the last few months. Having fun just didn't feel right. Then a month ago, after forcing herself to do it, she had gone to meet her friend at a seminar at the horticultural club. She was pleasantly surprised to find so many interesting people there from all walks of life and she loved the lecture. But there was another much more important reason to why she was so glad that she attended. Had she not gone, she would never have known about last Tuesday's talk on plant toxins, a subject dear to her heart and she would never have noticed the rather tall and attractive man, in his mid-thirties, who'd been watching her as she left. Kathleen found herself wondering, whether or not he was married. She was already out of the door when he caught her eye, but she was determined to see him again and wild horses couldn't have kept her away from last Tuesday's gathering.

The meeting had been great for all the right reasons. The speaker, Peter Wilson, was the very same man she'd noticed looking at her the previous month, and whom she'd been thinking about ever since. He was an expert on the toxins that could be made from plants, and how, in medieval times, some potions made from native flora had been used to assassinate political enemies and even monarchs.

Because he had given the lecture, Kathleen had the perfect opportunity to speak to him and, as soon as Peter stepped down from the rostrum, she made a beeline in his direction, armed with a number of questions guaranteed to keep him talking to her for ages. His knowledge of botany was vast and impressive, his answers, both in-depth and detailed, though in truth at the time, she couldn't have been less interested in plants, or more interested in him.

Over a glass of wine, they exchanged information and Peter told her he worked as a forensic scientist with the government, though his real interest was plant toxicology. When Kathleen revealed that she ran the family funeral business, she was pleasantly surprised when he expressed great admiration for her work. This was unusual. Most people shied away when she told them what she did, as though her occupation was some kind of taboo. Peter was engaging and easy company and he appeared genuinely interested in what she had to say, the bonus being that she found him incredibly attractive.

They had talked for almost an hour about anything and everything, the time flying and it soon became clear they had a lot in common.

It was with some surprise that she felt a gentle touch on her shoulder and heard the President of the club say, "I'm sorry to cut your evening short, folks, but the caretaker wants to close up now."

Looking around the room, she was astounded to see that all of the people had left, leaving just Peter and her, like some small island in the ocean.

The same look of disbelief was on his face as he said apologetically, "I'm sorry, Doug. I had no idea it was so late."

Doug gave a knowing smile and turned to leave.

"No problem. See you both next time?" he called over his shoulder, as he made his way to the main door.

Peter and Kathleen were walking towards the exit when he asked, "How are you getting home?"

"My Mini's round the corner, what about you?"

"I'm parked across the street. It's late, let me accompany you."

Once outside, they walked in silence until they reached her car. She unlocked the door and Peter opened it for her. Not a word had been spoken since they had left the building, yet both knowing there was more to say and that the evening shouldn't simply finish like this.

"I was wondering," began Peter as Kathleen sat behind the wheel.

"Yes?"

"I was wondering if, if…"

Peter was finding this difficult.

Kathleen didn't move.

"If?" she prompted.

"If… well, if maybe you'd like to go to dinner, perhaps next Saturday?"

There, it was out at last.

"Next Saturday?"

"Hey, if you're busy, that's OK, really, it is. It probably wasn't a good idea anyway. I mean, you've probably got a thousand things to do on Sat…"

"I'd love to have dinner with you next Saturday, Peter."

"You would?"

"What time?"

"Is eight OK?"

"Eight is fine."

Peter closed the door, smiling proudly and rising to his full height while stepping back.

"Well, I'll pick you up at eight."

He began to walk away.

She rolled down her window.

"Peter."

Stopping in mid-stride he turned to face her.

"The address!"

"Address?"

"My address."

"Sorry, sorry," he bumbled, "where do you live?"

"Above the premises of O'Neill's, on Brookstone Street. There's a separate entrance with an intercom buzzer on the door, you can't miss it."

"Great, see you Saturday."

He was now wearing a huge smile and waved as she drove away.

The invitation to dinner had taken her completely by surprise. There was something very nice about this man, a touch of the 'little boy lost' and the 'boy next door' and, until then, she'd never felt so attracted to anyone in her whole life. What was it about him? The answer eluded her like a spectre in a dream, just out of reach.

Saturday night had finally arrived and Kathleen sat in front of the dressing table mirror brushing her hair, light jazz coming from a nearby radio, contemplating the events of the previous week and the way her life had taken an abrupt but very welcome about turn. She couldn't wait to see him again.

* * *

Eight kilometres away and several hours later, Jerome T Spitz was making altogether different plans. It was after midnight and his mind was working overtime, frustrated by the lack of progress in his acquisitions programme. Cradling a large whisky tumbler, he stared at the fiery liquid, deep in thought. As he swirled the alcohol around, the sound of ice cubes knocking against the heavy crystal glass was the only sound which broke the silence. Radic sat patiently in the next chair, like a dog waiting for its master to issue a command.

"I think the time has finally come, Angel, my friend, to teach Messrs Humphries and Robertson a lesson. I've been quite clear about what I want and how unhappy I would be if I didn't get it. No one could be in any doubt about that, don't you agree?"

"Yez," replied the stocky Croat.

"I mean, I'm a *reasonable* man."

The word *reasonable* sounded like he was genuinely offended.

"I make a more than generous offer for their businesses and what do I receive? I tell you what I receive… not even the *courtesy,* the common courtesy of a reply!"

The tone was changing from hurt and offended to angry. The soliloquy continued.

"Well, my patience has run out! Try and do the right thing and where does it get you? Nowhere, that's where! These men need to be taught a lesson and I'm just the one to give it to them. They'll see. They'll see that messing me around is definitely bad for business!"

The remnants of the whisky disappeared down his throat. He turned to Radic.

"Angel, I think you should pay our friends a little visit. Both Mr Robertson and Mr Humphries have funerals on Monday. Perhaps the ill wind of misfortune should blow in their direction and cause them to reconsider my offer. What do you think?"

The henchman gave him a puzzled look.

"Infiltration, sabotage. You *are* familiar with these words, are you not?"

The puzzled look increased.

Spitz sighed.

"Angelo, listen to me very carefully."

"*One.* I want you to go to Gordon Humphries funeral parlour and find the garage area. His place has minimal security, so I'm sure with your past experience you shouldn't have any problems getting in. You should be there by 1am."

He paused so the Croat could digest this information. It was like watching the hour hand on a large clock move.

Radic nodded.

"Good!"

"*Two.* Do you see those two metal boxes on the shelf over there?"

Like a puppet, Radic moved his head, his eyes following Spitz's hand as he pointed to a small red container, and a slightly larger grey one next to it.

"Take the red box and, when you are in the garage, find the hearse and then place it under the engine. It's magnetic, so anywhere that is out of sight will be fine. I've set the timer to go off at 2.15am and all you have to do is push the red button on the side of the box and then leave."

He paused, watching Radic's face struggle with this last lengthy instruction. It was obvious the man was approaching information overload.

"Go to the garage, find the hearse, and put the red box under the engine. Push the red button and get out," Spitz repeated.

The précised information was apparently easier to understand.

"Hearse, box under engine," a lengthy pause, "push za button... leave."

"Red box," added Spitz. "We don't want the wrong box in the wrong place do we?"

Radic shook his head and then with a single nod uttered, "Red box."

*"Three.* When you are done there, go to James Robertson's undertakers. Like Humphries, his place has minimal security, so again you shouldn't have any problems getting in. Be there by 2am. Locate the person who is being buried. He only has one funeral that day, Jack Sullivan, the ex-mayor of Sydney, and the body will be in the viewing room on a stand covered in drapes. Are you with me so far?"

"Yez, I goddit. Roberrzons, find za stiff."

Spitz closed his eyes and sighed again. God, he needed another drink. This was hard work.

"Good. Do you see that small grey metal box on the shelf over there?"

Radic nodded.

*"Four.* Take the grey box and place it under the coffin, but not so it can be seen. I would suggest under the legs of the stand. I've set the timer to go off at 3am and all you have to do is push the red button on the side of the box. When you have done that, leave as quietly as you entered."

Spitz raised his eyebrows.

"OK?" Spitz asked.

"Put za box under za legs," Radic repeated with no small effort, acknowledging the instructions at their most elemental level.

"The *grey* box under the legs," reiterated Spitz.

"Grey box under za legs," regurgitated Radic.

There was a prolonged pause, followed by "Go quietly."

Spitz slapped a hand over his eyes. How could this be so difficult?

Unable to hide the exasperation in his voice, Spitz spoke very slowly.

"Angelo. What about the button?"

Like some ancient computer, Radic's brain digested this last piece of information.

"Push za button, zen go quietly?"

"Good."

It was like wading through treacle. Spitz breathed a huge sigh of relief and moved to the drinks cabinet to refill his glass.

With a look of complete concentration, Radic was repeating the instructions soundlessly to himself, his lips moving in harmony with his brain.

"Angel."

The Croat looked up, jerked out of his mental acrobatics. Spitz walked over to the man and handed him the red and grey boxes.

"Here," he said, "you'll need these, and don't forget – Humphries – 1am and then Robertson's at 2am."

He returned to the sideboard and poured himself another whisky, signalling the end of the discussion. Surprisingly, Radic took the hint and left, carefully cradling the two objects.

"So, Messrs Humphries and Robertson, it looks as you're both in for a little surprise," he said to no one in particular.

The idea of taking out Humphries' only hearse and setting a fire in Robertson's viewing room brought a smile to his face.

'Yes, that would certainly win hearts and minds, they'd both be more agreeable to speeding up the sale process under pressure like that'.

He swirled the amber liquid around the thick glass in his hand and grinned.

'Yes, much more agreeable.'

Swallowing a good measure of the whisky, he sat down and turned on the television. By chance, *The Godfather* was playing and, although he had seen it many times before, it was still one of his favourite movies. Part of him felt a strong empathy with the ruthless Vito Corleone. Johnny Fontaine had just finished telling his godfather about the movie part he had been denied and Vito Corleone was assuring him everything would be taken care of.

Spitz took a small sip of the whisky and assumed the persona of Don Corleone, "I'm gonna make him an offer he can't refuse."

He mimed to Brando's television image, while quietly wondering what effect Radic's little visits would have on his recalcitrant competitors.

# Chapter 11

## A Flashing Little "P"

Peter Wilson drew up outside 108 Brookstone Street, a simple neon sign announcing he was at the premises of O'Neill's Funeral Directors. Strangely, the thought of meeting someone who lived above such premises didn't make him feel at all uneasy. Locking his car, a small bunch of flowers in one hand, he approached the door at the side of the main offices and pushed the buzzer marked 'Flat A'. Feeling slightly nervous he waited for Kathleen to reply. Moments later her voice crackled over the intercom.

"Hello?"

Peter coughed and swallowed hard.

"It's me, Peter," a short pause, "Peter Wilson."

"Hi, Peter. Come on up."

A prolonged buzz freed the latch as Peter pushed the door and entered the small lobby, a flight of carpeted stairs immediately in front of him which took him to the entrance of her flat. Hiding the flowers behind his back, he knocked politely and the door slightly ajar was opened instantly revealing Kathleen in a beautiful green dress. The colour perfectly suited her peaches and cream complexion, complimenting her dark eyes and jet black hair. Peter was stunned. She looked so glamorous she had literally taken his breath away.

"Hello, Peter, I'll be with you in a moment," she greeted. "Come in."

She beckoned him into the living room and he followed like a puppy.

"I… I thought you might like… I mean these are for you," he stammered, revealing the flowers.

"Oh, Peter, they're beautiful," she replied with genuine surprise.

"How sweet. Let me put them in some water. Can I get you a drink?"

"No, thanks, I'm fine. I'll just wait here."

He was feeling like a nervous schoolboy.

"Please take your time, there's no rush," he said trying to regain his composure.

He had been taken completely off guard by her appearance, she looked amazing and he'd never seen her with her hair up before. Although he wasn't sure what she saw in him, he was very glad he had plucked up the courage to ask her out in the first place.

Sitting in a cream leather armchair, he looked around the room, which was simply, yet tastefully decorated in neutral colours. The subtle tone of the pale green carpet was set off by a large leafy plant in the corner and complemented by a large Kandinsky print on the wall. Soft jazz came from somewhere and the light from the table lamp was warm and gentle, creating a harmonious and rather seductive environment.

"Nice room," he called above the music.

"Thank you," came the reply from the kitchen, where Kathleen was arranging the flowers.

"I don't like busy rooms, so I tried to keep it simple – minimalist. Anyway, I like it, so I guess that's the main thing."

Holding up the beautifully arranged flowers for his approval as she came back into the room, then placed them on a side table.

"They look very professional," he remarked, "I'm impressed".

Her flower arranging class had its uses, she thought to herself.

"Now, I'll just be a minute."

There was an easy atmosphere between them and Peter felt himself naturally relaxing.

It had been a while since he had taken a woman to dinner but he'd never been out before with anybody he found as attractive or as captivating as Kathleen. He wondered if this date would turn out like the others. Starting well, but finishing badly. Madeline was the last woman he'd dated and that was almost two and a half years ago. A temp at his place of work, they had been flirting with each other for a couple of weeks and she had made the first move, inviting him to join her for a drink with a few friends. After that, he'd invited her out for a meal. The evening had begun promisingly, much like this one and then, over dinner, when Peter mentioned he looked after his mother at weekends, the tone abruptly changed. After that, the conversation dried up and the evening was to all intents and purposes over. He could still remember the restaurant setting and the uncomfortable silence which followed his revelation, his attractive date no longer attracted to what she undoubtedly saw as a 'mummy's boy'.

Of course it wasn't like that at the time. There was a crisis, but he never got a chance to explain and, after her cold reaction, he didn't really want to.

Superficial women were not his cup of tea, but because of his looks, he seemed to draw them like a magnet. His impatience with such shallow behaviour had made him wary of the opposite sex and so he had switched off and stopped noticing the signals which constantly came his way.

"Well, what do you think?"

Kathleen was standing in front of him, flirting shamelessly. She looked dazzling in the matching set of diamante earrings and necklace which set off her hair and dress. It was the second time in less than ten minutes he was rendered speechless. She was pleased by his reaction.

"You look beautiful," he said in awe.

Kathleen stopped, taken aback by the sincerity of the compliment. She smiled.

"Thank you, Peter."

There was electricity between them and they both sensed it.

"I've booked a table at Chez Nous. Do you like French food?"

"I *love* French food."

"Good!" he replied in a decisive tone. "Let's go."

At the restaurant, the Maître D' greeted them warmly.

"Bonsoir, Monsieur, Mademoiselle. Do you have a booking?"

"Yes," answered Peter, "table for two in the name of Wilson."

"Ah, yes – 8:30. Pardon, Monsieur, but your table is not quite ready. It will only be a few minutes. Would you like a drink before your meal? Compliments of the house of course."

"It's no problem, and yes, thank you, a drink before dinner would be nice."

Kathleen observed how quietly assertive Peter was. His dark hair framed a face where the features were in perfect proportion to each other, the tan setting off his piercing blue eyes. It was her turn to be mesmerised as he led her gently by the arm and followed the Maître D' into a small ante room.

"Mademoiselle?" the man enquired.

Kathleen looked a little perplexed.

"Would you like Champagne?"

"Yes, that would be lovely."

"And for Monsieur?"

"Champagne is perfect."

The Maître D' signalled to a nearby steward and two glasses of Moet arrived in seconds.

Peter held up his glass.

"Cheers."

"Cheers."

The clink of the crystal glasses was followed by a sip of the liquid and they looked at each other, their eyes meeting in a quiet understanding that something special was happening to them both.

Kathleen was the first to speak.

"So tell me about your family, Peter."

"Well, sadly, I don't have any close relatives. I'm an only child. My parents had me very late in life and I think I was a bit of a surprise for both of them. They're both gone now and the only other family I have left are an aunt and two cousins I've never met, who live in London."

Kathleen studied his face and nodded but said nothing. It was second nature to listen and let people speak. Silence almost always prompted the speaker to say more.

"My father was a doctor, but he died of cancer ten years ago and my mother was his practice nurse when they fell in love and got married," Peter continued.

"My mum adored my dad and she nursed him to the very end. She never really recovered from his death and she was very lonely after he'd gone. He was her life. After that, I had to step in and take care of her. She suffered from arthritis, which made it very difficult for her to get around."

"Arthritis is an awful disease," acknowledged Kathleen.

"It did depress her because mum was quite an independent sort and she hated having to rely on others, especially me, but she had no choice. She coped pretty well for a few years. I did the shopping and took her out, but then she started to go down-hill really fast, especially in the last year of her life."

"In what way?" she asked.

"She developed Alzheimer's – I noticed she was becoming quite forgetful, I mean she was always a little scatty, most of us are sometimes, I guess, but when one of the neighbours phoned to tell me mum had asked him where the post office was I knew we had a problem. I arranged for a carer to spend most of the day with her and I went after work and at weekends to look after her, but she declined so quickly that in the end she couldn't be left alone. I had to move back in with her so I could be there after the carer left."

Kathleen was listening intently, moved by his selflessness and compassion, a rare combination of qualities in anyone.

"That's amazing of you, Peter."

He felt himself redden – how different this reaction was to his last disastrous date with Madeline. Kath didn't see him as a wimp at all. Instead, she saw in him loyalty and integrity and it was like a breath of fresh air.

"I had to, Kath, she was so frail and I knew she didn't have long to go. At the end though, the carer couldn't cope with mum on her own and I couldn't give up my job to look after her full time, so I had no choice but to put her into a nursing home. I visited her every day, but she didn't really know who I was, it was heartbreaking."

"I know people who'd prefer to die than end their lives like that. It must have been awful for her as well as for you. I'm so sorry, Peter."

"If I'd been in her shoes, dependent on tubes and machines, I'd want somebody to pull the plug. If it wasn't against the law, I would have given her something myself, especially at the end."

Her heart skipped a beat at his words – they struck a resonant chord in her.

"She died two months later."

"How long ago was that?"

"Last year, in July."

Suddenly he felt embarrassed.

"I can't believe how much I've told you, I never talk about myself. This is hardly an appropriate conversation for a dinner date, is it?"

"It's OK, Peter, I seem to have that effect on people. I understand your feelings, perhaps more that you appreciate, I really do."

She reached across and touched his hand in an empathetic gesture, a surge of electricity coursed through his body and then she held up her champagne glass as if in a toast.

He mirrored her movement.

"What are we drinking to?"

"To a fresh start and the fact that none of us gets out of this world alive," she winked, immediately lightening the mood.

They both sipped their champagne.

"Uh, humm," a discreet cough from the Maître D' announced his presence, causing the two to sit upright as though caught in some illicit act. "Your table is ready, Monsieur, Mademoiselle. If you would care to follow me?"

Peter acknowledged the request.

"Yes, of course. Thank you," he said, getting to his feet and drawing back Kathleen's chair.

The main dining room was decidedly chic and up market with candles and a delicate flower arrangement on each table. "Mademoiselle?" a waiter pulled a seat out for Kathleen, replacing it under her legs as she sat.

Peter seated himself and in an instant another waiter was at the table with a wine list.

"Good evening, Mademoiselle, Monsieur. Would you like a drink?"

"Thank you," replied Peter. "Kath, what would you prefer, red or white?"

"Oh, I'm not bothered. You choose, I'm sure I'll like it."

Kath's mind was on other things. She felt she'd found her soul mate and she was praying that he felt the same.

The waiter extended the wine list to Peter.

"That's OK, a bottle of the Poilly Fume if you have it, please," ordered Peter.

"Certainly, Sir."

The waiter noted the wine on a small pad and with a curt nod of his head was gone.

"So, your turn now," began Peter. "You've heard my sorry tale, tell me about you."

"Not a lot to tell," replied Kathleen.

There were many things she wanted to tell him if she only could.

"I run O'Neill's. It's a family business. I had been helping to run it with my mother and father until my mum died of a stroke five years ago. Her death floored my father and he found it very difficult to cope without her. They were childhood sweethearts and they'd been together since the age of thirteen. He was never really the same after mum died and he often told me that he felt like a part of him was missing. I had to do a lot more than I had been doing, until dad felt stronger, but after a couple of years we settled into a nice routine, just the two of us, and, before I realised it, I guess the business just sort of took over my life."

"Haven't you got any brothers or sisters?" enquired Peter.

"No, I'm an only child too. I had a brother who was stillborn and then my mother couldn't have any more children after that."

Peter nodded.

"You get used to your own company when you grow up as an only child and it's hard to break the habit sometimes."

"I suppose that's true, I hadn't thought of it like that before."

Kath had never been one to share her most intimate feelings, except with her father. The wine arrived, distracting her for a moment and Peter inspected the label and tasted a small mouthful, nodding in agreement to the steward, who poured two glasses and left.

"What about your father, is he still alive?" Peter asked.

"No, unfortunately, my dad passed away quite suddenly a few months ago."

"Oh, Kath, I'm so sorry to hear that."

"I suppose in a way, compared to you, I was lucky, because he died peacefully at home in his sleep. I was pretty stunned, but, with a business to run, I just had to keep going. O'Neill's maintains a long tradition going back to the eighteenth century Ireland and I know my dad would have wanted this to continue. He was an immensely proud man and I loved him dearly."

"It must have been hard going for you, the last few months."

He noticed the moisture in her eyes as she nodded.

There was a quiet moment before Peter deftly changed the subject, sensing she didn't want to talk about it any more.

"I'm glad you said yes to tonight, I really am, we've got so much in common," he added touching her hand and her body tingled at his touch.

"I'm glad too, Peter," she replied and smiled.

A waiter arrived and greeted them both.

"Are you ready to order now, sir?"

Raising his eyebrows, Peter looked at Kathleen, an invitation to respond to the question.

"I'll send someone over straight away," replied the waiter and was gone.

A few moments later another waiter approached the table.

"Good evening, Mademoiselle, Sir. What would you like?"

Kathleen picked up the menu and quickly scanned it.

"I'll have the grilled Barramundi, please," she replied, "with a small salad." "No entree?"

"No, thank you, the fish and salad will be fine."

"And for Sir?"

Peter didn't even peruse the menu.

"The same for me, please," he answered, with a warm smile in Kathleen's direction.

"Great minds etcetera."

The waiter noted the order and withdrew the wine from its stand by the side of the table.

"That's enough for me, thanks, or I'll be over the limit," Peter said, putting his hand over his glass.

"Mademoiselle?"

"Yes, please, the wine is lovely."

Kathleen was impressed by the choice of restaurant. Its subtlety and elegance, the way things ran smoothly. Even the small delay in being seated had been pleasurable and she was enjoying this man's company immensely. To most people, Kath imagined Peter appeared as a shy and reserved scientist, but she was certain that this was a case of 'still waters running deep'.

Peter too was enjoying the company. From the first time he had seen Kath, he had been drawn by her poise and beauty. He studied her oval face, high cheek bones and ruby red full lips, which had a pronounced cupid bow. Her straight nose and a flawless complexion set off her deep brown eyes. He found her beautiful on the outside, but there was also an inner beauty which had attracted Peter from the start.

The remainder of the evening was accompanied by light conversation and Peter's dry, acerbic wit. They laughed easily throughout the meal and when, at last, they were at the street entrance to her flat, Kathleen didn't want to say goodbye.

She hoped he'd ask to see her again and said with sincerity, "Thank you, Peter, for a simply wonderful night. I haven't enjoyed myself so much for ages."

"I enjoyed myself too... perhaps I could call you sometime tomorrow... ah, I mean... if, if that's OK?"

Like a cat that got the cream, she beamed.

"I'd like that very much," she answered, then leaned across and kissed him on the cheek.

"Goodnight, Peter."

The door opened and she was gone.

Peter stood stunned by the gentle peck on the cheek. A moment or two passed before his legs would move, then he strode with a wide grin to his car and drove home smiling the whole way.

* * *

The alley was dark and quiet, a solitary car parked some eighteen metres from Humphries' premises. Angelo Radic sat quietly behind the wheel, waiting for 1am. He looked at his wrist watch. It said 12:57, just three minutes to go. Spitz had said 1:00 and that was when he was going to make his move and not before. A man of limited reasoning ability, Radic adhered to important things, literally, and, if Spitz stipulated a time, it meant on the dot. The red box destined for Humphries' place and the grey box for Robertson's were placed carefully on his lap and throughout the past ten minutes he had continually patted them with his left and right hands, repeating parrot-fashion to himself, "Humvries, Roberrzon, Humvries. Roberrzon," at each touch.

He glanced at his watch – 1:00am exactly. It was time.

Opening the car door quietly and completely absorbed in his mission, he failed to notice the two boxes still on his legs. As his feet made contact with the road, the two boxes slid off his lap and fell to the asphalt with a clatter. Radic froze, aghast at his own clumsiness and the noise the metal boxes had made. At any moment now, a police car would surely round the corner and he would have some explaining to do! However, after what seemed an age of standing like a statue, nothing happened and it was with some relief that he discerned nothing would. After all, it was one o'clock in the morning and people in this part of the suburbs would be asleep. Breathing a sigh of relief, he ran the back of his hand over his forehead, where small beads of sweat had broken out and looked at the red and grey metal boxes at his feet. The small hinged doors on both had sprung open in the fall, exposing digital timers which were now flashing 00:00 and 00:00.

'Stay calm,' he told himself. After all, no one had seen or heard anything. All he had to do was reset the timers and make sure the devices were set. Picking up the red box and turning a small thumb wheel on the side made the numbers advance. He stopped at 2.15, where a small 'p' was showing. 'No one would know of this small mishap', he thought.

Now for the grey box, what had the boss said about the time? In truth he couldn't remember but something close to an hour struck a resonant chord.

Turning the thumb wheel, he stopped at 3. The little 'p' was showing on the grey box too, but was again disregarded. He looked again at his watch – 1:05am, time to get going or he wouldn't get to Robertson's on time. Carefully placing the grey box back on the driver's seat, Radic quietly closed the door, walking towards the Humphries establishment and patting the red box, repeating over and over again, "Humvries, hearse, engine, leave."

He found his way into the garage area with ease. A strong magnet snapped the box to the underside of the engine with a loud "click" before he pushed the red button. Job done, mission accomplished and time to leave. Closing the side door behind him, Radic left quickly and quietly. The whole operation had taken just a few minutes.

Back in his car, Radic patted the grey box, repeating over and over again, "Roberrzon, stiv, legs."

A short drive later, he was at Robertson's Funeral Directors and, carefully, he took out the other box and walked silently to the side of the premises, searching for a suitable entry point. Despite the accident with the boxes, for a large man, he was surprisingly adroit. He tried the windows and found the first three were securely locked but the fourth was merely closed, the internal latch not properly fastened. A long thin screwdriver wrested the latch from its semi-closed position and the window opened easily.

Once inside, he stopped, listening intently for any activity. There was none. The viewing room was easy to find and the body of the deceased, due for burial later that afternoon, was laid out in its coffin, just as Spitz had said, the lid standing upright a few metres away. Carefully, taking the grey box from his left jacket pocket and placing it under the corpse's knees, he pushed the red button and stood back, the task accomplished. This was proving surprisingly straight-forward. With equal dexterity, he retraced his steps and, like a shadow, left the building as soundlessly as he had entered.

Humphries and Robertson were in for a surprise tomorrow, that was for sure. Exactly what kind of surprise he had no idea, for he had not thought to ask why he was placing the red box in the hearse and the grey box in a coffin. Like a faithful dog, all he understood was this was an important part of some greater plan which he didn't need to know, and, in truth, the very thought of trying to put the pieces of the jigsaw together made his head hurt. Radic started the car, and smiling quietly to himself, headed home, pleased in the knowledge that he had done his job and knowing his boss would be impressed.

Tomorrow's events however, would do far more than impress his boss; they would stun the whole country.

## Chapter 12


## Ashes to Ashes


James Robertson paced the floor in his office reviewing the plans for the afternoon's only funeral and, although it was only eight o'clock, this was the third time he had been over the list. His wife appeared in the doorway with a cup of coffee.

"James," she chided, "relax. Everything is going to go smoothly, like it always does. Drink this coffee and read your newspaper."

"This is the most important and high profile funeral we've ever arranged, Bet. I can't afford for anything to go wrong."

"I know, but while Jack Sullivan may have been a pillar of the community and a former mayor of Sydney, there still isn't anything more you can do, because you've done it all!"

There was a touch of exasperation in her voice. She had seen him behave this way just before very big funerals. Getting worried that this little thing wasn't right and that little thing wasn't quite as it should be, until he was a nervous wreck.

"But, Betty, what if I've left something important out? The whole thing is going to be televised. All of Australia will be watching if something goes wrong!"

There was an anguished look on his face. Placing her hand under his elbow, she led him to the settee and sat him down, handing him the paper and the coffee.

"James, while it's possible the whole of Australia may be watching, somehow I don't think that's probable and, even if they are, everything is going to be just fine, I know it. Trust me, have I ever been wrong? The funeral is going to go like clockwork, no hitches, no problems, alright?"

His frown deepened, making a sharp vertical crease and causing the eyebrows to move closer together.

"Alright?" she persisted.

"I guess you're right," he lied. The feeling of something going badly awry would not leave him. His whole body slumped as he exhaled deeply, the sigh mistaken by his wife as an unconscious sign of relaxation and acceptance of her argument.

"Good. You're not due to leave here until two o'clock, so there's plenty of time to relax and read your paper."

The last part was said in a cheery, almost patronising tone.

"I'm in the kitchen if you'd like some breakfast," she called over her shoulder from the hallway.

Robertson merely shook his head. The thought of breakfast made his stomach heave. Dutifully, he picked up the paper and glanced through it without reading until an article on page three leapt out at him. 'Funeral of ex-mayor of Sydney today'. His stomach did an involuntary roll and he put the paper down and walked to the table to go over his list once again.

It was arranged sequentially: One: check hearse and attendants' attire. Two: make sure all flowers have senders' cards on them. Three: ring priest and confirm time of service. The list ran to eighteen points and, when he had reached the last number, he began at the top again. He wanted the whole funeral to be perfect, without *any* hitches.

Gordon Humphries had no such misgivings concerning his day. By contrast, he had three funerals to organise, but they were all fairly low level affairs, no dignitaries or suchlike. The first was scheduled for 10:30am and the last, which was due to take place at 2:30pm, was to be held at the same cemetery as Jack Sullivan's funeral. In fact, they would probably pass each other at or near the gates, he leaving and the ex- mayor of Sydney arriving. Rumour had it that the ex-mayor's funeral may even be televised. Better make sure the Humphries & Co livery was very visible. Some free television advertising certainly wouldn't go amiss. He sat in his kitchen delicately sipping a cappuccino in his pink satin kimono, an ageing, overweight, long haired black cat on his lap. They suited each other perfectly, both soft, indulgent creatures with little interest in anything other than themselves.

"Oh, dear," he pouted, "what are we going to do with you, Lucinda, you naughty girl?"

A raft of black fur slid off the satin robe and fell to the floor.

"At this rate, you'll have nothing left and I'll be covered in black fur!"

He giggled to himself and squeezed the cat lovingly.

Humphries had fitted well into the funeral business, initially working as an administrative assistant for the previous owner, Howard Johnson. That was forty years ago. The young assistant had quickly learned that taking control in the bereaved's time of need was the key to a successful enterprise, something his predecessor had not fully embraced. Over the course of his first ten years, Humphries had assumed responsibility for the running of the business and it was with no small degree of satisfaction that Johnson, then in his eighties, accepted an offer to sell him the business. Arranging the finance had not been a problem – he could demonstrate a good working knowledge of the trade and his organisational skills were first rate and so when the sale was completed, he had changed the name to Humphries and Co and the rest was, as they say, history.

Charming and personable to clients, he personified a Gibraltarian rock that could be leaned on in times of need, dealing with funeral arrangements sensitively, but always ensuring style was never compromised. When it came to closing a 'deal' he was unmatched.

"Do you really think mother deserves anything less?" he would prompt, while steering the bereaved to a more expensive range of coffins, floral arrangements, choice of cars and so on. In some perverse way, people, especially women, trusted the effeminate Humphries in matters funerary and he had gained a reputation as man of discerning taste. His staff however saw a different side to him as he frequently repeated the minutiae of every task several times to make sure they had understood his instructions.

"Now, Arthur, don't forget to securely fasten the coffin lid before it's placed in the hearse," for example, could be mentioned several times in the space of an hour, making grown men feel like children.

Precise by nature and tolerable only in small doses, he invariably drove those who worked for him crazy. A little of Gordon Humphries went a long way.

Finishing his coffee, he picked up his beloved cat and nuzzled it between his cheek and shoulder while stroking its back.

"Now, Lucinda, you be a good girl and eat your breakfast while I get ready for work."

The cat purred loudly, the eyes closing on its chubby face before being carefully placed on the floor next to a bowl of freshly prepared chicken.

Humphries went into the bathroom and turned on the shower, a small "Oooooo!" escaping from his lips as the hot water cascaded over his soft white body.

* * *

James Robertson wiped his hands for the tenth time and addressed himself in the mirror yet again. He had tried to organise some accounts all morning, but his mind had been elsewhere. It was now ten minutes to two, his nerves were on edge and he felt nauseous. He would have to inspect the cars and make sure that his men were looking immaculate and sombre.

"OK… tie in place, hair neatly groomed, suit… suit yes, suit looks good."

'All I have to do,' he thought, 'is get in the hearse and arrive at the house by 2.15pm.'

His driver knew the way to the Sullivan place, his men were all ready… what could possibly go wrong? He had been doing this for years.

'I'll go onto autopilot,' he told himself, 'and it will be just like any other funeral, it will, it really will.'

He took another cursory look at the clipboard with the list of must-dos lined up like pins on a bowling alley. Everything was in place, that much he knew and recognised, but still he couldn't relax.

The memory of Spitz and Radic's visit had left him in a state of permanent paranoia. He had chosen to ignore the hideous American's threat, but now he was terrified of what the consequences might be. Try as he might, he couldn't imagine how they might interfere with a funeral but the sense of foreboding wouldn't leave him. He fought to compose himself. It was imperative he remained calm and professional.

"James!" the shrill voice of his wife snapped him back to the present.

His palms were still moist.

"James!" the urgency had increased twofold. "James, Arthur and the men are waiting by the hearse with the rest of the cars. It's time to collect Mr Sullivan's family. What are you doing?"

"Coming, dear."

The autopilot kicked in without him even realising it. Stepping outside, he made a final inspection of the cortege before seating himself in the passenger's seat of the hearse.

Slowly, the convoy of cars moved away, making their way to the large Sullivan mansion, people in the street stopping to stare at the long motorcade, until eventually it arrived at the appointed destination.

The front door was opened by Sullivan's granddaughter, a pretty teenager in a pony tail, her eyes red from crying. She directed Robertson to the lounge.

He walked up to the elderly Mrs Sullivan, seated in a high backed chair, and taking her hand in both of his said with great sincerity, "Mrs Sullivan, the cars are here. It's time to leave. Would you and your family follow me, please?"

She arose stiffly, a number of mourners, about twenty five in all, following her cue, as the group made its way towards the front door. This was the part that made Robertson the most anxious. When relatives were waiting to form a cortege to the church or cemetery, tension ran high and he would remain on edge until this part of the proceedings had been completed and the family was seated in their cars. Important funerals like this were, for him, the most unsettling of all.

"Is everyone here, Mrs Sullivan?" he asked quietly.

"We're still missing my son, Robert, and his wife, but I don't suppose he'll be much longer, he's usually very punctual."

"That's fine – there's plenty of time. We can wait for him outside. It's important to get people seated."

\* \* \*

Eight kilometres away, Gordon Humphries, on his last funeral for the day, was also organising a small group in readiness for the journey from the funeral parlour to the Crematorium. The atmosphere in the waiting room was subdued as they quietly sipped coffee, the click of spoons in coffee cups the only discernable sound apart from murmured conversation. Humphries approached the widow and her family.

"Mrs Campbell," he began, "we must be on our way. I'd like you and three others to sit in the lead car please. The second car will comfortably seat five more."

"Yes, of course, Mr Humphries. Ethel, Gladys and George are coming in the first car with me. John and his family are going in the second one."

The party walked to the waiting cortege parked on the street outside. When everybody was seated, Humphries walked to the front of the hearse, turned to face it and bowed his head respectfully before seating himself next to the driver.

"Off you go, Andrew," he instructed the driver, a pasty-faced 23 year old, "but nice and easy. Forty kilometres per hour, alright?"

"Yes, Mr Humphries," the youth replied with sarcasm, "forty it is. Of course I *will* have to stop at red lights and stop signs."

Humphries gave the man a despairing look.

"Well, of course you'll have to keep within the law, only don't go over forty."

The driver gritted his teeth and said nothing as the cortege moved slowly through the suburban streets.

"Henry, Joseph, Edward?"

Humphries turned to address the three pallbearers seated in the small fold down rear seats.

"Remember, when you take the coffin out of the hearse, make sure the flowers have been put to one side."

He paused for effect.

"We don't want an avalanche of wreaths tumbling from the coffin like they did at the Wilkinson funeral last week."

He focused his gaze on the nearest pallbearer and raised a solitary eyebrow, seeking confirmation of his instructions.

The hapless Joseph nodded his head a couple of times.

"I'm sorry about that, Mr Humphries, I must have missed that last small wreath, although I don't think anyone really noticed and it was just one very small arrangement, hardly an avalanche."

"Even so, let's not have the same situation, OK?"

The question hung in the air unanswered as he turned to face the front and shifted in his seat to read the speedometer.

"Forty, Andrew, not more than forty," he reiterated.

Andrew clicked his tongue and shook his head. Jesus, this man was driving him mad.

A loud bang, followed by the sound of grinding metal shattered the moment. The young driver braked and the hearse slowed before coming to a stop, the cortege following suit. Humphries immediately rounded on the driver.

"What was that?" roared Humphries.

"I'm not sure, Mr Humphries," replied the driver, "but it didn't sound too good."

"Could it have something to do with the speed? Perhaps you were going too fast?"

"I was doing forty, just like you said. This has nothing to do with the speed of the car, something else happened."

The hearse was now stationary, as were the two cars which had been following it. All five men stepped out and gathered around the now opened bonnet.

"Did you service the car last week like I asked you to, Andrew?"

"Yes, Mr Humphries."

"Are you sure?"

"Yes, I'm sure, very sure."

"Oh, dear, oh, dear" chanted Humphries.

"See if you can fix it while I speak to Mrs Campbell and the rest of the family."

The rear window of the first car unwound as he approached it.

"We appear to have a slight mechanical problem," he began with a nervous smile. "I'm sure it's nothing to worry about and we should be on our way in a few moments."

The self-assuredness and confidence he always displayed in his professional dealings were clearly dented.

"My driver is a trained mechanic and is attending to the matter now, so just sit tight and we'll have it sorted in a jiffy."

Moving to the second car, he relayed a similar message before excusing himself and returning to the hearse, bonnet now up with the driver peering inside.

"Well?" he demanded, "Is it fixed?"

"No," replied the young man evenly, "but it is fucked."

"What do you mean – fucked?"

Humphries uttered incredulously. The expletive was pronounced as though referring to some distasteful object.

'You really can be very thick,' thought the driver.

"It's a technical term, Mr Humphries, meaning rooted, arseholed, buggered, knackered. The gear box has just exploded and this hearse ain't goin' nowhere fast."

As the implication of the event dawned, the colour drained from Humphries' face and he lifted one hand to his forehead. Giddiness enveloped him as he fought to find a solution to the predicament. Nothing like this had ever happened before and he was completely at a loss for what to do.

Joseph had been listening throughout and drew closer to Humphries, who looked like he might faint at any moment.

"NRMA?" he offered.

"What are you on about?" sighed Humphries.

"The NRMA, the Motoring Service, the service that tends to roadside repairs, you know, they can be reached by telephone and they attend to cars that have broken down, like for example, this one."

Humphries eyes lit up.

"Yes, yes, of course, the NRMA! Good thinking, Joseph, ring them straight away."

"I'll need a telephone of course," the pallbearer asked in a droll voice while holding out his hand to Humphries.

The funeral director approached the two stationary cars behind the now immobile hearse.

"It seems we have a slightly more, er…" he fumbled, searching for the right words, "… a slightly more serious problem."

The colour in his face was rising, giving him a flushed look. He could hear Joseph talking to the NRMA on his mobile phone.

"However," he continued, "a member of my staff is at this moment calling the Motoring Repair Service who will be with us in a matter of moments. There shouldn't be too long a delay in getting to the cemetery. Everything is under control."

"Oh, Mr Humphries," called Joseph from the front of the hearse and holding up his mobile phone. "It's the NRMA. Could you spare a moment?"

"See," confirmed Humphries to the widow and pointing in the direction of the hearse, "all under control. Please, would you excuse me for a moment?"

Snatching the phone from Joseph's hand, he spoke into the mouthpiece.

"Humphries speaking."

"This is Veronica from the NRMA, Mr Humphries," came the voice, "your colleague has been explaining the situation to me, but I'm afraid we are very busy at the moment. Mr Humphries, and there are no vehicles available for at least an hour."

There was a silence as the gravity of the situation sunk in.

"I don't have an hour right now! I have a broken hearse with a body that has to be at the cemetery in fifteen minutes!"

"I see," continued the controller, "I could give you the number of a local garage who may be able to get there more quickly than us, but that's about as much as I can do at this point in time."

Humphries was feeling like a fish being driven into a net. There appeared to be little alternative.

"Very well," he sighed. "What is it?"

He instructed the driver to call first the garage and then the priest, to let the latter know they would be late, while he had the excruciating job of telling the relatives what had happened. In the circumstances, he thought they were remarkably sanguine. Grief generally manifested in one of two ways at times of crisis. People were either too shocked to react very much at all, or they were dangerously unbalanced and on this occasion, Humphries was lucky. Whilst obviously upset, they accepted that the man was doing all he could to solve the problem.

Ten minutes later, the recovery truck pulled up beside the hearse. A large man in dirty blue overalls got out and walked over to the raised bonnet where the funeral director and his staff were waiting.

"G'day, mate. What seems to be the problem?"

The driver was the first to speak.

"It's the gearbox, looks like it's blown up."

A few minutes poking around under the bonnet confirmed the original diagnosis.

"Yep," affirmed the mechanic, "bloody great hole in the side of the gearbox. Must have wrecked all the major gears."

"Can you fix it here, in, say, five minutes?" pumped an increasingly nervous Humphries.

The recovery driver grinned widely.

"Look, mate, I'm a mechanic not a magician. This car needs to go into the workshop for a few days, probably longer as it's a rare make."

Humphries shook his head, the sign of a desperate man with no solution to his immediate problem.

"Do you want me to tow the car to the garage?" prompted the mechanic.

"You don't seem to understand," snapped an exasperated Humphries and pointing to the coffin in the hearse, he said, "we have a funeral to see to."

The recovery driver scratched his chin, deep in thought, and then his eyes lit up with a solution to the problem.

"No worries. We can drop the body off first and then go on to the garage."

Humphries groaned audibly at the possible solution, the thought of being towed to the cemetery was too horrible to contemplate.

"Are you absolutely sure you can't deal with this here, now?"

It was a man grabbing at straws.

"Look, mate. If I could wave a wand and get it going, nothing would give me greater pleasure."

He paused to let the words sink in.

"But the fact of the matter is the gearbox on your car has gone to the great garage in the sky, it is no more, it has gone to its maker."

Andrew looked at the now completely distraught Humphries, nodded and raised his eyebrows.

"It's fucked," he repeated.

\* \* \*

Back at the Sullivan mansion, fifteen minutes had passed and the family was still seated in the cars lined up behind the hearse. The coffin containing the mortal remains of ex-mayor Jack Sullivan was covered in a massive display of white and red roses, spelling out the name 'Jacko'. James Robertson paced up and down the pavement, nervously looking again and again at his watch. The missing son was due to read the eulogy at the service and they couldn't really leave without him. At this rate, they were going to be late, and he was about to speak to the widow when a top of the range Mercedes convertible pulled up. A man and woman hastily got out of the car and hurried over to Mrs Sullivan. At last, Robert and his wife were here, the former kissing his mother on the cheek and offering an apology.

"I'm so sorry I'm late, mum. There was a tow truck blocking the road and the traffic was backed up for the length of the High Street, with nothing moving and no way out. It's taken forty minutes to get here from Staples Corner."

Robertson didn't like the sound of this. Today, of all days, a serious traffic jam was the one thing over which he had no control. Even though there were several police motorcycle outriders ready to accompany the procession, if the traffic wasn't moving, there wasn't going to be much they could do.

Robertson took control.

"We should set off, Mrs Sullivan," he prompted. "If your son and his wife would please join you in the first car, the rest of your family are already seated in cars two, three, four, five and six, so we can begin."

The hearse, headed by eight police motorcycles and six shiny black cars lined up behind it, was finally ready to take the Hon. J. Sullivan to his last resting place, a barrage of news cameramen recording every moment. Robertson walked to the front of the cortege, turned to face the hearse and bowed his head in respect before climbing into the front passenger's seat.

The procession set off at a slow pace, like a snake, growing longer as independent mourners in cars of their own followed behind. It wound through the suburban streets on its way to Westfield Cemetery, some six kilometres away, where a graveside service was scheduled as per Sullivan's last will and testament. Sullivan, ever the showman, had expressly forbidden a church affair. His vision was of an American-style funeral, filmed as he knew it would be, in the open, with hundreds of mourners weeping by his grave and all under the glare of the TV cameras. He was going out in style.

A television crew from the ABC had set up by the main gate to the cemetery, ready to film the arrival of the cortege of his ex-Worshipful Jack

Sullivan. Colin Douglas stood by the video camera waiting for the funeral procession to arrive while his colleague, Leo Matthews, tinkered with the sound equipment, fine-tuning the recording levels.

"Col, they say old Jacko Sullivan was a bit of a mongrel."

Colin was almost a generation older than Leo, a seasoned veteran who had covered much of Sydney's political in-fighting over many years.

"Well, I guess, Leo, he didn't get to be mayor of Australia's biggest city for twelve years without ruffling a few feathers here and there."

"Ruffling a few feathers, that's choice. I heard he was as hard as nails. Even caused some blokes to go to the wall when the city wouldn't deliver on some deals."

He checked the connections on the directional microphone one more time.

"Like I say, that's what I heard, wouldn't even be surprised to see some of the enemy here today, just to gloat." He nodded his head in self-agreement. "Yeah, wouldn't be surprised at all."

"It's so bloody hot, Leo, my mate, they'd either have to love him or hate him to be here today. I reckon they should be here any time now. I just want to get the footage and go home for a cold beer and a barbie. Let's scan the mourners, especially the ones that are crying a lot, see the old bastard in the ground, and get out of here, right?"

Leo nodded several times in quick succession.

"Yeah, sure, Col, no worries. Shall I..." the words died out in mid-sentence at the approach of a funeral cortege entering the cemetery gates. "Hey... check this out, will you?"

The yellow flashing light on the top of the recovery vehicle boldly announced the arrival of the late Walter Campbell esquire en route to his final resting place. He may have started the journey horizontally, but he was most definitely ending it at an angle of thirty degrees. The front wheels of the hearse were winched off the ground by a series of bulky chains attached to a formidable looking crane, situated at the rear of the dirty, orange-coloured recovery truck. Gordon Humphries sat in a semi-crumpled position in the passenger's seat, a look of deep humiliation on his ashen face, while the driver and three pallbearers maintained the presence expected of their profession and remained perpendicular, creating an odd juxtaposition with both the vehicle and their employer.

Douglas was the first to act, instinctively sweeping up the camera and recording even before the image was focused. Whatever was going on here, he wanted to record it, and even though it was not the Sullivan funeral, it was certainly news.

"Are you rolling, Col?" urged the anxious sound technician.

"I've got it, Leo," he replied, almost unable to control his excitement.

"This is a first. I've never seen this before!"

The camera scanned the scene and then zoomed in on the Humphries' livery as the truck drove the first twenty metres into the entrance then stopped.

The mechanic jumped down from the cab and walked back to the hearse, snagged like a fish on a line. Both cars of the Campbell family which were following the hearse, pulled over to the left of the entrance. He approached the passenger's door and the mortified Humphries.

"Where to, mate?" he asked with a sardonic grin. "I don't come here very often."

The priest, having been informed of the problem, was waiting at the gates, ready to calm the family, should it be necessary. He approached the two men at the door of the hearse.

There was a long pause.

"I'm officiating at the funeral of Mr Campbell."

His eyes moved to the right, indicating the coffin in the back of the dangling hearse. "You seem to have a small problem."

Humphries laughed nervously.

"*Small* is not an apt description, Father."

A handkerchief appeared from an inside jacket pocket and he mopped his perspiring brow.

"What we have here is not a *small* problem. What we have here is an *enormous* problem."

More fevered mopping.

"I have never been so embarrassed in my life; this kind of thing *just doesn't happen!*"

The priest suppressed a blossoming grin.

"It looks like it already has. The Lord does indeed move in mysterious ways! However, Mr Humphries," he continued, reverting to a more sober tone, "we both have a job to do now."

Humphries nodded dully, grateful to have someone take charge in a situation gone horribly wrong.

"Good. Fortunately there are no more cremations scheduled for today. Mr Campbell's is the last so we won't have to hurry the service. Do you know whether the deceased had a sense of humour? The line 'being late for your own funeral' comes to me mind, but I wouldn't want to upset anybody."

Humphreys looked horrified and started to raise his hands in a gesture of 'no'.

"Only joking," the priest soothed.

He turned to the mechanic and winked.

"Would you mind if I sat in the truck, that way I can direct you to the crematorium?"

"Sure, Father, but I wasn't expecting company – it's a bit messy up there."

"In the circumstances, I believe we should get this concluded as expeditiously as possible."

It sounded more like a Papal edict than a statement.

Fifty metres away, the television crew was riveted to the unfolding drama.

"Are you getting this, Col?" Leo pressed.

"Every bit, mate, every bit.

"Look!" squeaked Leo, "it's the Sullivan funeral. It's right behind the one with the tow truck. Oh shit... this is priceless."

Tears were running down his cheeks at the sight of a dignitary's funeral with a tow truck for a vanguard. There were eight motorcycle police now lining up behind the tow truck, followed by Jack Sullivan's cortege and the independent mourners. The motorcade had managed to get between the tow truck and the two cars carrying Campbell's relatives, blocking them in.

"Yeeeessssss," Colin said speaking to himself in a low voice; one eye glued to the eyepiece, the other closed in concentration.

Zooming in he continued, "Tight focus on the hearse. I bet old Sullivan never expected to follow a tow truck on his big day."

Father Burns climbed into the cab of the tow truck as the mechanic started the engine. A cloud of thick black smoke belched out of the exhaust pipe, engulfing the first four police riders and catching a section of the crowd, including a number of reporters and dignitaries waiting to follow the Sullivan cortege. The coughing and expletives began almost immediately as people shied away from the entrance road, waving their hands in front of their faces in a desperate attempt to shift the smoke.

"Still rolling, Col?" asked Leo, unable to take his eyes off the fiasco unfolding a short distance away.

Colin remained immobile, hunched over the camera.

"I've got it, mate, every second, every bloody second."

The Sullivan cortege, led by the dirty orange tow truck, yellow lights flashing, moved slowly off in the direction of the crematorium, followed by the police riders and the Sullivan cortege. Finally, the two cars carrying the Campbell family managed to join the convoy and trailed behind the Sullivan procession. Resembling a small flotilla the two funerals wove their way through the cemetery grounds. At the crossroads, the Sullivan party peeled off to its prearranged location while the Campbell group, bringing up the rear, finally caught up with the tow truck, which had turned left towards the red brick building housing the chapel and the crematorium.

Douglas, an award-winning cameraman, was already at the graveside as the Sullivan hearse drew up. James Robertson, like a conductor in front of a large orchestra, stepped from the passenger's side of the hearse and bowed deeply towards the casket before directing four pallbearers to remove the coffin and carry it to a waiting platform, draped in synthetic grass. A number of chairs arranged at the graveside were soon occupied by the family and a hush settled over the proceedings as the priest addressed the crowd.

"We gather here today to pay our last respects and give thanks for the life of Jack Sullivan, a man who stood out from other men as a visionary, a tireless advocate for the betterment of his peers and a loving husband and father."

The voice rose and fell melodically.

The cameraman suppressed a small grin.

'Betterment of his peers, loving husband... that was a joke,' he thought to himself.

Jacko Sullivan was about as greedy as it got and the only peer who benefited was himself. Despite a number of allegations of contract bribes, payoffs and work-related sex incidences, nothing ever stuck. The consummate politician, His Worship, the Mayor of Sydney, Jack Sullivan presented whiter than white to the public, but was in fact a money-grubbing letch with a voracious appetite for young female civil servants and a man who lined his own pockets at the expense of the public purse. A number of sexual improprieties had been covered up by female staff 'resigning' with generous bonuses but there was never sufficient hard evidence to make a case.

The priest continued his eulogy.

"Jack was well known for his support of charitable causes, in particular the Retired Racehorse Retreat. I know that this charity has helped hundreds of retired horses live long and peaceful lives, whilst also giving thousands of hours pleasure to young city children who visited the retreat and who might otherwise never have had the opportunity of being in close and safe contact with those magnificent animals."

A small cough from the rear of the crowd turned a few heads. It was rumoured that Jack Sullivan had received large amounts of cash from the racing fraternity in exchange for supporting liberal gambling legislation. There was also talk that the 3R charity, which it had been dubbed, was merely a way of presenting the relationship between some of the heavier sponsors of the industry and a public official in a rosy light. No one really knew the level of involvement of organised crime and racing, but it was rumoured that Jacko Sullivan had a finger deep in the pie and made substantial amounts of money from it.

Two councillors standing in the front row listened to the praise with contempt.

"A friend to the needy, a benefactor to the disadvantaged and a tower of strength to those less fortunate than himself, Jack Sullivan will be remembered as a man who always took time to listen and act with compassion."

"Yeah," muttered one of the councillors to the other under his breath, "like the compassion he showed to the homeless centre."

It was a reference to a failed planning application for a much-needed homeless centre in the heart of the city, where a large block of luxury flats now stood. One of the trustees of the 3R charity was a prominent investor in the development – it had caused huge controversy at the time but, like everything else, amounted to nothing.

"It makes my stomach turn to listen to this crap," whispered the other.

"If there's a God, I hope the old bastard gets his just desserts! If I didn't have to play the game, I wouldn't even be here."

"Look, count it as a day off," suggested his colleague.

A muted "Shhhh!" from a woman immediately behind the two silenced their conversation.

The priest droned on, extolling the virtues of the ex-mayor while all the while the digital counter on the little grey box, carefully concealed under the knees of His Worship Jack Sullivan, moved closer to zero. Each second registered a lower number – 135, 134, 133, 132...

"And so it is with great sadness that we say farewell to a pillar of our community, a man among men, and a man of our time, a friend. Let us pray."

The incendiary device went off at 3:00pm – exactly as timed – exactly as Radic had reset it. The small "pfffffff" sound it made remained unheard inside the heavy oak coffin. The lining caught fire immediately and within minutes the wood had begun to burn.

"Thank you, Lord, for the multitude of blessings you have bestowed on us and we entrust the soul of our beloved brother to you."

The priest bowed his head and in a solemn voice continued, "Earth to earth."

The first traces of smoke escaped from under the lid of the coffin and a noticeable burning smell now emanated from close by.

"Ashes to ashes."

Unnoticed by the minister, the first flames were beginning to appear through the corners of the coffin, licking the edges of the casket.

"Dust to Dust."

A number of mourners gasped incredulously, as black acrid smoke and flames spread rapidly, lighting the synthetic grass, followed by a loud 'whoosh', before exploding into an inferno. A frenzied scream from a large woman seated close to the priest bisected the "Amen" in mid-flow.

"Fuckin' Shiiiit!"

The casket was now blazing, flames dancing around the lid like some grotesque, out of control barbecue.

James Robertson looked on in horror at the spectacle unfolding before his eyes. Rooted to the spot, all he could do was watch as the fire took hold, while mourners fled in a blind panic, tripping over chairs and each other in a desperate rush to get away. The fire was now huge, flames leaping three metres into the air.

"I thought this was a burial, not a fucking cremation!" was heard above the crowd and picked up by the sound technician.

"I've never seen anything like it," gasped the councillor to his colleague.

The sound of the siren from the approaching fire engine was getting louder.

"Yeah. Reckon there is a God after all," the colleague replied.

Two emergency vehicles screeched to a halt at the graveside and several firemen jumped out, seizing the hoses and quickly doused the flames, leaving the charred and blackened casket smouldering on top of two trestles. The Astroturf had completely disappeared and a smell of burning plastic and wood hung over the entire area.

The sound technician, Leo Matthews, was speechless.

"Jesus Christ, Col," he asked the cameraman, "what the fuck happened there?"

"I have absolutely no idea, Leo, my son, but I have the whole thing on tape," he replied, switching off the camera. "Were you recording the audio?"

"Yeah. It's going to look and sound, like a bad day in Baghdad."

"That's what I was thinking!" he said winking one eye.

"Come on, let's get cracking. This can still make the six o'clock news."

Robertson remained immobile, incapable of any action and repeating over and over again, "This is not happening, this is not happening. This is a bad dream and soon I will wake up... this is not happening."

A small, recurring tick on the left side of his face was the most visible sign of an ongoing mental implosion.

But the nightmare wasn't over. Things were about to get worse, much worse.

## Chapter 13

## The Secret Killer

The following day, Peter Wilson was examining metal fragments retrieved from the cemetery where the mayor's coffin had burst into flames, DI Thompson looking on over his shoulder. Thompson chewed thoughtfully on a pencil, his notebook open and ready.

"Well?"

He edged closer to Peter, who was peering intently into the microscope and gave him a nudge with an elbow.

"I'm certain this was a deliberate act, Ian."

"I knew it!" replied the policeman, "coffins don't just burst into flames, except when they're in the crematorium of course."

A wry smile spread across his face at the unintentional wit. It was quickly cut short as the pencil broke in his mouth.

"Look," replied Wilson, "I'll have a clearer picture after a couple more tests, but on first inspection it looks as though there was some kind of detonation inside the casket."

"Detonation? What, like some kind of bomb?"

Bits of pencil were being blown from his tongue in the reply. Peter handed the man a tissue.

"That's the picture I'm getting. By the looks of things I'd say a small incendiary device."

Thompson scratched his head.

"So it was an attack on Sullivan's funeral," he paused taking in the information, "but nobody heard an explosion."

"This wasn't a bomb in the way that you are thinking, Ian, it was a device, timed to go off and start a fire."

"How?"

"I'll have a clearer picture a bit later on, Ian. Why don't you give me a ring this afternoon, after four-thirty? I should have the results by then."

Thompson had been writing in his note book with the remnants of the pencil, struggling to get the points on paper, as bits of the pencil crumbled away. The policeman slid off the lab stool.

"Thanks, Peter, you're a diamond."

He walked a few paces to the door and held it open while he considered the next line of enquiry.

"Think I'll go and have a little chat with our Mr Robertson. Maybe he's calmed down a little after yesterday's events."

The whole sorry saga had been screened on the state-wide six o'clock news, including a close-up of Robertson, eyes wide in horror as the coffin burned fiercely.

"Yes. I suppose the guy was pretty shaken up."

"If that was me, I'd certainly be shaken up. I'll ring you after four."

"Four-thirty," corrected Wilson.

"Yeah, that's what I meant, four-thirty. See you later, Peter."

* * *

Francis Sykes had been fixing cars for longer than he cared to remember, but this was the first time he had seen anything quite like this. The gearbox on the hearse had indeed blown up, which was why the vehicle had stopped, but looking at the inside of the gearbox showed that the explosion had come from the outside of the casing and not the inside, which was not what he had expected. Wiping his hands, he moved to the small cluttered office and dialled the number for Humphries & Co. The telephone was answered by Gordon Humphries after just a couple of rings.

"Good afternoon, Humphries and Co. Funeral Directors."

"Mr Humphries, it's Frank Sykes from the garage – we're fixing your funeral car."

"Did you manage to sort the gearbox out, Mr Sykes?" he asked hopefully.

There was an audible intake of breath followed by an exhalation before Sykes continued, "Well, not exactly. I can see what's happened, but I thought you ought to see for yourself before we go any further."

"Mr Sykes, I am an extremely busy man and frankly all I need to hear is that you have isolated the problem and fixed it. *You* are the mechanic, not I."

The irritation in his voice was hard to disguise.

"Let me try to explain, Mr Humphries."

The mechanic was now also becoming irritated.

"When gearboxes blow, and they do, although it's rare, especially in a large vehicle that isn't driven to extremes – like yours for example, the explosion comes from the *inside*. Your gearbox blew up from the outside."

There was a protracted silence.

"From the outside?"

The irritation had gone.

"That's right, from the outside."

"But how could that possibly be? Perhaps some other part of the engine broke and fell inside and caused the damage you're talking about."

"Look, Mr Humphries," Sykes was now talking in a slow, measured voice, "no doubt you are good at what you do and, if I needed advice about some, some," he searched for the right words, "some matter regarding a funeral, then I would talk to someone in your profession."

There was no response from the undertaker.

"I work with engines and have done so for many years now. I'm extremely good at what I do, so, when I say that this is serious, you ought to believe me."

"What *exactly* are you saying, Mr Sykes?"

"There was an explosion on the outside of the gearbox."

Humphries scoffed.

"Are you're telling me that a bomb blew up the gearbox?"

"I'd put money on it and that's why I'm going to call the Police. Now, do you want to come down here and see for yourself or not?"

"I'll be right down," replied Humphries, a second before slamming the phone down and ending the conversation.

* * *

Jerome T Spitz froze the video tape of the previous evening's news footage. The scene was one of utter chaos as horror-stricken people ran wide eyed and open mouthed in all directions, the burning coffin in the background clearly visible as the source of the chaotic scene. Turning slowly in his swivel chair he addressed the stocky Croat sitting on the nearby lounge, a vacuous look on his face.

"Let me guess," he began, "the grey box went *inside* the coffin."

"Yez, inside za coffin – under za legs; juz like you say."

Spitz groaned.

"Under the *table* legs, Angelo, the *table* legs. That's what I was talking about – not the deceased's legs."

Radic shrugged his broad shoulders and spread his hands, palms up in a gesture of supplication.

"Legs," was all he could say.

"The timer was set for 3:00am, Angelo. What happened there?"

"Just like you zay, Boz, I zet it at 3:00."

"You set it?"

"Yez, Boz, it fell and opened up, ze numbers vere flashing, but I remember vot you zed. I zet it for 3 o'clock."

"So you reset it, yes? Reset it for three, three am?"

Radic stared blankly.

"Am?"

The cloud of confusion was dispersing and now the picture of what had happened was becoming clearer to Spitz.

"And the grey box?"

"It break too, zame problem, but I zet it also like you zed, Bozz... 2:15."

"It's not really what I had planned," continued Spitz after a pause, "but when all's said and done, by a stroke of good fortune it has worked out quite nicely."

For once Radic's incompetence had proved fortuitous.

"I never imagined negative state-wide coverage. A simple fire overnight would have prevented the funeral from going ahead and destroyed the premises. It would have caused financial hardship, but this is better, much better."

Radic beamed.

"But next time, Angelo, if you're not one hundred percent sure of what I'm talking about, I want you to *ask*, is that clear?"

The henchman nodded.

"Yez, is clear."

* * *

Sitting in the main office at O'Neill's, Kathleen scanned through her diary, making mental notes of her commitments for the remainder of the week. The issue of Mrs Papadopoulos was still outstanding, but she hadn't felt able to deal with the matter since Michael's passing. However, it was an agreement O'Neill's had to honour and she was the only one left who could do it. It was quite likely that Maria's condition would have further deteriorated since her father's visit a few months earlier and Kathleen resolved to deal with the matter sooner rather than later. Today she was fully booked and she was expected at another nursing home after work this evening... and tomorrow was even worse, but Thursday... yes, Thursday would be perfect. Provided she made a couple of small alterations to her schedule, her receptionist, Tracey, could cover for her that day and there would be more than enough time to visit the Deepdene nursing home, where Maria was now a resident. If the coast was clear and so long as nothing had changed for the better since Michael had assessed her, Kathleen would complete the contract as agreed with Maria a little over two years ago, when the old lady's mind was clear and she knew what she wanted.

\* \* \*

"Good afternoon, Mr Robertson," announced the policeman holding up his warrant card for inspection. "I'm Detective Inspector Thompson from West Sydney police station. I wonder if you could spare a few minutes. It's about yesterday's unfortunate experience at the cemetery," he paused, searching for the right words, "the fire."

Robertson groaned and slowly shook his head.

"Unfortunate, doesn't even come close, Inspector."

He shook his head and shuddered.

"Please, take a seat. Would you like a coffee?"

Thompson began to smile.

"A coffee would be nice, thank you."

Robertson poured him a coffee from a cafétiere on his desk.

"Sugar?"

"Two, please."

Settling into an armchair and producing a small leather bound notebook from his jacket, the policeman continued, "Do you have any idea why the casket may have caught fire?"

Robertson shook his head.

"None, whatsoever."

"Some flammable material used in the embalming process that may have accidentally escaped perhaps?"

"No, Inspector, it doesn't work like that. There is absolutely no possibility of delayed combustion associated with any of the chemicals used in the embalming process, and in any event I have *never* heard of anything like this happening before, never. It's a complete mystery."

Thompson made a series of notes in the small book and continued.

"Can you think of anyone who would want to cause you or your establishment problems?"

Robertson shifted uneasily in his chair, thinking of the night Spitz and Radic had called.

"We have reason to believe this is not accidental, but I am keeping all lines of enquiry open, so anything you can remember no matter how small or insignificant, may be important."

The policeman waited patiently for a reply, sensing he had hit on a raw nerve.

"Well...er... I don't want to do or say anything for the moment."

Robertson cleared his throat with a small cough before nervously sipping a glass of water.

"Let me be frank, Inspector. A week or so ago I had a visit from a certain party. It seems his interests and mine are in conflict and he would rather I quietly... how shall I say... went away."

Another sip of water. There was a slight tremor in his hand as he raised the glass to his lips.

"I've worked hard over the last thirty years building this business," he continued. It's a lot to just walk away from. I did consider going to the police, I really did, but I thought this party and I would be able to reach some kind of compromise, you know, some kind of deal. Then this."

He shook his head and sighed heavily.

"Do you have any idea how much damage an incident like the one the other day can do to one's business? We haven't had a single enquiry since."

Thompson stared intensely into the undertaker's eyes. His initial thoughts were that one of Sullivan's enemies had sabotaged the event. However, this little snippet of information had been completely unexpected.

"People like that don't go away until they have what they want. You know that don't you, Mr Robertson? There is no deal to be done, no compromise, I can assure you, and it will only get worse. This is just the beginning."

Robertson exhaled deeply, but did not respond.

"If the person who did this is the same person who threatened you a week ago, then that's extortion, a serious criminal offence punishable by imprisonment. Give me a name and I'll make some enquiries."

Another sip of water.

"No one else knows of this, Inspector, not even my wife. These men are dangerous and I won't put her in harm's way. If it's all the same, I'll try and deal with this myself. I'm sure you can appreciate my position."

Thompson closed his notebook.

"Of course I can appreciate your position, Mr Robertson, but *you* must appreciate that men like these are persistent. They need to be *stopped* and the sooner they are stopped the better for all concerned."

He rose from the chair and extracted a business card from his wallet.

"Thank you for your time, Mr Robertson. Here's my card. Should you wish to talk, please give me a call. I can see myself out."

They shook hands and the policeman left.

* * *

"Mr Sykes?"

The question hung in the air as the burly, grease-stained mechanic extracted his torso from under the bonnet of a car.

"Gordon Humphries, we spoke on the telephone a short while ago. You were saying something about a bomb under one of our hearses."

"Ah, Mr Humphries, thank you for coming over. Your vehicle is over here," he said, pointing to a raised hydraulic platform. "Do you want to see for yourself?"

"I most certainly do," spat Humphries, the annoyance palpable in his voice.

He loathed these places, full of dirty, sweaty men, all of whom he regarded as lesser individuals.

"And then perhaps we can put this matter to rest and you can get on with the job of repairing my vehicle. I've had to hire another and I've been put to great expense and inconvenience."

"Right," replied Sykes sarcastically, "then we'd better get on with the job of repairing your vehicle. There's just the small matter of the Police."

"What?"

Humphries had literally stopped in his tracks.

"You can't be serious... just because the vehicle broke down?"

Sykes walked to a nearby hoist where the damaged hearse sat some two metres off the ground, its underbelly exposed.

"You see, Gordon," began Sykes, "may I call you Gordon?" a touch of false toadying in his voice.

"No, you may not!" snapped Humphries.

"You see, *Mister* Humphries," corrected the mechanic and pointing with his index finger to a large hole on the outside of the gearbox, "this damage was caused from the outside, not the inside, and from the way the metal has been twisted and fused, I'd lay money it was caused by an explosion of some sort."

'Could this possibly be the 'consequences' that Spitz had threatened?' Humphries dismissed the thought. 'Explosions? Here, in Sydney? No, not possible, not possible at all.'

"Perhaps a large rock or sharp piece of metal thrown up from the road was the cause?"

"Look, Mister Humphries, I know it sounds far fetched, but I used to be in the Army and I've seen this before. Large rocks and sharp pieces of metal don't do this kind of damage. Explosions do and I've called the Police. As you were so disbelieving over the phone, I thought you should see it for yourself."

There was little Humphries could say or do at this point. The hearse was clearly out of service and wasn't going to be fixed until the Police had, at the very least, attended.

"Frank, Frank..." the garage's middle-aged receptionist was calling from the office. Sykes turned to face the woman some ten metres away.

"What is it, Doris?" he called over the noise from the workshop.

"There are a couple of policemen here to see you."

The alarm in her voice was unmistakable.

The mechanic turned to face the undertaker and winked.

"Talk of the devil! Now, if you'll excuse me for a moment, I'll be right back."

\* \* \*

Peter Wilson studied the results carefully. Despite the activity on the third floor of the West Sydney police building, he remained impervious to all around him. The profile of the mass spectrometer reading showed the spikes of some of the elements appeared very similar to those recovered from the Sullivan funeral also sent to him for analysis. On that occasion his initial investigation of the coffin lining had suggested some kind of accelerant had been used. His first thoughts had been petrol or kerosene, but to get an accurate picture, he had run the sample through the mass spectrometer which identified all the elements present and presented them as a chart with spikes indicating their quantities. Reading particles at an atomic level, the results were indisputable and what he found deeply disturbed him. Instead of petrol or kerosene, there was the unmistakable profile of the high explosive C4 in sufficient quantity to burn slowly, but without the catastrophic effect of a compressed explosion. It also looked as though magnesium had been mixed with the explosive to sustain the burning process. Perhaps this also answered the question of why the remains of a small grey box, found in the coffin, had high residual concentrations of both substances.

That was two days ago. The results now before him were from pieces of metal sent to him yesterday. Apparently, the metallic fragments had been taken from the engine of a hearse – the police had been called after the garage owner had become suspicious. They had taken some small samples and sent them to the State Forensics Service for investigation. Retrieving those results, he displayed them and the burnt coffin spectrometer readings on a split screen monitor. Overlaying the two caused his heart to skip a beat.

The levels of high explosive from the metal fragments were considerably higher than those from the coffin, which made sense, given the outcome, but the profile of both was identical and there was only one conclusion to be drawn from this observation – the compounds were identical. Moreover, they had come from the same batch. He picked up the telephone and dialled an internal number.

"Keith? Hi, it's Peter Wilson. I was wondering of you could spare a minute or two, I've got something here I could really use your opinion on."

"Can we sort it out over the phone?"

"Well, it's concerning some results from the mass spectrometer and, to be honest, I'd much rather you saw them for yourself."

"OK, Peter, no problem. I'll come over. Give me ten minutes."

"Cheers, Keith."

Fifteen minutes later, Peter Wilson and the long-serving forensic scientist, Keith Somerset, were studying a monitor where both spectrographic results were displayed.

"Look Keith," began Peter, "see these spikes here and here."

Somerset nodded.

"They're C4 profiles."

"The high explosive C4?"

"Yes, the high explosive."

"The spikes are identical."

Peter nodded.

"That's what I wanted to talk to you about."

"Where did the samples come from?" asked the older man.

"The first one, this one here, is from the inside of Sullivan's coffin that caught fire just before it was about to be lowered into the grave."

" Jacko Sullivan's funeral?"

"The very same."

"Yes, I saw the whole thing on the six o'clock news on Tuesday. Quite bizarre. And the other?"

"This one," continued Peter, pointing to the second image, "was taken from the engine of a hearse. A hole had been punched through the gearbox."

"A hearse?"

"Yes. A hearse. The one that was towed in front of Sullivan's cortege."

"Mmm, interesting."

Somerset was scratching his chin and looking at the ceiling.

"Quite. But look, Keith, these profiles are identical, and that strongly suggests they came from the same batch, wouldn't you say?"

"Yes, it does, young man, unmistakably. Tell me, Peter, when did the explosion on the hearse occur?"

"Tuesday, forty five minutes before the Sullivan funeral."

"Mmm."

More scratching of the chin.

"It can't be coincidence, somebody set out to deliberately cause chaos, at least that's how it looks to me," offered Keith.

"It looks that way to me too. Ian Thompson is going to be very busy if he has to interview everybody with a gripe against Jacko."

Peter slid off the lab stool and patted Somerset warmly on the shoulder.

"Yeah, isn't that the truth? Thanks, Keith, you've been a real help."

"No problem."

Somerset turned to leave the room.

"Anytime," said the older man as he passed through the door and out into the main corridor.

It was time to speak to Ian Thompson. Peter returned to the bench, picked up the receiver and dialled. The call was answered after only a few short rings.

"DI Thompson."

"Ian, it's Peter. You know the fire at the cemetery the other day – the Sullivan one?"

"What about it?"

"Ian, I think this may not be a one-off."

The tone in Peter's voice stopped the policeman dead in his tracks.

"What makes you say that?"

"I've just finished another spectral examination on a different sample. The compound used in the Sullivan case is exactly the same."

"And?"

"And this one involves another funeral director, but both incidents occurred on the same day. It was the hearse being towed in front of the Sullivan procession."

"I see."

There was a prolonged silence.

"Ian, are you still there?"

The man could be exasperating, thought Peter to himself.

"Ian, did you hear what I just said?"

"Sorry, Peter, just thinking."

"Ian, I think you should come up here now. This is important."

Ten minutes later, Thompson was looking at the split screen displaying the spectral analyses from the fire at the Sullivan funeral and the gearbox from the damaged hearse.

"I see what you mean, Peter. They're similar."

"No, Ian, not similar, exactly the same, from the same batch. This is C4 high explosive residue, it's like a fingerprint."

He paused to let the importance of what he had said sink in.

Thompson turned to face the young scientist.

"You're quite sure of this?"

"A hundred per cent sure. I've even confirmed it with Keith Somerset."

Thompson was now analysing the evidence, thinking quietly to himself. 'One funeral director is intimidated and a prominent funeral reduced to chaos. Another man's hearse is put out of action and the common links are the explosive and perhaps Jacko Sullivan. It was either the work of Sullivan's enemies or someone out to cause trouble for the funeral directors.'

His guts told him it was the former and his guts were rarely wrong. He rubbed his lips with an index finger.

"Think I'd better have a chat with the owner of the hearse. I'll get the details from the case officer."

Thompson straightened up and addressed the younger man.

"Thanks, Peter, you're certainly on the ball. But you do look tired. Been burning the midnight oil here, in the lab, lately?"

Peter sighed.

"Yep, it's been pretty full-on the last few days, but that's the way it goes sometimes."

Thompson's eyes lit up.

"I've just had a great idea! Why don't you come over to my place tonight and have dinner? I'm not a bad cook and you look like you could do with some company."

Peter smiled.

"Thanks, Ian, you're very kind. Ordinarily I'd jump at the chance, but I'm off to the theatre tonight."

"The theatre can be a lonely place by yourself," the policeman mused.

"Well, actually, I'm taking someone."

"A lady?"

"No, Ian, a man."

He laughed.

"Of course it's a lady and a very beautiful one at that. To be truthful, I'm really attracted to her, but she's treating me more like a friend, than a boyfriend. I don't want be pushy, but I'd like to be more than a friend. I've bought her a nice present, but I'm afraid to give it to her, in case I scare her off."

"What is it?"

"A ring."

"You're a dark horse!"

Thompson tapped him playfully on the shoulder with a mock punch.

"I've never known a woman upset to receive a nice piece of jewellery. I've even know a few who'd kill to get some!"

Peter laughed.

"I don't suppose by any chance you have it with you?"

"As it happens, I have," Peter said, pulling a small black box from his trouser pocket.

He opened it and lifted out a small gold ring. It had a rather expensive looking diamond, sitting in a raised setting, beautiful and tasteful in its simplicity.

"Mmmm," smiled the policeman, "that looks like and engagement ring to me. Were you planning to give it to her when you propose?"

"I, I hadn't thought of that, Ian. It's not really that sort of relationship yet. I was just going to pick my time and give it to her as gift."

"Were you thinking about giving it to her tonight?"

"Oh no, Ian, not tonight. It's the wrong sort of play for anything that."

"What's the play about?"

"It's a murder mystery. It sounds quite good."

He looked at his watch.

"I'd better make a move, I've got a lot to finish and I have to leave this place by five o'clock. I don't want to be late."

Thompson smiled, "I won't keep you then, enjoy yourself tonight."

"Thanks, Ian."

As he walked away, Peter considered Kathleen's invitation to see 'The Secret Killer'. He was slightly surprised by her choice, but he should have paid more attention. It was the first clue to another side of her character.

## Chapter 14

## This Must Be Your Lucky Day

B reakfast at the Deepdene Nursing Home had finished and the last of the residents were filtering back to their rooms. Matron Banks kept a steely eye on the cleaning up, issuing a terse instruction here, and a verbal prod there.

"Come on, come on!" she urged one of the kitchen porters. "You'll have to move faster than that if you're going to get the rest of your work done and the tables set up in time for lunch!"

The porter swore under his breath and moved fractionally faster. No matter how quick or efficient he was, it was never good enough for this overweight tyrant.

"I'll just switch on the turbo, Matron," he scoffed.

"What was that?" she had radar-like ears and rarely missed anything.

"Nothing, Matron, nothing."

"Good. Then get on with it!"

She strode forcefully away down the corridor, a battle cruiser on the high seas looking to broadside the first errant employee within range.

The porter looked up from the table he was clearing, his eyes fixed on the woman as she barked a command at a young Asian worker. God, how he hated the cow. Still, he wasn't alone, everyone hated her and the thought, in some perverse way, brought a smile to his lips.

Maria Papadopoulos slowly made her way back to her room. It had been a couple of weeks since she had used the wheelchair and the severe swelling on her right leg had all but disappeared. With the infection gone, she was more mobile and chatty. The transition from wheelchair to Zimmer frame to walking stick had been relatively straight forward and she was now able to walk without assistance, albeit carefully. Breakfast these days was, for Maria, a fairly mediocre affair, and generally she simply went through the motions of presenting herself, along with the other residents at the appointed time, eating and returning to her room. Alternating between the real world and fantasy, she was still prone to periods of immobility, sitting in a world of her own, staring into the distance, unable to communicate with anyone around her. However, fantasy often propelled her back many years and the nursing staff had on more than one occasion prevented her from leaving the premises, when she imagined she was going shopping, to the beach and so on. Fortunately, their vigilance had kept her out of harm's way.

'I think I'll go to the pictures,' she thought to herself as she moved along the spotlessly clean corridor. 'Yes, the pictures, that new one with Clark Gable and Vivien Leigh... now, what's it called?'

Her memory searched for the title. She could see the poster – Gable with Leigh in his arms and with a southern mansion burning in the background. Gone... gone something. Gone with the wind! Yes, that was it – I'll go to the pictures and see Gone with the wind.'

Reaching her room, she went immediately to the wardrobe to select an outfit to wear.

A knock at the door diverted her attention from the small selection of clothes she had placed on the bed.

"Hello?" the door opened and Evelyn entered. "Good morning, Maria," she announced cheerily, "how was breakfast?"

"Breakfast?"

The old lady had already forgotten the scrambled eggs she'd just eaten.

"I'll have some, when I get back," she said.

Ignoring her confusion, Evelyn continued their conversation.

"Back from where, Maria? Is Nick coming to take you out?"

"Nick, who's Nick?"

Evelyn sighed, nodded her head slowly and smiled. With any luck, reality would return soon.

"Why don't I brush your hair for you, Maria? You like having your hair brushed, don't you?"

"Why, thank y'all, that would be nice."

The accent was deep Southern with a Louisiana drawl. *Gone with the wind* was already playing in the old lady's mind.

"Mah pleasure, M'am," replied Evelyn, playing the game and picking up a mother of pearl hairbrush that had seen nearly sixty years of use.

Maria sat on a chair in front of the dressing table, while Evelyn unfurled her long grey hair.

"You have lovely hair, Maria, so long and thick. I wish my hair was as nice as yours."

She moved the brush deliberately and slowly from the top of the old lady's head to the small of her back.

"So where are you going again?"

"To the pictures, to see Gone…"

There was a pause as she struggled to remember the name of the film. It was as though the words were shrouded in fog and couldn't be deciphered.

"It's a very good film, everyone says so. I've seen the posters. It's that new one with Clark Gable."

Evelyn maintained the steady strokes of the hair brush.

"Well, Maria, that sounds absolutely grand."

She had looked after many people like Maria, always treating them with respect and kindness, no matter what their frailties. Were her ethos the benchmark for all care homes, there'd be nothing to fear from needing care in old age or at any time for that matter. But, as things were, for many elderly and vulnerable folk, the thought of going into a home was the stuff of nightmares, where characters like Banks held sway.

While Evelyn found it heartbreaking to watch Maria alternate between reality and fantasy, she never doubted the old lady's capacity to feel sad, happy or afraid, even though her cognitive functions were severely impaired. Rare periods of lucidity, interspersed with complete inactivity had revealed this to be true. Evelyn wished some of her colleagues would recognise this, not only for Maria's benefit, but also for the sake of many of the residents at Deepdene.

Evelyn had little doubt that Maria would revert to her inactive state again before the day was through and she made a mental note to keep a closer eye on her.

"There we go."

The brush was returned to the dressing table.

"All finished."

Maria was wearing a blue pastel dress with a flowcry motif and her unplaited silver hair fell down to her waist. Evelyn directed the old lady to the nearby full length mirror.

"Oh, Maria, you look lovely and that dress is so pretty on you."

"From Stavros, it's his favourite."

Evelyn sighed. Maria's son had brought her the dress for her birthday, the previous month.

"Why don't we go down to the sun lounge? I hear they're having a bingo game at ten o'clock."

"I like bingo," chirped the old lady happily, all thoughts of 'Gone with the Wind' now forgotten.

\* \* \*

Gordon Humphries held the phone to his ear and glanced at the clock on the wall. It read 10:05am. A patient man, he had let the caller, Mrs Cook, babble on for a good ten minutes now – it was part of the way he handled his clients. He liked to think he knew people pretty well, especially the bereaved. After all, he had been in the business a long time and, when it came to making people feel good about the inevitable end of their nearest and dearest, he felt he was up there with the best of them.

"Yes, of course I understand, Mrs Cook. I think he would be delighted with your choice."

He was holding the telephone in his right hand while the index finger of his left hand traced the raised lettering on the small brown ceramic container in front of him on the desk.

"No – I wouldn't say it was at all strange or unusual. Special, loving, unique are the words that spring to mind."

The index finger had finished tracing the last letter and began with the first letter again.

S

"Yes, it's finished. In fact it's on my desk as we speak."

U

"I must say, Mrs Cook, it is very discreet."

G

"That's right. This way your dear husband can always be with you in your home."

A

"Absolutely. It's the perfect size for his ashes."

R

"It's up to you. Call anytime at your convenience. We'll keep it safe until then for you. My pleasure. It's all part of the service. Goodbye, Mrs Cook."

He smiled magnanimously and replaced the receiver.

"What a stupid woman!" he muttered out loud.

Bob and Margaret Cook's pet names for each other had been Sugar and Spice. Many years ago, they had made a pact that they would be together after death as a twin set. A jar for sugar and one for spice, a romantic testament of their love for all to see.

Humphries, however, thought the whole concept ridiculous, a thought of course he kept to himself.

He lifted up the ceramic lid and spoke to the dust inside, "Morning, Sugar."

It really did sound ridiculous.

Outside, Ian Thompson sat waiting patiently, leafing through 'Modern Living' magazine, smiling at the irony of the title, here, of all places. A clipped voice immediately shifted his attention from the glossy magazine. A small, immaculately dressed man stood to his left.

"I'm Gordon Humphries. May I help you?"

Thompson rose and faced the man.

"Good morning, Mr Humphries, I'm Detective Inspector Thompson from West Sydney police."

He held up his warrant card for inspection.

"I'd like to ask you a few questions about your hearse which I understand was damaged the other day."

"Yes, of course, Inspector," replied Humphries, holding open his office door. "Do come in, although I think this is just a storm in a teacup, so much fuss about a simple mechanical breakdown."

Humphries seated himself behind his desk, and, although Thompson had not yet taken a chair, the former continued to speak.

"I've been all through this with that wretched Sykes from the garage. It's quite clear to me all he wants is to justify an extortionate repair bill by whatever means he can conjure up, which incidentally has wasted a great deal of valuable police time, not to mention my own. Now the police have impounded my car and I've been forced to take out a long term hire contract on another hearse. It's costing me a fortune. It's not the kind of vehicle you can get from your local Hertz office!"

"Mr Humphries," interjected Thompson, seizing the moment while he could. "I'm afraid new evidence has come to light which has opened up another line of enquiry to this investigation."

"New evidence?" Humphries asked, the derisory tone was unmistakable. "What kind of new evidence?"

"The kind of evidence that tells me someone deliberately sabotaged your funeral car. Forensic tests have shown explosive residue around the damaged gearbox."

Thompson paused for effect.

"It seems your grubby mechanic was spot on in his assessment regarding the cause of the damage and did absolutely the right thing in notifying the police."

"Are you sure?" asked the undertaker meekly.

The wind had completely gone out of his sails.

"One hundred percent. There's no doubt at all."

Silence hung over the office as the gravity of the situation slowly registered with Humphries.

"So, Mr Humphries, can you think of anyone who would want to do this?"

"No. No one," spluttered the stunned man. "I'm well liked and respected. Ask anyone, they'll all tell you the same story."

"A rival, disgruntled ex-employee… perhaps a jealous lover?"

"Inspector!" fumed Humphries, "My private life is just that – *private*!"

Thompson had clearly broached a sensitive area.

"Forgive me, Mr Humphries, but I must explore all avenues, even if you find some of them uncomfortable."

The question remained unanswered.

"Can you think of anyone with a grudge against you?"

Humphries shook his head.

Thompson shifted slightly in his seat.

"We have reason to believe this is not an isolated event."

"What? You mean this has happened to someone else?"

"Not exactly. But we are investigating another incident with striking similarities."

"I don't understand, Inspector, what are you trying to say?"

The moment was interrupted by a knock at the door and Angela, the receptionist, entered.

"I'm sorry to bother you, Mr Humphries, but there's a client in reception. He's here about his father – we did the funeral last week."

The sentence ended on a higher note as though it were a question.

"He's very upset about the bill. Says he won't leave until he's seen you. He's being very unpleasant."

Humphries groaned.

"Tell him I'll be right out. I'm sorry, Inspector. This will only take a few minutes. Would you like some coffee?"

Thompson brightened.

"Actually, I would love a cup. Two sugars, please. Thank you."

Humphries called to the departing receptionist, "And make the Inspector a coffee, Angela."

He rose from behind the large desk and made his way to the door.

"I'll be right back," he offered by way of apology and was gone.

Thompson looked around the room. Certainly not a style he would have chosen for his office. The furniture was a little too ornate for his taste, but, then again he wasn't in the funeral business and he supposed this was pretty much the '*de jour*' standard for many such places. He was now pretty sure Humphries was a closet queen.

The door opened and Angela entered unannounced with a cup of coffee and a chocolate mint.

"There we go, Inspector," she said, placing the cup in front of him on the desk. "Mr Humphries won't be long."

"Thank you very much," Thompson replied, reaching for the drink.

The receptionist was opening the door as he took a small sip of the hot liquid. 'Ah! No sugar!' he thought.

"Excuse me, would you have any…" was all he could manage before the heavy door closed, leaving him alone again.

A brown ceramic jar in front of him with the words SUGAR in raised letters caught his eye. Saved!

Reaching across the desk, he lifted the lid and scooped two spoonfuls of the brown dust into the coffee, but not without noticing how fine the sweetener was.

"Must be some kind of new Demerara," he mused to no one in particular before replacing the lid.

The door opened as he was stirring the drink.

"My apologies, Inspector," announced Humphries. "Now, where were we?"

"I was explaining that this may not be an isolated incident," began Thompson.

"You see, that's the part I don't understand. Could you be a little more specific?"

"I'm afraid at this stage I can't, Mr Humphries. We need to keep both enquiries separate for now, I'm sure you can appreciate the need for discretion."

Humphries remained silent. This stupid policeman was wasting his time with scare-mongering stores of explosions and 'related' incidents. The arrogance began to creep back into him again.

"I'm afraid I can't help you, Inspector, if you won't give me the full picture."

It was a dismissive remark full of contempt.

Thompson then dropped the bombshell.

"Has anyone threatened or intimidated you recently?" he asked quietly, the coffee cup at his lips.

Humphries looked like he had been hit with a knock out punch.

Thompson recognised fear when he saw it and pressing his advantage, continued, "Personally, I find extortion leaves a bad taste in my mouth. It's also a very serious offence."

He sipped the coffee, wincing at the taste.

"If someone is making life difficult for you, I need to know."

"I, I don't want to say anything at this point, Inspector," stammered Humphries.

"I promise it will only make matters worse for you if you don't," countered the policeman.

Thompson took another sip of coffee.

'Christ! This was an unusual blend', he thought, while making small movements with his lips and tongue, a look of distaste on his face.

The funeral director observed the policeman expression and it alarmed him.

Clearing his throat and straightening his tie nervously, he replied, "I'm hoping to come to an arrangement with another party in the near future and I don't want to jeopardise any negotiations."

"You don't look like you're too happy with the situation, Mr Humphries."

Another sip of coffee, the taste was getting worse, the more of it he drank. How was that possible? Thompson was doing his best to agitate the man into revealing information about the 'other party', but was having trouble getting past the flavour of the drink, which by now was truly awful.

"No, I'm not happy, Inspector, but there's a bigger picture and right now I don't want to complicate it."

He produced a handkerchief from his breast pocket and patted his now perspiring brow.

"So you'll have to forgive me if I decline to say anything more at this point."

Thompson rose from his chair.

"Very well, Mr Humphries, thank you for your time, and the...," he waved his hand loosely at the half finished coffee, "... and the refreshments."

He removed a business card from his wallet.

"Here, this has my direct number. Please give me a call if you want to talk."

He moved to the door.

"I can see myself out, but don't forget – if you think this is just going to go away, you're wrong."

Humphries' heart was pounding in his chest as the inspector closed the door.

'It was Spitz, it had to be. So these were the consequences he had threatened.'

* * *

As Maria Papadopoulos stared blankly at the bingo card in front of her, Kathleen O'Neill, sitting behind the wheel of her car, focused at the small vial in her hand, a small vial which would be used to conclude the contract on the old lady.

The last few months had been amongst the most difficult she had ever encountered, her father's death not only causing immense sadness, but also shifting the entire responsibility of the business onto her shoulders. Maria Papadopoulos was of course part of that responsibility and the completion of the contract was long overdue. Starting the engine and clicking on her indicator, she pulled slowly away from the kerb moving seamlessly into the stream of traffic and on her way to the Deepdene nursing home to do what she knew she must.

Kathleen was a careful driver who rarely exceeded the speed limit and in all the years she had been driving, had never had an accident. By contrast, Jock Strapp never adhered to any speed limit and had been involved in countless accidents. According to the law of averages, it was amazing he was still alive. He gunned the Harley into life, let out the clutch and roared off down the road. Even after all these years, the thrill of zero to seventy kilometres an hour in first gear on a Harley Davison and the sound of the engine as the tachometer approached red line had never receded. Magic, pure magic.

The meeting of the Sydney Kings Cross Hell's Angels chapter had been arranged for twelve noon at a pub on the other side of town and, although he was an infrequent visitor at these meetings, in light of his recent diagnosis, he had decided to live every day as though it was his last. The irony was that, overall, he had never felt more alive. The predicted monster headaches had not yet materialised, although there had been a couple of days when the pain was definitely an issue and he had to take his little white pills from the hospital. That aside, he felt pretty good, especially on a winding road on his beloved machine and with the Doobie Brothers blasting, "Jesus is just all right with me," through his CD player's headphones.

\* \* \*

Bingo at the Deepdene nursing home had long since finished. The bingo caller had fought to maintain a level of excitement among the seven semi-interested residents throughout the hour-long session. It had proved to be a losing battle as, one by one, the seven conscious dwindled to two. Hypnos, arch enemy of wakefulness, claimed four residents, while Maria Papadopoulos drifted from the present to the past.

"Come along now!"

Matron Banks was rousing the sleeping ex-bingo players.

"It's lunchtime, ladies and gentlemen."

It was more like a dog herding a mob of sheep than an invitation to dine.

"Come on, come on!" she persisted like a stuck record. "Lunch will only get cold and we don't want that, now do we?"

Banks was the past master of the rhetorical question and any person, staff or resident, who was foolish enough to answer, invariably regretted it.

Unseen by the Matron, Maria separated from the small column heading for the dining room and went into her room to inspect her hair in the mirror. It was fine.

"Gone with the Wind, here I come," she announced to her reflection, then headed for the main lobby.

The Matron's office was immediately adjacent to the empty reception desk and the unfortunate receptionist who'd been summoned by her was in the process of receiving a tongue lashing from Banks, whose frame completely occupied the entire office doorway. All that could be seen was the back of the woman, a colossus in white, frequent hand gesticulations reinforcing each point she was delivering without mercy.

"Vigilance!" she shouted at the hapless receptionist. "That's what I expect from my reception staff!"

The tirade had just begun.

"Vigilance at all times!"

"But, Matron," replied the receptionist, "it was twelve o'clock. I hadn't had a break since I came on duty, at seven this morning, and I needed to go to the toilet. Ingrid was covering for me, when she was called away on an emergency. I had no idea the front desk was empty. I was only gone for a couple of minutes."

"A couple of minutes were all it took for Mr Peterson to walk past an empty reception desk and out of the front door! Out of the door... and thankfully right into his son, who just happened to be visiting him!"

She was now waving her arms wildly in the air.

The volume had increased considerably.

"Do you have any idea how that makes me and this establishment look?"

It was another rhetorical question, that much the receptionist understood, a question not to be answered under any circumstances.

She remained silent, hoping the verbal assault would end soon.

"No, I don't suppose you have *any* idea! Well, I'll tell you. Incompetent! That's how it makes me look, incompetent!"

The pitch and decibel had both risen dangerously close to unacceptable industrial safety standards.

"And I *refuse* to look incompetent!"

The receptionist was now partially deaf in one ear, and somewhat spared from the last salvo and any to follow. She hoped this wouldn't last much longer. Banks' reputation for epic chastisements was legendary.

Maria Papadopoulos, shielded by the white mountain in the doorway and by the sheer volume coming from it, shuffled quietly past the empty reception desk, through the main door and onto the waiting footpath on her journey to the cinema too see *Gone with the wind*.

\* \* \*

One mile away, Kathleen O'Neill was heading for the Deepdene nursing home, lost in thought on how to handle this particular visit. Whilst apprehensive, she certainly had no qualms of conscience – she was going to conclude a contract according to the client's own wishes, by an arrangement freely entered into when she was of sound mind. During the entire time, there had never been any suggestion from Mrs Papadopoulos she wanted to change her mind even though she knew Michael had asked her this while she was still in a fit state to reply. A part of Kathleen was hoping against hope that, when she arrived at the nursing home, the old lady would have made a miraculous recovery and simply decided to cancel the contract.

'Don't be stupid,' she chided herself, 'that's not going to happen. 'Be strong now and do the job you agreed to do. Dad wouldn't be thinking in such a cowardly, selfish way!'

Yet, despite the deliberate self-motivation, she remained a little scared. All her thoughts were focused on the imminent task, while her eyes remained glued to the road ahead, neither seeing nor hearing anything in the periphery.

\* \* \*

A mile and a half away and approaching Kathleen at right angles, Jock Strapp, on his way back from the Diamond Café, continued to maintain a furious pace on his roaring machine, passing cars with ease, and oblivious to the needs of other road users. A car on his left screeched to a halt as Jock sped through the intersection, disregarding the other motorist's right of way.

"Wanker!" the epithet barely audible above the noise from the Harley, as he left the fuming driver far behind and continued down the single carriageway.

\* \* \*

The old lady was only interested in getting to the pictures before the main feature began. She wanted to see the whole film without missing a single minute. It was already one o'clock and she was sure the show started at quarter past. The fact that the Hoyt's Theatre had been pulled down thirty years ago had absolutely no bearing on her desire to go there. For her, it was still real, fantasy and reality intertwined. Stepping out from between two parked vans to cross the road, she neither saw, nor heard the approaching motorbike. With tunnel vision, all she could see was the other side of the road and the corner, around which, was the cinema.

Involuntarily, Jock slammed on the brakes as the old lady appeared without warning immediately in front of him. His body leaned sharply to the right, causing the machine to pitch violently in that direction and into the path of oncoming traffic.

Kathleen was powerless to avoid the collision. All that registered was the screech from the motorbike's tyres and, in an instant, the bike shot diagonally across the front of her, leaving her no time to swerve out of the way. The bike slammed into the front of her car, propelling the rider into the windscreen and over the roof with terrible force and the last thing Jock saw was the grass verge rushing up to meet his airborne body.

The whoosh of the passing motorbike and the noise from the resultant crash rendered the old lady motionless. Stepping back in between the shelter of the two parked vans, she looked around her, confusion registering on her face. Her mind snapped back to the present.

"What am I doing here?" she mumbled to herself, all thoughts of the cinema now completely forgotten.

A vision of the Deepdene nursing home slowly crept into her consciousness and, with the very recent accident now also forgotten, she moved back to the footpath and began retracing her steps, 'lunch' being her overriding thought.

Maria Papadopoulos, the cause of the calamity, unseen and unnoticed by anyone other than Jock, shuffled slowly away from the scene, down the street, around the corner and through the entrance doors of the Deepdene nursing home. She walked back past the empty reception desk and the Matron's office, where the dressing down was still in progress and into the dining room, where she was greeted by the ever smiling Evelyn.

"Maria," she chided, "you very nearly missed out on lunch! Where *have* you been? Everyone's almost finished."

Guiding the old lady to a nearby table, she sat her down and picked up the menu card.

"Ooooo!" she squealed in delight. "Roast lamb! I know that's your favourite," and then touching her shoulder added, "this must be your lucky day!"

# Chapter 15

## O'Neill's Deadly Beauty

The sun was beginning to set as the taxi pulled up outside Kathleen's flat, yet even when the car came to a complete stop opposite her flat, she remained in a world of her own, lost in thought about the day's events. It had been one of the most distressing days she could ever remember, even when compared to the recent death of her father. The engine idled smoothly while the driver waited for some response and, sensing none, eyed the meter and turned to his passenger in the back seat.

"Twenty three dollars, fifty, please, love," he announced.

The driver's voice caused her to look away from the side window she had been staring through with unseeing eyes all the way from the hospital and focus on the driver in the front seat.

Kathleen fumbled in her purse and extracted a twenty and a five dollar bill.

"Thanks," she replied, passing the notes to the driver, who began by fishing for some change. "That's OK," she added, opening the door and getting slowly out of the taxi.

"Goodnight."

"Night," came the response, as she closed the door and the car drew away and continued down the road.

She stood, drained of all energy, watching the receding car until it had disappeared from view, then finally and with great effort, walked across the street to her flat. The air-conditioned ride in the taxi from the hospital had left her unprepared for the humid evening air, hot and oppressive, draining what little strength was left in her body. For the past six hours, she had been at the West Sydney Memorial Hospital's Emergency department being examined, X-rayed, prodded and poked and generally fussed over by what seemed like an army of health professionals and workers.

Her car had sustained substantial damage and the bottle containing the mixture for Maria had shattered and broken glass was everywhere inside. Despite the impact, she miraculously escaped with minor cuts and bruises. However, she was in shock, her upper body, especially the arms and neck, so stiff that every movement was slow and painful.

Unlocking the front door, she began the weary climb up the stairs to her apartment, pausing half way up. Once inside her flat, she never got as far as the bedroom, instead dropping exhausted onto the sofa, where she fell asleep almost immediately.

The telephone rang noisily catapulting her awake. For a moment, she had no idea where she was, the day or time or why she should feel so tired. With a great deal of effort, she picked up the receiver and uttered a weak "Hello."

The clock on the wall read 6:15pm. Bits of the day began coming together.

"Kathleen, it's Peter; are you alright?"

A mock laugh dispelled any notion she *was* alright.

"I was involved in a traffic accident this afternoon, Peter. I'm OK, a bit shaken up, but I'm alright. The car's been totalled though…"

There was an audible gasp from the receiver.

"Look, Peter, can we cancel tonight? I don't really feel up to going out just now. Don't feel much like doing anything, to be honest, except lying down on the sofa. Is it alright if we skip the restaurant tonight?"

"I'm not worried about the restaurant, I'm worried about you! You don't sound all right. I'm coming over!"

"I'll be fine, honestly, there's no need to fuss over me. I'm just a bit whacked."

His tone was insistent.

"Don't move. I'll be there in twenty minutes," and he hung up.

Fifteen minutes later, the downstairs buzzer rang.

"Kath, it's me – Peter."

The voice sounded anxious and urgent.

Seconds later he stood in the doorway looking agitated and, in an instant, was at her side.

"I was really worried – are you OK?"

"Yes, I'm a bit shaken but I'm OK."

Positioning himself next to her and still holding her hand he prompted, "So, Kath, what happened?"

He listened in silence for the next few minutes as she recounted the accident, being taken by ambulance to hospital and the barrage of tests she'd had before finally being discharged.

"You're lucky to be alive," he said at last, "but what about the guy on the bike?"

Kathleen shrugged her shoulders and shook her head.

"I don't know. I'm praying that he's alright. He took a terrible knock. It all happened so fast. I remember the bike coming out of nowhere, a terrible crash, then seeing a bearded man hit the windscreen and he was gone. I couldn't move for ages. The ambulance finally arrived, put a neck brace on me and the next thing I knew, I was on a stretcher on my way to hospital. I asked the casualty nurse, what happened to him, but she wouldn't say."

She began to sob quietly, overwhelmed by the events of the day. Peter held her firmly in his arms as she cried against his chest.

"Let it out, Kath," he whispered, "you've had one hell of a day, but now it's over."

Finally, she straightened up and drew back, wiping her eyes with her hands as Peter magically produced a clean handkerchief.

"Sorry about that," she said meekly, "I don't know what came over me. That's not like me at all. I feel quite embarrassed."

Peter rebuked her gently, but firmly.

"You're still in shock, Kath, and what you're going through right now is normal. You've had a lucky escape today, but you're very shaken, so don't beat yourself up any more OK?"

He wiped an errant strand of hair away from her cheek and smiled into her eyes.

"OK?"

Kathleen nodded slowly.

"OK," she whispered.

"Are you hungry? What have you eaten today?"

"Eaten? I had a piece of toast when I got up, around seven this morning, but that's all. I hadn't really given much thought to the matter, but now that you mention it, I am quite hungry."

Rising from the settee, Peter made his way towards the kitchen.

"No problem," he announced over his shoulder. "If we're not going out for dinner, the least I can do is fix you something here."

"Please, don't bother, Peter. I'll make a piece of toast or something."

"Stay there and put the telly on, or some music. I'll have something sorted before you know it."

The voice came from the kitchen amid sounds of cupboards being opened and closed, while he ferreted around, sourcing ingredients.

Gratefully, Kathleen acquiesced, picking up the remote control for the television. It sprang into life as a documentary about the sea unfolded, and she lay back, grateful for the care and attention.

Peter hummed to himself while preparing the meal amid the clatter of saucepans and bowls, occasionally bouncing a question or comment in her direction, more rhetorical than expectant.

He found some eggs and cheese and within ten minutes the omelette was browning under the grill. The fridge also yielded up a head of lettuce, an avocado and some tomatoes and, finding a couple of lemons in the pantry, he deftly prepared a dressing with olive oil. A small sample of the mixture on a teaspoon caused him to hesitate – it was good, but there was something missing... basil! He looked around for any herbs or spices, but he was out of luck.

It was only then that he noticed the leafy green plant with white lines sitting on the window sill, nestling among the spider plants and other variegated varieties.

He thought it resembled something he'd seen recently, but, for the life of him, he couldn't identify what it was or where he'd seen it. The shape and colour of the leaves and the way the parallel white markings ran from stalk to tip was a unique identifier, yet, no matter how hard he tried, he couldn't remember its name.

The timer from the oven broke his train of thought. He made a mental note to ask Kathleen about the distinctive plant later, as he pulled out the grill tray, lifting the frying pan out and placing it on the hob. It was perfect, a light golden brown colour.

Making his way to the lounge, he went over to Kathleen.

"Would Madame like to sit at the table, or eat here?"

"I don't think I can move – would you mind if we ate in front of the telly?"

"Great idea, I'll get the waiter to bring it over."

Dressing a couple of trays with clean tea towels, he laid out two portions of the omelette with a side salad and a paper napkin folded into a triangle under each fork.

"For Madame," he announced in a mock French accent placing the tray on Kathleen's lap, "compliments of ze chef."

"Peter," she gasped, "it looks amazing! You really are a whiz in the kitchen, aren't you?"

"Years of looking after my mum, I guess. Besides, I enjoy cooking – but it's much more enjoyable when it's not just for yourself."

As they ate their impromptu meal, the television providing a muted background, they chatted amiably in between mouthfuls of food. Kathleen's appetite had returned in full force. At length, she placed the knife and fork on her empty plate and let her head drop back.

"That was fantastic, it really was. Thank you so much for cooking – I didn't realise how hungry I was."

"You're welcome, I'm glad you enjoyed it," Peter responded, before clearing away the supper things.

"I noticed some ice-cream in the freezer – would you like some?"

Kathleen shook her head.

"I couldn't eat another thing."

"Coffee, tea?"

"I'd *love* a cup of tea."

"Milk, no sugar?"

"Yes, that's right, how did you guess?"

"No guess," Peter shrugged, "same as the restaurant last week. I figured that's how you preferred tea."

This time it was Kathleen's turn to smile.

She enjoyed the sound of the kettle boiling mixed with the clatter of plates being washed and dried as Peter tidied up in the kitchen. A few minutes later, he emerged with two cups of tea, and sat down beside Kathleen.

"Feeling better?"

"*Much* better. You've been very kind, Peter. I was pretty shaken up today. I would have felt much worse if you hadn't come over. Thank you, I really mean it."

"All part of the service – no extra charge."

They sipped their tea in silence, both sensing that the bond developing between them was deepening and both a little nervous about where this was going.

Peter broke the silence.

"I noticed a green leafy plant with white lines on the windowsill, Kath. I'm sure I've seen it in some book, but I can't remember where or what it's called. It's very unusual."

An involuntary shudder went through Kathleen's body and she tensed for a moment, before recovering.

"Oh, that, I don't know. My dad called it O'Neill's beauty – quite common in parts of Ireland, but is grows well here too. I hardly water the thing – low maintenance, so it's perfect for me."

She laughed nervously. However much Kathleen would have liked to tell Peter the truth, she knew she never could. It was family business and she was the only remaining guardian of the O'Neill family secret, entrusted to her by her father. It went back through generations of O'Neills, passed down by family members for a hundred and fifty years. It was a heavy responsibility, but also a duty and, if Kathleen had any qualms about it, her loyalty to her father stopped her from questioning his counsel. She had promised to continue the work of alleviating suffering and uphold the family tradition and that was exactly what she was going to do.

Deftly, she steered the conversation in a different direction.

"Do you mind if we watch the news? It's just starting on Channel Nine."

"Sure," replied Peter as she pressed the 'on' button on the remote control.

The news had indeed just started, the newsreader giving a précis of the stories to be covered – a growing political crisis in the Federal government, freak weather in India, a major financial collapse. And then the local news – rising hospital waiting times, league footballer arrested on cocaine charges and finally a story about the funeral of James A Hollickson – the circus impresario who had died suddenly. The funeral was certainly not a normal one and had apparently offended many people, with the mixture of carnival and mock solemnity which surrounded it. The newscaster was introducing the story against a backdrop of head and shoulders photographs of James A Hollickson and the undertaker Jerome T Spitz.

Peter made a mental note to speak to Kathleen at the end of the news. It seemed being in the funeral business these days had become somewhat precarious and he wanted to make Kathleen aware of the latest risks.

The newscaster continued with the story, "... and many are asking, 'is this the right way to conduct a funeral?' Our reporter, Sue Nelson, has the details."

A young, smartly dressed woman was speaking into the camera, while, in the background, a white hearse, followed by jugglers, fire eaters, dancing girls and clowns on stilts was driven from the cemetery gates to the crematorium. In front of the whole procession was Spitz, leading a brass band and waving a gold-spangled baton while dressed in a gold lamé jacket and matching top hat. As a drum major, he directed the bizarre cortege, past the camera and onwards to the crematorium.

"After the debacle of our ex-mayor, Jack Sullivan, this must surely be one of the most extraordinary funerals Sydney has ever seen. James A Hollickson, youngest son of James T Hollickson, who co-founded the world famous Hollickson Brothers Circus, was, like his father, larger than life and now, it would seem, equally eccentric in death as he completes his final journey."

The camera panned over the cortege, taking in the sideshow which went with it.

"Earlier this week I spoke with James T Spitz, the Funeral Director who is literally running the show."

The screen cut to the prior interview, Spitz talking earnestly and gesticulating forcefully against the background of his offices.

"Who says it has to be all black and sombre?" he began. "We, here, at Spitz & Co, believe in doing what the client wants, whatever that may be."

"But many people have expressed revulsion with the style of your services," continued the reporter. "Doesn't that concern you just a bit?"

"Not in the slightest."

Spitz was unshakeable.

"To each his own... and," he was on a roll now and that was exactly how it came across, "I intend to be the biggest provider of *all* types of funeral services in Australia within the next five years!"

"Five years?"

"That's right, five years – mark my words!"

He turned to face the camera, which zoomed in on his face.

Grinning into the lens he winked cheekily and said, "Funerals can be fun!"

The footage cut back to the funeral in hand, the reporter now summing up her story.

"So there you have it," she concluded. "Jerome T Spitz. Love him or loathe him, either way, the man looks certain to go on creating a big impression in this town and, if he is to be believed, the entire country."

This news segment was now over and the reporter, microphone in hand signed off.

"This is Sue Nelson, Channel Nine News."

Kathleen shook her head.

"I can't believe it," she said, "whatever is the world coming to?"

"It is pretty weird, isn't it?" added Peter.

"Weird isn't the word. In fact I can't think of an appropriate word. There's something about that guy that makes my skin creep."

"He's just a brash American trying to get some cheap advertising. Can you honestly see the average Aussie buying into *that*?"

"I suppose you're right, but there's still something about him I don't like – it's in his eyes."

Peter took one of her hands in both of his.

"Look, Kath, there's something I wanted to talk to you about."

The tone was serious. Kathleen, picking it up immediately, turned her head slightly to one side.

"There were a couple of incidents this week involving two separate funeral businesses," he said.

He had her full attention.

"What kind of *incidents*?"

"Do you remember the Jacko Sullivan funeral, on Tuesday?"

"I doubt whether anyone could forget it after being splashed all over the six o'clock news!"

"Well, it wasn't an accident."

Kathleen gave him a puzzled look. This was old news.

"I know. The papers are full of it. There's a story going around that one of Sullivan's enemies sabotaged the funeral. Personally, I don't subscribe to the conspiracy theory. I think somebody flicked a cigarette onto the Astroturf and set it alight."

"It may seem that way, but there was another incident on the same day. Do you know of Humphries & Co?"

"Gordon Humphries? Yes, of course I do."

"Humphries' hearse was damaged – that's why it had to be towed to the cemetery – it was just ahead of the Sullivan funeral. If you remember, it was also on the news."

"Yes, I remember."

He was looking intently into her eyes.

"The police were called to investigate both incidents. I ran the forensic tests and I found a common link."

"Peter, why don't you stop beating around the bush and tell me what's going on?"

There was a touch of humour in her voice, as though they were playing a game of charades.

"What I'm about to tell you is in the strictest confidence," he said looking at her seriously.

She returned his gaze and nodded.

"OK."

"I found traces of explosive, the *same* explosive used in both incidents."

Kathleen openly laughed.

"Peter, you can't be serious. You're winding me up, aren't you? This kind of thing doesn't happen in Australia and, besides, why?"

"I'm deadly serious, Kath," he replied, the emphasis in his voice unmistakable.

The laughter died on her lips as she took in the severity of the situation.

"Look, I don't want to scare you, but I do want you to be extra vigilant from now on, alright?"

She nodded, nervous at what she was hearing.

"The matter is being investigated by a senior policeman, a friend of mine actually, but I don't think he would be too pleased if he knew I was releasing this kind of information to the general public. I could get into serious trouble."

Peter paused for a moment before adding, "I'm sure we'll find the culprit soon. But, in the meantime, please take care and if you're worried by anything, anything at all, I want you to promise me you'll pick up the phone – agreed?"

He was nodding to her, a prompt for acknowledgement.

She nodded back.

"Sure, Peter, I'll keep my eyes open."

"And you'll call me if you're worried about anything unusual?"

"I'll call you if I'm worried," she repeated.

"Good."

He stood up.

"Are you going to be alright tonight?"

"I'm fine, really," she replied. "Actually I reckon I could sleep for a week, it's been a long, long day."

Leaning down, he kissed her tenderly on the cheek and stroked her hair.

"I'll give you a ring tomorrow. Night, Kath."

Peter straightened up, walked away from the settee and was almost at the door when she called out to him.

"Peter."

He turned around to face her.

"Thank you."

It was a simple and moving phrase and the feeling behind it was not lost on him.

"My pleasure, speak to you tomorrow."

The door closed quietly after him and she heard his footsteps descending the stairs.

There was a pause as the front door opened and then she heard the sound of it closing. The day had been traumatic, to say the very least, but Peter's visit had lifted her spirits and she was both nervous and excited by how much she felt drawn to him.

Normally, a strong and resilient woman, Kathleen had felt weak and brittle, but his gentle strength had made her feel safe and that was a nice sensation. She turned out the lights and made her way to her bedroom. Peter had shown himself to be a real friend, but she felt tortured. Her work was too important to stop and Peter was too nice to give up.

As she lay on her bed, she wondered how she could allow their relation-ship to develop and at the same time keep the family's deadly secret still a secret.

# Chapter 16

## Jock-no-Luck

Several days had passed since the accident and Kathleen rose wearily after a restless night. Talking about it to the police constable the previous evening had caused the whole episode to come flooding back and she hadn't slept. Though she had retired early last night around eleven o'clock, she woke in the small hours from a dreamless sleep, looked at the bedside radio clock and couldn't believe it was only 1:37am. And so it had continued, pockets of sleep followed by what seemed like hours of wakefulness and then the whole cycle repeating itself, until it was mercifully ended by the alarm at 7:00am.

Bending over the wash basin, she scooped up a handful of cold water and splashed it onto her face. The effect was immediate and snapped both eyes wide open. Now she felt awake. However, the cabinet mirror told a different story – bleary eyes with dark patches beneath them belied her exhaustion, something the cold water could not remove.

"Coffee!" she said aloud. "You need some coffee."

The small Mocha machine hissed and burbled while the news announcer on the radio droned on in an impersonal monologue about the events in the world during the last 24 hours. It was depressingly familiar – a cocktail of disasters, destruction, and woe, which did nothing to lift her spirits. What had the songwriter John Williamson said? 'Good news never made a paper sell'? She switched stations and instantly felt better as the soothing sounds of James Taylor floated across the kitchen. 'I'm your handyman…'

But nothing could take her mind off the news she'd been given the previous day by the young policeman, when he took the witness statement from her about the accident. When she asked the young PC about the injuries of the man on the bike who had collided with her, she was very upset to find out that he was now paralysed. The news had left her feeling unsettled and disturbed. Like an unwelcome guest, these feelings wouldn't leave. As a hospital visitor, Kathleen had no trouble finding out the name of the accident victim… it was James Strapp.

James Taylor finished, Roberta Flack started and the coffee was ready as she filled an espresso-sized cup and added two sugars. Within five minutes, she could feel the effects of the caffeine, but the urge to go and visit Strapp in hospital persisted. It had kept her awake for most of the night. She knew the collision hadn't been her fault, but nonetheless, felt guilty. If she hadn't gone that day to the Deepdene Nursing Home, the accident would never have happened.

Unknowingly, she was about to make a life-changing decision.

'I'll go and see him,' she thought. 'Don't know if it's going to change anything but it feels like the right thing to do.'

The unsettling feelings drifted away and she felt better, calmer and more focused. There was nothing in the diary for the day ahead, at least nothing that couldn't be handled by her able receptionist, Tracey. Tomorrow was different – two funerals in the morning and another in the afternoon with an equally busy schedule the day after tomorrow, so if she was going to look in on Mr Strapp, then today was her best opportunity to do so.

Kathleen made a couple of slices of toast and poured the last of the espresso from the Mocha pot, then spent the next hour showering, applying her makeup and dressing.

By 8:30, she was at her desk downstairs in the office. Tracey arrived promptly at nine with a cheery:

"Good morning, Kath."

She sat down and busied herself immediately, typing a handful of letters for Kathleen to sign.

"Trace?" Kathleen enquired, "I have a visit to make this morning for a couple of hours. Shouldn't be any longer than that, but if I am, will you be OK here?"

"No problem. Looks like being a fairly quiet one today – I'll be fine."

She held up one hand and crossed the index and forefinger, the universal sign for hope, and smiled.

The drive to the hospital in the hire car was uneventful. Kathleen had taken a couple of days to get used to the feeling of being behind the wheel again, but had quickly convinced herself that the accident would not become an impediment and these things, sadly, happened every day. The only thing to do after falling out of the saddle was to get back in it again and pronto.

Before leaving for the hospital, Kathleen phoned and spoke to a nurse to enquire about Strapp's condition.

"Comfortable and stable," were the words the ward sister had used, but when pressed about the extent of his injuries, she had elaborated with, "he's a very lucky man. By all accounts, he should be in far worse shape, but I'm pleased to say that he's awake and lucid and, to be perfectly honest, as grumpy as hell. He doesn't want to be here – just wants to go home, which, in nursing terms, is a very encouraging sign. He's being moved to a medical ward, as soon as there's a bed available."

Pulling into the hospital car park and turning off the ignition, she sat quietly for a moment or two, wondering whether this was the right thing to do. Would he object to her visit, would he even be *able* to have visitors? The answer was not long in coming – yes, it was the right thing to do, indeed it was something that *had* to be done. The day was shaping up to be a hot one, it must be in the high twenties already, thought Kathleen as she walked to the hospital entrance, and was rewarded with a blast of cool air as she moved through the revolving door and approached the reception desk.

A gormless young woman busied herself filling in a form of some kind and only looked up when Kathleen, who had been standing patiently for a number of seconds, said, "Excuse me, I'm looking for a patient, but I don't know what ward he's in."

"Name?"

Monosyllabic, dull and devoid of interest.

"Strapp, J."

"Statt, Statt, Stratt," the receptionist mumbled to herself while running a finger down the computer monitor, before announcing, "Not here."

"Strapp – S T R A P P, with a P not a T."

The receptionist returned to the monitor…

"Lewis Ward, eighth floor."

"Thank you."

Kathleen turned on her heel and walked in the direction of the lifts. At the entrance to Lewis ward she began walking down a long corridor, her shoes squeaking slightly with each step, until she reached the nurses' station. A sharp eyed sister greeted her warmly.

"Can I help you?"

"Ah… yes. Do you have a James Strapp on this ward?"

The Sister rolled her eyes upwards and smiled at the same time.

"Yes, we do – he's in room 823, second on the left."

"Thank you."

Kathleen walked the short distance to the room and stopped outside the closed door. She was about to knock, when her resolve momentarily faltered. Now that she was finally here, a hundred doubts rushed into her mind. 'Just do it,' she rebuked herself and gently knocked a couple of times on the door.

"Yeah?" came the response, as she gingerly opened the door and stepped inside.

From the voice, she was half expecting some kind of Hell's Angel, dressed in leathers and with a black crash helmet, despite her memory of James, eyes wide in terror, flying into her windscreen, as his motorbike struck her car with incredible force. Instead, she saw a man with long greying hair, wearing standard blue hospital pyjamas, his left arm in a sling, staring out of the window.

He continued looking away from the door, completely disinterested in who had just entered the room.

This was the moment Kathleen had dreaded and there was no turning back now.

"Hello, James, I'm Kathleen, Kathleen O'Neill. I'm a hospital volunteer."

There was an awkward silence.

"What do you want? I didn't ask for any help, except to get 'oot of here," he replied.

She faltered with the next words, unsure of how to begin.

Suddenly it was out.

"I was driving the car that hit your bike."

He studied her for what seemed an age and then smiled broadly.

"Well... that's nice, but you've got your facts arse-about, love. You didn't hit me, I hit you. Some silly old cow just walked right out in front of me. I don't know how I missed her."

He paused, stared at the floor and shook his head.

"Silly old cow!" He looked up at Kathleen, "You all right?"

"A bit shaken, but otherwise, no damage. The car's a write-off, but I don't care about that. It's insured. I'm more worried about you. I remember a tremendous bang and seeing you hit the windscreen. I wasn't sure what had happened, it was all so fast... I thought it might have been my fault and I wanted to make sure you were OK."

"That's good of you, lassie. Nay... it was the old girl who caused the accident. I told the police, but nobody saw her and they've put the whole bloody thing down to me – going too fast, lost control etcetera – you know, the usual. Sure, I was speeding, I always speed. I've been riding for over forty years now and my bike, or rather what's left of it, is built for speed."

He took a deep breath and sighed loudly.

"Bugger!" he added.

It wasn't the time to talk. Kathleen intuitively grasped that fact as the angry and embittered man lay on the hospital bed, lips pursed and looking away from her. At last, he turned his head in her direction and gave a wry smile.

"Sorry about that," he began, "it's all kind of falling to bits at the moment."

Kathleen remained silent.

"First the head thing… that was bad enough, but I could handle that and then, 'oot of the blue, this old woman just walks 'oot between a couple of parked vans, I swerve and then the next thing is I see is your yellow car and now I'm back in here."

"Back in here?"

"Yeah, some toe rag bashed me over the head with a bar stool and they brought me in unconscious. That's when they found 'oot about my brain tumour."

A hospital orderly, pushing a tea trolley, wandered past in the corridor outside, the sharp clattering sound creating a hiatus in the conversation.

Kathleen didn't know what to say for a moment and then she spoke, "Oh!" she looked at Strapp with concern, "you have a brain tumour?"

"Yeah, and I'm not going to be around for much longer. Pity you didn't finish me off. You should have been going faster… I did my bit, I was doing at least 70!"

He grinned bitterly, nodding his head.

"I'm terribly sorry to hear you're so ill," replied Kathleen, ignoring the last comment.

"Ill is do-able, paralysed is not."

Kathleen looked away. She'd already found out that James Strapp couldn't walk, but finding out he was terminally ill wrenched at her heart. She had robbed this man of the last few weeks, in which he might have had any remaining quality of life. Why had she picked that day to go to Maria?

"Look, lassie, I don't want to upset you. It's not your fault that I'm here and it's not your fault that I'm dying. I was riding way too fast when I crashed into you. I'm sorry I ruined your car. It's really nice that you came to see me."

"I'm so sorry, James. I don't quite know what to say."

"Please, call me Jock. Jock-no-luck," he added in his strong Glaswegian accent. "And don't worry yourself. There's nothing to say, is there?"

Before Kathleen could respond, the door opened and a nurse appeared at the foot of the bed and examined the chart suspended from the clip board.

"How are we feeling, Mr Strapp?" she enquired cheerily.

"We are feeling pissed off," he replied sarcastically, "really, really pissed off."

He stared at the nurse.

"I'll just take your pulse and temperature and then leave you and your friend alone again… shan't take a moment."

The voice was still rich with melody, the earlier, barbed response, having been completely ignored. Kathleen rose from her seat barely able to hold back the tears, as the nurse began flicking the thermometer. She didn't want Jock to see her crying, knowing that would make him feel worse. She imagined he was not a man who enjoyed pity.

Welcoming the excuse to leave, now that the nurse had appeared she spluttered, "I'd better be going. I'm just in the way here."

"Nay, you're not in the way. Thanks for coming. Really, I mean it. Thanks," the Scotsman said humbly.

Kathleen smiled, "That's OK, Jock."

The nurse manoeuvred herself into a position between Jock and Kathleen and was about to take his temperature when the Scotsman grabbed her wrist in mid action, his eyes focused on Kathleen.

"I don't get many visitors here… I'm so bored. If you have the time… I mean, if you are passing, it would be really nice to see you again."

He looked down at his legs, covered by the hospital sheet and then turned to face Kathleen.

"If you're too busy, I understand."

She considered whether this might be the first time Jock had ever asked anything of anybody.

Her heart went out to him.

"Of course I will, if you want me to."

Kathleen held his gaze. The nurse, now mute, her wrist held in Jock's grip a mere spectator to the scene, simply looked on.

"See you soon," she added.

Slowly, he released his grip on the nurse's wrist. She had been immobile throughout the brief exchange, unable to do anything.

Jock looked past the nurse and directly at Kathleen.

"I really hope so," he said.

* * *

While Jock's nurse went about the business of taking temperature and blood pressure readings from the now placated Scotsman, Peter Wilson was busily engaged in summarising his report on the Jack Sullivan funeral debacle and the sabotaged hearse.

Several hours later, Ian Thompson approached the young scientist as the latter crouched over his computer, tapping out a description of his findings on the casket fire and the hearse explosion.

"Peter, this business of the C4, you know, the fire at the graveside and the incendiary device on the hearse."

Peter looked up from the keyboard.

"Yes, Ian, what about it?"

"Are you certain?"

"Certain about what?"

"About it being the same?"

Peter nodded.

"Yes, Ian, I'm certain."

The policeman's head was cocked to one side and his eyebrows rose into small crescent shapes.

"Mmm."

He gave a long sigh and scratched the top of his head.

"There's no possibility of something like a friction build-up from some kind of chemical used in the funeral trade?"

Peter shook his head.

"I've identified a third compound. It's a fire accelerant polybutilehexaphosphate. It's used occasionally in the building industry to increase oxidation during the arc welding process. It's not used in the funeral business. Now, I'm not Hercule Poirot, but the chances of all these substances being the root cause of two separate incidents, on the same day I might add, and *not* being connected in some way, seem to me to be extremely unlikely."

"So C4, Polybute, phos... or whatever you called it, was used in both these incidents? And that means we have..."

There was a prolonged silence between the two men. Peter knew better than to interrupt when Thompson was working something out in his head.

Eventually the policeman spoke.

"That means we have two incidents with a common chemical denominator, linked to two funeral directors on the same day. That is at best highly unlikely to be coincidental and at worst, deliberate."

Peter wondered what could be left in between "at best" and "at worst".

He drummed his fingers on his chin.

"Would you say that was an accurate summation, Peter?"

"Yes, I would."

Thompson continued, "So what do you think of this as a hypothesis? On first inspection, it looks like someone with a grudge against Sullivan wanted to cause as much mayhem as possible and completely sabotage the old boy's send-off. That's what the papers are suggesting at least, and, if that were to be the case, I'd have to interview half the State to get to the bottom of this. Old Jacko had a lot of people who didn't like him."

Peter smiled. Jack Sullivan probably had more enemies than any one else in Australia.

"However, I've interviewed both of the undertakers concerned – Robertson, who conducted Sullivan's funeral, and Humphries, whose hearse provided the escort when it had to be towed into the cemetery, and I can tell you, both of them are holding something back and they're scared."

Peter looked perplexed.

"What could they be afraid of?"

"I don't know, but I've got a feeling somebody might be running some sort of protection racket. I'm sure they've been threatened."

"Why would anyone lean on funeral directors for protection money? It doesn't make any sense, Ian."

But to one funeral director, who would stop at nothing, not even murder, to get what he wanted, it made perfect sense.

# Chapter 17

## The Lone Predator

Jerome T Spitz loved his office. He especially loved positioning himself imperiously behind his desk and offering counsel to those who came his way – counsel which inevitably lined his pockets. On this occasion however, he was crunching numbers on a computer. The forecasts were not looking good – he was behind schedule on the acquisition of Humphries and Robertson's businesses, which were both taking longer than he had planned. The images of a catatonic Robertson, set against the backdrop of what could have easily been a bushfire and Humphries, seated inelegantly in his towed hearse, still made him smile.

However, all was not rosy in the Spitz camp. Cash flow, damned cash flow, it always amounted to cash flow. Sure, he had picked up business with his unusual approach to death. The circus impresario's send-off had given him great coverage, but the projected revenue was less than expected, partly due to the adverse publicity from the Christian moral right and also to an Australian culture, which was slower in accepting change in this area than he had anticipated. Robertson and Humphries, despite the havoc from last week, had not caved in, although he sensed the time was rapidly approaching when they would throw in the towel. He made a mental note to employ his 'Angel' one more time on these two and perhaps a more direct approach was called for. Now, that he had begun, there was no turning back. Onward and upward.

Unexpectedly, the office door opened and Radic strode in, completely shattering Spitz's train of thought. Startled, the undertaker looked up from his computer.

"Angelo, how many times have I told you about knocking before entering?"

The anger in his voice was barely disguised. Radic came to an abrupt halt, his brain trying to salvage the last conversation about the rules for entering the inner sanctum that was Spitz's office as his brow furrowed and his small beady eyes squinted in laboured concentration. Eventually his face relaxed as the answer came to him, heralded by a wide grin.

"Knock firzt?"

"Yes. Knock first, then wait for an answer. I could have been with a client."

"Sorry, Bozz, I won't forget nexzt time."

'Yes, you will,' thought Spitz, 'and the time after that and the time after that too.'

He turned to exit, when Spitz called him back.

"Angelo, you're here now, come and sit down, I have some things I need you to attend to. As it happens, we have work to do with our two friends, Messrs Robertson & Humphries."

Being needed by Spitz made Radic feel important and valued. With a wide smile on his rock-like face, he turned, grabbed the door handle and closed the door behind him with such force, two framed certificates on the adjacent wall shook. Spitz groaned and placed a hand over his eyes. He had been over this a hundred times and it was always the same. Were it not for the blind allegiance and the child-like acceptance of his strategy by Radic, he would have sacked this gorilla long ago.

"And, Angelo, when you close the door, try being gentle about it, OK?"

Radic looked puzzled.

"I vos being gentle, Bozz."

There was no getting around this and Spitz knew it. Letting the moment pass he beckoned Radic to the chair next to the desk.

"I've been thinking, Angelo," he began. "It is time to increase the pressure on our two competitors. They've been somewhat lethargic in their acquiescence to my original offer."

Radic was now totally confused. Big words did that to him.

"We have to see Humphries and Robertson again."

"Mmm, yez," the Croat nodded in acknowledgement.

It was amazing that the head could move at all with the absence of a neck – it simply sat on top of his bulging shoulders giving him the appearance of some mythological creature.

Spitz continued, "I think tomorrow night would be a good time for a little chat, but this time we should have it here. Much cosier and intimate, more conducive to changing hearts and minds and certainly the venue for focusing one's attention on matters immediate and imperative, wouldn't you say, Angelo?"

More big words.

"They'll feel more scared here."

Smaller words made more sense.

Radic nodded sagaciously.

"Mmm, yez. More scared."

"But first, there's someone to whom we should pay a little visit. I don't know why I didn't think of it before."

He stretched out in the high backed swivel chair, placing his hands behind his head.

"O'Neill's – small, family-operated funeral business, dad recently deceased and daughter now running the show all by herself. Perfect for us – should be a piece of cake. I think we should go and see her very soon."

\* \* \*

Ian Thompson was a man with a hearty appetite and he loved having lunch with Peter Wilson. The young scientist was a great sounding board for his ideas and somehow the policeman always felt clearer after talking to him. In the relaxed atmosphere of the Criterion Hotel, he was enjoying his meal, attacking the steak and chips on the plate in front of him, with gusto. The food was delicious, but he was having trouble with the blunt steak knife. Lost amid the clatter and noise of the busy pub, Peter struggled to catch each word, as Thompson determinedly sawed his way through the large sirloin with the dull knife, while simultaneously conducting a conversation with his mouth half full of food. Only parts of each sentence were intelligible. Wilson watched in amazement.

"So, Peter, only a matter of time before… the bottom of this, eh?"

A gulp of orange squash was the only interruption to the attack on the steak. Thompson continued with the same dogged determination, talking all the while.

"Something going on here, my boy… feel it in my bones. Something rotten in the state of Denmark and all that, eh?"

Peter was about to speak, but Thompson continued the monologue.

"… Robertson… holding back… damned sure of that!"

There was absolutely no point in trying to engage the hungry policeman until all the food had been consumed. It was as though Thompson had tunnel vision and the only thing in his sights was the plate before him. The mind however was working in a different direction, thinking about the recent events and trying to connect them. Peter sat patiently and watched the contents of the plate disappear. The final remnant of the steak was scooped into the waiting jaws.

"Humphries too… connected somehow… damned sure of that!"

A stifled belch signalled the end of the meal.

"Ahhhhhh, that's better. I was starving. Haven't eaten for days. Well, hours anyhow."

He glanced at Peter's plate – he was only half way through his meal.

"Not hungry?"

"I'm fine, Ian – I just don't eat as fast as you. Actually, I don't know anyone who does."

They both laughed, comfortable in each other's company.

Peter picked up the conversation.

"You mentioned something about Robertson? Holding back?"

"Yes, I went to see Mr James Robertson the day after the horrendous Jacko Sullivan funeral. He was pretty shaken up – Robertson, I mean."

Peter suppressed a smile. There was a certain irony to the entire fiasco.

"I had the distinct impression someone was leaning on him, but he wouldn't talk to me about it."

"Scared of what, of whom?"

"Wouldn't go into any details, polite and hospitable enough of course, but very guarded."

Peter listened intently.

"Paid a visit to the other fellow, Humphries. His hearse is very much the worse with a hole in its engine."

"Did you get any further with him?"

"Not really. Same problem. He said something about advanced negotiations and not wanting to upset the apple cart. Odd fellow… made the worst coffee I've ever tasted."

Peter was about to ask what bad coffee had to do with anything, but chose to let the matter drop. Thompson would often think aloud. The trick for the listener was to filter out the extraneous information and just retrieve the occasional nugget.

For the next quarter of an hour, the two chatted about matters unrelated to their jobs, while Peter finished his meal and the last drop of fresh orange juice had been consumed. The pub was becoming quieter, as lunch time patrons returned to work, and the serving staff collected empty plates, then wiped and reset tables for the next sitting. Peter enjoyed these times with Thompson and remarkably the lunch had been incident-free. The last time at this pub, a waitress had been inadvertently stabbed in the leg, as Thompson sought to catch a steak knife falling from her tray. Unbeknown to him and from that day onwards, the waiting staff had kept the sharper objects well clear of the man, supplying him only with blunted cutting implements.

Noticing the meal appeared to be at an end, a waitress approached the two men.

"Hi, gents, all done here?"

Thompson smiled warmly.

"Yes, thanks, love, we're finished."

"Everything alright, I trust?"

"Fine," answered Peter immediately, leaving Thompson to complete the affirmation.

"Steak was great and the chips fantastic, but I reckon you need some more cutlery. My knife was as blunt as a spoon."

The waitress blushed. Being new, her instructions were not to offer, under *any* circumstances, a regular steak knife to this man. Her predecessor had been less fortunate and had the scar to prove it.

"Oh, I'm sorry about that, I'll mention it to the Manager. I hope it didn't spoil your meal."

"No problem. It was very nice."

Thompson rose, signalling the return to work, while narrowly missing a passing steward with a tray full of empty glasses. Peter closed his eyes and said a small prayer. Ian Thompson was the most likeable of men, but dangerous to be around. Accidents followed him like the wake from a ship and the secret of not getting wet was to be vigilant at all times.

Peter held the door open for the policeman as they left the pub and walked out onto the busy street and the strong sunlight.

"Thanks for the lunch, Ian, I really enjoyed it. I'd be interested to know what you turn up. Please, keep me informed."

"My pleasure, I'll give you a ring later, OK?"

\* \* \*

It had been over a week since Kathleen first visited Jock. Despite promising to see him soon, the truth of the matter was that, apart from being extremely busy, she also had very mixed emotions. She was still quite traumatised by the accident and these thoughts were running through her head as she parked in the hospital car park. However, Kathleen had made Jock a promise and the O'Neills didn't break their promises. His situation was truly awful and, given the part she played in it, however unintentional, she felt compelled to visit as often as she could. Opening the car doors, despite her nerves, she stepped out into the bright sunlight. It was cranking up to be a real scorcher as she made her way to the entrance, through the revolving doors and into the lift up to the eighth floor.

"Good morning," the salutation from a nurse at the nurses' station was bright and cheerful.

"Good morning. I've come to see Mr Strapp. How's he doing today?"

The nurse raised her eyes briefly upwards and shook her head slightly.

"That is one determined man. He wants to go home yesterday, which by all accounts is a good sign, but there are a few things we need to get right first."

"Are they serious?"

"Are you a relative?"

"No."

"You're the only visitor he's had, which is why I thought you might be related."

Kathleen blushed slightly.

"No, I'm a volunteer."

"Well, you probably know then that he's been in a nasty accident, and, although he's recovering well, the doctors would like to see him completely stable before he's discharged. Social Services also have to be sure that his accommodation is suitable for a wheelchair and all these things take time. We can't discharge him until it's safe to do so. Perhaps you might like to help him take that on board. I shouldn't think he will be with us for much more than a couple of weeks, maybe less."

"I understand. I'll do my best."

Kathleen knocked on the door to Jock's room and was greeted with a very firm "Go away!" from inside.

Perplexed, she called out, "Jock, it's me, Kathleen O'Neill. If it's not a good time, I'll come back later."

There was clearly confusion and anger inside the room, as several expletives floated out into the corridor. Concerned, Kathleen made her way back to the nurse she had just been talking to.

"I think there may be a problem with Mr Strapp. Can you take a look please?"

The nurse was immediately on her feet and at the door to Jock's room in an instant. Without bothering to knock she went straight in with Kathleen right behind her, to find Jock sitting on the floor akimbo, trying to get back into the high hospital bed, but obviously without success. He was clearly agitated and swearing loudly.

Quickly taking charge of the situation, the nurse turned to Kathleen,

"Would you ask a couple of my colleagues from the desk to come here straight away, please?"

It was more of an order than a request. Kathleen did exactly as she was told and, within a minute, two extra nurses were in the room and had their patient back in bed. Kathleen waited quietly outside until finally all three nurses left.

The lead nurse was the last through the door.

"All sorted now. I told you he was determined! Still, it's OK now. You can go in if you like."

Jock was sitting up in bed, an intravenous line attached to the back of his left hand, an angry look on his face.

"It doesn't look like I've come at a very good time. I'd better go," said Kathleen meekly.

She had one foot inside the door. Jock sat immobile, his lips pursed and breathing in laboured fashion as though he had been running.

Kathleen turned to leave and was halfway out of the room when he called out from the bed.

"Nay! Don't go... please... don't go."

He beckoned her in with a movement of his head. She returned to the bedside and Jock pointed to an arm chair next to the bed.

"Why don't you sit down?"

"Thank you, Jock, are you OK now?"

"Yeah, yeah... Look, sorry again. Jesus, that's all I seem to be saying to people these days, sorry!"

Kathleen drew the chair slightly closer.

"Jock, it's OK, honestly, I imagine it's not much fun being here."

He laughed ironically.

"Ms O'Neill, that is the understatement of the century."

The last statement broke the ice and suddenly the atmosphere was lighter.

"So, Jock, what was that all about?" nodding her head in the direction of the door and the nurses station just outside.

"Needed to get 'oot of this bloody bed, fed up being stuck here like a beached whale, it's driving me mad. I'm sick of calling a nurse every time I need anything. It's making me feel like a little kid. I hate it!"

Kathleen sat patiently, not speaking. She knew when to listen and this was one of those times.

He continued, "Anyway, I managed to unplug the drip and I used the stand to drag the wheelchair over to the bed – thought that was kind of inspired, actually. Getting into the wheelchair from the bed should have been the easy part, but you know what they say about pride before a fall?"

He smiled ruefully.

"Forgot to engage the brake, didn't I? Slipped 'oot of bed, and half onto a moving wheelchair. Knocked a couple of monitors over and dumped myself on the floor in the process."

He shook his head in annoyance.

"Useless bloody legs!"

Kathleen reached out and gently touched his forearm.

"Jock, it's alright to be angry. You're clearly an independent man and this must be very frustrating for you. I'm not surprised you find it difficult being here, in this place, with all of its limitations and restrictions, but the nurses I've spoken to are concerned that you're fully stabilised before you try and do too much."

The words and the touch had a soothing effect on him, there was genuine concern from this woman and it was not lost on him.

The anger slowly began to dissipate.

"I know. I just wanna' get 'oot of here. Life has been full of nasty surprises lately. I never counted on the heed problem, but I was kind of getting used to the fact that there's an end for all of us, even me! And then this," he said, nodding his head in the direction of his legs. "I thought I'd at least go 'oot like a man, not like some pathetic cripple."

Kathleen gave his arm a small squeeze.

"I don't think you're a pathetic cripple, Jock. I think you're a very courageous man who needs a little time to take in the situation and, if that means being fed up or getting angry from time to time, I think that's perfectly understandable."

He sighed deeply, grateful for the company.

"Thanks, Kath, thanks. I really mean it. I guess you're right and the sooner I'm patched up, the sooner they'll let me go."

"That's the spirit, Jock."

The conversation drifted onto the subject of Jock's youth and his adventures as a schoolboy in Glasgow, before his family migrated to Australia. Despite his terrible circumstances, Jock was a great story teller and had

Kathleen in stitches. His dry, gritty humour and unpretentious ways made his plight all the more poignant. Kathleen confided some of the mishaps that had occurred in her business and Jock laughed raucously, enjoying the shared confidence. He sensed instinctively that this was not a woman who confided in just anybody and was flattered by her openness with him.

The door opened and an orderly entered wheeling a dinner trolley.

"Dinner time," he announced.

Kathleen stood and pushed the chair to one side.

"I'd better get back and do some work. I've really enjoyed this time... thank you, Jock."

"Nay, fine lady, the pleasure is mine."

The orderly pushed the rolling table from the foot of the bed up to Jock's chest and put down the tray containing the evening meal.

"Guess that's my cue."

Kathleen moved out of the way.

"Enjoy your meal, Jock. I'll see you again soon."

"Cheers, Kath, see you and thanks for coming."

* * *

If Jock and Kathleen were enjoying their time together, the opposite was true for Spitz, the lone predator. Irritation was leading him back to his former ways and a dark side, once unleashed, knew few boundaries.

# Chapter 18

## Love Birds

Spitz sat in his office, nursing the remains of a whisky and ice and contemplating his options. Neither Robertson, nor Humphries had crumbled, despite the recent misfortunes which had befallen them both, but this, he concluded, was not entirely unexpected.

A patient man, Spitz had a contingency plan for every eventuality and now, he reasoned, was the time to step up the pressure, starting with Robertson. Yes, he would get the man here, on home ground where he would have the advantage and twist the screw a little tighter, make the issues a little more... *personal*... yes, that was it – personal.

It was after five o'clock and Radic was outside in reception, leafing through a magazine with lots of bright pictures. He liked the pictures, mainly landscapes depicting country scenes with the occasional bit of wildlife to complete the rural image. The accompanying words, he disregarded, they were too difficult to derive any meaning from and they did not form part of the overall visual experience.

"Angel!"

It was Spitz calling from the office.

"Would you come in, please?"

The door opened forcefully as Radic entered the office. He closed it with equal vigour, shaking the framed certificates hanging on the wall.

The Croat froze. He had done it again.

"Sorry, Bozz."

Spitz shook his head dully. It was no good trying to get through to this moron.

"Yes, Angelo, I know. However, we have more important matters to attend to."

He downed the remnants of the whisky and pointed to a chair.

"Sit down, my friend. I have a job for you."

Radic positioned himself on the edge of the chair. He liked doing jobs for the boss, it made him feel special and important. He listened attentively, concentrating on Spitz's words.

"I want you to call on our friend, Robertson, and ask him firmly but politely, to accompany you, whereupon you will bring him here, in order that I may have a little chat with him. Is that clear?"

The blank look on Radic's face said it all.

Spitz sighed and thought of the last time his gorilla had visited Robertson's establishment alone. He had been confident then his instructions were straight forward, but he had of course been wrong. Time for words of less than one syllable.

"Robertson – he owns the place you visited last week, grey metal box under the legs… does this ring a bell?"

It most certainly did and the Croat beamed.

"Yez, Bozz – I remember."

He could manage small numbers.

"Good. I want you to go there right now and bring Mr Robertson here. Do you understand?"

"Yez, Bozz," he said frowning.

"What is it, Angelo?"

"He may not want to come."

"Then convince him otherwise."

The furrow in his brow deepened and then swallowed slightly as the solution to this possible problem came to him.

He nodded slowly to himself, acknowledging his brain's message.

"I'll break his legs."

Spitz was aghast.

"No, Angelo, don't break his legs."

"I'll break an arm."

"Angelo, don't break his arm, just go there, I'm sure he will see reason."

"Some fingers?"

This was proving to be more difficult than he had originally envisaged, yet it was important that Robertson be delivered there without any obvious or undue influence that could be traced back to himself.

"Angelo, no bones, OK? Don't break *any* bones. Just show him to the car and I'm sure everything will be just fine."

Radic nodded slowly. He thought the idea of breaking some bones was quite a good one, but his boss knew best, he always did.

Rising from his chair, he walked to the door and opened it.

"OK, Bozz, I'll go now."

"Good, Angelo, I'll expect you back here in about an hour with our friend."

The door closed with such force, that the whole room shook.

\* \* \*

A few kilometres and a different world away, Kathleen stared at the paperwork on her desk, yet saw none of it. The events of the last week had taken their toll. In a world of her own, her mind was racing between Mrs Papadopoulos, Jock, Peter, her father and where her life was going, when the knock at the door jerked her back to the here and now.

"Come in."

Peter Wilson entered the room and looked with concern at the figure behind the desk.

"Kath, are you alright?"

"Peter," a grateful smile spread across her face. "Am I glad to see you? It's been a long couple of days."

There was weariness in her eyes.

"Take me out somewhere, Peter, somewhere away from here for a while."

He moved towards her and gently took both her hands in his, raising her from her chair.

"Great minds think alike! That's exactly why I called. It's nearly five thirty. Come on, let's get out of here. Can Tracey lock up for you?"

Kathleen nodded.

"Good, then I know the perfect place!"

Fifteen minutes and a short taxi ride later, they were in a Hawaiian-style cocktail bar. The décor created a tropical island effect, with large murals depicting coconut trees against a backdrop of an azure-blue ocean while soft-slide guitar music discreetly floated over the whole scene. There was even a large brilliantly coloured parrot on a stand near one of the corners.

The contrast from her office at O'Neill's couldn't have been more pronounced as she felt herself unwinding.

Peter was the first to speak.

"Apparently they make fabulous cocktails here, the best in Sydney, so I'm told."

As they sat at the bar, he perused the cocktail menu.

"This looks good – 'Tidal Wave'… rum, brandy, a touch of grenadine and lemon poured over crushed ice."

He was deeply engrossed in the menu as Kathleen looked warmly at him. She reached out and took his hand in hers, causing him to look up.

"You're very sweet, do you know that, Peter?"

She leaned across and kissed him gently on the cheek.

"Thank you for calling by and bringing me here. I think I sometimes don't get out enough."

He grinned broadly.

"Well, you're out now and that's the main thing, OK? You know what they say, all work and no play etc. Anyway, the really important question is what cocktail do you fancy?"

The conversation flowed easily. Light banter about this and that, day to day events with nothing deep or heavy. Kathleen was grateful for the inter-action and the setting, the effects of the cocktail making her relax without realising it. They blended in easily with a number of other couples sitting at the bar. It was a good feeling being here, with this man, in this place.

Peter glanced at his watch, it was seven o'clock and they had both finished their drinks and felt a bit tipsy.

"Hungry?"

"Hungry? I'm starving! I've only had a salad today."

"Good. How does Russian sound?"

"Russian? I've never eaten Russian food before."

"Neither have I, but some of the guys at work said there's a new place just opened. It's supposed to be brilliant and it's not far from here. What do you say? Shall we give it a go?"

"I'm game."

The cocktail had made her feel a little extroverted.

"Take me to Russia!" she laughed in an Eastern European accent.

Peter was already on his feet.

"Da! Your vish is my command. Lezz call a taxi!"

\* \* \*

By a lucky coincidence, Radic arrived at Robertson's office as the under-taker was about to lock up for the evening. Seeing the thug approaching was like an action replay of the last visit and the fact that Spitz was not present made him feel very nervous. At least Spitz could control the brute.

A huge hand clapped him on the shoulder.

"Za bozz wants to zee you – now."

Robertson was in a state of sheer panic. His feet felt like they were glued to the ground and the sounds that came out of his mouth were weak and feeble.

"Wha… what are you talking about?"

The hand moved from his shoulder and grabbed his upper arm. It was like having his blood pressure taken by a boa constrictor, the force cutting off the blood flow to his fingers and making them tingle.

"Za Bozz – now."

The pressure increased and he sensed the man had lots more in reserve – this was just a gentle urging. In the event, there was no chance to reply, as Radic began to walk in the direction of his car, parked a few metres away. Robertson walked too. There was little option with his arm in the vice-like grip.

"Ged in."

It was a command, not a request and Robertson did exactly as he was told. Radic sat heavily behind the wheel, the medium-sized car sinking noticeably under his weight.

The door slammed with customary force as he turned to face his passenger sitting centimetres away, shooting him a menacing look. Robertson felt his bladder give way, as a small wet patch appeared on his crotch.

"Zeet belt."

With a momentary sense of relief that he was not going to die there and then, he quickly fastened his seat belt and offered a tentative smile to the Croat.

Radic nodded in agreement, a small grunt, the only audible response of acknowledgement as he started the car and drove off to deliver his charge.

\* \* \*

Deciding to eat Russian had been a complete impulse, but it had proved to be a most pleasant surprise. Peter was finishing the last of the borscht as the waiter came to their table.

"Did you enjoy the soup, sir?"

"It was absolutely delicious," he replied, holding up his hand so the thumb and index finger formed the letter O. "I must have the recipe," he joked.

"Ah, I'm afraid my mother never reveals her cooking secrets, especially when they've been handed down through the generations. So sorry, but you are certainly not the first to ask and hopefully not the last. Now, shall I bring the main course and a little more chilled Vodka, yes?"

Peter nodded and the waiter, having cleared the table withdrew to the kitchen.

Kathleen sat back in her chair, the effects of the day melting away in the subdued lighting and low background conversation of the restaurant.

·"What a fabulous find, real home-cooked food, great décor and I just *love* the music."

A trio with violin, balalaika and accordion played softly from the corner.

"Thank you, Peter, you're so kind to me, I was feeling pretty low when you called."

The waiter returned with two small shot glasses of vodka, placed them on the table and left.

"Ah… the healing powers of alcohol."

Peter raised his glass, Kathleen did the same.

"Nostrovia," said Peter.

The glasses clinked.

"Nostrovia," she replied, as they both took small sips.

Kathleen leaned across the table and took his hand in hers.

"You're a kind and special man, Peter, and I just love your company."

"I… I…," he started, "I love your company too, Kath, you make me feel good inside and you're fun."

He gave her hand a gentle squeeze.

"God knows there's been precious little of that over the past couple of years."

They held each other's gaze until Peter broke the silence.

"Listen to me, won't you – getting all maudlin. Must be the vodka!"

Kathleen's voice was serene and level.

"You're not being maudlin and it's not the vodka, Peter, you know how to express your feelings and I think that's one of the things that I love best about you."

Did he hear her say the word 'love'? His heart raced a little, but the moment was interrupted when the waiter arrived with the main course, a tasty goulash with rice and a dusting of paprika. Peter and Kathleen released each other's hands and sat back.

They had shared an unexpectedly close moment and it set the mood for the rest of the night. With their remaining inhibitions falling away, they spent a great evening together, telling each other stories and making one another laugh.

The flickering candle on the table lent an intimate mood to the occasion and, as the hours passed, and encouraged by the effects of the vodka, their jokes and conversation became more and more risqué.

The plates had been cleared away and the empty espresso cups sat drained of their contents.

"Some more coffee?" Peter asked.

"No, that was just lovely, the perfect ending to a perfect evening."

Kathleen looked at her watch, thinking of only one thing that would make it better. Peter took the cue and caught the waiter's eye making small writing movements on his hand, the universal sign language for 'bring me the bill.'

The waiter appeared from nowhere with a small salver containing a small piece of paper, which he placed on the table, and before Peter could find his credit card, he placed two small glasses of liqueur on the table.

Peter looked confused.

"We didn't order these," he said to the waiter.

"They are with my compliments."

The accent was unmistakably Russian. An older, stout woman had now joined the conversation.

"I am Anna and this is my restaurant. Did you enjoy your meal?"

Kathleen was the first to respond.

"It was fantastic, all of it."

"Especially the borscht," Peter added.

"Thank you, you are too kind."

"I don't suppose you could let me have the recipe?"

There was a hopeful tone in Peter's voice.

"Cheeky boy!"

The rebuke was playful as the matriarch touched him lightly on the shoulder.

"I've been watching you, love birds, all evening and, believe me, there's magic at this table tonight."

A quick nod of her head brought the violinist and the accordionist to the table.

"Play something romantic for this lovely couple," she ordered.

It had been a perfect evening and Kathleen felt good all over.

Meeting Peter was the best thing that had ever happened to her.

* * *

By contrast, meeting Spitz was definitely *not* the best thing that had ever happened to Robertson and, although he didn't yet know it, his life would soon be in mortal danger.

## Chapter 19

## Come Up For a Coffee

"Mr Robertson, thank you so much for stopping by." Spitz indicated a chair with an open hand.

"Please, do make yourself comfortable. I thought we might have a little chat, you know, iron out any *misunderstandings*."

As usual, Radic sat by the door, dashing any thought of escape. Robertson resigned himself to the meeting and had decided in the course of the journey from his office to Spitz's with the henchman, to go through the motions and simply get through this. After all, he considered, it wasn't as if they were going to kill him.

Suddenly, the thought terrified him, maybe they were and perhaps what he should be doing now was fighting for his life. But how? He was clearly no match for Radic and, besides, they were two and he was just one and...

"Don't worry Mr Robertson, you will not be harmed."

It was as if Spitz was reading his mind. Was he that transparent?

"But I do think it is in everyone's best interest we reach a common understanding, don't you agree?"

"What do you want?" the question lacked any backbone.

"You know what I want. I thought I made that clear two weeks ago. I want to acquire your business. The problem seems to be *when* and that is where I think we have a little mis-un-der-stand-ing."

The syllabic response was accompanied by a specious smile.

"Even if I were going to sell, these things take *time*," protested Robertson, "papers need to be prepared, solicitors instructed, a dozen different tasks. The list goes on and on."

A touch of indignation was creeping into the response and it was stiffening his resolve.

"In any event, I don't want to sell my business, not just to you, but to anyone."

"Been busy in the last week, have we?"

Spitz was examining a fingernail with great concentration.

"March is always quieter than other months."

"That's not true and you know it. Word on the street is that you made a real mess of the Sullivan funeral and, if you can do that with such a notable client, well, it's not rocket science, is it?"

"What are you driving at, Spitz?"

This time there was anger in the question.

Spitz's mood changed instantly, the fake bonhomie and all interest in the fingernail now gone. In his peripheral vision, Robertson saw Radic stir in the corner. Suddenly both Spitz and Radic were on either side of him.

"What I'm telling you is that, after the Sullivan debacle, you don't *have* a business, because people don't want that happening to their loved ones. Let's face it, Robertson, you don't have anything to sell. You're history in this town, your days are over."

Robertson was on the ropes, he knew it.

Both Spitz and Radic leaned closer to their prey.

"You're finished!"

Radic sneered.

"Fffffffinised!"

Spitz slowly rotated his head to look at the Croat and silenced him by holding up his index finger.

"Don't speak, Angelo. Don't say anything. Just sit quietly over there."

Robertson still looked dazed as Spitz delivered the coup de grace.

"The end of the month. I want this concluded by the end of the month and, as it's now the sixth, you have plenty of time to get things moving. After all, we wouldn't want to have any more problems, now would we?"

"Problems?"

"I should hate to think another adverse *incident* might occur with any of your clients. Or indeed, that any harm should befall either you or your lovely wife. Make no mistake, Mr Robertson, you are in over your head, and if I have to get rough, Jack Sullivan's funeral will look like a picnic. I have some very unpleasant friends, who like hurting people."

He looked at Radic.

"Trust me," he continued, "when I tell you, you wouldn't want to provoke them, by trying to hold on to your little business. Do you understand what I'm telling you?"

He paused to let the words sink in, while Robertson, stared blankly ahead, caught between a rock and a hard place.

"I think Mr Robertson understands, don't you, Angelo?"

Spitz looked at Radic and nodded in the direction of the door.

"Don't forget, the end of the month. This discussion is now over."

Radic held the door open, as Robertson stumbled through and out onto the street to hail a taxi.

* * *

It was nearing midnight as the cab pulled up outside O'Neill's. Peter got out first and opened the door for Kathleen, taking her hand as she stepped out.

"Kath, I've had a great night, one I'll remember for a long time. Thanks."

He was about to get back into the cab when she said, "Why don't you come up for a coffee? It's really not that late."

Though he longed to take her up on her offer, he hesitated.

"I don't want to outstay my welcome."

"Believe me, you aren't. Besides, tomorrow's Saturday. You've got the whole weekend to recover!"

Peter spoke hesitantly.

"If you're absolutely sure, I mean, I don't want to be a nuisance and it's no both..."

Kathleen cut him short.

"Peter, pay the driver and come up for a coffee."

He turned to the taxi driver and fished into his wallet for some notes. The cabbie looked at the meter.

"Twenty five bucks, mate."

Peter pulled out three ten dollar notes and passed them through the open passenger window.

"Cheers. Keep the change."

"Thanks, mate."

The driver gave a knowing wink, pocketed the fare and drove quietly away.

The kettle in the kitchen clicked itself off as Peter and Kathleen sat together on the settee.

"Did you really have a great night?" she asked.

"I think great is probably a poor description. I had an amazing night."

She moved close to him so that their hips were touching, her perfume strong and pleasant as she gently touched his forearm.

"I had an amazing night too."

Both felt the charged atmosphere and neither spoke. Words seemed unnecessary in the situation.

Kathleen looked into his eyes and brought her lips close to his.

"Amazing," was all she could say before he kissed her tenderly, his arms now around her shoulders and holding her tight.

"Amazing," he mimicked.

They kissed again, Kathleen relaxing in his strong embrace.

"Stay with me tonight, Peter, please stay with me tonight."

He smiled broadly as he stood up, took her hands in his, and pulled her gently onto her feet, before leading her into the bedroom.

\* \* \*

Being summertime, the sun rose early in the southern hemisphere. At 4:30, the first feeble glimmers of the impending dawn were faintly discernable in night sky. An hour later, the sun had breached the horizon and begun its ellipse through the eastern skies. Peter and Kathleen saw none of this while James Robertson saw it all.

The man looked terrible. He hadn't slept a wink all night and couldn't stop thinking about yesterday evening's conversation with Spitz and his pet gorilla. Any idea that these two would back off had since disappeared and he was in a quandary what to do. Walking around his office, after a sleepless night, he considered his options, none of which were particularly appealing.

One: acquiesce… roll over and let Spitz buy him out. He'd probably have to sell well below the going price, but, as things stood, there wasn't much goodwill left anyway. The Sullivan incident and the nationwide television coverage it attracted had seen to that. An iconic head and shoulders photograph of Roberstson, eyes wide and staring with a look of utter shock on his face had also appeared in the Sydney Morning Herald on page four, under the caption, "Funeral goes up in smoke".

The same photo had been picked up by the local papers. Business had been almost non-existent since those publications.

Two: do nothing. But Spitz's overt threat to him and his wife, he concluded, was genuine. The man had no regard for others and an obvious contempt for the law. Why else would he risk a police investigation, unless he was sure that it would never see the light of day? This wasn't going to go away, the thug with no neck would surely see to that. He looked like the sort of man who could take on a rugby team and come out on top and, besides, he had never felt strength or known breath like that before. His wrist and arm bore the reminders of last night. No, doing nothing wasn't a serious option. He and his wife wouldn't stand a chance to win against someone of Radic's size and temperament. Besides, unlike his foes, he wasn't a gangster. He was just a simple undertaker.

Three: go to the police. This was the path down which he had not wanted to travel, initially at least, but was now feeling somewhat driven in this direction. It was of course fraught with risk. Once the cat was out of the bag, there would be no turning back. It was an all-or-nothing approach and would certainly mean involving his wife. She would have to know all the details, but he was in real fear for her safety and his own.

He had to make a decision, and sooner rather than later. The American would be sure to up the ante next time and make life even more difficult for him and his wife.

'Come on,' he thought to himself, 'think of something or make a decision and get this over with.'

The intercom on his desk buzzed. It was June, the receptionist.

"There's a Detective Inspector Ian Thompson to see you, Mr Robertson."

Robertson stopped pacing the floor, the message having taken him completely by surprise. He stood immobile in front of the desk.

"Mr Robertson? Are you there?"

No reply.

"Mr Roberston?"

He poked at the 'connect' button and said, "Yes! I'm here June!"

"There's a Detetcive Inspect…"

"I heard you the first time! Give me a few minutes. I'll be out shortly."

The receptionist released the intercom button and turned to Thompson.

"Mr Robertson will see you in a few minutes. Please take a seat."

She began to rise from behind her desk.

"Do you want anything to drink while you're waiting, a tea or a coffee?"

Thompson stiffened slightly, the memory of Humphries' coffee still fresh in his mind.

"No! I've just had one, but thanks all the same."

He sat in a nearby chair, picked up a magazine from the coffee table and began leafing through it.

In a short while, a door adjacent to the receptionist's desk opened and Robertson came out.

"Good morning, Inspector, please come in."

They shook hands as Thompson entered the main office and both men seated themselves.

Thompson was the first to speak.

"Are you alright, Mr Robertson?"

"No, not really, Inspector."

He furtively rubbed the back of his hand over his mouth several times, as though the action would initiate some explanatory words. None came.

"Would you like to tell me what the problem is? I've been a policeman now for over thirty years, Mr Robertson, and it's pretty obvious you're scared. The question is of what... or whom?"

The question hung in the air as Thompson patiently waited for a response.

"I wasn't completely honest with you the last time we spoke, Inspector, or should I say, I didn't make you aware of all the facts."

There was a tremor in his voice.

"And, frankly, I'm not entirely sure I should be revealing what I'm about to tell you. The fact of the matter is I'm in a bit of a jam and I'm not certain how it's going to turn out."

"Go on."

Robertson poured a small glass of water from a carafe and took a deep gulp. He pulled his chair closer to the policeman's and lowered his head slightly. It was reminiscent of a penitent and priest in the confessional.

Robertson spoke in a muted voice.

"There's this man, you see, he wants to buy my business, only I don't really want to sell, but he's not giving me any alternatives. My wife and I have worked hard to get this far and I don't want to just give it all up, but he's dangerous, you know what I mean, *dangerous* and, as for that body guard of his, well, I mean, it's not looking good and... "

It was all coming out in a rush.

"Slowly, please."

Thompson held up a hand.

"I need to write all this down."

The undertaker ran the back of his hand over his mouth again.

"Sorry, sorry. It's been going over and over in my mind. I haven't been sleeping much since this all began, even less since the fire."

Thompson had withdrawn a small notebook.

"Tell me from the beginning what has happened so that I get the full picture."

"They came to see me about two weeks ago, as I was closing up. One of them had a knife. It happened again last night."

"What happened again, last night? Who is threatening you?"

The timing of Thompson's arrival was uncanny. Robertson hadn't meant to blurt it out, but he already had and there was no turning back.

"Names, Mr Robertson, I need names."

"You can't begin some half-baked investigation and then leave me out to dry, Inspector. If I give you names, you have to promise me you'll see this through. I'll need police protection."

"If you were in any danger, we would protect you, but I can't just go around arresting people without evidence and I can't collect evidence if I don't know where to look. You give me somewhere to look and you have my word, I'll see this through. Extortion is a very serious offence."

Robertson shot Thompson a nervous, worried look.

"For what it's worth, I'll be very discreet. I don't want to stir up the dust at this stage," said Thompson.

"It's Spitz."

"The American funeral director, Spitz?"

"Yes."

"Good. You've done the right thing. Now, help me fill in the details."

At last, he was getting somewhere. Thompson finally had a suspect for the sabotage. He had Spitz in his sights and a finger on the trigger. It was a shame his aim was so poor. He was about to fire at the wrong target.

# Chapter 20

## A Romantic Picnic

An hour later, Radic, who had been summoned by Spitz, was taking a careful note of what his boss was saying.

"I have a very special job for you, Angelo."

"Vot is id, bozz?"

These times made Angelo feel very special.

"I want you to bring Humphries over here, for a little chat. Only this time I don't want you to go to his office. I've an extra surprise for our closet friend. He needs to feel completely isolated, not safe anywhere, not even on familiar ground. I want you to go to The Pink Mussel bar – on Duke Street. He goes there every night at seven, after closing, and stays for an hour or so. Get there before him and, when he arrives, join him for a drink – he'll be like a petrified rabbit in front of a snake, you won't have any trouble. Convince him it is in his very best interests to go with you, only don't show any aggression, don't draw attention to yourself in that way, the rest of the patrons will make some obvious conclusions when you leave together, which is what I want. It's the perfect cover."

Radic had looked perplexed.

Spitz translated.

"Bring him here, but don't break any bones."

His face relaxed visibly.

"Yez, Bozz, I goddit. No bones."

Later that day, Radic made his way to Duke Street and arrived early as instructed, fifteen minutes early, to be exact. He was unprepared for the scene that greeted him, as he walked through the door. Pink walls, adorned with portraits of handsome, muscle-bound young men, deep maroon floor tiles and cerise table tops were set off by the long bar to his right, which was bathed in pink lighting. The sides of the bar were covered with smoked glass and the metallic stools, with violent pink, shiny leather tops, completed the scene. Radic felt awkward and out of place in these surroundings, especially when the man at the bar next to him was drinking from a long, dainty glass full of pink, yellow and green liquids topped off with a small umbrella embedded in a peach slice. When he had asked for a beer, the barman had simply sniggered.

"No beer served here, sweetheart. We only serve cocktails."

The response had been accompanied by a long, lascivious top-to-bottom look.

Ordinarily, he would have broken several bones or, at the very least, a few, before walking out, but the Boss had said to wait for Humphries to arrive and, under no circumstances, draw attention to himself. The simple act of ordering a beer was proving to be a major obstacle.

"So…?"

Radic had never drunk a cocktail, let alone ordered one and the effort in choosing from the list on the bar was proving extremely challenging.

The barman stood waiting, the back of one hand, on his hip.

"First time, is it, dear? You do want a *cock*tail, I presume?"

"Yez. I vant cocktail."

Radic's brain was working overtime deciding what to choose and yet, somewhere in the deepest regions of his cerebrum, a dim memory stirred. Miraculously, it came to him – mental gymnastics were not his strong point.

"Give me prawn cocktail," he grunted.

Suppressing a laugh, the barman shook his head and pointed to the list.

"I'm sorry, love. I meant what cocktail would you like to drink? You'll have to choose another."

Radic waved at the list.

"Give me anyzing."

"Well, for a big boy like you, why don't you try a 'big package'? I'm sure it's right up your alley, if you get my drift."

He gave a small wink and set about preparing the drink.

"Take a seat and I'll bring it over."

The Croat nodded and found a table in the corner from where he could watch the door. He sat down and waited for Humphries to arrive.

Radic toyed with the little umbrella in his multi-coloured drink, wishing all the while he was somewhere else, a normal pub, surrounded by normal people, with a glass of Krenna. Certainly not here, in this place, with its stupid little sweet drinks. Still, a job was a job. His boss always knew best and, whatever he had been asked to do, it was sure to be part of some larger plan. That was about as far ahead as he was able to think. Any more caused his head to ache, but at least he was better off than before. The paint factory was certainly no match for working as an "associate." Yes, he liked the term. He felt important, looked more important too, now, that he wore a suit, although that had taken some getting used to – it was tight across the shoulders and when he moved his arms, the sleeves rode up. Even wearing a tie was less of a problem now that he had mastered the art of the tie's knot. A slim man in tight fitting trousers and a floral shirt drew up a chair and sat next to Radic, breaking his thoughts about suits and ties.

"I do hope you don't mind, but you looked so... so *sad*. Poor love. At any rate, I thought I'd just pop over and cheer you up, buy you a drink and make you all happy again."

The man extended a hand towards Radic.

"Justin de Witt at your serv..."

Despite his size and lumbering thought processes, Radic was surprisingly fast, especially when an unexpected move was made towards him. His right hand shot out like a striking snake and completely engulfed the hand moving towards him. The look of terror and pain was immediate as De Witt's hand was trapped with enormous force, just a few centimetres above the table. The man was speechless, as Radic glowered at him, lips pulled back to expose the front teeth and a low, primeval growling noise coming from somewhere deep in his throat.

"Go avay."

The sound of the little umbrella breaking somehow reinforced the command.

"Yes, yes, of course, I didn't realise, sorry to bother you..."

The grip relaxed and De Witt carefully withdrew his hand and rose from the table. All his fingers were tingling.

The apologies kept coming.

"Sorry, sorry," he said as he backed away from the Croat.

Humphries, who had just arrived, observed the whole thing. He hadn't noticed Radic at first, but the sudden movement had drawn his attention to the table in the corner. A hundred thoughts rushed through his mind, none of which made any sense. What was Spitz's henchman doing here? Looking for him? Surely not. He hadn't pegged the man as gay and even now, in this setting, it didn't make sense. What did make sense was that he didn't want to be here with the thug in plain view. Nervously, he took a step back towards the exit, hoping not to be recognised. However, like some kind of telepathic message, the instant he did so, Radic looked in his direction and he knew then, the game was up. The brute rose from his table and made a bee line for him at the bar. A huge hand wrapped itself around his upper arm as Radic nodded in the direction of the door.

"You come viz me, talk to Bozz."

"I don't understand," Humphries spluttered, "talk about what?"

The nervousness in his voice unmistakable.

"You come viz me, talk to Bozz."

There was no reasoning with the man. He had instructions and they were going to be carried out. He stepped away from the bar and towards the door, a quivering Humphries in tow.

A man standing at the bar watched the two men walk to the door and leave. He turned to the man next to him.

"Oh, I just *love* the forceful type. Makes me go all weak at the knees. Lucky boy."

Nursing his hand, De Witt said nothing.

\* \* \*

Kathleen had always loved the feeling of the wind in her hair and the sense of freedom that being in an open-topped car always brought. It felt good to be out of the city and in the hills. The air was fresher, the bush a welcome change from buildings and concrete as they drove along a winding road.

The memory of their shared passion the previous night had left Kathleen with a warm glow. Peter felt the same and driving his pristine Mk I MGB roadster with Kathleen beside him, her right hand lovingly stroking the back of his neck, he felt happier than he'd ever been before. Though the car wasn't fast, it was the fun of driving it Peter loved as he instinctively changed into third gear to round a gentle bend and drive deeper into the Blue Mountains.

His mind was completely absorbed with the memories of yesterday. Too shy to make the first move, he had been surprised and delighted by Kathleen's invitation to stay with her and it felt so right for them to be together. After making love for half the night, they stroked and caressed one another's bodies until sleep came. When they awoke, neither could tear themselves apart, unwilling to let the moment end. They were hooked. Uncharacteristically, Kathleen took the day off work and decided to join

Peter on his day off. After delegating the day's work to Tracey, she agreed to a drive in the Blue Mountains with him.

It was after midday when they pulled into the beauty spot overlooking the Three Sisters, some twenty kilometres away.

Peter turned off the engine. The view was spectacular and the silence amazing. Being alone and high above the valley view felt good, the quiet invoking a calm almost surreal atmosphere.

"Can you hear it?" Peter ran his hand through her long black hair.

"Hear what?"

"Nothing, that's what, no cars, no people, no hustle and bustle. Sounds good, doesn't it?"

Kathleen leaned across and kissed him tenderly.

"I'm in love with you, Peter."

"I'm in love with you, too," he replied thickly, "I think I loved you from the moment I first saw you."

"Oh, Peter, I just can't believe this has happened and it's happened so fast. I've never felt like this before."

"Nor me."

He leaned across and kissed her passionately, before releasing her and looking lovingly into her eyes. A crow, the epitome of the Australian bush, called in the distance. They held each other in a long embrace, enjoying the beauty of the place and the intimacy of the occasion.

An hour had passed before Peter drew Kath away from him and said playfully, "I have a little surprise for you."

"Ooo, I love surprises."

"Are you hungry?"

"I'm starving!"

"OK then, close your eyes and I'll tell you when you can open them again."

Peter got out of the car and opened the boot.

"No peeking," he ordered as he gathered a woollen blanket and spread it on the grass. Then he took out the hamper and opened it.

"OK, I'm going to help you get out of the car," he said, opening the passenger door, "but you can't look until I tell you."

Kathleen giggled.

"What on earth are you up to, Mr Wilson?" she said, as she stood up.

"Mademoiselle," he announced, "you may now look."

Kathleen looked in amazement. A romantic picnic, with wine and all the trimmings had magically appeared and were laid out before her.

"How did you, I mean when did you get all this together?"

"It's nothing special really, just a couple of bits and pieces from the fridge I threw together this morning."

The hamper held plates, serviettes, knives and forks, glasses and a cool box with a selection of cold meats, salad, cheese and biscuits. Kathleen looked on in amazement.

"You're fantastic. Do you know that, Peter Wilson?"

He blushed slightly at the compliment and flexed a bicep in mock ac-knowledgement. Kathleen pushed him playfully. They sat down on the blanket, had a leisurely lunch, talking and laughing like a couple of teenagers.

Afterwards, they laid down, completely relaxed, Kath lying on her back with her arms folded behind her head, Peter on his side facing her, leaning on one elbow and resting his head on his hand.

"Kath…"

"Yes, Peter."

"Kath, there's something I want to ask you."

She turned towards him, so their bodies were touching.

"Mmm?"

He hesitated before Kathleen prompted, "What is it, Peter?"

The rustle of the leaves in the gentle breeze and the birds singing were the only audible sounds apart from their breathing, which was heavy with desire.

He wrapped his arms tightly around her and kissed her again.

When he released her, the love in his eyes made her melt.

"Kath, I've waited for someone like you all my life and now that I've found you, I don't want to lose you."

"Don't be silly. How could you lose me? I love you."

There was a pause, while he searched for the right words.

"It's a big thing I know, but…"

"What is it, Peter?"

Peter put his hand in his pocket and retrieved a small black box.

He lifted himself up, first into a seated position and then onto one knee. Kathleen sat up.

He looked at her lovingly as he opened the box, revealing the ring, the diamond, sparkling in the sun.

Kath's eyes widened.

"Kath… will you marry me?"

She was stunned, the surprise unmistakable, and then her eyes watered, as she blinked several times, trying to hold back the tears. A broad smile spread across her face. Nothing had ever felt so right.

There was no hesitation, as she replied, "Yes, Peter, I'd love to marry you," and kissed him passionately on the lips.

He placed the ring on her finger. It was perfect.

Kath held out her hand to admire her ring and waved it left and right to watch it sparkle.

"I love it. It's beautiful and it feels like it was made for me."

Holding her tightly in his strong embrace, he murmured, "Are you sure, Kath? Am I moving too fast?"

"Yes, I'm sure, and no, you're not moving too fast. This feels right, Peter. Don't ask me why, it just does."

"It feels right for me too."

They wrapped their arms around each other, two people fused into one, and kissed again.

\* \* \*

Ian Thompson was by nature a patient man. Experience had taught him, the more one rushed an investigation, the more one missed and particularly where witness cooperation was essential. You could lean a little, but never rush, so, when it came to interviewing Gordon Humphries for a second time, he was quite content to sit in the waiting room and browse through a copy of Home & Garden.

The unannounced visit was quite deliberate. He thought it was the best way to put someone on the back foot and, when it worked, he thought it more than made up for a few wasted journeys, when the people he wanted to see were out.

A buzzing sound at the reception desk was followed by a short, muted conversation.

"Inspector?"

It was the receptionist.

"Mr Humphries will see you now. Would you come with me, please?"

Thompson rose slowly from the chair and followed the woman, rubbing the backs of his legs. He was having greater difficulty getting up from soft sofas these days.

She knocked briefly then opened the door, announcing the policeman at the same time.

"Mr Humphries, Inspector Thompson."

Humphries had clearly been taken off guard by the impromptu visit, that much Thompson could sense, but there was something else, something lurking just under the surface.

"Good morning, Inspector."

There was a slight quaver in the salutation. The man looked really unnerved.

"Take a seat, please. I must confess, I'm a little surprised to see you again and so soon after our last little chat. I thought I'd given you all the information you required, to fully investigate the damage to my hearse."

"Well, there have been some recent developments, you see, and these developments have taken the investigation into a different and, frankly, more *sinister* direction."

"Sinister? Aren't you being a little melodramatic?"

"Do you know James Robertson?"

"James Robertson, the funeral director?"

"Yes."

"Why do you ask?"

"Do you know Jerome T Spitz?"

Humphries stiffened. It was the reaction Thompson had been looking for. It meant he was going in the right direction.

"Yes, Inspector, but professionally, not socially. Look, what *is* this all about? I've a busy day ahead and I'd appreciate it if you got to the point."

"Extortion, intimidation, blackmail, obtaining money by menaces, Mr Humphries. I'm not sure how many of the above you have to deal with, but I know that Spitz is playing the same game with others and I'm certain he's leaning on you too."

Humphries was panicking. He was tantalisingly close to finalising the sale of his freehold to a developer. He had no desire to provoke any reaction from Spitz, by talking to the police and needed to keep him at bay for just a little while longer.

"As a matter of fact, Mr Spitz did come to see me with his associate and he told me that he wanted to buy my business. I declined and that was the end of it," he lied.

He reached into a cabinet drawing out a decanter of sherry and a glass.

"I know you're on duty, Inspector, so I won't offer you any," said Humphries, as he poured himself a drink, unable to conceal his shaking hands.

Thompson sat quietly and watched while the man took a sip.

"Did Spitz threaten you in any way, Mr Humphries?"

"No."

"Do you have anything at all to say about Mr Spitz's conduct?"

"He was a perfect gentleman."

'Well, this doesn't fit the picture,' thought Thompson. Was Robertson telling him the truth or was he trying to discredit his rival? The policeman had no way of knowing and the only way to find out was to confront Spitz with the allegations and watch his reaction.

Clueless as to how dangerous Spitz could become, when challenged, Thompson decided it was now time to pay him a visit.

## Chapter 21

## Last Wish

For Maria Papadopoulos the Monday morning breakfast was a distant memory, even though it had taken place but a short hour ago. Sitting in the lounge area of the Deepdene Nursing Home, she was transfixed by the movements of the birds immediately outside the floor to ceiling windows. She watched them as they splashed and fluttered in the large bird bath. They were all there. Willy wagtails, finches, brilliantly coloured parakeets and even the occasional budgerigar, all enjoying the cool water. Maria had long forgotten their names, but she liked watching them all the same. A handful of other residents milled around, talking quietly, reading or just dozing, but none of them registered in her mind. The birds, just the birds held her full attention. It was something about the freedom such animals enjoyed. When they wished, they simply took to the air. The kernel of such an idea took root as she watched a magpie shake a shower of water from its head and take to the sky. Freedom. Out, away and gone.

"Maria?"

The voice at her side brought her back to the present. All thoughts of flying away were shaken off, like the water from the magpie's head.

"Maria? You have some visitors," called Evelyn.

"Visitors?"

"Yes. It's your son and his family. They're just outside."

Nick, Diane and the two children entered the room. Nick was holding a large bunch of flowers.

"Hello, mum," he announced cheerily. "How are you?"

He kissed her warmly on the cheek.

Diane was right behind him and moved forward to the old lady.

"Hello, mum."

Another kiss on the cheek.

"Look, we've brought James and Sue to see you."

The children dutifully approached their grandmother.

James, aged ten, gave her a perfunctory kiss on the cheek, while his sister, three years younger, flung her arms around the old lady, squealing with delight, "Nanny, nanny!"

Nick drew up a chair alongside his mother's and held her hand.

"You look well, mum. I think this place agrees with you."

The old lady looked into her son's eyes.

"Stavros?"

"It's Nick, mum, Nick."

Her son looked distressed. There was no hint of recognition in her eyes.

"Stavros was your husband, our father. Do you remember now?"

"Where have you been, Stavros? You said you'd be straight home after work! I've been waiting for ages. I thought you were going to take me shopping?"

Diane and Nick exchanged a knowing look.

Diane was shaking her head.

"Nick, she has no idea it's you. At least last time, there was the occasional recognition, but she's getting worse."

Nick shook his head in despair.

"Keep it down, will you?" he said to his wife in a low voice. "Not in front of her and the kids!"

Diane raised her eyes to the ceiling and shrugged her shoulders at the same time, in a gesture of mechanical compliance.

Nick reached out for the little girl.

"Sue, come here, love, and show Nanny what you made at school."

The child approached her grandmother and produced an odd-shaped coffee cup, with a heart painted on the side and the word "Nanny" inside the heart.

"Look, Nanny, I made this for you!"

"Oh," the old lady took the cup in her bony hands and examined it closely.

"It's beautiful, Androulla, you're a clever girl, aren't you? I'll make this my special cup. A special cup from a special daughter!"

The young girl looked quizzically at the old lady, unsure of what was being said, while her father and mother simply shook their heads in frustration.

The old lady beamed and turned to Nick.

"Look what Androulla made, Stavros, just look."

Her smile broadened to show a row of gleaming dentures, the top plate clearly loose and coming away from the roof of her mouth.

The cup was now just beneath her chin as she displayed it to her son, the dentures, extricating themselves further from their rightful place and changing her speech.

"Juth look!"

The growing look of horror on the two children was unmistakable, as Maria Papadopoulos' teeth now protruded from her mouth.

"Ith bootiffff…"

In the middle of a broad smile and propelled by the "f" sound in "beautiful", her top denture plate continued its journey, out of the old lady's mouth and into the cup she was holding up, for all to see.

"Good morning!"

It was Matron Banks, conducting her morning rounds with military efficiency.

"And how are we all today?"

Nick, Diane and their two children sat like ice statues, captured in the depressing scene, which had just unfolded.

The old lady looked up at the bulk in white which was Banks and held up the cup for inspection.

"Androulla haff may a luffly cup for me – look, look."

A small stream of saliva, unchecked by her dentures, was now running out of the corner of her mouth. Although Banks took all of this in, her main preoccupation was ensuring her presence was noted.

She barely broke stride as she continued her inspection of the day room.

"Yes, it's lovely."

A nurse in the corner, tending to another resident, suddenly became the focus of her attention and, like a heat-seeking missile, Banks headed towards the corner of the room.

A curt "Excuse me" over her shoulder was directed at the Papadopoulos family, as she moved towards the unfortunate employee.

Her visit had ended as quickly as it had begun, brief, impersonal and unannounced.

Nick regained his composure, reached into the cup and retrieved the dentures.

"Mum, here, put these back in."

The old lady did as instructed and turned towards the window, her attention fixed again on the birdbath and the birds splashing around in it.

"Look at that cheeky little bird. He just *loves* the water."

The events of the past few minutes had been consigned to obscurity and again she was oblivious to everything, save for the activity immediately outside the window.

Nick's heart sank. Her condition was getting worse each time he saw her. There was always another small piece of his mother which seemed to have gone and this time the change had been dramatic. Sure, there had been occasions when she hadn't recognised him for a moment or two, but he had put that down to brief spells of forgetfulness and she had always bounced back to the mother he knew and loved. But this time it was different and now he was having serious concerns about this place. Judging by the attitude of the matron, it was starting to feel more like an army camp than a residential care home.

He turned to his wife, struggling for answers.

"Perhaps if we took her back with us, Di, just for a while, you know, things might get better?"

Diane turned to their two children and pointed to a small settee, near the entrance to the day room.

"James, sit over there with your sister for a minute, will you?"

When the children were out of ear shot, she turned to her husband.

"We've had this conversation before, Nick. You know how I feel about it. You're at work all day and I've got two kids to look after. I don't need another one!"

"Di…"

There was real anguish in his voice.

"Jesus, Nick, she doesn't recognise anybody – not you, not me, not even the kids. It's like she's living in the past. I tell you, I can't do this. Don't make me."

"I just wish there was someway to, to…" he was now lost for words, unable and incapable of bringing back the mother he had known as a boy and young man.

"You've done all you could, Nick. She's in the best place, twenty four hour care, seven days a week and, to be honest, I don't think she's really all that bothered."

She turned to the old lady who had begun to nod off. Diane raised her eyebrows.

"I'm right, Nick. Trust me on this. Bringing her back to live with us wouldn't make any real difference to your mum, but it would turn our lives upside down."

She took him gently by the elbow.

"Come on, love, let's go home."

\* \* \*

Even though it wasn't even eleven o'clock, Monday was shaping up to be a busy one as Kathleen was on the phone arranging a funeral for the coming week and speaking to the priest from the St John's Methodist church.

"That's right Father, 2:30pm at the Elton cemetery. I've just received confirmation from the office there. No, there's no need. I'll contact the family and give them the details. Fine, yes, that's about it, I think, nothing more for you to do. See you next Wednesday at two thirty. Bye."

She replaced the receiver in the cradle and was about to telephone the family of the deceased, when there was a single knock at the door.

It opened without acknowledgement and Tracey, the receptionist entered. Once inside, she closed the door behind her.

"Kath, there are two men outside to see you. One of them is Jerome Spitz, the other guy gives me the creeps. They want to see you. I told them they need to make an appointment, but they're not buying it. What do you want me to do?"

She was clearly nervous.

"It's fine, Trace. I'm sure there's nothing to worry about. It'll be alright. Send them in, please, but stay outside in case I need you, OK?"

Spitz entered the office followed by Radic.

"Ms O'Neill, thank you for seeing us at such short notice. I'm Jerome T Spitz, perhaps you've heard of me? And this is my associate, Mr Radic. I wonder if we might have a little chat."

Both men drew up chairs and sat down.

"Yes, I've heard of you, Mr Spitz. But today isn't a particularly good time. I've some urgent matters to attend to. Will this take long?"

"That is entirely up to you, Ms O'Neill."

Radic grunted and nodded his head.

"Perhaps you'd like to be a little more specific, Mr Spitz?"

"You're obviously an intelligent woman, so I'll come straight to the point. I've made no secret of my ambition to become the largest provider of funeral services in Australia and, dare I say it, eventually in the entire Southern Hemisphere. I've already entered into negotiations with a number of Funeral Directors here in Sydney, which should be concluded in the very near future."

He paused for a moment, relishing the theatre. Kathleen remained silent, unimpressed by the man and waiting for him to finish. She had very definite thoughts on where this was going.

"I always get what I want, Ms O'Neill, *always*."

As if on cue, Radic's eyes narrowed as he stared menacingly at Kathleen. "Alffays."

Spitz returned to his theme.

"Precisely, Mr Radic, and, so it is, Ms O'Neill, that I have come this day to make you a generous offer for your business. I know times have been difficult for a number of my competitors, especially for those who...," he gazed at the ceiling, searching for the correct word, "who... *unwisely* chose not to accept my initial offer. Bad luck seems to follow them around. I should hate to see any adverse occurrence befall either yourself or your business. Do we understand each other, Ms O'Neill?"

Kathleen straightened in her chair and looked squarely at Spitz.

"I understand perfectly, so I'll come straight to the point too and, for the avoidance of all doubt, let me be blunt. I have no intention of selling a business, which has been in my family for over one hundred and fifty years, but, if I did, that decision would be mine and mine alone and, in that event, *I* would choose the purchaser, not the other way around. Furthermore, I don't take kindly to threats, veiled or otherwise and I'm certainly not intimidated by your *associate*."

The contempt in her voice was unmistakeable.

"In short, Mr Spitz, I'm not interested in being a party in any way to your grandiose plans and I'd like you and your associate, to leave immediately!"

Like a bullet, Radic shot up from his chair, reached across the desk and seized Kathleen by the throat with one huge hand. She was, like most that saw the man in action, completely taken off guard by how fast he could move.

Spitz looked on, unperturbed by the situation.

"I don't believe I heard you correctly, Ms O'Neill. Would you like to repeat that last bit?"

Radic released his grip, causing Kathleen to slump back in her chair. She was clearly shaken, but furious at the assault too. Radic remained standing, a dim-witted smirk on his face. It worked every time. Apply the frighteners and they always saw sense. Spitz lounged back in his chair and crossed his legs, one knee over the other.

"You were saying...?"

Kathleen leaned forward, and, before anyone could stop her, she flicked a switch on the switch board.

"Are you still taping this, Tracey?"

She paused.

"As I was saying, Mr Spitz, I'm not interested and, believe me, I'll have no hesitation in sharing the details of this little *chat* with the police, unless you and your thug get the hell out of my office. Now!"

She was breathing heavily, fire in her eyes.

Radic took a step towards Kathleen, but was halted by a bark from Spitz.

"Angelo! Stop!"

Spitz was now also on his feet, surprised by the sudden change in dynamics.

"Very well, Ms O'Neill, as you wish. It would appear that this has been an unfortunate misunderstanding. I trust there are no hard feelings."

He turned to the door, a nod of his head indicating for the Croat to follow.

"Until we meet again."

"We won't be meeting again, Mr Spitz, not here, not ever!"

They left without another word.

Kathleen sat down in the now empty office. Her hands were trembling and she felt a little light-headed. Her own reaction had surprised her, where had the bluff about the tape recording come from? She had no idea what they might do and Peter's warnings came to mind.

At first, she had felt frightened by Radic, his hand around her throat, but when he had released his grip, she felt the anger rise up in her, unstoppable and overtaking all other emotions. Now she was nervous. Would they attack her or her premises? Kathleen wished her father were still here.

After toying with the idea of calling the police, Kathleen thought better of it, considering the nature of her business and, with the imminent completion of the contract with Mrs Papadopoulos, she didn't feel inclined to bring any unwanted attention to herself. Were Peter to find out about Spitz and Radic's little visit, he would definitely go to the police, so after considering all her options, Kathleen told herself it was unlikely they would come back and decided to let the matter rest for now.

Tracey entered without knocking, a concerned look on her face.

"Are you alright, Kath?"

"I'm fine, Trace, fine."

"They were so rude... stormed out in a real huff. The tall one looked furious and the stocky one nearly broke the door when he slammed it. I was glad to see them leave. What did they want?"

"Nothing really. Don't worry."

"Do you think they'll be back?"

"No, I don't think they'll come back, but if by some chance they do, call the police immediately. OK?"

Tracey looked as if all her worries were confirmed, but she only said, "OK, Kath."

Kathleen looked at her watch. It was only 11am. God, she needed somebody to talk to. Reaching for the phone, she dialled Peter's number. After several rings, it went to voicemail.

"Hi, this is Peter Wilson. I can't take your call right now, but please leave a number after the beep and I'll call back as soon as I can. Thanks."

A long beep sounded as she slowly replaced the receiver and let out a long sigh.

"Get a grip, girl. You're made of sterner stuff!" she said, rebuking herself. "You stood up to them and they're gone. You've got work to do and a business to run."

She opened the bottom drawer, selected a suspension file and turned on the computer.

\* \* \*

DI Ian Thompson continued to leaf through his notes. There was no question, based on the forensic evidence, that in the cases of Robertson and Humphries, a person or persons unknown had deliberately sabotaged their businesses and property. With Robertson's statement, Spitz was definitely a suspect in the sabotage, as he had something to gain. But sabotage could just as easily be the work of one of Jack Sullivan's enemies, who had a grudge and who took revenge on him by ruining his send off.

Thompson decided to look more closely at Spitz and Radic. Going through the notes, he realised he knew precious little about either man.

'Better to know at least something about the people you intend to arrest,' he thought.

The National Police Database produced no results on Spitz, apart from his basic immigration file and one complaint by an estate agent, alleging threatening behaviour, which was subsequently withdrawn.

By contrast, apart from one failed prosecution for burglary, Radic had a number of convictions for assault, none of which had resulted in a jail sentence, though he did have a spell of probation ten years earlier. He had not been arrested since.

Some general information was needed and the detective decided to look on the internet. As soon as he put Spitz's name into the computer and pressed the search button, dozens of links appeared. He clicked on the on 'My Way' website and searched under Proprietor: Jerome T Spitz.

'Born in New York in 1950, Spitz opened his first Funeral Director's office in The Bronx in 1981 and, from this humble beginning, a number of other branches soon followed. In the short space of twenty years 'My Way' had over fifty offices on both East and West Coasts of the United States. Jerome T Spitz opened the door of opportunity for hundreds of dedicated entrepreneurs by franchising these operations and is now successfully extending his business empire in the southern hemisphere.'

No mention of a Mrs Spitz, past or present, in fact, there appeared to be little room for anyone in Spitz's life, but the man himself. One thing was certain. He had an ego the size of Everest. The web site was full of accolades to the man. The text peppered with adjectives like *trailblazer*, *far-reaching*, *intuitive* and so on.

Returning to the main search page, he clicked on another couple of links. These were less flattering and taken from a number of newspaper and magazine articles and completely at odds with the image on 'My Way's website. The criticisms, which painted an entirely different picture of the man and which matched the details given by Robertson, were fairly consistent, with allegations of sharp practice and ruthlessness. There was no mention anywhere of the sidekick, Radic.

'Not surprising really,' thought Thompson. 'You wouldn't want to advertise *him.*'

Continuing down the list, Thompson saw a link to The Chicago Times. He pressed the button and was surprised by the headline.

LOCAL UNDERTAKER ARRESTED IN BODY DISPOSAL CASE.

'Jerome T Spitz, a local funeral director, was arrested on suspicion of disposing of a body. Antonio Divinos has not been seen for several weeks and is thought to have been murdered. A witness, who is under police protection, has testified that he saw Spitz in the company of Giovanni Calabria, a well known mobster, immediately after Divinos' disappearance. The missing man was last seen at a bar with Calabria and Spitz, in the downtown district of Chicago.

Spitz is alleged to have lured Divinos to the meeting and the following day, he arranged a cremation of an Alfredo Conti, at the request of Calabria.

When questioned, Calabria claimed that Conti was his uncle, but a closer examination revealed major inconsistencies in the paperwork. According to a police source, Conti's death had not been registered and the death certificate had been forged. The question 'Whose body was cremated?' remains unanswered.

The article was dated September 1998. Thompson switched back to the Police database, where Spitz's immigration file was still open. His first entrance in Australia was registered in November 1998.

'So the man is on the run,' he thought.

He leaned across and switched off his computer.

It was time to pay Mr Spitz a visit.

\* \* \*

The morning had not started well for Jock.

"Hello, Mr Strapp," the nurse greeted him as she approached the bed. "We're just going to take you downstairs for another scan, OK?"

His head was splitting and all he could do was to manage a slight nod.

Jock was wheeled to the lift in his bed by a young porter, who, apart from his short commentary of where they were going, said little.

"Going down," he announced, as he pressed the button.

The Scotsman felt the lift descend and closed his eyes.

When the doors opened, he was wheeled into the waiting area, where illuminated signs indicated the X-ray, Ultrasound and MRI rooms.

"I'll leave you here, Jock. Somebody will come when they're ready to do the scan. You shouldn't have to wait long," explained the porter.

Jock nodded acknowledgment and stared at the ceiling, the décor faded and in need of a fresh coat of paint.

"Well, well," came the voice from behind him.

Jock craned his head to the right to see who it was.

"Fancy seeing you here, you old bastard?"

A thin, young man on crutches, his head in a bandage, leaned over him, sneering menacingly. It was the lout he'd decked at the Railway Hotel.

"This is priceless! Wait 'til I tell Kev that you're still laid up after he hit you. It'll make his day."

"Fuck off!" was all the Scotsman could manage, before two staff members in overalls appeared at his side.

Pickersgill moved away, still grinning. Jock grabbed the bedrails tightly, furious that he couldn't get up and hit the little prick again. What was he doing down here anyway? One thing was clear... he looked like he'd been run over by a steam roller.

Car accident? Possibly. A fight with another young punk? Probably. Or had the boys from the Diamond Café paid him a visit? Hopefully.

The last thought brought a smile to his face as the bed was wheeled toward the lighted sign saying MRI.

The scan took about 15 minutes and, before long, the porter was back to take him to the eighth floor. Jock was grateful to be in a private room and not on the main ward. As the lift reached its destination, the doors opened and the porter, deftly manoeuvred the bed out of the elevator and down the corridor, towards Lewis Ward.

As they approached the double doors, he heard, "Allow me."

It was the same voice as downstairs. Had the thug followed him?

Pickersgill appeared from behind and, leaning on one crutch, opened one of the doors for the porter with his free arm, enabling the latter to push the bed into the ward.

'I don't need this,' thought Jock.

Pickersgill followed the porter, chatting to him as though Jock was invisible.

"I'm just down the corridor," he offered, knowing his enemy could hear every word. "I got attacked by four blokes, but I beat three of them up, before they managed to put me in here. They came out of it much worse than I did," he said, sneering at the Scotsman.

Jock returned the look.

"Karma is a fucker, eh, laddie? I guess what goes around comes around," he said to Pickersgill. "Wouldn't have been a bunch of old guys riding bikes by any chance?"

The sneer on the young thug's face fell away. The two old dudes had given him a pretty good work over, his three other mates too, but he was the one who came out worst. Still, at least he could walk, despite the crutches and broken leg. The Scotsman, on the other hand, wasn't going anywhere.

As Jock was wheeled back into his room, helped by the nurse on duty, he heard Pickersgill call, "I'm only down the corridor. I'll call in and see you. It can't be much fun not being able to get out of bed."

Jock could hear the sarcasm and the venom in his voice, but the porter didn't notice and left, leaving him with the duty nurse, who set about adjusting his bedding.

"Seems like a pleasant young man," she commented, "at least you won't be all alone. Friend of yours, is he?"

Jock shook his head and gritted his teeth, but said nothing.

"OK, Jock," she continued, oblivious to the enmity between the two men, "the doctor will be in to see you shortly. Would you like anything?"

The Scotsman shook his head. The only thing he wanted was to get his hands around Pickersgill's throat and squeeze tightly.

"I'll check on you later, after the doctor's been, alright?"

Later that day, the news from the doctor was not good. The latest scan had shown the tumour was spreading more quickly than the worst estimates. His days were numbered, the pain was worse and, as if that weren't bad enough, he knew the coward who had hit him from behind would soon be in to gloat, once Pickersgill told him where he was.

\* \* \*

A few hours had elapsed since Spitz and Radic had called at Kathleen's premises and, after the initial shock following their departure, Kathleen had buried herself in paperwork. The time had passed quickly and, glancing at her watch, she realised with some surprise that it was almost half past three in the afternoon. A growl in her stomach reminded her she hadn't eaten since breakfast, a couple of slices of toast being the only food she had taken the whole day. Walking to the reception area she approached Tracey.

"Trace, I'm stepping out to get a bite to eat. Can I get you anything?"

Tracey looked up from a letter she was typing.

"No, thanks, Kath, I've already eaten. It's pretty quiet here. I can hold the fort for the rest of the day if you like. Why don't you have an early one? I can lock up and I've got your mobile number if I need to get in touch."

Kathleen raised her eyebrows. The thought had never crossed her mind.

"Actually…"

"You looked a little upset this morning after those two men left. It might be nice to get out in the sun for an hour or two. Have a break, you know, some time for yourself. You're always working."

Kathleen sighed and nodded her head.

"Are you sure you don't mind? To be honest, I'd love to get away from here for a couple of hours."

"Not a problem. I'll see you tomorrow, OK?"

"OK. And thanks again."

Opening the office door and stepping out onto the busy street came as an enormous relief. It was with some reluctance that Kathleen then conceded that perhaps the morning's unannounced visitors had left her more shaken than she'd cared to admit. She entered a small café and sat by the window, watching the passers-by. Half an hour, a sandwich and cappuccino later, she felt much more like her old self and ready to face the world again.

However, for some unknown reason, Jock Strapp entered her thoughts. Although it had only been a couple of days since she'd last seen the bed-bound Scotsman, she had a strong feeling she should go and see him again today. Kathleen had grown enormously fond of the man in the brief time they'd known each other. He was a rascal, but he always made her laugh with stories of his exploits and adventures. She decided to pay him a surprise visit.

A short drive later, she was at the hospital and outside his room. She knocked gently on the door.

"It's Kath," she said quietly.

"Come in," she heard.

"Jock, I thought you might like to see a friendly face. How are you?" she announced cheerily.

He hardly raised his head, barely acknowledging her presence.

Immediately concerned, Kathleen drew up a chair next to his bed and placed a hand lightly on his arm.

"Jock, what is it, what's wrong?"

Slowly he shook his head, sighing deeply at the same time.

"I canna' be doin' this nay more, I canna'."

"Canna' be doing what any more?"

"He came by today, the specialist, the one who's dealing with this thing inside ma heed."

He pointed to his brow with an index finger.

"Tells me the tumour has spread into other parts of my brain. Seems I can expect seizures, memory loss and the whole shooting match. Great news, eh?"

Kathleen squeezed his arm in a gesture of sympathy.

"Oh, Jock, I'm so sorry, I don't know what to say."

"I found it hard enough coming to terms with being a bloody invalid until 'D' day, but I had kind of reconciled myself to that. Now this… this is too much… jerking around and not knowing I'm doing it. Nay, nay way. That's not how I wanna' go 'oot. Not me, nay way!"

Kathleen stared intently at the man's face. A mixture of anger, resentment and fear at the cruel trick the growth inside his head was playing on him.

"Are they certain, Jock?" she asked quietly.

"Positive, nay doubt at all."

There was a long pause.

"Did they give any indication of when your condition might start to… to deteriorate?"

This was extremely sensitive ground and Kathleen was treading lightly.

"It already has. I won't be here much longer."

"How long?"

"Weeks," came the reply. "Six to eight weeks, if I'm lucky."

The irony in his voice was unmistakeable.

"If I could move 'oot of this bloody bed, I'd end it all right now! I'm never going home. I'm never going to ride my bike again and, to top it all, I've just met the young punk I got into a fight with, the one whose mate put me in here in the first place. Would you believe it? He's on the same ward as me and had a good laugh seeing me like this. Now I can expect a visit from his pal, the one who hit me from behind with the bar stool and I'm gonna have to put up with him gloating at me. I hate people seeing me like this anyway, but I canna' stand the thought of those two little bastards having the last laugh. I've had enough! There must be a hundred pills right ootside this door that would do the job. There's even a balcony down the corridor, but they've taken the wheelchair away, in case I try and get into it again. I don't wanna' go 'oot like this! If I had some arsenic, I'd end it all here and now."

Kathleen moved her hand down the Scotsman's arm and took his hand in hers. It was rough and calloused, yet felt like a defenceless child's.

She leaned across and spoke softly into his ear.

"I had a feeling I should come and see you today. I'm so sorry, Jock, that you're having such a hard time. I'm really glad I'm here. You shouldn't be on your own right now. Shall I tell anybody about the other guy on the ward? Do you think they might try to hurt you?"

"Nay, Kath, please don't say anything. I'm not afraid of them, it's just my pride that's hurt. I canna' stand the idea that they can laugh at me, when there's nothing I can do about it. I canna' even get 'oot of bed. I want this to be over. Couldn't you get me some pills, Kath? I know it's not fair to ask you, but there's nay one else."

Kathleen stayed silent, stunned by the request. It was what her father always told her was the first requirement. Never suggest the 'family remedy', people who need it will always ask.

'What should I do?' she wondered.

Seeing her shock, Jock spoke.

"I'm sorry, Kath, I've put you on the spot, but I canna' bear this any more. I'm much more afraid of living than of dying and I wouldn't ask you to help if there was any other way. Nobody would ever suspect you."

Although he was pleading with her, she was torn. Bound by the tradition of the generations before her and the promise she'd made to her father, she was fearful of providing the fatal drink and being caught. And what about Peter, if things went wrong? She would lose him.

Her father warned her that the first time it happened she would hesitate, but she must be strong and put the needs of the dying first. She cared for Jock and didn't want to see him die, even though he wanted to. Weren't Jock's needs more important than her own?

"Please, Kath, don't make me beg."

Now she knew what she had to do.

Talking with her father, sometimes for hours into the night, about just such a scenario had prepared her for this situation and finally she responded.

"Jock, I'm going to tell you something, something you must not repeat to anyone."

She looked him in the eye and he held her gaze.

"I want you to listen very carefully to what I am about to say."

He straightened up slightly, the gravity in Kathleen's voice commanding his full attention.

She began quietly, speaking in slow, measured tones.

"If I *could* alleviate what you say is going to happen, and I'm not talking about a cure, would you really want me to?"

She paused.

He turned his head slightly to one side, a confused look on his face.

"Do you understand what I'm saying, Jock?"

"What exactly do you mean by *alleviate*?"

"I mean I could offer you an option, a painless, happy, *final* option."

The significance of what she was offering him slowly dawned on the man. It was that last word, *final*.

"Go on."

There was silence in the room as several seconds slowly ticked by. He gripped her hand.

Eventually she spoke.

"I can get you something, Jock, if that's what you want."

"You'll get me some pills?"

"Not pills. A drink that'll make you high as a kite."

He looked at her intently. 'Is she serious?' he thought.

"You really are full of surprises, aren't you, Kath?"

The laugh was feeble and weak and did nothing to dispel the intensity of the moment.

Kathleen remained silent.

"Are you interested?"

"Yes, I'm interested, Kath. Tell me more."

"Do you want to hear it all?"

"Yes, I wanna' hear it all."

"This is dangerous for me, Jock. I'm talking about assisted suicide, the law is quite clear on such matters."

There was a long pause.

Finally, Kathleen asked the question, "Do you want me to help you end your life?"

"Yes. I can handle the dying – it's the thought of turning into a vegetable I canna' bear, especially in front of an audience like the little bastard down the corridor and his mate."

Kathleen looked intently at the man.

"Are you absolutely sure?"

"I'm absolutely sure."

Kathleen gave his hand a comforting squeeze.

"Alright, I'll do it."

"Thanks, Kath," he sighed with relief.

"Shall I tell you what's involved?"

Jock nodded soberly.

"When you're ready, I'll bring you a bottle with a small amount of a liquid. It's odourless and colourless, so you won't notice it at all. I can mix it with anything you like. It is however, very strong and a small amount is all that's required."

She paused.

"Shall I go on?"

He was listening intently.

"Yes."

"A few minutes after drinking it, you'll start to feel happy, a bit like being tipsy. The feeling of happiness will grow stronger as the minutes pass, until eventually you'll feel the happiest you've ever felt in your entire life and then you'll simply go to sleep. No suffering, no pain and no fear. That's it, it's that simple."

Silence enveloped the room once more.

Jock cleared his throat.

"That's it?"

"Yes, Jock, that's it."

The quizzical look returned to his face.

"How can you be sure there's nay pain – you know, happy chappie and then the big sleep?"

"Trust me, I know. That's how it works."

"How do you know, Kath? What is this drink?"

"This remedy has been in my family for over a century. It was invented by my great, great grandfather, back in Ireland, and we have been using it ever since to relieve the suffering of the dying. Grandpa Patrick hated seeing anyone suffer, but, in those days when people were poor, they often died in agony, because they couldn't afford medicine or doctors. After watching his mother die like that, he resolved to stop it ever happening again to anybody he loved, so being a keen botanist and an amateur herbalist, he turned to plants and began experimenting with pain relief remedies. After many years of research, he found a plant which had strong opiate properties. The drink made from its leaves was a natural painkiller and gave his patients a fantastic sense of euphoria and worked incredibly quickly. But the roots of the same plant were highly toxic and, once in the blood stream, caused instant unconsciousness and death. So, for patients who were at the very end, he combined the extracts from the root and the leaves in a way that, by the time the toxin caused death, the patient was so high, he could feel no pain. That's how it got the name 'The O'Neill remedy'. It's ironic, I know, but it's helped people die painlessly, for over a century. In fact, it's helped them to die happily. My family brought a number of these plants with them, when they came over from Ireland. Using cuttings, we have created more plants and it's been my job to tend them. I even have one in my kitchen, and I've been making the drink for the last five years, to help people like you. My father confided the secret to me after my mother died, because he wanted to pass it on, and he taught me how to prepare the remedy, which has been passed down from generation to generation. I'm the last person in the world to know the secret ingredients and that's why I know how it works."

The Scotsman was silent for a few moments. He hadn't expected this at all. Jock was in awe.

"You've done this before?"

"Not personally, but my father did several times."

"When can you get me the drink?"

"Whenever you want me to."

"As soon as you can get it. I'm getting worse, the pain in ma heed is unbearable and the medicine's not working. I canna' move my legs and the nurses literally have to wipe my arse. It's not the way I wanna' to check 'oot. Your way sounds much better."

Kathleen smiled gently.

"What would you have said if I changed my mind?"

"Nothing, and I'd deny that we ever had this conversation," she replied evenly.

"Kath, you're a real friend. What you're doing shouldn't be illegal, but I know it is, and I canna' tell you how grateful I am, lassie, that you're prepared to take such a chance for me. Can you get it for me tomorrow?"

"If that's what you want," Kathleen nodded, "but are you sure you don't want to sleep on it for a night or two?"

"Nay lass, the sooner the better for me."

"Alright, if that's what you want, we'll do it tomorrow, tomorrow evening?"

Jock smiled.

"Thanks, Kath."

He paused as a thought entered his head.

"Won't they find traces of the stuff in me, you know, after I've gone?"

"No, it breaks down completely in the body, and, apart from the smile on your face, there'll be no indication that you took anything at all. I've been making it up for long enough to know. Our motto, 'Dignity in Death', is something my whole family passionately believed in and, even though I'm the only one left now, I feel duty bound to keep our tradition going. I believe that people such as you should have that choice."

"God, you're a dark horse," he said and paused for a few seconds. "You said you could mix the drink with something?"

"How does whisky sound?"

Jock's face beamed.

"Sounds perfect to me!"

"OK, Jock, until tomorrow then."

She rose from the chair and hugged him. As he hugged her back, she felt the deepest sadness. She would have loved to give him something else, something that would make him whole again, but the only way should could make a difference to him was to respect his wishes and help him die.

"Tomorrow," he said, as he released her. "Thank you."

\* \* \*

Waiting in funeral directors' reception areas was getting to be somewhat familiar for Ian Thompson. During the last couple of weeks, he had called on Robertson, then Humphries, and now it was time for a little chat with Spitz. He'd arrived unannounced and had asked the receptionist if he could speak with the proprietor.

"Mr Spitz is terribly busy. What's the nature of your enquiry? Perhaps I could help?"

Good staff were hard to find and naturally formed a necessary line of defence between the public and their employers. Thompson had produced his warrant card and simply announced, "Routine enquiries."

That had done the trick and he was directed to a small adjacent waiting area, while Spitz was informed.

The room was large enough to fit a couple of two seater settees, plus two armchairs arranged around a rectangular coffee table, on which a small pile of magazines lay casually scattered. A non-descript print hung on the wall opposite the door, while the other three walls were adorned with certificates from a number of organisations Thompson had never heard of, together with photographs of Spitz in various funerary garb – head mourner with top hat and tails, chief pall bearer and so on. He guessed the display was designed to impress, although his first thought was how tacky the whole arrangement looked, style and chic being completely absent.

Without notice, the door opened. A tall thin man with a hooked nose, pencil-thin moustache, thin lips and wearing a shiny grey suit entered.

"Inspector! Jerome T Spitz at your service."

He offered a hand. The handshake was surprisingly firm.

"Won't you come this way?"

He followed Spitz into his office.

"Please, take a seat."

Once seated behind his desk, he asked, "How may I help you?"

"We're making enquiries into a couple of incidents that occurred recently to two other undertakers. A fire at ex-Mayor Sullivan's funeral and, coincidentally on the same day, a hearse which suffered a major malfunction. Both matters were covered on the evening news, perhaps you saw the broadcast?"

Spitz remained motionless, like a lizard on a log.

"No, Inspector, I can't say that I did, however I am familiar with the events. They were widely reported in the local paper. One couldn't help but notice."

"I see."

Thompson searched in his suit coat pocket and withdrew a small leather-bound notebook.

"Do you know the funeral directors Mr Robertson and Mr Humphries?"

"Yes, I know them."

"Exactly, how do you know them, Mr Spitz? Professionally? Socially?"

Spitz stifled a snigger.

"Hardly the latter, Inspector. Thankfully we don't mix in the same circles, but I did meet both of them recently to discuss business."

Thompson was taking notes in the small book.

"And what form did this business discussion take?"

"I hate to appear uncooperative, Inspector, but where is all of this going? Have I broken some law or fallen foul of some code?"

He didn't wait for a reply. "I went to discuss the possibility of a possible merger, a proposition I felt could be of benefit to all concerned."

"I see. Was it a harmonious meeting?"

Spitz was now clearly irritated.

"Look, Inspector. I'm a busy man. There are a million and one things I have to do today. Surely, my business dealings hold no interest for the police, so, unless you get to the point of your visit, I'm not prepared to waste any more of my time!"

"Mr Spitz, my enquiries lead me to believe that your meeting with Mr Robertson was less than harmonious, unpleasant sinister even. I understand that a Mr Radic was also present."

'So Robertson, had been talking,' thought Spitz, 'that wouldn't do at all. He would have to be severely punished for that. When witnesses got talkative, they simply had to be silenced. He wouldn't be the first and it wasn't as if he hadn't been warned.'

A prominent vein had begun to visibly throb on Spitz's temple and his face was reddening by the second. If he were an engine, he was getting ready to blow a gasket. Thompson pressed on.

"My information leads me to believe that acts of sabotage were made to deliberately disrupt funerals conducted by each of these undertakers. Our forensics department discovered incendiary devices were used in both incidents and, as a result, the trade of both funeral directors has suffered. As a party interested in acquisitions, I imagine this would put you in a favourable position to negotiate highly favourable terms of sale for their respective businesses and would certainly give you a motive. So, in the light of this information, to the contrary, your business dealings hold immense interest for me. Mr Spitz, do you remember where you were on the evening of February 16th, between the hours of 10pm and 3am the following morning?"

The engine exploded as Spitz rose from his chair, gesticulating wildly. He'd anticipated this situation and had a perfect alibi.

"This is preposterous! I am an honest businessman and I shan't be besmirched in this way! I was at a civic meeting on that day, not that I need to explain myself or my movements to you, Inspector." He was breathing heavily and was highly animated. "I'm a funeral director. What would I know about explosives?"

Thompson stood up and began to walk to the door. He grabbed the door handle and turned to face Spitz.

"You use explosives, Mr Spitz, in some of your funerals. I've seen the advertisements of Granddad's ashes going up in a sky rocket!"

Spitz was a little taken aback. He hadn't expected that response.

"Am I under arrest?"

"No, Mr Spitz, this is just a simple chat, but I may wish to speak with you again, perhaps a more formal interview at the police station."

Spitz could take no more. He wanted this policeman out and right now.

"Angelo!"

It was an order, not a request.

The door opened with enormous force and slammed into the toe of Thompson's right shoe before recoiling back onto the bull-like head of Angelo Radic now half way through the entrance to the office. Thompson was caught completely unaware and fought to maintain his balance.

Radic fared less well. His head was no match for the heavy wooden door moving at the speed of a prize fighter's left hook as door and skull collided with terrible force. The impact made a circular indentation in the wood and rendered Radic instantly unconscious as he dropped like a stone to the floor.

Silence hung over the office. Spitz was amazed, Thompson dazed and Radic out cold. It had all happened so fast. The policeman looked across at Spitz.

Spitz stood dumbstruck. If there was only a way to channel Radic's brute strength. It was like training an elephant. A very large, incredibly stupid elephant. Thompson stood over the prostrate Croat and looked down with some concern.

"Perhaps we should call an ambulance?" he offered to Spitz, at which point Radic groaned and opened his eyes.

"Vot happened?"

"You bumped your head, I think," replied Thompson. "Are you alright?"

Radic slowly rose unsteadily to his feet, holding onto the door frame, until he was at last upright. It was all he could do to nod a couple of times. Like a drunk, he wobbled into the office rubbing his temple and looking questioningly at Spitz, unsure of the significance of the policeman's visit.

He was getting a headache.

Thompson turned to see Spitz, seated behind his desk with his head in his hands.

"So, Mr Spitz, I'll be on my way then. I'm sure we'll be speaking again soon."

Spitz looked up and scowled at the departing policeman.

"In your dreams," he muttered under his breath.

He rubbed his head.

He was getting a headache.

Apart from the accident as he was leaving, Thompson was pleased with the outcome of the meeting at 'My Way'. Peter's observations about Spitz's use of explosives were very astute and he knew he'd caught the undertaker off guard.

But the reality was different. Now, that Spitz had this information, he needed to prevent any more careless talk and deal with Robertson. The acquisition of the man's business was now secondary to the need to get him out of the way… permanently!

# Chapter 22

## The Guest of Honour

It had been a long day. 9:30pm and Kathleen had finally finished preparing the mixture. The leaves of the plant had been carefully boiled and then discarded. Small sections of plant root were then added to the remaining liquid and allowed to sit for several minutes. The resultant mixture was then sieved through muslin and placed in a teacup. Although she had done this a number of times, the simplicity of the operation and the resulting potency of the finished product never failed to surprise her. So simple, yet so effective. If one had an earnest desire to leave this world painlessly and happily, this was surely the perfect choice. Apart from Jock, there was still Mrs Papadopoulos to consider.

Reaching into the cupboard, she selected two small bottles of Bell's whisky. Both were about a quarter full and, into each, she carefully poured equal amounts of the mixture, one for Jock, the other for the old lady.

She stared intently at the two bottles.

Though it was not long since she had set out to conclude the contract on Mrs Papadopoulos, the contract her father had been unable to fulfill, it felt like ages. The fears and reservations she felt on that fateful day had not completely receded, but somehow they were now less acute. Talking to Jock had helped her come to terms with the work. It felt like a rite of passage, something she must do. Despite meeting Peter and their recent engagement, ideologically, her stance had not changed – it was the right and honourable thing to do. It took courage to risk one's own liberty in order to deliver the ultimate act of caring – a release from suffering.

The irony was that in attempting to honour the old lady's wishes, she was now planning to help Jock, the very person who had stopped her doing just that. Fate, it seemed had intervened in a very forceful way. Kathleen was now on a path from which there was no turning back. She stared at the two bottles which would have such profound consequences and suddenly felt deeply tired. While her father was alive, they could discuss their clients. Now Kathleen had to carry the burden alone. Peter was due soon and all she wanted to do was to curl up on the sofa with him and watch mindless television then fall asleep in his arms.

A knock on the door broke her train of thought.

"Kath?"

It was her fiancée. He had an uncanny knack of appearing or calling like some kind of genie when she was thinking of him.

"Peter!"

She ran to the door and threw her arms around his neck.

"Now, that's what I call a welcome," he managed to say before she kissed him and hugged him tightly in an embrace that showed no signs of ending.

"Is everything alright, Kath?"

"Yes, everything's fine. It's just been a long day and I'm so glad to see you. Please, stay tonight."

"Sure" he hugged her back. "Have you eaten yet?"

She shook her head.

"Hungry?"

"I haven't had time to cook."

"No problem, I'll sort out something."

Peter led the way to the kitchen, Kathleen a step behind, holding his hand.

"I've had a pretty busy day too as it turns out. The full gamut from electron microscopy analysis of clothing fibres to toxicology tests. I was glad to leave the place."

He pulled out a chair from the nearby table and sat her on it.

"So, lovely lady, what would you like for dinner? Something spicy? Italian perhaps? Rest assured, whatever is in these cupboards is just waiting to be transformed into a veritable feast for two."

He made a grandiose, sweeping gesture with both arms like a conductor calling up the string section of an orchestra, but cut it short at the sight of the two small whisky bottles on the worktop.

"Hello... what have we here?" he announced, reaching for one of the bottles. "I didn't know you liked whisk...."

"Don't touch that!"

Kathleen was out of the chair in a flash and snatched up both bottles, stopping Peter dead in his tracks and taking him completely unawares.

She'd been so lost in thought, she'd forgotten to put the bottles away. A puzzled look spread across his face.

"They're for someone else, a… a special present… a bit of a private joke, with one of my customers. I'm sorry, darling. I should have tucked them away. I forgot. I didn't mean to startle you. It's been ever such a long day."

She opened a cupboard and placed them inside.

"Why don't we just order a take-away? You look bushed and I'm really tired too. I'm sorry I snapped."

She opened the refrigerator, withdrew a bottle of opened white wine and poured two glasses.

"Come and sit with me for a moment. I've missed you."

He followed Kathleen to the couch, his mind still going over her reaction to the whisky bottles. It was strange to make a present of not one, but two bottles, with so little in them. 'What kind of private joke?' he wondered, but didn't ask. They sat down together, but the reservation in Peter was obvious as she drew close to him, taking his hand in hers.

'Was she a secret drinker?' he found himself wondering.

"It's been hard with dad gone, I've got to keep an eye on everything now and sometimes it gets to me. I know it shouldn't, but it does. I love you very much Peter Wilson. I wouldn't do anything to hurt you and I'm sorry if I was a bit over the top just now. I'm glad you're here, you make me feel safe."

Mollified and largely reassured, Peter kissed her on the cheek. If Kathleen needed a drink and didn't want to share the information with him, that was her business. All he knew was that he'd never smelled alcohol on her breath, except when she relaxed with a glass of wine in the evening.

"That's OK," he reassured, "I've been feeling pretty stressed all afternoon as well. There's too much to do and not enough time in which to do it. I am glad I'm here."

They sat close together for half an hour, the small talk and wine melting away the tensions of the day and in particular the recent awkwardness in the kitchen. By ten thirty, the Chinese takeaway they had ordered was gone and an hour later they were in bed, curled up spoon-style, sleeping soundly.

\* \* \*

It had been a particularly busy day so far and it wasn't even two o'clock. Spitz had already seen five clients, four of whom had opted for 'My Way' as a direct result of the television advertisement. The fifth had come via a local doctor to whom "inducements" were offered, when the bereaved needed an undertaker and asked for a recommendation.

A Mr Harris had called to ask the undertaker to visit him at home, to take out a funeral plan. He was a wealthy old man. Clients like that were the best. They couldn't take the money with them and it was easy to get them to spend. He had slotted the appointment in for that afternoon, at four pm, which meant he would have to let Radic go to the morgue by himself. Letting Radic fly solo wasn't Spitz's first choice, but rich clients didn't come along all that often and he wasn't about to look a gift horse in the mouth. Collecting a body should be child's play, even for Radic.

After all, what could possibly go wrong?

Spitz picked up the telephone and pressed the key to the motor pool where Radic was polishing the hearse.

The telephone rang half a dozen times before it was picked up.

"Yez?"

"Angelo, would you come to the office please? I have a job for you."

"OK, Bozz, I come n..." was all he managed to say before the phone hung up.

Spitz often cut him short, yet he never took offense, reasoning in some skewered way that it was simply how his boss was. Important, busy people were, he concluded, like that.

Radic entered the office without knocking and, in his inimitable and forceful style, flinging the door back on its hinge. The SAS in a hostage rescue situation could have taken lessons from the man.

"Bozz?"

Angelo stood before Spitz like a dog that had just retrieved a ball. The latter had eventually conceded he was never going to win the "knock before you enter" battle, but took comfort knowing that the prints and diplomas on the wall were finally safe and secure. A handyman had lined the door jam with a small strip of foam and fitted a door closing mechanism. Slamming doors were now thankfully a thing of the past.

"Vot you vont me to do, Bozz?"

"An elderly gentleman, a Mr Turnbull, has sadly passed away and is laying *prostratum morte* in the morgue of the West Sydney Memorial hospital. His family have requested 'My Way' handle the arrangements; *ergo,* Mr Turnbull needs to be transferred here so we can fulfill his family's wishes. Everyone else is busy and I have an appointment this afternoon, so you'll have to collect the deceased yourself."

Radic's brow knotted in deep concentration. More big words.

Spitz sighed heavily. There was certainly a price to be paid for employing

Angelo. Unswerving loyalty coupled with the intellectual capacity of an amoeba. Unswerving loyalty won most of the time, but sometimes he wished Angelo was just a little more sharp on the uptake. *C'est la vie.*

"There's a stiff in the hospital, an old stiff. Take the van, go to the hospital, pick him up and bring him here."

The furrow in Radic's brow deepened as he processed the information, his lips moving as he replayed the instructions in his mind.

"OK."

Spitz nodded once.

"Good. Finish cleaning the hearse and then use the van. I've arranged to collect the body after six pm so I'll expect you back by…" he glanced at his wristwatch, calculating the expected time to perform this task, "…by seven, OK?"

The Croat nodded.

"OK, Bozz, seven. Goddit."

Spitz picked up the telephone to make a call and stopped in mid- stream, glancing up at Radic, nodded to the door, thereby dismissing him.

Walking back to the car bay, Angelo replayed the instructions in his mind… van… hozbital… Timble… back… van… hozbital… Tunkle… back… van… hozbital… Trumball… back.

The instructions were clear, all but the name. He almost had the name and repeated it until he felt confident of carrying out his employer's instructions. Opening the rear door of the hearse, he picked up the vacuum cleaner and resumed hoovering the inside of the vehicle.

\* \* \*

Spitz made his way to his BMW convertible and got in. He turned the key, stopping for a moment to listen to the engine. 'An exquisite machine,' he thought as he headed for the hills towards the Bondi Coast Road. Harris must be loaded to live up there. He was already formulating a number of ways in which to part the old boy from his cash.

As he drove past a rather grand mansion, its boastful façade, with pillars at the front and statues of lions at the gates, suggested a Greek occupant. The road continued to rise, carved out of the limestone cliffs, offering magnificent views of the bay.

Eventually, turning right to Mackenzies' Point, he reached what must have been the entrance to Harris' place. He derived this by the two decrepit walls, with enough room between them for him to drive through. He imagined that once there must have been either a door or a gate, but that would have been a very long time ago. It was at least another five hundred metres, before he reached his client's place, at the top of the cliff.

The house was an old weatherboard construction, with broken fly wire on the windows and a corrugated iron roof. It looked out of place here, in this beautiful location and, though the property had little value, the land would have been worth several million dollars. Spitz felt excited. In a place like this, he could make a killing.

The old red door, its paint peeling was opened by a short, stout, balding man, before Spitz reached it. He smiled and held out his hand to Harris, wondering why such splendour was wasted on an old man like this?'

"I'm Andrew Harris," he said.

"Good afternoon, Mr Harris, Jerome T Spitz at your service."

\* \* \*

Kathleen had just finished talking with a middle aged couple… the father of the man had passed away after a long and protracted illness.

She opened the office door and as they were leaving the man extended his hand.

"Thank you, Ms O'Neill, you've been so kind."

Kathleen shook it firmly but gently,

"We'll take care of everything, Mr Trumball, don't worry about a thing. I'll give you a call tomorrow with all the details, but, if you have any questions before then, you have my card."

The man's wife smiled and shook Kathleen's hand.

"Thank you, dear, thank you."

Kathleen returned to her desk to organise the collection of the body from the West Sydney Memorial Hospital. Today was going to be challenging – she had never concluded a contract before, while the collection of a body from the morgue she had either done or organised many times. She picked up the telephone and dialled the hospital's number and, after a short hold, was put through to a mortuary attendant.

"Morgue. Smith speaking, can I help you?" the tone was flat and lifeless, stereotypical for the job.

"Yes. My name's Kathleen O'Neill, O'Neill's Funeral Directors. I believe you have a Mr Trumball there, he died this morning and would have been transferred down from E Ward?"

"Just a moment."

The sound of the phone being placed on a desk was unmistakable, as was the sound of shuffling paperwork. After a few seconds, the man was back on the line.

"Sharpe, Stockton, Tasker, Turnbull... yes he's here."

"No, not Turnbull, Trumball, Trumball!"

The exasperation in her voice was obvious.

"Tasker, Turnbull, Vickers... hang on a sec – Trumball, yeah, he's here too. Some clown didn't file it in the right order."

Kathleen sighed heavily. She wondered who 'some clown' could possibly be.

"Fine. I'll need to collect the deceased this evening, say after around 7:30. Is that alright?"

"Do you have the paperwork? We can't hand out bodies to just anyone, you know. You'll have to bring the paperwork with you, ID as well – photo ID."

The attendant, obviously new in the job, must have been old Jones' replacement and didn't know the regular faces.

"Look, Mr... " she fought to control her rising irritation. "Mr Smith. I've done this many times before and I'm completely familiar with the procedure. Now, if someone will be in attendance around 7:30 this evening, I'll turn up with all the necessary paperwork together with a suitable form of identification, *photographic* identification, so that I may collect Mr *Trumball*. Is that OK?"

"Half past seven, I'll make a note in the register."

"Thank you."

Kathleen replaced the telephone receiver and shook her head.

'Where did they find these people? Not an ounce of independent thought and, following the rules to the letter, only able to think by numbers. Still,' she reasoned, 'it took all kinds to make the world go around.'

Her thoughts turned to Jock and what she must do this evening, a question-and-answer session playing in her head.

'Was it the right thing to be doing, given his circumstances?'

'Yes.'

'Should I have offered him a way out in the first place?'

'Yes.'

'Should I tell Jock to reconsider?'

'Perhaps.'

These were the fundamental questions that had been dogging her since she had left the hospital yesterday afternoon and, even though she had prepared the mixture, she needed to be clear in her mind that this was still the correct thing to do.

Peter, dear Peter. Her heart skipped a beat when he had reached for the small whisky bottle. Did he suspect anything? She couldn't be sure. He was very sharp and she knew he had sensed something was not right, although, by the end of the evening, the event had not been mentioned, presumably passed off as just 'one of those things'. Still, if they were to be married, there may come a time when he might stumble across the family's dark secret and her role in its perpetuation. If that happened, how would it affect them? Would he leave her? Go to the police? Her mind was racing, trying to ascertain every conceivable scenario and how she would deal with it. What she would say, how she would act and how best to mitigate any negative outcome.

"Stop!" she said out loud. This was not helpful. 'Cross that bridge if and when you come to it,' she said to herself.

"What's that, Kath?"

Unnoticed by Kathleen, Tracey had entered the room.

"Oh, nothing. Just talking to myself."

"You know what they say, don't you?" Tracey made the sign of a circle against the side of her head with an index finger.

Kathleen laughed.

"Well, I know I'm a bit mad, but I'm not quite that bad, not yet at any rate!"

Tracey handed her a small pile of papers.

"There's a few letters and some forms from the Registrar's office for you to sign. I'm just going to pop down to the bank to deposit this morning's cheques. Do you need anything while I'm out?"

"I'm fine, Trace. Do we need any tea, coffee, that sort of thing?"

"No, there's plenty. See you in a bit."

\* \* \*

Half an hour had passed since six o'clock, when the hospital porter had left a tray of food across Jock's bed, but tonight Jock had little appetite. His mind was on far more important things. It was, after all, going to be his last day on this earth. He wouldn't see the sun rise tomorrow morning and, while that thought was one which wouldn't go away, it was counter-balanced by the dread of becoming so debilitated, that he would have no control over his movements and suffer terrible pain, without being able to ask for help. Despite the medication, the pain in his head was already unbearable and, if the prognosis was to be believed, would get even worse. It was no contest. He continued to look at the covered plate, knowing he had made the right decision, and waited for Kathleen to arrive.

Downstairs, in the hospital basement, a spotty, bespectacled mortuary attendant who had just come on duty, sat reading a girlie magazine. There wasn't much to do in the morgue after five thirty. Most of the pathologists had completed their post mortem examinations during the day and had left for the evening. The only activity was the occasional visit from a member of staff, usually bringing down some poor soul who had died or an ambulance with the victim of a fatal accident. Funeral homes also called, but they had to make an appointment. This was recorded in the Collections register and it was this book to which he now turned his attention. There were two such scheduled collections tonight; at 6:00pm a representative from 'My Way' was to collect a Mr Turnbull – ID No 10898 and then at 7:30 O'Neill's were sending someone to collect ID No 10889 – Frederick Trumball.

It was going to be a quiet night.

He read the first entry again and looked up at the wall clock.

"Five past six," he muttered out loud. "You're late, Mr 'My Way'. Good job I'm not the strict type!"

In fact, the attendant was anything but the strict type. He had the perfect job – evening shifts meant little or no interaction, with any other person. The dead, after all, were quiet by nature and never complained. By all accounts, that meant he was left to his own devices for most of the time and, that was how he liked it. Picking up the girlie magazine, he resumed ogling the topless models in provocative and suggestive poses. He began to fantasize about a particular girl with large breasts when the door buzzer sounded a sharp series of calls and pulled him back to the present.

Quickly hiding the magazine in the top drawer, he walked to the door and opened it. A stocky man with no neck, wearing an ill-fitting suit, stood in the entrance.

"Yes?"

Radic produced a business card which read 'My Way' Funerals. Angelo Radic – Associate.'

He liked showing and giving out his business card. It made him feel important.

"Come to get D,D,D..." the furrow in his brow deepened as his pea brain struggled to remember the name of the body he had to collect. A scowl spread across his face with the effort. It was an intimidating sight and the mortuary attendant took a step back, unsure of what was about to happen.

Suddenly Radic had the name and he blurted it out with gusto, "Drumbull!"

"Yes, yes," the attendant retreated further into the morgue. "Let me check the register."

Nervously he ran his finger down the list of names. Drumball – it sounded familiar. Angelo stood close beside him, peering over his shoulder at the register.

"D, D, D... nothing here for Drumbull, I'm afraid."

And afraid he was. Angelo had this effect on many people, even when it wasn't intentional, but now he was getting annoyed. The traffic to the hospital had been terrible, he had arrived later than planned, his boss was expecting him back by seven and this kid couldn't find the stiff.

"Drumbull!"

A blast of the garlic breath caused the attendant to wince and double his efforts – he wanted this man out of here.

"Yes, yes, it's here. Trumball, Trumball, 10898 – not Drumbull."

He laughed a nervous laugh.

"Yez – Drumbull."

The scowl on Radic's face remained.

"Where is your van parked?"

"In za road."

"Yes, well, if you'd like to bring it around to the side entrance, I'll open the door." Another nervous laugh escaped his mouth as Radic did an about turn and went to get the van.

Though it was cold in the main mortuary area, the mortuary attendant was sweating. He wanted to get this over with as soon as possible. The large man scared him, there was something almost machine-like about him. He looked like the sort of person who would break your neck and not give it a moment's thought. Scanning the piece of paper in his hand on which he had written the reference number, he quickly located No 10898. A knock at the side door signalled Radic's arrival. The attendant nervously opened the door and the Croat wheeled in a gurney on which an empty open coffin was placed.

The attendant glanced at the piece of paper in his hand and pointed to a wall which contained a row of stainless steel doors, each measuring about 60 centimetres square.

"Your man's over there," he managed nervously.

The young man opened 10898 and slid out a stainless steel drawer. A white linen sheet covered the body.

Radic wheeled the gurney next to the drawer and, removing the lid of the coffin addressed the attendant, "I take legs, you take head."

The man willingly complied and, in one swift movement, the cadaver was transferred from the tray to the coffin.

"You'll... you'll have to sign the collection papers."

He held up a clipboard with a set of papers in triplicate, marked the spot where Radic should sign and handed him the clipboard and a pen. In almost child-like fashion, slowly and with deliberation, Angelo wrote his name next to the X and handed the pen and papers back.

'Almost done, he'll be out of here in a moment,' the attendant thought to himself.

Radic secured the lid with a few small brass latches and wheeled the gurney to the side door.

He was almost out of the building when the attendant cried out:

"Wait! The paperwork, you need to take the blue copy."

Angelo stopped in his tracks and, for one small moment, the attendant thought he had in some way unwittingly antagonised the Croat. Radic abandoned the trolley and strode purposefully back to the man, who was holding up a blue copy of the collection document. His hands were trembling.

Angelo was only centimetres away from the man's face.

"Vot?"

The response was weak and muted, affected no doubt by the garlic which had become the Croat's trademark.

"Your copy... you should keep it... for your records."

Radic snatched the proffered blue collection note from the shaking hand and marched back to the gurney. Half a dozen more steps and he was out of the door and into the side alleyway.

It wasn't until the attendant heard the sound of the van starting up that he was able to move. The whole experience with Radic had completely unnerved him. He walked quickly to the side door and closed it firmly, turning the key and securing the top and bottom bolts for good measure and breathed a sigh of relief. God, he needed a drink. Returning to his desk he opened the bottom drawer and reached into the back part, retrieving a small bottle of vodka, hidden under some papers. The bottle clinked as it made contact with the empty coffee cup, into which he poured a good measure of the fiery liquid. He downed the spirit in one and then wiped his brow with the back of his hand. With some surprise, he realised he was still sweating and couldn't stop his hand from shaking.

* * *

Jock had resigned himself to do what he knew he must do. He had come to the conclusion he was, after all, a lucky man – lucky to have been given this chance, but also mindful of the risk Kathleen was taking. All day it had been going around and around in his head – the end was inevitable and his condition would deteriorate. Taking matters into his own hands and ending it here and now was the only bit of control he held over his life since the accident.

His eyes were focused on the framed print of a sailing ship on the opposite wall. There was something about the way the sails billowed, pushing the pitching ship through the stormy waters. It was the movement that had captured his attention and all he could think about was riding his Harley through the countryside, the wind in his face and the feel of the powerful machine as he guided it through the winding roads.

A gentle knock at the door disturbed his thoughts.

"Come in."

It was Kathleen. He had been expecting her.

"Hello, Jock." Kathleen smiled kindly and gently touched the Scotsman's hand.

"Hello, Kath."

There was a silence for a few seconds, eventually broken by Jock.

"Did you bring it?"

Kathleen nodded.

"Yes, I have it here. Listen, Jock. It's OK to change your mind. You don't have to do this."

Jock smiled and shook his head slowly.

"Nay, lassie. I'm not gonna' change my mind, this is what I want. The throbbing in ma heed is terrible. I canna' stand it any longer."

He pushed himself slightly higher up in the bed.

"I didn't sleep much last night. Kept turning it over in my mind, but the more I thought about it, the more I realised I'd made the right decision. I couldn't bear the thought of being like this for the next few weeks. The pain is getting worse and they don't seem to have a handle on it in this place. I've had enough, but, were it not for you, I'd have nay say in the matter, nay say at all. I guess what I'm trying to say in ma hamfisted way, is 'thank you'. Thank you for giving me the chance to be a man again."

Kathleen was hoping he'd change his mind, but he was resolute. She nodded and reached into her handbag, withdrawing a small bottle of whisky, five fingers full and, with her heart racing, and a lump in her throat, she passed it to the Scotsman. Jock held the bottle in his hand.

"Bells, eh? My favourite, as it happens. You reckon this'll do the job?"

"Yes, Jock."

She looked away. She didn't want him to see the tears.

"Wow! So this is it. Looks just like the real thing, eh? I'd never have guessed, not in a million years. No chance of getting a hangover, I suppose?"

He laughed at the comedy of the situation, an innocuous bottle of whisky, except for one small thing: it was anything but benign. It wasn't going to give him a hangover. It was going to kill him.

Kathleen was quick to sense the change of mood.

"Jock, why don't we talk about this another time?"

She reached for the bottle.

"Nay!" The response was firm and unequivocal, as Jock pulled the bottle away from her.

"It's OK, Kath, really, it's OK. I guess I expected something, something, you know… different, a bit more dramatic."

"Something like a sorcerer's potion?" she offered.

"Yeah, I did. Stupid, eh? Didn't know what it was going to look like, but I didn't figure on something as ordinary as this."

Kathleen had mixed feelings. It wasn't too late to change the outcome, not wanting him to die and yet compelled to respect his wishes. Like her father always told her, "Sometime, you have to care enough for someone to let them go." But, if there was any sign that Jock was hesitant, she would take the bottle back.

Jock cradled the bottle in his hand, staring at its latent potency and turned to face Kathleen.

"Thirty minutes, half an hour done and dusted?"

"Less. It works fast. After a couple of minutes you'll feel happy. Believe it or not, most people laugh and that feeling only gets better and stronger, the closer you get. There'll be no pain, no suffering, only a sense of complete well being and joy. You'll be happy."

"Kath, I need just a few minutes alone. Is that OK?"

Kathleen squeezed his hand.

"Of course that's OK, Jock."

"I'd better take this with me."

"Nay – I'd rather hold it for a while, if that's alright," he responded, drawing it close into his body, like a mother with a child.

He gazed up and saw the concern in her eyes.

"Don't worry. I won't do anything until you're back, promise."

He held up the bottle.

"After all, we don't want to leave this lying around, do we?"

"Sure, Jock."

Kathleen glanced at her watch.

"Look, it's seven thirty now. I've got a couple of things to do. Why don't I sort them out and come back here at eight? Would that be alright?"

"Perfect. See you at eight."

Kathleen stood up.

'He still might change his mind.'

"You won't do anything, will you?"

"Madame, you have my word as a Scotsman."

Kathleen paused by the door, a questioning look on her face, as she turned to face him. He caught her gaze.

"My word as a Scotsman."

\* \* \*

Radic pulled into the garage, killed the engine and looked at his watch. 6:58 – not bad. He'd made good progress back from the hospital despite the traffic and an unusually high number of older drivers who seemed hell bent on slowing him up. Well, his boss wanted him back by seven o'clock and here he was, back in one piece and bang on time. The coffin rolled easily out of the van onto the waiting trolley and Angelo smiled to himself as he pushed it through the rear of the building and into the embalming room, where Spitz was busy mixing a number of chemicals. The smell of formaldehyde filled the air.

"Ah, Angelo, I see you have our man and you are back on time to boot. Well done! I've had a very good day today."

He gestured to the now beaming Radic to bring the trolley over to the preparation table.

"Yes, just here is perfect."

The coffin was aligned parallel to the stainless steel table, about fifteen centimetres away. Spitz was releasing the four brass swivel fasteners one by one as he spoke to Radic, as though delivering a sermon.

"When it comes to creating the appearance of life, there aren't many who can hold a candle to the great JTS. I'm not one to boast, but the facts speak for themselves…"

One latch undone, three to go…

"You wouldn't believe the number of people who have said 'Mr Spitz, Aunt Betty, Uncle Bill, whomever… looked twenty, thirty years younger. You are a genius!"

Two latches free, two to go…

"I've never seen skill like that before. No wonder they call you the King of Funerals!"

Three latches loose, one remaining…

"And most important of all, Mr Spitz, you care, you really do care. It shows in everything you do…"

With the last brass latch undone, Radic stepped forward and removed the coffin lid. Spitz was still in another place, a place where his ego had massively expanded like some over-inflated balloon. His head was turned towards heaven, arms open in supplication, the monologue nearing its conclusion.

"Mr Spitz, we're so lucky to have found you. You've turned a sad situation into a joyful celebration of Aunt Betty's life and she would have loved it, we know she wa… "

Spitz was looking at the body in the coffin and his self-adulation died in mid-delivery, as lifeless as the corpse before him.

Silence filled the room.

At length, he spoke, the tone, suspicious and questioning,

"Angelo, Mr Turnbull is, or rather was, an eighty seven year old Caucasian man. Height, a hundred and eighty-seven centimetres, weight, approximately a hundred kilos, hair, abundant and completely white and, in his younger days, was favourably compared to John Wayne."

Spitz was keeping his temper under control but clearly finding it difficult.

"Is any of this getting through, Angelo?"

Radic was dimly aware that something was not right, yet he couldn't quite put his finger on it.

"John Vayne?" was all he could offer.

"Yes, that's right Angelo, John Wayne – and I was going to transform our beloved Mr Turnbull into John Wayne again. It was going to be another JTS work of art."

Radic now had no idea where this was going. Spitz continued, hand open, palm exposed and indicating the body in the wooden coffin.

"Does this man look like an older John Wayne?"

Radic was now completely confused, unable to grasp the problem. It showed on his face.

"Let me help you, Angelo, help you spot the differences and then you can draw your own conclusions, alright?"

Angelo nodded, grateful for the help.

"Mr Turnbull was a hundred and eighty-seven centimetres. This man would be scraping to make a hundred and seventy-five on tip-toes. Mr Turnbull was a heavy man, whereas this gentleman might easily blow away on a windy day. Mr Turnbull had white snowy hair and was clean shaven, but our friend here is bald and sports a curly beard."

The trembling in his voice was now becoming more acute.

"Is it starting to come together yet? No? Well, how about another clue? Mr Turnbull was white. This man is black!"

Spitz could hold it back no more.

"Angelo, you moron, this is not Mr Turnbull!"

"But Bozz... I did ged za right stiv. Look, I write it down on peez of paper, juz like you zay."

"What *exactly* did you write down, Angelo?"

Radic searched in vain through his pockets, unable to locate the note.

"I lozzed za paper, but I get za right stiv, no vurries. Look, za man give me blue paper."

Spitz took the crumpled collection note from the hospital mortuary and smoothed it out on the table, his eyes darting across each line as he read the form.

"Angelo, this is a collection note for a Mr Trumball, whereas I was expecting a Mr *Turnbull*. Can you explain this to me?"

Radic shrugged his shoulders.

"Muz be mix-up."

"Mix up... yes – I think that would pretty much cover it."

Spitz was counting silently to himself, his lips barely moving in an effort to control the frustration that refused to go away.

"A mix-up, which meant you collected the WRONG FUCKING BODY!"

Angelo now looked somewhat sheepish. He still had no idea how this had happened, but his boss was clearly disappointed and this made him feel bad.

"So, my friend, what do you think we should do, eh?"

Angelo shrugged.

"OK, I'll make it easy for you. Choose one of the following two options. One: take Errol Brown here, give him a shave, stick on a wig, pad him out a bit and, not forgetting, paint him white, or… two: take him back and get the *real* Mr Turnbull."

Angelo was pondering the options, looking for the trick question, his brain working furiously.

"Would it help if I said option one was NOT, repeat, not the right one?"

Radic gave an audible sigh of relief.

"Ve take him back?"

"Yes, we take him back and get the right body. Now put the lid back on the coffin and return it to the van. I'm coming with you this time!"

\* \* \*

Jock looked at the clock on the wall – 7:50 pm. Kath would be here shortly. Visiting hours finished at 8:30pm, that would be enough time to spend quietly with Kath before he drank the mixture and then said goodbye, goodbye to everything including the cruel path fate had laid out before him. He needed this quiet time to be alone with his thoughts. Time to take stock of what he had achieved in his life, the missed opportunities, regrets and achievements, highs and lows. An emotional balance sheet of his sixty-odd years on the planet.

He hoped there was a God. As a child, his mother had taken him to church, but even oblivion would be a better option than the pounding in his head. A movement at the door pulled him back to the here and now, a touch of annoyance sweeping aside the reflective mood. Kathleen had always knocked before. He was about to speak when the door swung open and a young man entered. Jock recognised him instantly as the man from the Railway Hotel.

"Well, well. If it isn't our wee Scottie man. What a coincidence! I was just visiting me mate down the corridor and he told me you were here.

Priceless! I just had to come and see for myself. I knocked you a right corker, didn't I?"

Cosgrove sauntered across to the bed before stopping at its end and picking up the clipboard with the medical notes. He eyed Jock, a look of utter contempt on his face.

"Umm, can't get out of bed, eh, it's not looking chipper, laddie, now is it?"

The words oozed sarcasm as he taunted the Scotsman.

"What do *you* want?" retorted Jock, furious at the timing of this little creep's visit.

"Nothing. Nothing, except to see you having an absolute shit of a time. Jesus, if I'd have known you were here, I'd have called in ages ago!"

"Fuck you, Cosgrove. Go on, piss off or I'll get security to chuck you out!"

"No, you won't."

Cosgrove had moved from the foot of the bed and was now standing next to the bedside table.

"You won't do anything of the sort because you'll need this first to call a nurse."

He held up the red button connected to the nurses' station outside. Cosgrove's eyes fell on the small bottle of Bell's whisky in Jock's lap.

"Hello, hello, hello. What have we here?" sneered Cosgrove as he snatched it from Jock's grasp.

Jock pushed himself back against the bed head, raising his body higher.

"Give me that!" he swiped weakly at the bottle, Cosgrove holding it out of his reach.

"Got to be faster than that, old man, if you want a little drinkie."

He held the bottle up in front of Jock, goading him.

"Need a nip, do we? Frankly, I'm surprised they let you have this stuff here at all. Still, in a private room, I guess you can get away with murder, eh?"

A wry smile spread across Jock's face. Cosgrove's tone and attitude changed as he sensed the defiance.

"Think I'll have a little nip myself, actually. Little kick start to the evening. Not that you can do much about it, tucked up in bed like a baby. Come to think of it, I might even have the whole lot!"

He slowly unscrewed the bottle and moved it in a circular motion, the golden-amber contents swirling around and catching the light from the lamp above the bed. Cosgrove was deliberately making a dramatic display – he had control, the victor and the vanquished in close theatre.

"Cheers."

Cosgrove took a tug on the liquid, wiped his mouth with the back of his hand and exhaled a throaty sigh.

"Ahhhh!! Nice one! I do like Bell's, especially when it's on the house, know what I mean?"

"Gonna drink the lot, are you? Not going to spare some for a sick old man?"

"Why should I give you any? It's mine now – possession being nine tenths and all that."

"Look, pal, I know you canna' help being an arsehole, I just want one swig, that's all, and then you can go on being the person you are – no change."

"Sorry, mate. I'm not into sharing and the question still stands. Why should I give you any?"

Jock gave a despondent sigh and lowered his head in a gesture of submission.

"Because I dinna help the cops press charges against you."

It was a good answer and it worked.

"Well, I suppose that does deserve a little drinkie. As you've been such a good boy, I'll let you have some of *my* whisky."

He passed the bottle to Jock, the latter eagerly reaching out with one hand. At the last moment however, Cosgrove withdrew the prize, an anxious look spreading across Jock's face. It was all part of the cat and mouse game, cruel to the last.

"Go on, you sad old bugger, I can't be bothered."

There was a derisory tone in his voice as he passed the bottle to the Scotsman.

"It was much better when you were up and about. Should have seen the look on your face when that bar stool connected! Shit, that was priceless!"

A small chuckle bubbled to the surface.

Jock drank deeply and finished the bottle.

"Easy on, easy on! Be careful, that stuff might kill you!"

A fit of the giggles had spawned in Cosgrove's throat and it showed no signs of abating.

Jock too was smiling, but for different reasons, his mind focused on the young punk standing by the bed, openly taunting him.

'Thought you'd get the last laugh did you, pal? Got to be up earlier, if that's what you want. Well, now you're laughing, but I'm laughing louder!' he thought.

"Jesus, I feel good!"

Cosgrove could suppress the giggles no longer, everything was funny and he couldn't hide it.

"Look, old man, I'm going to push off. Got to see me mate. A short burst of laughter. "We must do this again some time – really. It's been... *awfully* good!"

The adverb was spoken in an upper class accent and immediately followed by a burst of uncontrolled laughter.

Jock raised his thumb – the 'everything's great' symbol.

"Top, ho, what?"

He too had begun to chuckle helplessly.

"What, ho?" mimicked Cosgrove, who was now staggering to the door, holding his sides, in a vain attempt to suppress the play on words.

"What, ho indeed?"

Jocks' face became flushed in an effort to hold back his private joke, "Arsehole, more likely!"

The contagious laughter burst forth, instantly infecting Cosgrove as he fumbled at the door, tears now running down his cheeks.

"Arsehole, what, ho, top, ho!"

The alliteration proved too much for the lout as he bumbled through the door, unable to contain himself any longer.

"See you again, old man!" he called over his shoulder. "Next time the drinks are on you!"

Cosgrove staggered out of the room and down the corridor outside, the laughter getting louder even though it was further away.

Peels and squeals reverberated around the ward, as visitors and patients came to the doors of the side wards, to see what was going on.

"I don't think so!" Jock spluttered after him, while Cosgrove staggered down the corridor.

As the liquid took effect, Jock was hooting as loudly and uncontrollably as Cosgrove. He had never felt so good or laughed so much in his entire life. The pain in his head was gone, replaced instead by an overwhelming sense of joy and happiness. If this was death, it was the most wonderful experience he had ever had. He'd heard people talk of a white light and a feeling of joy, but he'd always thought they were fools.

Now he knew differently, as his mother and father appeared waving and smiling, looking young again. A few of his old friends were there and also emerged from within the brightness. It was a surprise party and he was to be the guest of honour. The light was the brightest he had ever seen.

\* \* \*

Kathleen was patient, empathetic and reasonable. They were, after all, essential qualities of her vocation, but on this occasion all of those characteristics were fast receding. She glanced at her wristwatch for the fourth time in as many minutes – seven forty five pm – as the drumming of her fingers on the counter top became louder and more pronounced. She'd been waiting now for over fifteen minutes and was very conscious that Jock was expecting her back at eight. After what seemed ages, the mortuary attendant returned to the desk, a sheepish look on his face.

"Well?" the annoyance in her voice was unmistakeable. "Can I now please sign for Mr Trumball and I'll collect him in about forty five minutes?"

"I'm afraid there seems to be a slight problem, Ms O'Neill."

The drumming stopped.

"What kind of problem?"

"Mr Trumball has already been collected."

"What?" Kathleen's mouth hung agape. There was a long, awkward pause. "I'm not sure I'm hearing this correctly. You're telling me that the body of Mr Frederick Trumball, my client's father, is not here and has been collected by someone else? Is that what you're telling me?"

"Yes, I'm afraid so, Ms O'Neill, it looks like there has been some kind of mix-up, I'm dreadfully sorry."

The man was clearly nervous and had begun to sweat. A mistake like this could cost him his job. He took off his glasses and wiped his brow with a handkerchief.

"Dreadfully sorry doesn't help much, now does it? What would help however, is for you to get Mr Trumball back here, tonight, say… within the hour… so I can do my job, as you should have done yours!"

She was furious and made little effort to conceal the fact.

"I'll get on it right away, Ms O'Neill, right away."

He began to scramble through the paperwork on his desk. Panic replaced methodical search as the attendant frantically tore through the pile of original, duplicate and triplicate forms on the desk. Kathleen immediately saw this was not the way to correct the error and she quickly took control of the situation.

"Stop, stop!"

She placed a hand on the man's arm and spoke in a calm and commanding voice.

"It's going to be alright… what is your name again?"

"Tom… Tom Dodd. It's here, the paperwork, it's here I know it is!"

"Tom, it's not going to get found like this. Tom, look at me."

The gentle but firm instruction had the desired effect as the attendant stopped his panicked rifling through the multi-coloured pile of papers.

"Tom, has anyone collected a body in the last few hours, perhaps someone with a similar name? It's just a thought, but if it's any consolation, it sometimes happens."

Dodd's eyes lit up.

"Yes, yes! About an hour and a half ago. Name started with a T! Yes, it's possible!"

The relief on his face was manifest as a glimmer of hope prodded at his memory.

"The clipboard! The paperwork's on the clipboard. It's in the other room. Wait here, I'll go and get it."

A moment later he reappeared with a clipboard containing a white and blue sheet.

"I've got it! It's all here! Mr Trumball, collected by another funeral director. I'll phone them straightaway. Leave it to me – I'll get it sorted. Don't know how this could possibly have happened."

The man was racing, still in panic mode.

"Tom."

No response.

"Tom."

This time louder.

Still no response.

"Tom!" it was a command and had the desired effect.

Dodd stopped running and looked up.

"Yes?"

Kathleen gently prised the clipboard from his hands and guided him to his chair.

"Sit down, Tom. Take a few deep breaths and get a grip. You won't get anything sorted running around like a headless chicken. Now listen to me – OK?"

He nodded in acknowledgement.

"I've got a couple of things to see to and I'll be back in a short while. While I'm gone, you pick up the phone and talk to the funeral director keeping Mr Trumball. You have the telephone number, I trust?"

Dodd nodded vigorously.

"Good. You talk to the funeral parlour that has Mr Trumball and explain the mix-up. I'm sure they'll understand completely."

Dodd nodded again.

"Just tell them that the funeral director for Mr Trumball is here now and would they kindly bring him back so she can get on with her job? They'll understand. Can you do this Tom, are you OK to do this or do you want me to stay?"

"I'm OK." The voice was shaky but calmer.

Control had returned to the situation, and Kathleen breathed an audible sigh of relief.

"Good, Tom, good."

She glanced at her watch – seven fifty.

"I'll be back in about in about half an hour or so, alright? All you need to do is telephone the parlour that collected Mr Trumball and it can all be sorted."

Kathleen walked to the door and opened it.

"Half an hour, Tom, I'll be back in half an hour."

Dodd nodded.

"See you in half an hour."

As the door was closing behind her, he reached into the bottom drawer and withdrew the bottle of vodka. With shaking hands, he managed to unscrew the cap and lifted the bottle to his lips.

So much for a quiet night.

But if Dodd's night had been alarming, it was nothing compared to the shock waves reverberating around Lewis ward on the eight floor.

# Chapter 23

## Prime Suspect

K athleen pushed the button to call the lift and glanced at her watch again –seven fifty five pm – she'd promised Jock to be back by eight. The mix-up in the mortuary would have been bad at any time, but why tonight? Had she not taken charge of the situation, no doubt the man would still be faffing around, trying to find the collection slip that he had so obviously messed up.

Still, that was now in the past. There were more important matters to tend to now. After what seemed like ages, a 'ping' announced the arrival of the lift. 'Not many people visited this part of the hospital,' she thought as she entered the empty lift and pushed the button for the eighth floor.

There were butterflies in her stomach as she contemplated what lay ahead. She was about to find out. The lift arrived at the eight floor and Kathleen walked straight to the ward. There was no one at the nurses' station when she walked past, which was unusual. A loud commotion from another room on the ward made her ears prick up. People were shouting, but she couldn't make out the words. Rounding the corner, she came upon Jock's room and knocked gently on the door. No reply. She knocked again, this time slightly louder but still there was no response from inside. Slowly, she turned the handle so the door was ajar and called through the narrow opening.

"Jock. It's Kathleen, may I come in?"

Nothing.

"Jock, it's Kath, I'm coming in, OK?"

Once the door was open, her heart skipped a beat. It was obvious what had happened… Jock was half sitting up in bed, eyes open and a wide grin on his face, an empty quarter bottle of Bell's whisky on the side table.

Kathleen sighed heavily.

"Oh, Jock, why didn't you wait for me to come back?"

Despite his assurances, the Scotsman had obviously taken matters into his own hands, single-minded to the end. She approached the bed and gently stroked his hair then stooped to kiss him tenderly on the cheek.

"Goodbye, dear friend, goodbye."

Although she'd only known him for a short time, Kathleen would miss him dreadfully. He had profoundly affected her life, but what she didn't yet know was that he was going to have an ever greater affect on her future.

There was nothing more she could do, except retrieve the empty bottle and quietly leave, before anybody saw her. The nurses' station was still unattended and, judging by the commotion, there was some kind of crisis on the ward, which probably accounted for it. Kathleen walked unnoticed to the bank of lifts and pushed the 'down' button. Alone, she travelled back to the basement, with a heavy heart and a touch of guilt that she had not been with Jock at the end. He had given his word not to do anything, but clearly, for whatever reason, had decided otherwise. Perhaps he would have found saying 'goodbye' too painful. She would never know.

An illuminated letter 'B' signalled the basement. Kathleen walked into the mortuary. An involuntary reaction caused her to take a small step backwards, as the two men at the attendant's desk turned around at the sound of the opening door.

"Why, Ms O'Neill, what a surprise. How delightful to see you again."

Jerome T Spitz, effusive as ever, made a slight nod of his head in greeting. Radic could only manage a grunt.

"And what pray brings you to here at this hour?"

Before she had a chance to reply, the mortuary attendant interjected from behind the bulk that was Radic. Two cadavers, each on a gurney and covered up to the chin, were either side of him.

"It appears, Ms O'Neill, that Mr Trumball here was inadvertently collected by Mr…" he gesticulated towards Radic who glowered back at him, "by Mr, Mr," the name had completely escaped him, his mind swamped by a rising fear of Radic, "by the gentleman here from 'My Way'. However, it was Mr *Turnbull* who should have gone to the 'My Way' funeral parlour."

He was now sweating again.

"Trumball, Turnbull, the names are similar, it's an easy mistake to make, don't you think?"

He laughed nervously, anxious for all of this to be over.

Kathleen had regained her composure and walked up to the attendant, flanked on either side by a body.

"My client, Mr Trumball, is of Afro-Caribbean descent," Kathleen stated calmly. "His father, the late Mr Trumball, is also of Afro-Caribbean descent, so if I had to make a snap decision, I'd say that this man," pointing to the black corpse, "is Mr Trumball."

The attendant stood mute. There was little he could say at this point.

"Is this perchance Mr *Turnbull*?" asked Kathleen, pointing at the other body with an exaggerated movement of her arm.

Dodd nodded.

"So, Mr Turnbull is white, Mr Trumball is black. Is that correct?"

Dodd nodded again.

"And the release form, if I'm not mistaken, had a section which states the ethnicity of the deceased, is that correct?"

"Yes, but in the circumstances…"

"In the circumstances, Mr Dodd," Kathleen interjected, "I think it was a stupid mistake to make, not an easy one and, in any event, Mr Spitz, how could you possibly collect the wrong body? Didn't something as obvious as the wrong name and the wrong ethnic group ring any bells?"

Kathleen, emboldened by the presence of the morgue attendant, had now gone on the attack. She hated Spitz and Radic and would have loved to be able to report them for intimidation. But then, given what she'd just done, talking to the police didn't seem like an intelligent thing to do.

It was now Spitz's turn to eat humble pie, something he did not do easily or often.

"What can I say, Ms O'Neill? It was a mix-up and unfortunately these things happen."

He was looking squarely at Radic, speaking through clenched teeth.

"Thankfully though, no harm has come of it and the situation has now been resolved, so, if you will excuse us, we'll be on our way."

A quick movement of his head to Radic indicated an instruction to leave.

The Croat's brow furrowed in confusion.

"Wiz za stiff?"

Spitz sighed, this was not doing his blood pressure any good. It was taking all his self control not to explode in front of the O'Neill woman.

He pointed to the white cadaver.

"Yes, Angelo, put Mr Turnbull, *that one*, in the van," he commanded, before turning on his heel and walking swiftly out of the room.

* * *

Back at her flat, Kathleen kicked off her shoes, poured a large glass of wine and sat down heavily on the sofa. It had been a long and taxing day, leaving her emotionally drained. Kathleen had always worried how she would feel, when it was her turn to take over this part of the family business.

Now she knew. She'd often imagined feelings of guilt or fear. Instead she felt incredibly sad, but knowing Jock's wishes had been fulfilled, relieved some of the pain. It had hurt her to see him so desperate, unhappy and suffering. Helping him when he couldn't help himself and knowing he was in a better place was a good feeling.

She had done nothing morally wrong or bad – illegal, yes – but it was the law that was wrong, not her. She now knew that the O'Neill legacy was a blessing and not a curse. It would do more good than harm.

* * *

"Inspector Thompson."

Joanne, a WPC on the next desk was holding the telephone, a hand over the mouthpiece.

"Inspector Thompson," she called again.

Thompson looked up from a case file he had been preparing on the acts of sabotage against Robertson and Humphries.

"Yes, Jo, what is it?"

"I've got Dr Tagashi, the pathologist from West Sydney Memorial Hospital on the line. He's concerned about something that's just turned up." She offered Thompson the phone. "Would you mind? This sounds a little out of my league and all the other case officers are out at the moment."

"Sure, Jo, I'll speak to him."

Thompson rose from his chair and took the outstretched telephone receiver.

"Detective Inspector Thompson speaking."

"Good morning, Inspector."

The man spoke perfect English, but with a pronounced Far-Eastern accent.

"My name is Satoro Tagashi. I'm the senior pathologist at West Sydney Memorial Hospital."

"Good morning, Dr Togoshu. What can I do for you?"

"It's Tagashi. I have two patients with disturbing similarities, which are quite out of the ordinary and frankly I'm at a loss as to what might be the cause. I've never seen anything quite like it."

"I don't see how this involves me, Dr Tamashi. I'm a policeman, not a doctor. Have you talked to the two people, perhaps they could offer some insight into their conditions?"

"Tagashi, my name's Tagashi, Inspector, and I'm a pathologist. The two patients are both deceased."

"Oh, I see. Or rather, I don't see. I still don't understand why you think this involves the police. Do you suspect some kind of foul play?"

"I've run all the tests I can think of and foul play is becoming a very distinct possibility."

"Ah... now I understand. Would you like me to come down and see you?"

"That would be helpful. Could you come sooner than later? I've a busy schedule today, the afternoon is booked solid."

Thompson nodded.

"Very well, Dr Tag..."

"Tagashi."

"Yes, quite, my apologies. Never been good with Chinese names. I'll be with you in about an hour."

Joanne turned to Thompson, a puzzled look on her face.

"Is everything alright, Sir?"

Thompson was shaking his head.

"Fellow sounds a bit spooked. Got a couple of bodies that don't quite fit the bill, so thought he'd phone the local nick... wants me to go and meet him, give my opinion, know what I mean?"

The WPC looked even more confused.

"I'm sure it will all become clear in due course," continued Thompson, "probably a storm in a bathtub."

"Teacup, Sir."

"Yes, thanks, Jo, I'd love one. Milk, two sugars please."

The WPC was shaking her head as she went out to get the Inspector the beverage, while he turned his attention back to the case file.

"Now, where was I... ah, that's right. Jerome T Spitz... you're definitely in my sights, sunshine, definitely in my sights."

An hour later, Thompson arrived at the main hospital car park. Ten o'clock and already the temperature was in the high thirties. Like the past fortnight, today was going to be insufferably hot, that was for sure.

The hospital information desk was a busy, thriving place, the two staff continually dealing with a succession of telephone calls, and over the counter enquiries. Eventually, it was Thompson's turn.

"I'm looking for a Dr Tangeshu."

The receptionist ran her finger down a list of names, before looking up and replying.

"Sorry, no one of that name here. Next please!"

"Look, I might have got the name slightly wrong. He's a Chinese man, said he was the head pathologist, he's expecting me."

"Ah… that would be Dr Tagashi. Dr Tagashi, the *Japanese* head pathologist."

"Yes, that's the one. Where would I find him, please?"

"His office is in the basement, next to the mortuary. Lifts and stairs are over there. Next!"

The basement felt cooler than the ground floor, the fluorescent lighting, green walls and floor reinforcing a sense of isolation and detachment. Thompson followed the signs to the mortuary and adjacent to it came across a single door with a name plate – Dr S Tagashi, Head of Pathology.

Three knocks were rewarded with a "Come in!" from inside.

"Doctor Tagushi?"

"Tagashi, it's Tagashi. You must be Inspector Thompson?"

"Yes."

Tagashi looked like a pathologist. White coat, jet black hair parted neatly on one side and a studious look on his face. The wire-rimmed glasses completed the analytical persona. He looked up from the report he had been studying, came around from behind his desk and extended his hand.

The handshake was firm.

"Thank you for coming at such short notice. Please, take a seat."

Thompson settled himself in a chair opposite the desk and addressed Tagashi.

"You mentioned two deceased people and the possibility of foul play, Dr. Taneg… doctor. Can you be a little more specific?"

"Both are male, one in his sixties and the other in his twenties. Both Caucasian, one an in-patient here at West Sydney Memorial, the other appears to have been a visitor, although not connected to the patient, as far as we can ascertain. Both men died last night on Lewis ward on the eighth floor and both present striking similarities."

Thompson had taken out his notebook and was jotting down the important points.

"Some kind of infectious disease?" he suggested.

The pathologist rose from his chair and began to pace the room.

"There's no evidence of any such pathology and, even if it was something of that nature, it has only affected these two unrelated people. There is a witness to the younger man's death. The deceased was visiting his friend, and according to the nurse, he had been out onto the balcony to smoke a cigarette and later had come into the room laughing hysterically. He laughed for several minutes, unable to speak or explain what was so funny and then, all of a sudden, he stopped, but he wouldn't speak. His friend was concerned and pressed for the nurse and, when she came in, she couldn't find a pulse. She called the crash team of course, but they couldn't get his heart beating."

"A suspect batch of drugs? Or perhaps something they both ate?" offered Thompson.

"No, it's nothing they ate. We've taken of samples of their stomach contents and there was no evidence of any toxin, and, if it's drugs, I can't find any residue of anything in either body. There's no toxicological evidence at all which is extremely unusual. Frankly, I'm running out of options, Inspector. But the thing that puzzles me most of all, apart from the fact that they are the happiest corpses I've ever seen, is why just these two? What connects them? That's why I telephoned the police, as I said... I'm running out of ideas."

Thompson closed his notebook and looked up at the pathologist quizzically.

"May I see the two men?"

"Of course. Follow me, please."

Tagashi opened the door to his office, walked three metres to the next door and opened it.

He paused at the entrance, the door half open.

"Inspector, I'm obliged to say that this is an area I'm very familiar with. You may not feel so comfortable. Are you certain you want to do this?"

Thompson was a foot behind the pathologist.

"It's not my first time in the morgue, doctor, and I'm sure it won't be the last. Believe me, it's not a problem."

"Very well, Inspector, let me show you what we've been discussing."

Tagashi walked over to two examination tables, each containing a body covered with a white sheet. With a quick movement of his hand, he uncovered the face of the first corpse and an instant later, the second.

Thompson's sharp intake of breath was reflex-like.

"Jesus!"

The grinning face of Jock Strapp and Kevin Cosgrove, both wide-eyed and displaying looks of utter joy, were in stark contrast to their surroundings. The similarity of the expression was indisputable.

Tagashi nodded in agreement.

"Quite."

Recovering from his initial surprise, Thompson slowly began to digest the situation, the first thought crossing his mind being a connection between the two in the living world.

"There's definitely a link here."

Tagashi smiled.

"I think that's a given Inspector, wouldn't you say?"

Thompson shook his head vehemently.

"No, that's not what I'm saying. These two men were connected in real life, I just can't put my finger on it right now, but I know both of them."

"You knew both men?"

"Yes. I never forget a face, not even when it's dead and smiling."

The pathologist couldn't suppress his smile. There was a certain ironic humour in the situation.

"This is Kevin Cosgrove. I've been trying to put him away for a couple of years now, but he always seems to slip away from me. He's a drug dealer, mixed up with the Donatello brothers and, although we've never been able to prove it, our information is that the fire at the Traveller's Inn, last year, was set by none other than our smiling dead friend here, in revenge for the failure of one of the residents to pay a debt. It's a miracle no one was killed, though the owner was very badly burned. And then six months ago, a mother came to me to complain that Cosgrove was selling class 'A' drugs, outside her son's school. Her tyres were slashed and she withdrew the complaint, afraid for her safety. No one has been prepared to give evidence and Cosgrove was getting more powerful on the streets, by the day. If this is foul play, somebody's done society a real favour."

Thompson pointed to the older of the two.

"What's this man's name, Doctor?"

Tagashi scanned a clipboard at the head of the examination table.

"Strapp, James Strapp."

"Yes… it's all coming back now. I arrested Cosgrove after an attack on this man, at a pub. Strapp, James Strapp. Two witnesses to the attack picked Cosgrove out from the mug shots and I finally thought I'd got him. It was pretty much cut and dried, except our friend here wouldn't press charges and Cosgrove walked free again."

The policeman shook his head and smiled ruefully.

"Well, something's clearly going on here. The chance of both these men coming unstuck in the same way by accident or coincidence is unbelievable. There must be a common cause."

He paused to stroke his cheek, a gesture he often did while engaged in deep thought.

"You say you've run a few tests?" he continued.

"Several tests, actually," replied Tagashi. "Both of these men simply stopped breathing, but we have no idea of the cause. It would appear that they both laughed themselves to death. I've never come across anything quite like it."

Thompson was still stroking his cheek.

"Do you think this could be drugs related, doctor?"

"I would say it's the most likely cause, but, whatever it is, it has left no trace at all. Inspector?"

Thompson was miles away, his mind jumping from theory to theory.

"Sorry, doctor, I was just thinking about somebody who may be able to help you. Would you mind if I got one of the Forensic Science chaps to give you a ring? He's an expert on toxins and he might want to run a few tests himself. Maybe he'll come up with something that's been missed, would that be OK with you?"

Tagashi shook his head.

"No problem, but I'd be surprised if he finds anything, I've been over both cases with a fine tooth comb."

"No offence, doctor, but sometimes a different pair of eyes can uncover something that was missed the first time around."

"None taken. Of course, we'll be happy to cooperate in any way we can. I take it this is now a police matter?"

"Yes. I'll need to speak to the people who discovered the deaths and take their statements. I also need a report from you as soon as possible."

"Of course, Inspector. Here are some photographs I have taken for you," he said, passing him an envelope, "thank you for coming to see me so promptly."

He shook the pathologist's hand and moved to the door.

"Thank you. I'd like to see Mr Strapp's medical history. Who should I speak to?"

The pathologist followed the policeman to the door and they walked to the bank of lifts.

"Mr Strapp was on the eighth floor. His notes will still be at the nurses' station, and someone there should be able to help."

"Well, I guess there's no time like the present. Eighth floor, you say?"

A small 'ping' signalled the arrival of the elevator. Thompson thanked the pathologist again, entered the empty lift and pushed the button marked eight.

The following thirty minutes yielded some useful information. Though the medical records were meaningless to him, Thompson did manage to get a statement from a nurse, who was able to tell him that Jock had a regular lady visitor called Kathleen and that she'd visited the night Jock died. It was a promising start, but he needed to find out more. Thompson made a mental note to call back in the afternoon when the new shift of nurses came on duty. He thanked the duty sister and headed back to the car park.

It was just after midday when he called on Peter Wilson, the latter engrossed in the microscopic examination of some hair strands.

"Morning, Peter."

"Hello, Ian, how are you?"

"Fine, fine. Look, Peter, I know you're probably pretty busy, but something's come up and I wonder if you wouldn't mind taking a look."

Peter looked away from the sample he was studying.

"Never too busy to help out, Ian, you know that. In fact, I'm just finishing up here. What are we talking about?"

Thompson drew a stool closer to the bench and leaned forward, opening an envelope containing the mortuary pictures of Cosgrove and Strapp and spreading them on the bench.

Peter gasped at the sight of the two photographs.

"Jesus!"

Thompson smiled knowingly.

"My words exactly, Peter."

Recovering his composure, Peter looked closely at the two pictures.

"I take it this was no accident?"

"Don't know yet, but my nose tells me not."

Pointing to Cosgrove, he went on, "I arrested this one here, Kevin Cosgrove, for GBH on this one, a James Strapp," he proclaimed, tapping Jock's photo.

"Seems the old boy was an in-patient at West Sydney Memorial and the other fellow was visiting a friend on the same ward as James. This one, Cosgrove," he was pointing at the thug, "according to witnesses, collapsed laughing after returning from smoking a cigarette on the balcony, outside the Lewis ward and then simply stopped breathing. Not long after, this man here," his finger was on Jock's grinning death mask, "was found alone, propped up in bed, stone dead and looking like he'd won the lottery… so apart from their mysterious demise, minutes apart, at around 8 o'clock yesterday night, on the eighth floor of the hospital, we have no clues. We don't know what killed either man. These don't look like natural deaths to me. If we don't find out what caused this, it may be put down to natural causes, especially in the case of the Strapp, because he had a terminal illness."

"I've never seen anything like this before, Ian. I'm not sure I'd know where to start."

"It could be some sort of stimulant that killed both these men. What about the autopsy?"

Thompson considered Peter's comments.

"The post mortem examinations didn't find anything. The pathologist there has ruled out infection, food poisoning and all that sort of stuff. The only remaining option he could think of was some kind of new drug they'd both taken, or foul play with a hitherto unknown poison, but he couldn't find a trace of any known toxin in either man. For what it's worth, given that so many causes of death have been eliminated, I'm inclined to believe, there may well be a dodgy new drug on the market they both got their hands on the night they died. I thought with your knowledge of toxins, you might be able to point me in the right direction."

Peter looked perplexed.

"Who's the pathologist?"

"Tam, Tamash… some Chinese guy."

"You mean, Tagashi – he's very thorough and I doubt he'll have missed much. By the way, Ian, he's Japanese."

"Whatever. I just thought it wouldn't do any harm to have another pair of eyes look over the case. Would you mind taking a look at this for me, Peter?"

"So it's a police matter then?"

"Yes. I told him one of the forensics people would be giving him a call later."

Peter smiled at the policemen.

"No stone unturned, eh, Ian?"

"I'd really appreciate a second opinion, Peter. I have a few lines of enquiry to follow up and a number of statements to take, but the forensics are the key to the whole investigation. These are more likely to be drugs related deaths because there is no obvious motive for murder by poisoning, but if somebody is selling dangerous drugs, then at the very least, the supplier would be guilty of manslaughter and we have to get to the bottom of this before anybody else dies."

"OK, Ian, I'll give the hospital a call after I've had lunch and look into this. I'll get back to you tomorrow, is that OK?"

Thompson slid off his stool. A lone technician, carrying a tray of reagents gave the policeman a wide berth.

"Thanks, Peter. I'll speak to you tomorrow."

* * *

At the end of the day and back at his desk, Thompson ran the events of the past twelve hours over and over in his head. He liked the quiet of a semi-deserted office. The hubbub had usually died down after six pm and it was in this relative calm that he liked to think. He had spoken to Strapp's doctor late that afternoon. The mysterious lady visitor was identified and it was none other than Peter's fiancée, a volunteer hospital visitor. As a suspect, she never even crossed his mind, but as a witness who may have seen something, he considered that she may have been an important part of the investigation.

Thompson had later pulled out the report of the assault on Jock, but it yielded no clues. He considered Strapp's refusal to press charges and found himself wondering whether Strapp might have something to hide and Cosgrove had something over him. The witness reports however confirmed that Cosgrove was a newcomer to the Railway Hotel, where the assault had taken place and that nobody had seen him before that day. That line of enquiry was a dead end.

He had then opened the police file on the motorbike accident, information which had come to light after he had spoken to the doctor at the West Sydney Memorial. Scanning the Road Traffic Accident report, Thompson was trying to find anything which might suggest the possibility that somebody may have previously tried to kill the man. He gasped with surprise, when Kathleen O'Neill's name came up for a second time in relation to James Strapp. After thoroughly reading the report and the witness statement taken from Kathleen after the accident, it was clear that there was nothing more sinister to the crash, than an unlucky accident. It appeared that Kathleen had visited the poor chap after the crash to check on him.

The second surprising piece of information he'd uncovered that day was that a senior staff nurse had positively identified Spitz as being on Jock's ward, the night the Scotsman had died. She had gone to close the doors leading to the balcony, as cigar and cigarette smoke was coming into the ward. She saw Spitz on the eighth floor balcony, standing next to another man, and smoking a cheroot. The nurse had recognised him from his TV commercials. The man standing next to Spitz was none other than Cosgrove. Of course, at the time, the nurse had no idea who the second man was, but found out moments later, when she tried to resuscitate him after he collapsed laughing in a side room and died.

This little snippet of information opened up a completely new line of enquiry.

What was Spitz doing on the eighth floor and why was he on the balcony with Cosgrove? Both were extremely unsavoury characters. What had they been up to?

These and a hundred other questions bombarded his brain. He shook his head and stood up. This was turning into a complicated case and he had absolutely no idea where it was going. It was enough for one day. His mind was going round in circles.

"Pack it in, Thompson," he said out loud to the empty room. "Pack it in and go home."

Reaching for his jacket, he walked to the main door and turned off the lights.

* * *

The direct line telephone on her desk jangled into life, snapping Kathleen out of her day dream. It had been a long day and she had been thinking about the previous night and the confrontation in the mortuary with Spitz and Radic and then Jock and how the end had not gone completely as planned.

"Kath, it's Peter."

There was a pause before the voice sounded again.

"Kath, it's Peter, are you there?"

"Sorry, Peter, I was a million miles away. I'm really glad you phoned."

Peter immediately sensed the tension in her voice.

"Is everything OK, Kath?"

"Everything's fine, really. It's just been a busy day and I've had a lot on my mind. Are you coming over tonight?"

"You must be a mind reader, Ms O'Neill, because I was going to suggest a movie."

"I'd rather stay in with you, if that's OK. Why don't I make dinner and we'll see where the night leads us?"

"Well ... since you put it that way..."

The tone was now lighter, less sombre.

"What way, kind sir?" she replied in a playful tone.

"I'll see you later. Seven, alright?"

"Seven is perfect. Love you."

"Love you too."

\* \* \*

Spitz's day was far from over and his mind was buzzing. The incident at the mortuary had only served to sharpen his focus on the take-over plans for O'Neill's. Bumping into the O'Neill woman like that made him re-evaluate both his time scale and his approach – he had certainly been too lenient and things were moving too slowly for his taste.

The old ways were best. His former acquaintances in Chicago did business in a way that ensured *nobody* ever dared to cross them, for fear of meeting with an 'unfortunate' and untimely end.

He should know.

Luring people into dangerous situations was a piece of cake. The last time he'd disposed of a 'problem', he was arrested, but the charges were withdrawn. There was no physical evidence against him. It had all gone up in smoke!

Now Robertson was talking to the police, he had become dangerous to his dreams of expansion and so Spitz had no option but to revert to his earlier ways. These had helped him climb the ladder of success. He'd been legitimate for long enough. It was time to get his hands dirty again.

If something should happen to Robertson, something that couldn't be tied to 'My Way', that would terrify his competitors and they would give him what he wanted. If it worked in Chicago, it would work in Sydney too. He may not have had his old cronies around him now, but he knew how things were done.

Getting rid of Robertson was the key to increasing the pressure on his rivals. The germ of an idea began to form. How could Robertson turn up dead? How? It would have to look like an accident, that's for sure, or maybe not an accident, suicide would be even better.

His business was still in the headlines for all the wrong reasons, mainly because of threatened litigation by the Sullivan family and the impending action had been announced on the latest news bulletin. But some of the most recent press coverage had been blaming an anonymous saboteur for what had happened at the Sullivan funeral and Robertson was given a sympathetic write-up in one of the leading tabloids. The Daily Herald portrayed him as a victim, rather than an incompetent undertaker. As a result, his trade had picked up again. Spitz would have to act quickly for a 'suicide' to be convincing.

He began painting the picture in his mind. He could see the headlines:

'Undertaker James Robertson Kills Himself after Shame of Ex-Mayor's Funeral.'

It was plausible – depression since the business of the Jacko Sullivan fiasco, the shock of seeing the coffin on fire, embarrassment, a downturn in his business, nowhere to turn – suicide the only way out – perfect!

And Spitz knew the perfect spot too – the old Harris place by the sea, isolated and remote, with no other houses nearby. Harris had confided to him that he was going to hospital the next day and that he was worried about squatters, because he had nobody to look in on the place. Nobody would be there. If Spitz posed as Harris, he could get Robertson up to the dilapidated house easily. The cliff was a stone's throw from the property and, with a suitable suicide note conveniently situated at the site, it could be found after an anonymous tip off and then... 'so long, James'.

It would only take a hint of the truth behind the tragedy to terrify his rivals into compliance and all their businesses would be his for a song. It would save both time and money.

Robertson's fate was sealed.

Spitz glanced at his watch – five past six pm. Maybe he was still there. He picked up the phone.

Robertson answered, "Good evening, Robertson's Funeral directors."

Spitz had placed a handkerchief over the mouthpiece to disguise his voice and mimicked the Australian drawl.

"Is that Mr Robertson?"

"Yes, how can I help?"

"Mr Robertson, my name is Andrew Harris. I wanted to take out a funeral plan with you."

"That's fine, Mr Harris, thank you for calling us. We would be very pleased to help. When would you like to come in and discuss the matter?"

"Well, there's a problem. I'm confined to my home and I'm afraid I can't get out without making a lot of complicated arrangements."

"I see, Mr Harris. Would it help if I came to see you?"

"Is that possible?"

"Yes, of course it is. Where do you live?"

Spitz smiled, this was proving to be so easy.

"I've got a small house at the end of the Bondi Coast road. It's the last one there at the end of the road."

'End of the road for you too,' thought Spitz to himself.

He could hear Robertson taking down the details.

"OK – I've got that. When would you like me to meet you, Mr Harris?"

Spitz coughed the sound of an elderly, infirm man.

"I suppose Saturday morning is out of the question?"

"As it happens, Saturday morning is fine. I'm going to be busy myself for the rest of the week, so that would fit in perfectly. Shall we say about 9:15?"

"That would be good. Thank you, Mr Robertson."

There was warmth in Robertson's reply as the conversation drew to a close.

"I'll see you Saturday morning then. Goodbye."

"Goodbye, Mr Robertson."

Spitz replaced the receiver and smiled quietly to himself. The arrangement to lure Robertson to a deserted spot had proved unbelievably easy – a suicide in a deserted spot – no witnesses, it was the perfect plan.

The sound of Radic's footsteps in the reception area momentarily distracted him from his thoughts.

"Bozz, I'm going to za shop – you want I get somezing for you too?"

"Angelo, how many times have I told you to…"

Spitz could not finish the sentence, there was absolutely no point; nothing would change.

Sensing something was not quite right, the Croat shrugged his shoulders.

"Sorry Bozz, I forget again. I go now, leave you alone, kill zum time. Back later, OK?"

Radic left and moments later the outer door shut with a definite 'click'. With silence pervading the building once more, Spitz, turned his attention back to his murderous plan.

He would start by first applying pressure to the O'Neill woman and decided to pay her an unannounced visit on Saturday morning, before his appointment with Robertson. He would warn her not to think of going to the police until she'd read the next day's headlines. By then, Robertson's suicide would be all over the papers. She'd be terrified and give him what he wanted. With O'Neill's in his hands, Humphries would follow very quickly.

He switched on the laptop and poured himself a large whisky while the machine was booting up, then turned his attention to the suicide note. It would have to be to his wife... what was her name? He'd seen it in the papers... Betty, yes that was it. How to begin? It should be short, perfunctory and to the point, while focusing on the ills that had befallen the hapless undertaker. As Spitz considered his master plan, he smiled slyly to himself – 'Yes, suicide would be a very believable option. Not only would Robertson be out of the way, Betty would be vulnerable and alone'.

He started writing:

"My dearest Betty,

Please forgive me but I can't keep the show going any more. Ever since the Sullivan funeral, things have gone from bad to worse and I can't stand it any longer. I'm sorry for the hurt I've have caused you.

I love you.

Goodbye, my darling.

James."

Spitz read the note. It certainly was short... short but effective. He clicked the 'print' button. The printer whirred into life and, in a few seconds, the printed note was on the desk. Spitz scrawled Robertson's name at the end.

Holding it up in front of him, he was reading the short text when the door opened and Radic entered unannounced.

Sheepishly he said, "Sorry Bozz – forgot again."

The expected rebuke however, never materialised. Spitz was feeling very pleased with himself.

"It's alright, Angelo, my friend. I have just changed the dynamics of the whole game, upped the ante, positioned myself for an imminent check mate and driven our unsuspecting quarry into a cul-de-sac!"

The Croat's face said it all. What the brain could not fathom was written indelibly on his countenance.

"I've found a way to get Robertson out of the picture – permanently."

Radic breathed a sigh of relief.

"He gonna leave za country, Bozz?"

"No, Angelo, he going to leave the planet."

The look of consternation returned as before.

"He's going to commit suicide, on Saturday."

"Are you zure, Bozz? You talk to him?"

Spitz slowly shook his head. It really was pointless trying to explain all but the most simple and straight forward of premises to Angelo and he wondered why he had even tried to do so – again – tonight. 'Perhaps we all live in hope,' he thought.

"No, Angelo, I didn't talk to him and, before you ask *how* I know our Mr Robertson is going to top himself on Saturday, let me say that he is going to get some help."

He pointed first to himself and then to the Croat.

"Help... know what I mean?"

A large smile grew on Radic's face as he touched the side of his nose with an index finger.

"Ahhh. I zee. Help."

\* \* \*

Kathleen stirred the gravy for the pie in the oven, while Peter sat at the kitchen table recounting the events of the day.

"Ian came over this afternoon. He had something unusual he wanted me to look into."

"Ian?"

"Ian Thompson, Detective Inspector Ian Thompson, you know, the copper I've told you about. Nice guy, a real diamond, although things have a tendency to break and catch fire around him."

"What?"

"The last bit's not important, well, unless you happen to be within range of course."

Kathleen stopped stirring.

"Peter, what *are* you talking about?"

"Sorry, got sidetracked there. Anyway, Ian wanted me to take a look at something. Seems a couple of guys at West Sydney Memorial checked out last night and the pathologist thought it looked a little strange."

She started stirring again.

"People die in hospitals all the time, Peter, they're full of sick people, remember?"

"These two were different."

"In what way?"

"Well, for starters they both looked happy and I mean *really* happy. Huge smiles. Quite spooked me at first, if you want to know the truth. Very strange, no apparent connection, except for the fact that one of the guys had been arrested for assaulting the other and of... course that grin."

Kathleen had stopped stirring the gravy. It began to bubble and rise to the top of the small saucepan, a look of bewilderment now on her face. Unnoticed, the gravy spilled over onto the electric hotplate with a loud hiss.

"Kath!"

Peter jumped up from his chair and moved the saucepan off the heat.

"Kath? What's up?"

Kathleen blinked her eyes several times, the gravity of what had been said slowly sinking in.

"You said there were *two* men?"

"That's right, two. Are you OK?"

"I'm fine, I was just thinking of something else. I think the gravy's done. Do you want to lay the table?"

Peter opened the drawer containing the knives and forks. The atmosphere had suddenly changed and he wasn't sure why. Maybe discussing work wasn't such a good idea. During the meal and for the remainder of the evening, he kept the conversation light, but the atmosphere remained the same, even with the distraction of the television.

At length, Peter looked at his watch and stretched.

"I'm going to turn in, Kath, it's been a long day. Are you coming to bed?"

"What?"

"I said I'm going to bed. Why don't you come too, you seem to be pre-occupied. Was it something I said?"

Kathleen threw her arms around him and hugged him tightly.

"No, darling, it's not you, it's me. I'm sorry to be a bore. I've got a lot on at the moment. I just need to think a few things over, that's all."

"About us?"

There was real concern in his voice.

"No silly, not about us. That's the one thing I'm certain of. Just some work things. Go on, you go to bed. I'll join you shortly."

She kissed him tenderly.

"I love you, Peter Wilson. You're the best thing that ever happened to me."

He returned the kiss and stood up.

"And I love you too, Kathleen O'Neill. I'll keep your side of the bed warm, OK?"

Sitting in the quiet, Kathleen tried to piece together the events of last night. What had gone wrong? Jock's passing had been planned, but the second man, well, that had come as a complete shock. What had gone wrong?

The bottle was empty when she got there. If there were two men, then somebody shared his drink. Who?! It had to be the guy on the ward, the one who'd attacked Jock. At least she prayed it was, because, whilst she hadn't set out to kill anybody, she would never be able to live with the thought that a wholly innocent man was dead because of her. If it was Jock's attacker, then it was Jock and not her who bore the responsibility of the second man's death, but even that thought made her feel sick. Did the other man really deserve to die?

What if it had been one of Jock's friends, who'd decided to visit, and he had nothing to do with the attack on Jock? It didn't bear thinking about. The thought was just too horrible.

Now the police were involved. It wouldn't take them long to establish her link with Jock or that she had seen him that final evening. Peter was bound to find out now and would want to know why she hadn't mentioned that she'd visited the Scotsman. What would he think? Would he put two and two together? If he found out what she'd done, it would be over between them. She'd be locked up. It was all becoming too much and her head was spinning, trying to untangle what exactly had gone wrong.

Enough! The rebuke stopped the machinations cold. Enough for one night. Get some sleep, and pick it up tomorrow, she tried telling herself. Peter was breathing deeply and evenly as she slipped in beside him. Unconsciously, he rolled towards her and slipped a protective arm around her shoulders, his warm body melting away the fevered concerns of the past few hours.

'Tomorrow,' she thought to herself, 'deal with this tomorrow,' but she didn't sleep all night long.

\* \* \*

The following morning, Peter was at his desk by nine am and going over the lab reports from the hospital. They'd certainly done all the standard tests and some additional ones as well. In fact, it was pretty much what he'd expected from someone of Tagashi's calibre – thorough, systematic and organised. The blood reports looked normal, no obvious evidence of any kind of pathogen, viral, bacterial or fungal and no obvious toxicological signs or markers. In short, a complete mystery, yet something had dispatched two men within a very short space of time. The question though, was what?

By midday, he had completed his own analyses of the blood and tissue samples provided by the hospital and he was no further ahead than Tagashi. He had reached a brick wall and needed to apply a different logic as he ran the details over in his mind.

'Come on, Wilson, think. What's missing, first principles go outside the box... what's the most likely cause? Virus? No. Bacterium? No. Fungus? No. Poison? Yes.' Already, his mind felt more flexible as he explored the last possibility.

'OK – poison, what kind? Which poisons are the most potent? Mineral? No! Animal? No! Plant? Yes! Haven't seen this before, so maybe it's a new one or a very old one. How does that feel? It's possible, but where to start?'

His mind was now running like a finely-tuned machine as he considered the next step.

'Old books... need some old books. The library downstairs, as good as any a place to begin.'

There were dozens of Toxicology books in the Forensics library, many of them quite old and if the answer lay buried in the past, there was a fair chance he would find it there.

Several hours later, Peter had narrowed his search down to four likely candidates, none of which he had ever come across before. All four plants grew in moderate climates, fared poorly in the winter months but were widespread throughout the British Isles and Ireland. The leaves of all had euphoric properties, but in one, the roots contained a dangerous neuro-toxin and would cause the heart to stop beating almost immediately, once the poison reached the blood supply. There was no further information on how the toxin was extracted or indeed measured and no drawing of the plant.

Deciding to pursue this one species further, he scoured another three specialist books, until at last he came across a telling phrase. 'The active ingredient in the leaves has a euphoric effect, but the roots of the plant contain a deadly neuro-toxin. Any contamination of the extracted plant juice with the root will form a lethal combination. It was used as an analgesic in the Middle Ages, but fell out of favour due to frequent contamination by the roots which often proved fatal. Accidental deaths, caused in this way were determined by an expression of intense happiness on the faces of the deceased at the time of death."

There was a drawing of the variegated leaf, showing the veins, which had small purple flecks. It was related to the Belladonna family and he recalled a very similar plant he'd seen in the wild, when gathering samples, as a student. His lecturer had told him that the Australian wild flower was related to a European variety, which was highly toxic and used as a poison in the Middle Ages.

Bingo! This had to be worth following up – it ticked all the boxes – the grin, the potency, all the symptoms.

However, even if he could identify the plant, because of the way it appeared to break down in the body, leaving no trace, it would still be impossible to verify his theory. A thought persisted at the back of his mind, and wouldn't go away. He had seen a plant with leaves very similar to this recently, he couldn't quite put his finger on when and where. Or was it a drawing? It would come to him.

A voice behind him made him look up.

"They told me I'd find you down here."

It was Ian Thompson. He had seemingly appeared from nowhere, while Peter was trolling through the stack of old books.

"Ian. I didn't hear you – had my nose buried in these dusty covers for the past few hours, but I think I may have found something – not sure yet, but it looks promising."

"What have you got?"

"I've found something very interesting here, but I want to do a bit more research, before I get too excited. I haven't got anything new to add to Tagashi's results yet. If these deaths, strange though they are, are no more than coincidence, and I find that hard to accept, a drug of some kind would look like the most likely culprit, but I have to try to identify what substances might have been used to make it. We have no clues from the autopsy, only the fact that these men looked deliriously happy when they died. Most poisons, such as arsenic or wolfsbane leave a trace – there's always a small amount, microscopic sometimes, which remains in the cells, hair, blood, that kind of thing. But, in this case, there's nothing, nothing at all. With no chemical evidence, I can only guess at what the origin of such a substance might be, and whilst I think it's most likely to have come from a plant, it's just speculation at the moment."

"I'd say you're on the right track, Peter."

In fact, the Inspector didn't have a clue.

Thompson continued, "I can't see a motive for any deliberate poisoning. I've still got an open mind, but it looks as though Cosgrove got high on his own supply. Maybe he was using something new. There are a few new legal herbs on the market and we never know their side effects, until something like this happens and we make them illegal."

This theory still had gaps and Thompson knew it. How did Strapp come to get his hands on the drug and end up dead? Surely, Cosgrove wouldn't have sold any to him. That would be very unlikely if there was bad blood between them. This would indicate the existence of a third party with access to the substance, who supplied it to both men.

Could it have anything to do with Spitz? It was unlikely because, whilst he was seen with Cosgrove, other people were outside on the balcony at the same time and other than that, Spitz had no connection to Strapp.

Nothing fitted, and with no forensic evidence, it was hard to know where to begin. The policeman was good at gathering information, but putting it all together was a lot harder. He generally followed the most obvious path.

Peter picked up a leather-bound book and passed it across to Thompson, his index finger pointing to a description of a plant.

"This one here – *Morticius Aberaeum* – what you might call the prime suspect."

Thompson read carefully the description of the toxins that came from the plant.

"How old is this book, Peter?"

"Printed in 1901 and probably not in circulation anymore. There are lots of nuggets like this down here."

The policeman continued to read, his eyes widening when he came to one sentence.

"The subjects would display an expression of intense happiness at the time of death."

Peter smiled.

"Yes, that caught my eye too. What do you think?"

"Interesting, very interesting," smiled Thompson.

"It's a start, wouldn't you say?"

"Yes, it's a very promising start. Thanks for your help, Peter. You're the best man for a job like this. I'm lucky to have you. Do you mind if I photocopy a couple of pages?"

"Sure, I'll sort that out for you."

Standing by the photocopier, Peter had no idea just how dangerous he was going to make all this for his fiancée.

## Chapter 24

## Suspicions

Thompson rose early the next morning. He was keen to make progress in the investigation and wanted to speak to Kathleen sooner than later. He telephoned just after 9am and made an arrangement to call at O'Neill's around ten thirty. He had placed a similar call to Spitz and was due there at midday.

Kathleen was bright and pleasant when she came out of her office to greet him.

"Inspector Thompson, good morning. Please, come in. Tea? Coffee?"

"I'm fine, thanks, Ms O'Neill."

She gestured him to a comfortable chair and drew up another beside it.

"Please call me Kathleen or Kath, I mean, if that's alright. I know this is official business, but Peter has told me so much about you and it feels strange being this formal."

"That's perfectly fine, Kathleen it is then, and I guess while we're on the subject, please call me Ian. Peter is a lucky man."

She blushed slightly at the compliment.

"The reason I wanted to see you this morning, Kathleen, is to ask you a few questions about Mr James Strapp. He died suddenly in hospital two days ago."

Kathleen's shoulders sagged.

"Yes, I know. I had asked the nurses to inform me if there was any deterioration in his condition, and they called to let me know he'd died."

"I understand from the nursing staff, that you were his only visitor. What exactly was your relationship with Mr Strapp?"

"I'm a hospital volunteer, Ian. I had a rather bad car crash recently and I decided to find out how the other person was. I knew he'd been taken to the West Sydney Memorial, because he was on the stretcher next to mine, and I realised that he was badly injured. With my contacts, it wasn't hard for me to find out who he was and which ward he was on, and even though the accident wasn't my fault, to be honest, I felt responsible for what had happened. Did you know that the accident left him paralysed from the waist down?"

"Yes, his doctor told me when I spoke to him, but it wasn't your fault, Kathleen, I read the report and he was speeding. It's lucky for you that you weren't more seriously injured."

"I know, but I still felt awful, when I found out, and then when I went to see him, he told me he was terminally ill. The poor man. He was so brave and he asked me to keep visiting him. I really felt I had to go. We grew very close in the short time that I knew Jock. I was sad when the hospital phoned to tell me he'd died."

"Jock?" queried the policeman.

"It was his nickname. I guess being Scottish and with a surname like Strapp it must have been the obvious choice," she laughed.

Thompson smiled.

"Did you visit him in hospital last Tuesday evening?"

Without flinching Kathleen replied, "Yes. I had to arrange for the collection of a client's father who had just passed away in the same hospital. While I was there, I thought I may as well pop in to see Jock."

"What time was that?"

Thompson wanted to find out if Kathleen had seen anybody either with Jock or near his room.

"I popped in for only a few minutes around 7.30 because I had to go down to the morgue," she lied. She was pretty sure nobody had seen her go back upstairs afterwards.

"How was Jock when you saw him?"

"Do you mean was he happy, sad, that kind of thing?"

"Yes, what state of mind was he in? Did he seem anxious or upset? Was he different from the other times you saw him?"

Kathleen smiled.

"Ian, Jock was one of the most irrepressible characters I've ever met, despite his circumstances. He grappled with life head on, but he was very angry to be so incapacitated and annoyed that he couldn't ride his bike. In truth, both of those things seemed to bother him far more than the fact he had a terminal illness. But he still had a great sense of humour and always made me laugh when I visited. I shall really miss him."

"So he confided in you a lot. Mmm, that brings me to my next question. Did he ever talk to you of wanting to commit suicide?"

Thompson took her completely off guard. She recovered well, coughing slightly, and helping herself to a glass of water.

"Are you OK, Kathleen? This must be very upsetting for you."

"I'm sorry Ian, I think I'm coming down with something, I've got a slightly sore throat."

"Are you OK to continue?"

"Of course. I want to help in any way I can. No, he never mentioned taking his own life."

"Did you ever see any other visitors while you were there, or did he mention anybody else who came to see him?"

Kathleen decided not to reveal any more than she had to.

"No. Jock was a very private man. I don't know if he had any other visitors. I'm sure people would have come to see Jock, but I think he was so embarrassed by his disability, he didn't tell anybody he was in hospital."

"Did he ever mention the name 'Kevin Cosgrove' to you?"

"No. That name doesn't ring any bells."

Her father had warned her, if questions were ever asked about a client who'd used their service, never to reveal anything that she didn't have to, but be totally open about everything that could be found out. This would draw the least attention and though Michael had never been in such a situation, here she was, being questioned after only the first time.

Thompson jotted down her reply in his notebook.

Kathleen leaned slightly forward.

"Is there something else, Ian, something I'm missing?"

"You're very astute, young lady."

"In my profession, what's not said can be equally, if not more, important than what is."

Thompson nodded and smiled.

"Touché. Yes, there is another aspect to this investigation. A second man also died on the same night and we think in very similar circumstances."

"But, Ian, it's a hospital. People die in hospitals all the time and West Sydney Memorial is huge."

"The other man was the one who attacked our Mr Strapp, two months ago. He was just visiting a friend of his, on the same ward as Jock, when he died and, when I said 'in very similar circumstances' to your friend, I mean *very* similar."

Kathleen gasped.

"You believe there's a connection?"

Whilst she feigned surprise, she could now guess what had happened. The man Jock had told her about had gone into his room, perhaps to taunt him. Whilst she wasn't glad, a second person had died, at least it wasn't a completely innocent visitor, something which she would have found almost impossible to live with. The second man was Jock's assailant and it was almost certainly Jock who had poisoned him, deliberately or otherwise. It made her feel a little better knowing that, but it was a lesson for her never to leave anybody alone with a bottle of the remedy again.

The policeman was contemplating her question.

"Obviously, I can't say too much at this point, the investigation is at an early stage, but yes, I believe there is a connection."

"Oh, my God!"

"Quite. Kathleen, there's something else I need to ask you about. Do you know Jerome Spitz from 'My Way' Funeral Home?"

Kathleen shuddered involuntarily and this time she couldn't hide it. The reaction wasn't lost on Thompson.

"Know is not a word I would choose, Ian. I know who he is of course, but from what I see and hear, he is not a man I would care to know."

"Have you ever spoken with him?"

"Yes, he and another man, approached me recently to ask to buy my business and I told them I wasn't interested in selling."

Thompson said nothing. He now deduced that Robertson must be telling the truth after all, but couldn't understand why Humphries was lying. Was he in cahoots with Spitz?

"Then I saw him again, this Tuesday, when I went to make the collection arrangements for a client's deceased father, Mr Trumball."

"You met Spitz in the morgue?"

"Yes, him and a foul-smelling brute. There'd been a mix up by the mortuary attendant. Spitz collected the wrong body – Mr Trumball no less, the one I had gone to collect. They'd brought it back to get the right one and we all met in the basement."

"What time would this have been?"

"Oh, around eight, I think. I was down there for about thirty minutes, trying to sort out the forms, before they arrived. I went out for a few minutes to the ladies and when I got back to the morgue, Spitz and his 'associate' were both in there."

"And that was only the second time you met Mr Spitz and Mr Radic?"

Kathleen nodded.

"Yes. Is Radic the sidekick?"

"I think Mr Radic would prefer the term 'associate', but yes, that's his name."

"Nasty type."

"Yes, so I've heard," confirmed Thompson.

This was a moment of further enlightenment. The inspector now knew that Spitz was trying to get his hands on three funeral directors in his patch. Might he after all have something to do with the death of Jock and Cosgrove? Did he know that Kath visited Jock? Did he have her followed? Had he set up a hit that back-fired? Perhaps he was trying to frame her. In any event, he would be speaking to Spitz next.

Kathleen rapped her fingers on the desk and raised her eyebrows.

"Would there be anything else I can help you with, Ian? It's just that I've got a really busy day and…"

"Of course. No, I'm pretty much done for now."

Thompson rose from his chair and extracted a card from his wallet.

"Thank you, Kathleen, you've been very helpful. My direct number's on here. If you think of anything, even if you think it's unimportant, give me a call, OK?"

Kathleen also rose and they walked to the door.

"Sure, Ian, if anything pops up, I'll let you know."

They shook hands, while Kathleen held the door open for the policeman.

"Goodbye, Kathleen."

"Goodbye, Ian."

Back inside the sanctuary of her office, Kathleen breathed a sigh of relief. For a moment, she thought the policeman had been on to her, but his manner and the disclosure about the second man suggested otherwise. The picture was much clearer now than before. Either the wily Scotsman had tricked Cosgrove into drinking some of the mixture as a payback for attacking him or perhaps the lethal cocktail was taken from Jock before he'd finished drinking it. Whether by invitation or force, Cosgrove and Jock had shared the O'Neill family remedy, with fatal results. By all accounts, Cosgrove was a nasty piece of work and she got the sense that Thompson was glad to have him out of the way.

Ironically, she realised that Cosgrove's untimely death had probably removed more suspicion from her than it had created. The links between Jock, Cosgrove and her were obscure and disconnected.

What Kathleen had been completely unprepared for were the questions around Spitz and Radic. Peter had told her that the Sullivan funeral and a hearse belonging to Humphries had been deliberately sabotaged. Given Spitz and Radic's attempt to intimidate her and the clear interest Thompson had in them, it suggested a dark involvement between those two and the corresponding problems suffered by her colleagues in the funeral trade. Was it possible they were leaning on other undertakers as they had tried to do on her?

She had the sense that events were unfolding outside her control and that gave her cause for concern, but, at this present point in time, there was little she could do but maintain a consistent, low profile. She had no desire for Thompson to put her under the microscope because, despite his clumsiness, Peter was working with him quite closely and he was a lot sharper than the detective.

* * *

Thompson arrived at 'My Way' Funeral Home promptly at noon.

A middle aged receptionist greeted him as he entered the office.

"Good afternoon, may I help you?"

"Yes. Detective Inspector Thompson. I have an appointment with Mr Spitz – twelve o'clock."

She brushed an errant strand of bleached hair from over her eyes and picked up the intercom.

"Take a seat, Inspector. I'll let Mr Spitz know you're here."

A moment later the main office door opened and Spitz appeared.

"Inspector Thompson, please come in."

The bonhomie was gone and Thompson instinctively felt the man was on his guard.

"No Mr Radic?"

"I'm afraid he's attending to other matters at the moment. You didn't indicate you wanted him present too. Shall I call him?"

Thompson had settled himself in a chair and was searching for his notebook in his jacket pocket.

"No, that won't be necessary, Mr Spitz. I'm sure you can give me all the information I need."

"So what is this all about?"

"Last Tuesday evening two men were found dead at the West Sydney Memorial Hospital in very unusual circumstances."

Spitz could not suppress a short laugh.

"Inspector, it's a hospital, a very large hospital, and people have been known to pass away in hospitals. Or maybe that hadn't occurred to you?"

The sarcasm irritated Thompson and he made little effort to hide it.

"Do you know a James Strapp or a Kevin Cosgrove?"

"Are these the two deceased you're referring to?"

"Yes."

"No, I didn't know them, should I have?"

"Were you at West Sydney Memorial Hospital on Tuesday evening?"

"Yes, I was there with Mr Radic to collect a body from the mortuary."

"At what time?"

"Around eight pm, although there will be a record, but I suppose you've already checked that."

Thompson was writing in the small leather bound book.

"Did either you or Mr Radic go to the eighth floor that evening?"

"I enjoy an occasional cigar, Inspector, and there's a roof terrace on the eight floor. As I recall, I may have smoked a small cheroot while Mr Radic was finalising the collection."

Thompson was surprised that Spitz admitted he'd been up to Jock's floor. If he did have anything to hide, then he was a very cool customer.

"The eight floor? That's rather a long way to go for a smoke, wouldn't you say? What's wrong with the alley outside?"

"The view, Inspector. The view from the alley is less than gratifying, while on the other hand, the view from the eighth floor is quite spectacular."

"I see. Did you go anywhere else on that ward apart from the roof garden?"

"No, just the roof terrace!" Spitz was now irked. "Are we almost done here, Inspector?

Thompson ignored the question and pressed on.

"Do you recall the man you were talking to on the balcony on the eighth floor?"

"What man?"

"Mr Cosgrove, one of the deceased!"

Spitz was irritated. He wasn't sure where this was going.

"I didn't speak to anybody on the balcony. People come out all the time for a cigarette, but I didn't notice anybody in particular," he a paused for effect, "now I really do have a lot to be getting on with, so, unless there are any other questions you have for me...?"

The sentence trailed in the air and Thompson stood up.

"Just one. Apart from last Tuesday evening, when you were bringing back the wrong body to collect the right one," it was the policeman's turn to be sarcastic, "have you ever met Kathleen O'Neill of O'Neill's Funeral Directors?"

Without missing a beat, Spitz replied, "I did have occasion to speak with her a short while ago on a business matter."

"Was that at her premises?"

"Yes."

"Was Mr Radic also present?"

"Yes. You said *one* question Inspector and that makes three. Now, if you've got something to say, why don't you stop beating around the bush and come out and say it? Have I committed some crime? Am I under arrest?"

Thompson returned the notebook to his jacket pocket, and looked Spitz squarely in the eye.

"Not yet, but I'm working on it, Mr Spitz. I'll see myself out. Good day."

A vein on Spitz's temple had begun to throb. Thompson was on to something, he was sure of it. Had that bitch been talking as well? And what was all that palaver about Strapp and Cosgrove? Things going pear-shaped often had the Radic touch about them. Maybe there was something about that night he didn't know, something connected to the initial, bungled collection.

Picking up the intercom and asking the receptionist to send in Radic never even crossed his mind.

Instead, at the top of his lungs, he simply screamed, "Angelo! Get in here *now*!"

He appeared in seconds.

"Bozz? You vanted me?"

Spitz's sat down heavily, holding his palm over his forehead. His head was hurting.

* * *

"Kath?"

It was the early hours of Friday morning and Peter was wide awake and the bedside digital clock read one thirty seven. They had made love and fallen asleep almost immediately, but now sleep eluded him.

"Kath, are you awake?"

"Mmm," she rolled into his arms, her head on his chest.

"Tell me about the O'Neill crest."

"What? Not now, Peter, I'm tired."

"Please, then you can go back to sleep, I promise."

"From my great, great grandfather," her voice was still thick with sleep, "always been in the family. Go to sleep, Peter, go to sleep."

She turned over and drew the covers around her and was instantly asleep again.

But Peter could not sleep, something about the crest suddenly came into his mind and, for the life of him, he had no idea why it should have entered his thoughts now, when all was still and quiet, with a beautiful woman sleeping by his side. But it was there, and it would not go away. What *was* it about the O'Neill crest? The Latin inscription – no that wasn't it. The Irish colours? No, not that either. The garland? The garland, it was the garland! But *what* was it about the garland? It looked familiar. He had seen it before somewhere, somewhere recently.

'Come on, *think.*'

The revelation, when it came, made him gasp involuntarily. Kathleen stirred slightly but remained deeply asleep. The book, the old book in the Forensics library – there was a drawing of a leaf. It was the same as the garland, on the O'Neill crest, he was sure of it. All those years of studying Botany had taught him to note similarities between the species. But there was more – an actual plant... he'd seen it recently, a plant with leaves that looked the same as those on the O'Neill crest... but where had he seen it? He looked at the bedside clock – two thirteen am, and the illuminated digits made him think of the clock on the cooker, in the kitchen. That was it! The kitchen, he'd seen the plant in the kitchen nestled in among several others. All at once, a coldness enveloped him, washing away the euphoria of the discovery. An actual plant was in *Kathleen's* kitchen, not just a description in some dusty book. A toxic plant that induced a smiling death mask was in his fiancée's kitchen. He remembered asking her about the plant ages ago and she'd told him it was her father's. He knew it looked familiar then, but now he'd made the link.

'Calm down, Wilson,' he told himself. 'There's probably a perfectly reasonable explanation for the whole thing. Wait. Maybe it's not the same plant. The description could match a million plants. Well,' he thought, 'there's only one way to find out.'

Slowly, he slid out of the bed and wrapped a towel around his waist before heading into the kitchen. The clock from the cooker covered everything in a pale green light, including the plants on the window ledge. Peter snapped on the extractor light and lifted the leafy green plant, almost buried beneath the thriving spider plant next to it, onto the work surface. Carefully examining it under the strong white light, he noted the shape of the leaves, their size, the distinctive markings and variegation at the leaf edges. It was unmistakable. They matched both the O'Neill's crest and the written description, and drawing, in the library book. This was indeed *Morticius Aberaeum.*

"Peter?" it was Kathleen, calling from the bedroom in a sleepy voice.

The sudden sound startled him, almost causing him to drop the plant. He saw that a number of leaves had been removed… at least six and the soil looked a little raised as though the plant may have been re-potted. Following a hunch, he gently prised the plant away from its pot. His heart sank as he spotted, just below the surface, a small piece of a root tendril, which had been broken off. Quickly, he pushed it back down and packed the earth back as it had been. Carefully, he replaced the plant back onto the window ledge, leaving it as he'd found it nestled, among the other plants. His mind was racing as he made his way back into the bedroom.

Now he remembered the *two* whisky bottles and the way Kathleen had jumped up and grabbed them from him. Her explanation that they were presents, despite the fact that both bottles were almost empty, didn't make sense even at the time. In fact, nothing made sense any more. The evidence was pointing to Kathleen, but how could the woman he loved be a serial killer? He must be losing his mind.

"Peter?" she called again.

"I was just getting a glass of water, Kath."

He tried to sound normal. He felt anything but.

Back in bed, her warm body snuggled up to his.

"I was dreaming, I thought you'd gone away, far far away."

"No chance, I'm not going anywhere."

Tenderly, he kissed her on the cheek and gently stroked her hair.

"Now go back to sleep, it's late."

In a few minutes, she was fast asleep while a hundred questions raced through his head. He looked at the clock again – two fifty five am – and made a determined effort to clear his mind and think about these things tomorrow, tomorrow in the cold light of day. When at last sleep came, it was intermittent and troubled, punctuated by visions of green plants with distinctive variegated leaves and smiling faces.

The alarm by the side of the bed announced the beginning of a new day as Kathleen fumbled to find the off switch. Peter was still deeply asleep as she rose from the bed, wrapped a dressing gown around her and headed for the kitchen. Even though it was just before seven o'clock, bright sunlight poured through the window, causing her to squint, as she mechanically turned on the small radio and filled the electric kettle. The radio announcer was wrapping up the last hour of the breakfast show.

The kettle boiled and Kathleen made two cups of tea and returned to the bedroom.

Peter was still very much asleep, sprawled across the bed with his head half under the pillow. Kathleen placed the tea on the bedside cabinet and sat down next to him.

"Hey, sleepyhead, it's time to wake up."

Gently, she nibbled his earlobe and ran her fingers through his hair. Slowly, he began to stir into life and rolled onto his back.

Instinctively he reached up and drew her towards him.

"Come back to bed, Kath."

He needed to be close to her. He wanted to dispel the horrible suspicions from his mind. Kathleen drew away and removed his hands from her shoulders.

"Peter, you've got to go to work. Come on, wake up."

Seeing her with the morning sunlight in her hair, he felt ashamed of himself. He must have been mad ever to think that Kathleen would hurt anybody… It was a coincidence, it had to be. Jock and Cosgrove's demise were more likely to be drug-related than anything to do with plants or toxins. Even Thompson thought so. He'd let his imagination run away with him and he felt guilty for having entertained such dark thoughts.

"Come back to bed, Kath. I'll call in sick."

A wandering hand reached up and cupped her breast.

Kathleen giggled and stood up.

"Well, there's nothing wrong with you, that's for sure. There's a cup of tea by the bed. I'm going to jump in the shower. You'd better drink it and get up or else you'll be late for work."

Peter was dimly aware of Kathleen walking down the passageway and into the bathroom as he propped himself up on one elbow. A sip of the strong, hot brew helped him back to consciousness as he shook the sleep from his eyes. By the time half the cup was gone, he was fully awake. He sat up in bed, contemplating the events of last night, when Kathleen returned from the shower dressed in the bathrobe and with a towel wrapped around her head.

Seeing Peter awake she smiled broadly.

"Well, that's an improvement. Another cup?"

Peter shook his head.

"No, thanks, love, I'm fine."

"Looks like it's going to be a lovely day, not a cloud in the sky and not too hot either. At least that's what the forecast says."

She removed the towel and rubbed her long dark hair vigorously before brushing it with several long strokes. Peter watched in silence, she was so beautiful and natural, it sometimes took his breath away. Yet, though he'd calmed down, he was still troubled by what he had discovered last night and he had to talk about it.

Had she given anybody any cuttings from the plant? Could that explain the missing leaves?

"Kath, the plant on the window ledge in the kitchen."

"What?"

"The one on the window ledge in the kitchen, with the funny coloured leaves, next to the spider plant."

The brushing stopped.

"What about it?"

"Where did it come from?"

Kathleen resumed the brushing.

"It was my dad's, he loved it. Frankly, with my green thumbs, or should I say lack of them, I'm surprised it's still alive. Anyway, why the sudden interest?"

"No special reason, really, just that it's different. Can't say I've ever seen a species like it before, have you?"

"Never gave it much thought. Dad loved to potter around with exotic plants and flowers. I guess this was just one of the ones that survived."

She gave nothing away. Years of practice had taught her to protect the family secret.

Kathleen placed the brush on the dressing table and selected a pair of panties and bra from a drawer.

"It's seven thirty. If you don't get going soon, you'll be late for work. Come on, throw yourself in the shower and I'll make us some breakfast."

She slipped out of the robe and stood naked before him, the small pair of knickers in one hand.

"God, you're beautiful, Kath."

"I bet you say that to all the girls!"

"No, I don't and yes, you are."

Quickly, Kathleen slipped on the underwear and began rummaging in the wardrobe for a dress.

"Peter Wilson, I can feel your eyes all over me," Kathleen said giggling.

Peter threw back the sheet and stood up. He wished it was the weekend, but he knew he had to get a move on or he would be late.

"Think you're right, I'll grab a shower."

Kathleen turned around, her eyes drawn to his groin and the growing erection.

"Think you'd better make it a cold one!"

Peter smiled as he walked into the bathroom and turned on the shower. He was very much in love with this woman and she with him. On the surface, it was the perfect match, but his emotions were oscillating between faith and fear. There was something in the shadows, something indefinable he couldn't quite put his finger on, something that was lurking and waiting to rise up and torpedo it all. Stepping into the shower, he felt the hot water wash away the anxieties of the night and soothe his body.

Things that were larger than life in the darkness of the night often felt less ominous in the brightness of the morning. As he stood under the hot, cascading water, he began to relax and the conscious, rational mind took charge. What *was* he thinking about last night? Logic and fact had always been his credo and suddenly two plus two equalled five. Kath had answered all his questions about the plant without a hint of hesitation or guilt. Was he seriously entertaining a link between Kathleen and the deaths of two people in hospital?

"Wake up, Wilson," he spoke out loud stopping the train of thought in his mind.

'She's the best thing that's ever happened to you. The sweetest, kindest and most beautiful person God ever gave breath to. Kathleen involved with the two bizarre hospital deaths? I must be going mad.'

He shut off the water and reached for a towel. The shower had sharpened his senses and washed away the remnants of sleep. Quickly, he dried and berated himself at the same time for thinking the unthinkable.

"Peter, breakfast's ready."

"Coming."

He wrapped the towel around his waist and walked into the kitchen.

Approaching her from behind, he gently placed his hands on her hips, and turned her around to face him.

She responded by slipping her arms around his neck.

"What is it? Is everything OK?"

"Everything's perfect, Kath. I just wanted to say I love you."

"Oh, Peter, you're so sweet."

She kissed him tenderly.

"I love you too. Now come on. Your breakfast's going to go cold."

Peter sat down, a warm glow spreading through his body. This felt good, good and right.

"Coffee?" Kathleen had the percolator poised above a coffee cup.

Peter was looking at the green plant on the window ledge as a chill ran down his spine. Something in the shadows was still there.

"Peter? Would you like some coffee?"

"Ta, Kath. That would be great."

The plant seemed to look back at him and, there and then, he had an instinctive feeling that whatever secrets it held, they would soon reveal themselves.

Two hours later, Peter was at work but unable to completely shake off the nagging worry that had been with him all night. He had been staring at his monitor for the past twenty minutes and had only managed to draft the first sentence of a report due for completion that afternoon. What troubled him most was the conflict that had arisen between his brain and his heart. His mind had deduced that the most probable cause of death in the Strapp and Cosgrove cases was a toxin made from the *Morticius Aberaeum* plant. The effects were text-book. The fact there was a connection between one of the deceased and Kathleen and that it was almost certainly one of these same rare plants growing in her kitchen, gave rise to a multitude of conflicting emotions, disbelief being the prime one, disbelief that she could be involved in any way at all. Certainly, her explanation that the plant was simply her father's was entirely plausible and it was within the realms of possibility that others may have had cuttings, but yet there was an element of... doubt. Yes, that was it, doubt.

Peter's mind was in turmoil, torn between the suspicion that, in some way, Kathleen may be involved in these two inexplicable but clearly connected deaths and the immense love and trust he felt for her. After all these years, he had found someone whom he loved and who loved him in return and now this part of his life felt like it was in imminent jeopardy and that scared him, scared him more than he could bear.

He needed to talk to someone and sooner rather than later. There was only one person who entered his mind and, without hesitation, he picked up the telephone and dialled an internal number. The voice at the other end was clipped and no-nonsense.

"Thompson," immediately followed by a small clunking sound and a muted expletive.

"Ian, it's Peter. Is everything OK?"

"Bloody coffee, it's gone everywhere. Just a moment."

The sounds of desktop items being shuffled about and suppressed angry noises were picked up by the handset.

Eventually, Thompson came back on the line.

"Sorry about that. Some clown put my cup right by the telephone cord – that was an accident waiting to happen. Still, no real damage. What can I do for you, Peter?"

"Hi, Ian, I was thinking about the Strapp – Cosgrove case. I was wondering if you'd come up with anything new."

"I've been turning it over in my mind now for the last few days and the whole thing is clear as mud," responded the policeman. "I've got a couple of interesting new leads, but nothing solid. What about you, have you got anything for me in that lab of yours?"

"Well, Ian, I think I may have come across a likely candidate for your anonymous poison. Can you spare an hour if I pop down?"

"Of course. When?"

"How about now?"

"Fine. I'll put the kettle on."

"That's great, Ian. I'd love a cup."

A distinctive smell of coffee greeted Peter as he approached Thompson's desk, which was now neat and ordered. People often took Thompson for a bumbling fool, yet once he had latched on to a case, he was like a relentless terrier that never gave up. Peter admired his tenacity, if nothing else and, despite his chaotic character, the inspector often came up with good leads, even though he found it challenging to make any sense of them. Yet, despite all of this, Peter couldn't help but like the detective.

"Ah, Peter."

Thompson moved to the flip chart.

Peter couldn't help but notice the box with 'O'Neill's' written in it. A dotted line connected that box to another – 'My Way'.

"What's this about? O'Neill's and 'My Way'?"

"You know me, Peter, I think better using boxes. I'm just trying to get a visual picture of the main witnesses and how they all fit together. It turns out that, on the evening Cosgrove and Strapp checked out, Kathleen and Spitz from 'My Way' were both at the same hospital on or about the same time the two men died, hence my two little boxes."

Peter's heart missed a beat.

"As it happens, both had a verifiable reason for being there. The records showed that they each had to collect a body from the morgue, but there was a mix-up when 'My Way', collected the body that O'Neill's were meant to collect. Other than that, there's nothing strange about either of them attending the morgue."

"I'm not sure where all this is going, Ian?"

"I uncovered a very interesting new fact. When I spoke to your Kathleen, she confirmed that Spitz and Radic had approached her too about buying her business and that she'd told them she wasn't interested."

Peter hid his surprise really well. Kath hadn't told him either about Spitz's offer to buy O'Neill's or about the mix-up in the morgue. He felt that a dark and mysterious side of this woman was emerging. Peter was asking himself why Kath hadn't mentioned any of it before. Hadn't he told her to call him if anything out of the ordinary happened? He was hoping Ian would be able to fill in some of the gaps in his knowledge of his fiancée's life. Thompson broke his line of thought, unaware of the can of worms he had just opened up.

"I have spoken to Robertson and Humphries, you may remember it was Robertson who handled the Jacko Sullivan burial, the one that turned into a cremation and it was Humphries' hearse where a bomb blew up the engine?"

Peter nodded.

"Yes, of course, I did the tests."

"Well, it appears our Mr Spitz has been leaning pretty heavily on Robertson though I can't prove it yet, but Humphries is pretty guarded and hasn't told me anything about attempts at extortion. I suspect our American friend had something to do with the explosives and the problems with Jacko's send off. I wanted to be sure that Kathleen hadn't felt intimidated like Robertson, so I interviewed the morgue attendant and I asked him to tell me how Kathleen had behaved around Spitz. According to him, Kathleen gave Spitz a piece of her mind for collecting her client instead of his own, so I don't think you have anything to worry about. I'd say your girl can stand up for herself."

"Kath is soft, but she's no push over, Ian. I'm sure she would have told me if she thought she had a problem," Peter responded, hoping the reason she hadn't mentioned it was that she hadn't thought the incident important enough to discuss.

"After I'd spoken to Kath, I interviewed Spitz. His reason for being at the hospital corroborated the statements I'd been given by Kathleen and the morgue attendant. However the previous afternoon, I had also interviewed one of the nurses, who had been on duty when Jock and Cosgrove died and she positively identified Spitz as being on the eighth floor. He was outside on the balcony with Cosgrove, immediately before he died. When I asked Spitz whether he'd gone to the eighth floor, he admitted it straight away and told me he'd gone there to have a smoke… said he liked the view."

"That's a bit strange," Peter commented.

"That's what I thought, but what's interesting about that is that it puts both Spitz and Kathleen on the same ward as the two men who died."

This was making Peter very nervous, but he knew Ian well enough to know that he didn't suspect his fiancée of anything or he wouldn't have been discussing the matter with him. Peter scratched the side of his head. He was certainly surprised that Spitz had gone up to the eighth floor, but he was much more surprised that Kathleen had been there at all.

"I've also been doing a lot of thinking about these two," continued Thompson pointing to another two boxes labelled 'Strapp' and 'Cosgrove'. "After Cosgrove's assault on Strapp, the Scotsman was taken unconscious to the West Sydney Memorial and the brain cancer was discovered purely by chance. He was discharged, but then found himself back in hospital after the crash. It's uncanny that the accident brought Kathleen and Jock together, isn't it?"

"What accident?"

"When Jock crashed into your girlfriend, didn't you know?"

Peter's mind was racing. Kathleen had told him about an accident, but hadn't mentioned it was Jock. Perhaps she hadn't known who it was.

"Yes, she called me when it happened. We were supposed to be going out on a date and she cancelled."

Satisfied with the explanation, Thompson continued.

Peter's stomach was in a knot.

"She's a great girl, my friend, visiting him so regularly after the accident, despite all her commitments. Especially as it wasn't her fault. Strapp admitted he was riding too fast, but I think Kathleen still felt responsible, even more so when she found out he'd been paralysed from the waist down."

Peter had no idea and this time from the undisguised look of shock, Thompson noticed.

"You didn't know, did you?"

"I can't remember. She's always visiting people in hospital, she's a volunteer."

Thompson gave him an unexpected life line.

"The mark of a true Samaritan. Helping the needy in a quiet way and not drawing praise, even from their own loved ones. She's very special that girl, Peter. You keep hold of her now."

"Yes, she is."

He swallowed hard.

'Why hadn't she told him about Jock Strapp?' he thought, but before he had time to process the information, the policeman continued his update.

"I did some snooping around," continued Thompson. "Cosgrove was a nasty piece of work and he had been arrested several times for assault, but it seems he'd recently graduated to class A drugs – supplying no less. There's big money involved in that business, but big risks as well. Spitz was seen with him, immediately before Cosgrove died. There may be a more sinister connection between the two, something involving drugs, perhaps?"

'So, Cosgrove was dealing and maybe the predatory American was involved,' he thought, however, despite Thompson's suspicions about Spitz, his own mind was going in a different direction.

Thompson could have asked him more questions about Kathleen, but thankfully, it never occurred to Ian that Peter may be holding back a vital clue in order to protect his fiancée. Kathleen was one of the last people to see Jock alive, though Peter couldn't think of any reason why she might have wanted to kill him even though he had suspicions about the plant in her kitchen. And what about Cosgrove? Maybe this had something to do with Spitz after all.

Thompson broke his train of thought.

"Now, my boy, I'm going to need your expert knowledge of toxicology, to get to the bottom of this. Without the poison, I have only circumstantial evidence. I need proof and, unless I can identify the toxin and actually tie this to a supplier, whoever that may be, I'm no closer to getting the answer than I was when it first landed on my desk."

It looked to Peter as though the plant on Kathleen's window sill may have been the proof Thompson was looking for, but he was torn. With his knowledge of plants, he knew that the trail led as easily to Kathleen as it did to Spitz or Cosgrove, more so in fact, because the plant provided the missing link, though it didn't explain why Cosgrove and Spitz were on the balcony together. He desperately wanted to believe Ian's theory, but there were now so many questions surrounding Kathleen... the missing leaves, the fact that she had not told him about Jock. These questions were not going away. In fact he had more questions than answers.

"So, Peter, now you have my update, have you got any more information about the plant you came across in the library?"

Peter needed more time.

He had to speak to Kathleen before going further down that road with Thompson.

"No, not yet. I may have been a little over enthusiastic, Ian. I thought I had something there, but, in light of what you've told me, I need to reconsider some of the data. It is possible that there is some new drug out there doing the rounds."

"Yes, that's my first line of enquiry."

Peter rose to leave.

"What you've told me changes things a bit and there are still a number of options I've yet to explore. Let me come back to you in a day or so, OK?"

"Thanks, Peter. You're a great help. Keep in touch, eh?"

"Sure thing, Ian. If I turn up anything, you'll be the first to know."

"Cheers."

"Cheers, Ian."

Peter walked slowly back to his office. The conversation with Thompson had done little to allay his fears. In fact, quite the opposite had occurred. As fond as he was of Thompson, he knew imparting the knowledge he had unearthed about *Morticius Aberaeum* would only create suspicion on Kathleen and that thought he could not bear. Fact was fact and suspicion wasn't relevant.

Or was it?

* * *

Spitz flipped through his filing cabinet until he came across a suspension file with the tab marked 'Contracts' and selected two blank forms titled 'Contract of Sale'. Humphries had had long enough to think things over and now it was time for action.

Spitz glanced at his watch – 2:35pm – time to pay Mr Humphries a surprise visit. Radic was in the motor pool polishing one of the cars, the concentration on his face unmistakable. The paradox between Radic, the brute, and Radic, the cleaning devotee, was amazing.

"Angelo."

Radic looked up, surprised to see Spitz standing a few metres away.

"Yez, Bozz?"

"Angelo, we need to pay Mr Humphries a visit, now. Why don't you finish that later? Clean up and bring the car around the front. I'll wait for you there. This shouldn't take too long."

Radic gave one last buff with the polishing cloth before putting it on a nearby bench.

"OK, Bozz, I come."

During the short drive to Humphries' premises, Spitz outlined his plan.

"I've been far too tolerant with this closet queen. He's had sufficient time to come around to my way of thinking and enough *persuasion* too. Well, enough's enough. No more dilly dallying Angelo my friend. Today our Mr Humphries signs on the dotted line... or else."

Radic gripped the wheel tightly in concentration. He wasn't good at inference or deduction.

"Or else vot, Bozz?"

"Or else he'll be sorry, very sorry he didn't sign."

The grip on the steering wheel became tighter.

"That's where you come in, Angelo. I want you to make him, how shall I say... *reconsider* his options, his limited options."

Radic stared straight ahead, his eyes squinting in concentration. Spitz formed a fist and smacked it loudly into an open palm.

The Croat's face visibly relaxed. He nodded in agreement.

"I geddit, Bozz, I geddit."

"When he's finished reconsidering his options, he'll sign. There's not a doubt in my mind."

"I take care of it, Bozz, leave it to me."

Spitz sighed. Angelo could not be trusted to come on strong at the right time.

Like a powerful dog, he needed controlling.

"I'll decide if and when to apply the pressure, Angelo. Wait for my instructions. Is that clear?"

Radic nodded.

"Sure, Bozz. I wait."

A mile later, they were at Humphries' premises. Spitz waved an index finger at a vacant space between two cars.

"Pull in here."

The car glided to a halt and both men got out, but it was Spitz who first noticed the sign appended to the exterior of the building. He stopped dead in his tracks as he carefully read the notice.

'Acquired for redevelopment,' followed by the name of the agent and their details.

A vein in his temple began to throb as the colour rose in his face. It was like watching a pressure cooker building up steam, the outburst came sooner than expected.

"What?!" it was an angry scream rather than a question.

Radic looked at his employer. Something was definitely wrong.

"Vot?" he enquired, unsure exactly what was happening.

Spitz caught the question and turned to face the Croat.

"What?"

"Vot, vot, Bozz? Vot?"

"What do you mean what?! What are you talking about, you idiot? Can't you see what's happened?"

Radic scrutinised the sign intensely. He hated big words.

"Ak, ak, ak...."

The wind had been taken out of Spitz's sails, cheated at the last moment by a side-sale and he was in no mood to tolerate imbeciles like Radic.

"Oh, *do* shut up, Angelo! We've been beaten to the punch. Our Mr Humphries has negotiated a sale behind my back and probably flown the coop as well!"

"Vot?"

"He's sold his business premises, Angelo, which means now I can't buy it."

A furrow appeared in Radic's forehead. Some of this was beginning to make sense.

Some, but not a lot.

"OK, Bozz, I geddit. We still go in?"

Spitz shook his head.

"No, Angelo, you idiot, we don't go in, we go back. There's nothing to be done here. But let me tell you, I'm not going to be cheated out of what I want. That O'Neill bitch is top of my list."

# Chapter 25

## Sign or Die

Kathleen hadn't slept well. Most of the night had been spent thinking about her visit to Mrs Papadopoulos the previous afternoon, a visit necessary to establish the well being or otherwise of the old lady and whether it was, as her father used to say, "time" – time to honour the promise.

The Deepdene Nursing Home did little to live up to its brochure. It was neither warm nor friendly, thanks in no small measure to the goliath of a woman who ran it like an army barrack. Matron Banks had managed to crush all but the most indomitable spirit, resident and staff alike. In some twisted way, most families of the elderly perceived this strict regime as efficient care. 'The white uniforms worn by the staff transforming them into medical professionals who knew best must be helping,' she thought. Kathleen had seen this many times, but never as intense as at Deepdene. Yes, the premises were spotlessly clean and, thankfully, devoid of the tell-tale smells of the incontinent, but for all its cleanliness and efficiency, it was a soulless institution, where real love and care had no place or part to play.

Seeing the old lady yesterday and particularly in such an environment had greatly saddened her. There had been no response when Kathleen had tried to engage her in conversation. Blank to the outside world, and impervious to any external stimuli, the sparkle in her eyes had gone and Maria looked deeply unhappy and depressed. By chance, Banks had passed by and Kathleen had mentioned to her that the old lady's general health and mobility had deteriorated considerably since she had first joined them at Deepdene.

Banks' reply was almost a throw-away comment.

"It happens."

That was all she uttered before resuming some important inspection.

The staff now had to use a hoist to transfer the old lady from her bed to a wheelchair and she was now also doubly incontinent. It was clear that Mrs

Papadopoulos had reached a stage she had specifically wanted to avoid and, in Kathleen's heart, she knew the time had indeed arrived to honour the promise.

That evening, she had retired early, wearied by the day's events and wanting time by herself in which to think. Peter telephoned around five o'clock suggesting dinner, but she had feigned a headache and made it clear she was going to get an early night. Peter, dear sweet Peter. Would there ever come a time when she would reveal the darker side of her work to him? That was a question that would not leave her mind and so the night which had begun with a shallow, restless sleep had been dominated by issues about the old lady, Peter, their future together and finally the police investigation into the Strapp and Cosgrove deaths. Lying awake, in the early hours of the morning, with these questions running around in her head, made sleep difficult and answers impossible.

Sleep had finally come around four o'clock and, a few hours later, the alarm starkly announced Saturday's arrival. It jerked her out of a deep slumber to face the challenges the new day would surely bring. Kathleen lay in bed, semi-awake for the next half an hour, not wanting to get up, thoughts of the old lady and what must be done turning over and over in her mind. Finally, she threw back the covers and, awake but exhausted, sat up and planted both feet on the floor. Trudging to the bathroom, she stood under a hot shower until sleep had finally left her head and then all she could think of was strong, hot coffee. Sitting at the kitchen table in her dressing gown, with the radio barely audible, she stared at the small bottle of Bell's whisky placed carefully on the worktop next to the bread bin, while the percolator made plopping sounds, the aroma of fresh coffee filling the room.

Rising from the table, Kathleen opened a cupboard and retrieved a small vial into which she carefully poured some of the lethal plant mixture, masquerading as whisky. The vial was securely sealed with a screw cap and placed in her handbag. She would call at the Deepdene Nursing Home after they had finished breakfast, but before lunch, and carry out the old lady's wishes. In a strange way, having filled the vial, she felt less confused and reticent. Instead, she felt purposeful, secure in the knowledge she was about to fulfill the earnest wishes of another human being. It was by all accounts a sacred duty. She glanced at the wall clock and was astounded to see that it was already 8:40. The last hour and a half had passed as though it were just a few minutes.

"Come on, Kath!" she chided herself. "Get a move on. There's a lot to do today!"

The buzzer from the downstairs front door startled her interrupting her train of thought.

She went to the intercom and spoke through the mouthpiece, "Yes?"

"Delivery of flowers for Ms Kathleen O'Neill," came the disembodied voice.

"Please leave them inside the door," she replied, pressing the buzzer. 'They must be from Peter,' she thought, smiling to herself.

A few seconds later, there was another knock at the door from the hall outside.

"Flowers, miss."

'Didn't I just tell him to leave them downstairs?' she thought to herself as she opened the door.

She froze in horror as Angelo Radic barged past her and into the flat, Jerome Spitz following up the rear and calmly closing the door behind him.

"What on earth do you think…" was as far as she got before a huge hand clamped itself over her mouth, stifling all sound.

Spitz held up an index finger, the universal 'stop' signal. The finger waved from side to side like a metronome.

"No shouting, if you please, Ms O'Neill. We can have a civilized discussion, but without the volume, understood?"

Kathleen felt both furious and terrified. Radic maintained an iron-like grip with one arm around her shoulders from behind and preventing any movement at all. The other hand remained over her mouth.

"Do we understand each other?"

Kathleen nodded once.

"Good. Angelo, you may let her go now."

Radic released his grip and removed the hand from her mouth, but stayed dangerously close. For a big man, he moved surprisingly fast, and that intimidated her.

"Why don't we all have a nice cup of coffee?" Spitz raised one arm, palm up, "I presume you have a kitchen?"

Composing herself, Kathleen rearranged her bath robe and ran her fingers through her hair.

"Yes, I have a kitchen," she said with some defiance mixed with fear. The latter emotion was not lost on Spitz. It meant the surprise tactics had worked.

In the kitchen, Spitz and Radic sat down at the table as an awkward silence descended over the three.

It was broken by Spitz.

"I'd like a coffee, milk, two sugars, the same for my associate here."

It was an instruction, not a request and designed to reinforce his authority over the situation.

Kathleen remained immobile. The events of the past few minutes had left her shaken.

"Now!"

The command made her jump and she dutifully turned on the kettle and found two cups. Radic grinned – he liked the way his boss had taken control of the situation, with his help of course. They made a good team.

Spitz reached into his jacket pocket and withdrew a silver cigarette case. Taking out a cigarette and lighting it he turned his attention to Kathleen.

"The last time we called I told you of my intention to purchase your business. I was prepared to offer you a fair price, but I haven't heard a word from you since that day. No telephone call, no letter, nothing. That's very disrespectful, Ms O'Neill, very disrespectful indeed."

He took a long drag on the cigarette.

"You've had plenty of time to consider my generous proposal, but instead, chose to ignore me. Well, I'm afraid time has run out. I won't be messed about anymore, which is why we're having this little discussion right now."

Kathleen was quickly regaining her composure and she could feel the anger rising in her with every word that came out of Spitz's mouth.

"Just exactly what *do* you want?"

"It's simple, a signed contract of sale. You will sell me your business at an agreed price of twenty thousand dollars, which, in the present economic climate, is more than generous."

Spitz took another drag on the cigarette and reached into his jacket pocket to produce two legal documents.

"And, by pure good fortune, I just happen to have two contracts, one for you and one for me."

"You filthy little worm!"

Kathleen lunged at Spitz, hands outstretched like a cat pouncing, but she never saw Radic, who, in some primeval way had sensed an imminent reaction.

Two strong arms grabbed her by the shoulders and flung her to the floor. Kathleen crashed over a chair and landed heavily, knocking the wind out of her. There was near silence for a few seconds, the only audible sound coming from Kathleen, desperately trying to catch her breath. Spitz was the first to speak.

"Really, Ms O'Neill, you do surprise me. I'm not a violent man, in fact I abhor violence. Mr Radic, on the other hand, is no stranger to, how shall we say, more *vigorous* methods of communication."

Spitz stubbed out his cigarette on the table, leaving a small burn mark. As Radic grinned at Kathleen, both men knew she was completely powerless in this situation. Slowly, she picked herself up off the floor, righting the chair knocked over in the fall and carefully sat down rearranging her dressing gown which had been pulled open in the assault. A trickle of blood ran down the side of her face.

Spitz gazed nonchalantly around.

"Now, where were we?" he said.

The two contracts for sale were displayed on the table.

"Ah, that's right, the contracts."

Kathleen wiped away a small streak of blood, which had found its way into her left eye.

"You'll never get away with this, you know that, don't you? Even if I sign the contract, the moment you've gone I'll phone the police and tell them everything. You'll both go to prison."

Radic was instantly at her side a deep growling sound rumbling in his throat. The garlic breath was almost too much to bear.

Spitz's tone also changed.

"Don't push me, young lady, you don't know what I'm capable of. Take a look at tomorrow's papers. Believe me, you'll sign and you won't go to the police. It's better to be above ground than below it, do I make myself clear? I always get what I want, always!"

Radic brought his face close to Kathleen's so that their noses were almost touching.

"Alffvies!"

"Sign it!"

Spitz had pushed one of the contracts in front of her and a pen was rudely thrown on top of the document. Kathleen felt faint. This was madness. Things didn't happen like this, it was all going too fast. Panic was starting to overtake reason and she felt powerless to stop the rising feelings of helplessness.

"Sign it!" he shouted.

A vice-like grip grabbed her by the throat. Radic was applying his own subtle form of persuasion.

Dumbly she nodded her head.

A feeble "OK..." was all she could manage.

Radic released his grip, but stood close by. Spitz smiled contentedly.

"Good, good. Both copies please."

Was this really happening? Kathleen's mind fought to make sense of it all. Dazed and shaken, she slowly signed both sets of papers, dropping the pen from her hand when she had finished. Spitz snatched up both sets and examined them carefully.

"Good. It's settled then. I shall make arrangements to transfer the sum of twenty thousand dollars to your bank this afternoon and I'll be here tomorrow morning to collect the keys to the premises. I expect you to be gone by tomorrow night."

"What? I don't understand, I, I..."

"There's nothing *to* understand, Ms O'Neill. In a falling market and with a failing business, you wisely chose to sell at a generous price and to a buyer who could move quickly. No agent or solicitor's fees have made this a more attractive proposition. In the circumstances, you'd be hard pressed to find anyone who would have done otherwise, wouldn't you agree?"

Kathleen sat motionless, her head slightly bowed, clearly in shock.

He paused to let the words sink in.

"And as regards speaking to the authorities. My advice is don't. You'll never make it to the witness box, that much I can guarantee."

A small tear rolled down her cheek, mixing with the blood from the gash on her forehead.

"Come now, Ms O'Neill, there's no need to be unhappy. I've done you a favour. Later on you'll thank me for it."

His eyes fell on the bottle of Bell's whisky a few metres behind her on the counter.

"I know it's early, but to show you there's no hard feelings, why don't you let me buy you a drink? Angelo, get some glasses."

Easily visible through the glass door of one of the wall units, Radic grabbed three small glasses. Kathleen remained frozen to the spot as they were placed loudly on the table.

"Good. Now pass me that bottle."

Spitz poured three measures from the bottle and pushed one of the glasses towards Kathleen. He held up his glass, Radic following suit. Her heart was in her mouth. There were going to be two more smiling corpses, maybe three. She didn't know if they were going to force her to drink the concoction as well.

"To a successful acquisition. Cheers," toasted Spitz.

Both men downed the amber liquid in one gulp while Kathleen simply stared at the glass before her. She had still not moved a muscle. Spitz looked at her with contempt.

"Too early for you, is it? Well it's much too good to waste. You don't know what you're missing," he sneered.

Taking what was left in Kathleen's glass, he poured half of its contents back into Radic's now empty one and raised her glass to his lips.

"Cheers, my friend. To 'My Way'."

"My Vay," intoned the Croat.

The men clinked glasses and swallowed the contents in one gulp.

A wry smile was developing on Kathleen's face.

Spitz rose from his chair, picking up the whisky bottle, which still wasn't completely empty, and handed it to Radic. Gloatingly, he folded the contract of sale into two and placed it in his jacket pocket.

"It's been a pleasure doing business with you, Ms O'Neill."

A small rogue snigger came from nowhere.

"Remember what I said about the police."

He waved an index finger loosely in the Croat's direction.

"You don't need any extra trouble."

Radic also seemed to be finding the situation amusing.

He tapped the side of his nose with a finger, a broad grin on his face.

"Mum's za vord!"

An involuntary chortle escaped from his mouth. Spitz broke out in sympathy with a snort. Chuckling, both men walked to the front door and were gone.

Kathleen remained at the table, a dozen emotions swirling through her head, fear, anger, helplessness, satisfaction, regret and many others rendering her incapable of action or coherent thought. Above all, she felt confused. It had all happened so fast, they had entered uninvited, under duress she had been forced to sign away the family business and been assaulted in the process. Now two very happy looking corpses were going to turn up sometime soon, with a contract containing her signature and today's date, and there was nothing she could do to stop it and no way to explain it away.

God, she needed to talk to someone. Peter immediately came to mind and numbly she reached for the telephone and dialled his home number. The answering machine kicked in and she knew he must be at work or at least on the way to work. Robotically, she dialled his mobile number.

After a few rings, Peter picked up the phone.

"Peter Wilson."

"Peter, it's me. Something…" a flood of tears prevented her from going any further as she sobbed helplessly into the receiver.

"Kath! What's wrong? Are you alright?"

"Oh, Peter, they called, I couldn't stop them, it was awful…"

It was all coming out in one uncontrollable rush.

"They made me sign, I didn't want to, but they made me…"

"Slow down. Who called? Signed what? Speak to me, Kath, what happened?"

"Oh, Peter…"

"Don't move. I'm coming over. Lock the door! Do you hear me? Lock the door and I'll be there in ten minutes!"

\* \* \*

The lonely property, at the end of the Bondi Coast road, looked almost dilapidated. The garden was littered with broken bits of furniture and car parts. Robertson had stopped at the Greek mansion en route to Harris's place and asked the postman, who was heading away from the house, how much further he had to go, before he came to the old man's property.

In a few minutes, Robertson arrived at the run-down house. The view was amazing, yet the property looked out of place in this spot. There was no sign of any activity.

He knocked on the door and waited. Nothing.

Pacing up and down the front porch, with the sound of the broken flywire flapping incessantly in the breeze, the waves crashed against the cliff face forty metres below, making him feel isolated and vulnerable.

He checked his watch for the tenth time – nine fifteen exactly. Harris had said he was housebound without help, yet the place appeared to be deserted.

Maybe someone had taken him somewhere and they were late coming back.

But something didn't feel right. It was strange that there was no one around.

'OK,' he thought to himself, 'let's give this another ten minutes. If it's going to be a no-show, then I'm not going to wait around all day. Nine twenty five, come what may, I'm out of here.'

The act of making a decision bolstered his confidence and made him feel better. If he was honest, this place gave him the creeps, it was just too far from anywhere and being here all alone, waiting around like this, made it all the more foreboding.

A distant sound stopped his pacing back and forth. Was the wind and crashing surf playing tricks on his ears? He strained to hear the sound again.

There it was! A car! some way off, but unmistakably the sound of a car's engine. The sound of the car's engine was getting louder. It must be someone bringing Harris back to the house, after all. Robertson laughed nervously. He felt stupid getting all flustered for nothing and jumping at his own shadow. Like most things in life, the most obvious answer was usually the correct one. Harris must have been taken into town by someone, for some bits and pieces, and they were simply running late. Nothing sinister about that.

A small dust trail was now visible in the distance and the engine's noise was much louder, rising above the sound of the wind and waves. Robertson stepped off the porch and walked to the front gate. It opened with a pronounced creak and he walked a few paces past the decaying wooden fence and onto the track, ready to greet the arriving Mr Harris.

He first saw the approaching car, when it was about two hundred metres away and was instantly struck by its speed. Old men were usually driven much more slowly and less dangerously, whereas this car was bombing along and weaving from side to side, on the narrow gravel track. The other thing that struck him as the car became closer was the fact that it was a convertible – and for some obscure reason to which he had no insight at all, that just didn't fit. Now he could make out two figures in the car, both seemed to be shouting or singing – he couldn't make out which, and waving their hands in the air. His first thought was that they were drunk and this too made absolutely no sense at all.

Closer now, he could make out the type of car – a BMW convertible, which showed no signs of slowing down. As it sped towards him, he heard the occupants laughing hysterically, but he didn't manage to see their faces because the car swerved away from him. Frozen by fear, he had expected at any moment to feel the hard metal crash into his legs and catapult him into the sea.

The car braked suddenly, fishtailing violently for ten metres or so before crashing into a tree at the edge of the cliff. The gravel dust cloud wafted past Robertson, covering the car and making him cough.

Slowly, he shook his head incredulously, patting himself with open hands across his chest, not quite believing that he was unharmed. His heart was racing. He was lucky to be alive. At that moment, he never realised just how lucky.

Still shaking, he walked towards the car, now badly dented at the front, the tree trunk making a 'V' shape in the bonnet. If the tree hadn't been in the way, the BMW would certainly have gone over the cliff edge and crashed on to the rocks below. As he reached the vehicle, he gasped at the sight which greeted him.

"What the…?" he said out loud.

The car's engine had stalled as he gingerly approached the mangled convertible which had almost killed him. One metre from the driver's door he stopped in disbelief.

"Spitz?"

The head of Jerome T Spitz was pushed back, his open eyes gazing into the skies, a look of absolute joy on his face as the head of his passenger rested face down in his crotch.

Instinctively, perhaps after years as an undertaker, he knew the man was dead. Carefully, Robertson felt the side of Spitz's neck for a pulse. There was none. He repeated the test for the passenger – none there either. With some effort he pulled the passenger's torso back so he could see the face. Radic! With the same joyous look! If the look on Spitz' face looked out of place, on the gnarled Croat it was positively macabre. Shocked, he let go of Radic's shoulders, as the head fell back to where it had been. His mind was now racing. Radic's face in Spitz's groin was an unsavoury image. He had never figured them to be gay.

Where was Harris? Why were Spitz and his henchman here and why had they tried to run him over? All he knew for certain was that following the accident, two people were now dead and that never, in all his years, had he seen two happier looking corpses. It was time for him to call the police. Grabbing his mobile phone, he prayed for a signal. Yes! Not strong but hopefully adequate. He dialled triple zero and waited for the operator.

A faint voice answered.

"Emergency. Who do you require, Fire, Police or Ambulance?"

"Police."

A moment or two later a man's voice answered.

"Police. What is the nature of your emergency?"

Robertson looked at the BMW and at the grinning corpse which was Spitz.

"There are two dead men in a car at the end of Bondi Coast Road. Please send somebody immediately."

\* \* \*

Kathleen had sat motionless for what seemed like an age and, although the intrusion with Spitz and Radic had both terrified and angered her, she was panicking now that she had called Peter. It had been her first instinctive reaction, but how was she going to explain herself to him? It had all happened so fast and she'd signed the contracts just to get them out of her flat. She would have gone to the police, but watching the two men drink the family remedy was something she hadn't counted on. She could have stopped them, that would have been easy, but what then? The secret would have been out in the open and the idea that Spitz of all people should be privy to such information was unthinkable. Anyway, they probably would have forced her to drink it. And, if she was being brutally honest with herself, there was a part of her that wanted to hit back, there and then. Radic had hurt her physically, but then she had also felt degraded and that made her angry.

Angry enough to withhold a warning? Angry enough to justify murder – a crime by omission? Does anybody deserve that level of retribution? There were no immediate answers to these questions.

Two more grinning corpses were about to turn up and, from the signed contract in their possession, it would be perfectly clear that they had left her premises immediately before. It would also be clear that she was one of the last people to see them alive. With her connection to Jock and her presence on the ward the night he and Cosgrove died, how was she going to explain Spitz and Radic? She knew now that it would only be a matter of time before the truth would be unearthed. Peter had been asking her questions about the plant and he'd seen the whisky bottles. How long would it take him to piece the whole thing together?

The more she thought about everything, the more confused she became. It was like wrestling with a wild beast in a closed room. No help, no advice, alone and without support.

The sound of a key in the front door made her look up from the table surface she had been staring at. The door flew open as Peter rushed in. The moment she laid eyes on him some barrier inside her broke and she burst into tears.

Kneeling beside the kitchen table chair, he flung his arms protectively around her and held her tightly.

"Kath, what's happened?"

It was all she could do to speak, the sobs punctuating her reply as it all came out in one huge rush.

"Spitz came around… early this morning… just barged in… had his henchman with him… no warning… out of the blue…"

"Are you all right? Did they hurt you?"

"I couldn't do anything… he was too strong… I tried, really, I tried… he threw me over the chair… I couldn't stop him."

Peter magically produced a handkerchief and began mopping up the flow of tears.

"It's alright, I'm here now you're safe, slow down."

Peter was trying to be calm for her sake, but he felt murderous.

"You've a small cut on your forehead. Do you think anything is broken? Did either of them assault you in any other way?"

Kathleen was slowly calming down, the sobbing less erratic her breathing deeper and more regular.

She covered her face with both hands and shook her head from side to side.

"No, no, it wasn't anything like that, nothing like that. They came to deliver a message."

"A message? I don't understand."

"Spitz wants the business. The first time he called was downstairs, in the office, one afternoon. Made me an offer I couldn't refuse."

She laughed sardonically at the reference.

"I told them where to go and put it out of my mind."

"Oh, Kath, why didn't you tell me from the start? We could have had them arrested!"

"I didn't want to worry you."

Peter held her at arms length and examined her face.

"I wish you'd told me. I suppose Spitz wanted to buy O'Neill's at a knock-down price. Ian suspected they'd leaned on you, but he didn't think you were afraid or in danger."

"I wasn't afraid of them and I never really expected them to come back."

"Did you know, Spitz was trying the same thing with Robertson and Humphries too?" revealed Peter.

"No, I had no idea and I thought I'd scared them off. I didn't want the matter to escalate and get out of control. And then this morning, he brought some papers with him – contracts of sale. They threatened me again and forced me to sign them. Spitz told me to watch the papers tomorrow. He said I'd be reading something that would convince me not to go to the police."

"You signed the contracts?"

"I had to. He was acting like a crazy man. I was scared. Radic was very rough."

The gash in her forehead and bruising around her throat were evidence enough. Peter was furious.

"But the contract isn't valid. You signed under duress, no court would uphold that as a legally binding document."

"They threatened to kill me, if I tried to get out of it."

Peter could barely contain the anger he felt rising inside him.

"That's it! I'm calling Ian Thompson. This is an open and shut case of intimidation, assault and extortion. We'll get them arrested."

Peter stood up and reached for the telephone on the kitchen wall.

Kathleen was now also on her feet. She grabbed Peter by the arm.

"Stop, you can't."

Peter had punched in part of the telephone number and turned defiantly to her.

"Watch me."

Kathleen's finger on the cradle ended the dialling sequence.

"Peter, please. I can't go to the police," she pleaded.

A perplexed look came over his face.

"Why can't you go to the police, Kathleen, what's going on?"

Kathleen's eye filled with tears as she fought to control herself.

"There's something I have to tell you."

"What?"

"You've seen the family crest, and I'm sure you've understood the Latin phrase on it."

"Yes, and…?"

Peter had gone cold all over, he wasn't sure he wanted to hear this.

Her voice was breaking.

"You also recognised the flower," she looked him in the eye.

Peter looked at the flower with the distinctive leaves on the window ledge.

"That one, over there, your father's plant?" he asked.

Kathleen nodded.

"You knew it was the same plant as the one on the family crest, didn't you?"

"I knew, but not right away. I couldn't understand why you didn't tell me."

"It's because the family makes a drink from it, have done so from the beginning."

"Oh, God, the one you told me not to touch?"

His heart was breaking. He couldn't reconcile what was unfolding and what it would mean for their relationship.

"Did you know?"

"I've had my suspicions," he said flatly.

Peter's eyes narrowed.

"What kind of drink?"

"A drink that helps people to die."

Kathleen paused so that Peter would understand exactly what she was about to say.

"I help people who ask for my help to die. My family's been doing this for generations."

Peter gasped involuntarily and stepped back.

"What?"

"I made some last night, it was in a small whisky bottle. I was going to take it to an old lady, Mrs Papadopoulos, this morning, but Spitz and his thug turned up out of the blue and took the bottle with them."

Peter could scarcely believe his ears.

"You were going to poison an old lady, this morning?"

"She lived in constant fear of becoming a burden to her family and, more importantly, she couldn't bear the thought of losing her dignity, near the end of her life. It was her fervent wish this should not happen and she came to us two years ago and asked for help. We made a promise and I was going to honour that promise."

Peter's mouth hung agape.

"What are you talking about? This is unbelievable, you can't play God. It's murder!"

"No, it is *not*! It's a selfless deed with huge risks to the person who puts an act of love and mercy for someone they care about above their own personal liberty. It's been the family's credo for a hundred and fifty years."

"You're telling me this is not an isolated incident? That O'Neill's have been bumping people off over the generations?"

"No, it's not an isolated incident and we haven't been 'bumping people off', as you put it, because *we* think they should die. We've helped them die as and when they've wanted to. It's far more cruel to take that decision away from a human being when they are powerless to do it for themselves. That's judgemental. Who are we to decide somebody's end? If there's any choice at all, the only person who can make that decision is the person him or herself. I'm not 'bumping people off' who want to live, I'm honouring the wishes of those who want to die."

Peter's tone had changed, the outrage was absent.

"The old lady, Mrs Papa… Papa… what if she changes her mind?"

"Mrs Papadopoulos can't change her mind, that's the whole point. She made her mind up while she still *had* a mind. She didn't want to live when she didn't know who her son or grandchildren were or who was changing her incontinence pad. That's why she came to us two years ago and begged for help."

"Kath, it's not right."

"Of course it's not right. It's not right to let people get that way when they'd choose not to if they could."

"Kath…"

Peter was pleading with her.

"Look what you went through with your mother. You told me yourself she would have hated to see herself as she became. You said you were sure she would have ended her life if she could have. You said you understood how some people consider euthanasia, but you never had the courage to go down that road. You're one of the few people who could have given her something that could never have been traced. It would have looked like a natural death. You said it to me yourself."

"Just because I thought about it and even though I wished it, it didn't give me the right to do it."

"So you think it's an act of love, to watch your nearest and dearest suffering, when they've no quality of life left? You think it's right to leave them in a condition they'd never allow themselves to be in, if they could do anything about it?"

Peter paced back and forth.

"It doesn't matter *what* I think. It's against the law. It's murder."

"Is it murder or is it setting someone free from suffering, when the end is inevitable and sometimes only a matter of hours away? No one would let an animal suffer like that. They would say it's cruel to let it go on in pain, but we do it to people all the time."

"Animals can't decide for themselves, people can."

"And it's only for people who've decided for themselves that I help. I'm not making their decisions, they are. They're making those decisions and getting our help while they still can, before they get past the point of no return and are no longer able to determine their own end."

Peter was still pacing up and down, still trying to come to grips with the enormity of what they were discussing.

"What about the families? Without any intervention, they would have more time with them."

"That's just it. All the people we've helped can't bear the thought of putting their families through the torture of watching them decline or they're terrified of pain and their needs come first. Why should people near the end have to prolong their own agony for anybody else's sake? No one who really loves someone would wish needless suffering on them."

Peter nodded his head in agreement.

"That much I understand, believe me."

"Peter, whatever happens, a family is going to have to face the loss of their loved ones, but surely that doesn't make it right to let the one they love suffer for longer than they have to. These people are very near death and many of them, in their final days, don't have the strength to end their own lives and then suffer dreadfully. I'm not changing the inevitable. I'm making it easier for the terminally sick, because, by asking me to help, they don't put the burden on the ones they love. They can go to their end more peacefully, knowing their suffering won't be prolonged and no one they love will get into any trouble."

Peter had stopped the pacing and sat down, rubbing his forehead.

"You have to tell Thompson that Spitz and his heavy were both here this morning. Tell him everything – the forced entry, the assault, signing of the contract with duress, the threats, all of it. But, if you mention the bottle of whisky, then everything changes. It's out there now and you don't know who's got it or who's going to drink it. With luck, we'll find it when we find Spitz and hopefully before someone else dies."

The clock on the wall ticked audibly, reinforcing the temporary silence. Peter was furiously thinking of how to circumvent the immediate problem in hand when Kathleen dropped the bombshell.

"They drank all of the liquid in the whisky bottle."

Peter's head snapped up, eyes wide and shocked.

"They did *what*?"

"They thought it was whisky and both had a toast after I'd signed the contract. I could have said something, but I didn't."

"Oh, *shit*! Is there an antidote?"

Kathleen shook her head.

"No, it's very effective."

"How long?"

"How long what?" asked Kathleen.

"How long before the poison takes effect?"

"It's fast."

"*How* fast?" The exasperation in Peter's voice was palpable.

"Fifteen minutes… max. It depends upon the person – age, size, weight, health, that sort of thing."

Peter groaned and shook his head.

"Jesus, Kathleen, what have you done?"

Kathleen sat beside Peter and took his hand in hers.

"Peter, I have to go and see Mrs Papadopoulos, it should have happened months ago. I have a small vial ready for her."

Peter was dumbstruck. It had been a day full of surprises.

"You can't be serious. After all that's happened this morning?"

"I have to – she begged and we made her a promise. She couldn't stand the thought of losing her dignity in front of her son and his family the way her mother had with her."

"Kath, you can't. We've got to phone Thompson before anything else happens. If you slip the old lady your Mickey Finn and get caught, you'll spend the rest of your life behind bars. And where does that leave us?"

He was desperately trying to find a solution to the ever increasing dilemma they were now both in.

By contrast, Kathleen appeared focused and resigned.

"This has gotten way out of hand and I'm probably going to jail anyway, but I have to do this or it will all have been for nothing. My father died on the morning he had planned to go to Mrs Papadopoulos and that was six months ago. I tried to finish the task last month and I was on my way to see her at the nursing home with the drink, when Jock rode into my car trying to avoid an old lady."

"Jock?"

"Jock Strapp."

"Jock Strapp, the now dead Jock Strapp?"

Kathleen nodded.

"He had to spend his last weeks paralysed. He begged me to help him, so I gave him the night cap I'd prepared for Mrs Papadopoulos."

"So it *was* you!"

"It was the act of a friend, Peter. He knew exactly what he was doing."

"Does the body appear peaceful after death?"

Kathleen nodded again.

"Happy, dead happy actually. They go out smiling. It's quick and painless."

Peter nodded as another piece of the jigsaw fell into place.

"That explains Cosgrove. He had some too."

"What are you talking about?"

"There were two people who died that night in strikingly similar circumstances. You obviously know about Strapp, but why did you give the drink to Cosgrove?"

"I didn't give it to Cosgrove, Peter, I swear I didn't."

"Then how did he manage to get his hands on it?"

"I don't know. When I got back into the room, Jock was gone and the bottle was empty. Nobody else was there. Thompson told me when he came to see me that the other guy who'd died was the one who had attacked Jock, and Jock told me that he'd seen Cosgrove's friend on the ward the day before. He told me that he was expecting them to give him grief. It would explain Cosgrove being in Jock's room. I don't know exactly what happened. Either Jock decided to get even and offered him the drink, or Cosgrove decided to help himself."

"How could you leave anyone alone with something so lethal? What if another visitor had decided to take a tipple?"

"I know, Peter, that was a terrible mistake, but I've never done this before."

"I'm glad to hear that."

"Jock asked me to leave him on his own for a bit. When I left the room, I was really hoping he would change his mind about suicide. I thought having the option to die when he wanted to might make him less desperate. He promised not to do anything 'til I got back."

Peter looked at her. She wasn't evil, but she was terribly misguided. There had been absolutely no malice in anything she'd done, but he knew that the law wouldn't see it that way.

"Well, if it had to be anybody, I'm glad it was someone like Cosgrove," said Peter. "He made a lot of enemies and it was only a matter of time before he would either kill somebody or get himself killed. Thompson had been after that villain for ages. Strapp's testimony could have put Cosgrove away for a good number of years, but he wouldn't give evidence. It looks as though he went one better, but he should never have had the stuff in the first place. This stops now."

"No, Peter, I can't stop my work. I promised my father. It meant everything to him that I continue. He said to me that one day the law would change, but until then, it was our duty to help people if they wanted help to die. After helping Jock, I know he's right. I'm just a fool for leaving him alone with the stuff. I won't ever do that again."

"You won't ever do this again under any circumstances. It wasn't fair of your father to emotionally blackmail you like this."

"It's not blackmail, it's my duty, and I'm not just doing this because of my father. The O'Neills have always been right about this. We are just ahead of our time."

"Listen, will you, Kath? Right now Thompson can't understand how two smiling bodies turned up in the morgue at the same time. There was no explanation and no trace of anything from the autopsies, as to what killed them. He thinks it's a new drug on the street and he believes Cosgrove is behind it, though he doesn't know where he got hold of it and he doesn't know who gave it to Jock. You're not a suspect. You've made a terrible mistake, Kath, and I can understand how it happened, but you have to promise me you will never do this again."

"I can't make that promise, Peter. I have to go to Mrs Papadopoulos this morning. I can't let her down again."

"Don't be mad, Kath. There's still a way out of this for you. At this point in time, Thompson suspects that Spitz supplied some dodgy drugs to Cosgrove."

Kathleen gave him a puzzled look.

"Yes, Spitz. But if any more happy corpses turn up, after *he's* dead, even Thompson will eventually put two and two together, especially when they find him with a contract signed by you and dated today."

Kathleen stared into Peter's eyes and he returned the look. Neither blinked.

"Listen to me, Kath," he pleaded, "if you pull one more stunt like this, the whole thing will be over – for you, for us, forever."

Her look told him they had reached an impasse.

The mobile phone in Peter's pocket sprang into life. Without shifting his gaze, Peter opened it up and spoke into the receiver.

"Wilson." The tone was sharp and curt.

He listened intently for a few seconds before replying, "I see. At the end of the old Bondi Coast road – yes, I know it. Tell them not to touch *anything*. I'll be there in fifteen minutes."

He shut the phone off and replaced it in his pocket.

His eyes had not left hers.

"That was Ian Thompson. I have to go. You mustn't leave here under any circumstances. Stay where you are and promise me you won't do anything or call anyone, not 'til I come back."

She remained motionless, her heart thumping. Spitz and Radic were now also dead and smiling and Thompson was on the case.

Peter stood up and walked briskly to the door and was half way through it when Kathleen called after him, "Peter..."

He turned and pointed a finger at her.

"Just stay here. I'll be back soon."

\* \* \*

Peter arrived at the Harris property in twelve minutes. The drive had been frantic, as his mind tried to make sense of all that Kathleen had been telling him, but the only thing he could focus on was a way of stopping this madness without pointing the finger of suspicion at the woman he loved. What was certain was that another two people would turn up dead and this was now completely out of hand. What was also certain was that Thompson wouldn't take long to figure it out and, when he did, any life he and Kathleen might have enjoyed together would be over – forever.

He brought his car to a sudden halt on the dirt road, as a small trailing dust cloud swept over it. Thompson was already there and talking to a middle aged man near the farm house. A number of uniformed police officers were milling around and a blue and white plastic tape reading 'Police Crime Scene – Do Not Cross' cordoned off an open top car containing two men.

"Peter," said Thompson, beckoning him over with a wave of his arm, "over here."

Peter walked over to the policeman, his forensics bag in one hand.

"What do we have here, Ian?"

Thompson pointed to the convertible twenty or so metres away.

"Two dead," he explained.

"Any idea who the deceased are?" asked Peter despite knowing exactly who they were.

"Yes. One, Jerome T Spitz and one, Angelo Radic."

"Spitz, the funeral director?" Peter tried to sound surprised.

"None other," replied the inspector.

Peter swallowed deeply and shook his head.

"Well, I guess we'd better get on with it then."

He opened his bag and withdrew a thin disposable jump suit, mask, gloves and hat.

"Has anyone touched anything?"

"No, apart from Robertson. He checked both men for a pulse, before he dialled triple zero from his mobile."

"Robertson, the undertaker?"

"Yes, the one who did the Sullivan funeral. Apparently these bozos tried to run him over. He had a phone call a couple of days ago from an old boy who lives in the house, asking him to come over this morning to make a funeral plan. I've spoken to the nearest neighbours and the old man's in hospital."

"So you think that Spitz had set a trap for Robertson?" Peter asked, now slightly incredulous.

They were approaching the blue and white cordon as Thompson nodded.

Thompson lifted up the plastic tape. Both men ducked under it and were soon near the car.

"A couple of uniformed officers who responded to the triple zero call also examined the bodies and then called me, whereupon I called you and also the Coroner's Office. I arrived a few minutes before you did and had a look for myself. I had this area roped off to preserve the crime scene. The representative from the Coroner's office hasn't turned up yet."

Peter nodded in acknowledgement.

"Well done, Ian. It makes a pleasant change to get to a scene this quickly. So, let's see what's happened here shall we?"

He moved closer to the car.

"Jesus!" said Peter, jumping back involuntarily.

Spitz's head had been thrown fully back by the impact with the tree, his eyes open wide and mouth pulled back in a ridiculous grin.

Thompson could not help but smile slightly.

"My sentiments exactly," said Thompson. "The strange thing is he looks exactly the same as Strapp and Cosgrove did and that was just a few days ago."

"Have you checked out the other man?" Peter asked.

"He's smiling too. It looks as though my hunch about Cosgrove was near the mark. He must have got hold of some bad drugs. Clearly, this puts the meeting on the hospital balcony in a different light. Whether Spitz supplied drugs to Cosgrove or whether it was the other way round, they've all died from the same thing, but the thing I still can't figure out is who gave them to Strapp. It's a complete mystery."

Peter knew, that the minute Thompson saw the signed contract from Kathleen in Spitz's possession, the answer would be obvious. He had to find it first. How was he going to get Thompson away from the scene?

"Ah," said Thompson, "what's this?"

Peter's heart stopped.

"What?"

To his horror, the inspector was putting on some gloves and reaching down the inside of the door, to Spitz's side.

Suddenly Thompson held up a whisky bottle, there was hardly anything in it, but it was the detective's first clue to the mystery. Kathleen's fingerprints would be all over it. Peter hadn't thought of that until now and there was a lump in his throat. He should have known that it was too good to be true.

His fiancée was going to go to prison for a very long time. It was over. There was nothing he could do. As Thompson proudly held his prize up to the sunlight, examining the bottle, he heard the sound of a car coming up the bumpy drive.

"Ah, that must be the Coroner."

The detective spun round and lost his footing. Trying hard to stay upright, he stumbled on the uneven terrain, almost falling and then regaining his balance.

"That was close," he said, slightly breathless, "I almost dropped it."

He was gesturing towards the bottle with his head.

"I'd better put it down before I break…"

The ground seemed to disappear under his feet, as he put his foot forward. Stumbling into a pot-hole he was catapulted towards the edge of the cliff, with a forty metre sheer drop to the rocks below. Peter's heart was in his mouth, as Thompson flew through the air, arm outstretched, the bottle still in his hand.

As Thompson landed, his chest hit the edge of the cliff and forced his head over the abyss. The momentum of his forward motion, propelled the bottle from his grasp and it commenced its parabolic trajectory, over the cliff and into the sea, where it sank without trace.

Thompson coughed and spat out a mouthful of dirt.

"Ian, are you OK?" said Peter anxiously, rushing over to the prone policeman.

He got up on to his knees and dusted himself down, as Peter guided him to his feet and away from the dangerous drop. Remarkably, Thompson was unscathed, the mound of soft earth where he landed protecting him from serious injury. He was a bit winded and had a small scratch on his hand, but that was all. It was true what they said about him in the nick… God protects drunks, small children and Ian Thompson.

"That was rather close, Ian. You almost fell off."

"I couldn't hold onto the bottle, Peter," he said apologetically, "it just flew out of my hands."

"Thank God it was only the bottle that went over the edge."

Peter looked down.

"You're lucky to be alive, Ian. I reckon you must have a guardian angel. You should count your blessings. I do."

"I'd better go and talk to the Coroner, Peter. I'll leave you in peace to get on with your work."

Peter couldn't have felt more relieved and, for the first time since he'd met Thompson, he was eternally grateful that, for once, his clumsiness had served a useful purpose.

"I'll be fine Ian, leave this to me."

As the Inspector made his way back towards the house, Peter got to work.

As soon as Thompson was out of the way, he started to go through Spitz's pockets. The sale contract wasn't in his right pocket. It had to be in his left, but Radic was lying across him.

In death, Radic was no lighter than he was in life. With some difficulty, Peter fumbled around the Croat's torso, until his fingers located an envelope. Glancing quickly over his shoulder, Peter saw Thompson talking to Robertson and two other men. They weren't watching the crime scene. Seizing the opportunity and with a Herculean effort, he hauled Radic off Spitz's lap and back into the seated position. Peter immediately saw the large folded brown envelope and pulled it from Spitz's pocket. He looked again in the direction of the group and they were still talking with Robertson, the latter gesticulating wildly and showing how he had to jump out of the way.

Deftly, Peter manoeuvred Radic back to his original position letting him fall over Spitz, the look of ecstasy on Spitz's face providing an extraordinary backdrop, while Peter opened the envelope below the line of sight of any witnesses.

It was the contract. He had crossed the line and knew it, interfering with evidence from a crime scene. There was no turning back now. Opening his briefcase over Radic's lifeless body, he placed the envelope which would have put Kathleen firmly in the frame, carefully inside.

Thompson was walking back towards him with the Coroner and his assistant. As Thompson approached, Peter's feelings were a cocktail of guilt, anger and relief. Guilt because he didn't want to deceive his friend, anger because Spitz and Radic had threatened his fiancée and relief that Kathleen was now safe.

"I just need to get some saliva samples, then I'm done, he said, removing some things from a bag. The pathologist can do the rest in the autopsy."

Thompson nodded.

Peter took the swabs and was placing the saliva samples in his bag.

"What's that?"

The voice startled both Peter and Thompson. It was the Coroner, standing behind Thompson and pointing at the open glove box to a handwritten envelope with the word "Betty" written on it.

In his panic to find the contract, Peter hadn't even seen it. He extended a gloved hand, picked up the envelope and handed it to Thompson, who began to read.

When he had finished, he looked squarely at Peter. Peter's heart was beating so strongly in his chest, he was certain Thompson could hear it. A cold sweat had broken out on his forehead and his mouth was dry. He tried to speak, but all he could do was mouth the word 'What'.

Thompson gave a knowing look, before picking up the letter and walking away from the car to where Robertson was standing, thirty or so metres away.

He spoke briefly to a uniformed policeman before approaching the undertaker.

"Mr Robertson?"

The man had been sitting on a rickety wooden chair on the porch, gazing into the distance. On hearing his name being called, he looked up at the approaching policeman.

"Yes, Inspector?"

"Mr Robertson, what is your wife's first name?"

"I beg your pardon?"

"It's a simple question, what is your wife's first name?" repeated Thompson.

"Betty, it's Betty. Why do you ask? Has something happened to her?" A feeling of rising panic enveloped him.

"Mr Robertson, would you mind writing your signature on this piece of paper?" he requested, handing the man a pen and a notebook.

Taking both, Robertson looked at Thompson with alarm.

"What's going on?" he asked, as he scrawled his name in the notebook.

"Your wife is fine, Mr Robertson, please don't worry," he responded, as though reading the man's mind, whilst looking at the signature on the note from the car and comparing it to Robertson's. "You, my friend, are very lucky to be alive. I believe these men were here to kill you. I guess you have a guardian angel."

Robertson looked shocked.

"I'm told an ambulance should be here shortly. The paramedics will take care of you, but I'll need to get a full statement at some point. Do you feel up to coming down to the West Sydney station later on this afternoon?"

Robertson nodded.

"Yes, of course. I'm a bit shaken, but apart from that, I think I'm OK. I'll go home and let my wife know what's happened. What time shall I come to the station?"

"Three should be fine. I'll see you this afternoon."

Peter watched all of this without moving from where he stood, waiting in silence as Thompson walked back to him to reveal some dreadful revelation that would identify Kathleen as the perpetrator of this horrible crime.

"It's a suicide note."

Thompson passed the note to Peter.

"What? I don't understand," asked Peter, looking confused.

"It's a suicide note signed by James Robertson over there, only it's not his signature."

"I'm sorry, Ian, I still don't understand."

"It appears Robertson was lured here by Spitz, and, from the look of this note, he and Radic were planning to kill him and leave this behind. I'll know more when I've taken a formal statement from Robertson this afternoon."

An ambulance, followed by a vehicle from the Coroner's office, drove around the corner close to the front of the house.

"Ah, the cavalry!" he patted Peter on the shoulder. "Why don't you get back to your lab and see if you can identify the plant that's being used to make this drug? It looks as though some lunatic has been making some dangerous stuff with it."

Peter breathed a huge sigh of relief.

"Sure, Ian, no problem."

The drive back along the old Bondi Coast Road was almost relaxed… almost. His mind had been on overload. So much had happened in so short a time. Right now, the only important thing was to make sure Kathleen was alright. She had been through one hell of an ordeal this morning. Thanks to him finding the contract before Thompson, she was in the clear. His friend had got it wrong for sure. But Peter wasn't about to let him know that. Driving with one hand on the wheel, he opened his mobile phone and called Kathleen's home number. The phone in the flat rang and rang, but there was no reply.

An uneasy feeling was building in him as he dialled the office number. It was now quarter to eleven. Maybe Kathleen had gone downstairs and was at her desk.

After a couple of rings, Tracey the receptionist answered.

"Good morning, O'Neill's. May I help you?"

"Trace – it's Peter Wilson. Can I speak to Kath, please?"

"Oh, hi, Peter. She's just popped out for a while. Something to do with visiting an old lady. She should be back in an hour or so. Shall I get her to give you a ring when she gets in?"

Peter was fighting hard against the rising panic.

"I'll call her later. Thanks," he said and turned his mobile off. "No! No! No!" he screamed to himself. "Not now, now you're in the clear. Oh, Kath, not now!"

His right foot pushed down on the accelerator pedal as the car gained speed along the narrow gravel road. What was the name of the nursing home where Mrs Papa – whatever her name was? Deep something – it was on the tip of his tongue, yet it remained tantalisingly close. A kangaroo darted out of the bush in front of the car. Peter braked hard and swerved causing the front wheels to lock up. The car skidded for several metres, before stalling and coming to a stop on the other side of the track. The palms of his hands were sweating and he could taste the bile in his mouth as he forced himself to relax, breathing deeply and regularly. All at once, the name popped into his head.

Deepdene! Yes, that was it – The Deepdene Nursing Home, over on Philimore Street. That's where the old lady was. He looked at his watch and calculated he could be there in around twenty minutes, traffic permitting. Starting the engine, Peter straightened up the car and planted his foot on the pedal. The car leapt into life as he drove like a man possessed towards the Deepdene Nursing Home.

"Hold on, Kath, hold on." He said out loud. "Don't do anything silly. I'm coming!"

\* \* \*

Matron Banks was always in charge, especially on occasions like these.

"Oh, *do* stop your snivelling, Evelyn! Old people die in nursing homes. It is a simple fact of life. It happens all the time and you should be used to it by now."

There was a look of defiance in the nursing aide's eyes, as she delved into her pockets in search of a tissue. As usual, Banks had missed the point. An experienced and capable woman in her forties, Evelyn was no stranger to the passing of old people, but each such occasion brought sadness with it.

"I've worked in many nursing homes, Matron, and yes, you *are* right, but this is a person we're talking about here, not just a number on the register."

"Was," corrected Banks. "The important thing is to deal with this efficiently and professionally. There is a waiting list you know."

Evelyn shook her head in disbelief. The woman had no empathy at all. She may as well be in charge of a factory churning out engine parts.

"You're incredible," she said under her breath.

Missing the sarcasm, Banks swelled with pride, her ample bosom threatening to burst several buttons.

"Thank you, Evelyn. It's nice to know *someone* around here recognises that. Now, get on with sorting out the body and the room, please. I'll notify the next of kin."

Even with the door closed, the diminishing sound of the Matron's heavy footfall down the corridor was unmistakable. Evelyn was glad to have this quiet time with one of her favourite charges. She had only known Maria Papadopoulos for a brief period, months rather than years, but she had warmed to the old lady instantly and the affection was mutual, she had always felt it to be so.

Thinking of how she would gently brush the old lady's long grey hair with her treasured mother-of- pearl hairbrush, she was overcome with a mixture of great sadness and relief. Her decline had been incredibly rapid at the end as the Alzheimer's had taken over. A series of mini strokes had reduced her mobility to practically zero and she had to be hoisted in and out of bed and fed like a baby. Moments of lucidity were the exception rather than the rule as her condition worsened, but even during those clear windows, where part of the real Maria surfaced, she appeared deeply depressed, clenching her teeth, refusing food and drink. She'd decided to go and she'd picked her own time at the end. Death had at last brought relief to her suffering and, for that, Evelyn was glad.

Though it was over, the real tragedy was that she had been allowed to suffer for so long. 'Why do we let this happen when the end is obvious and the patient wants to die?' she asked herself.

Gently, she touched the old lady's cold cheek with the back of her hand.

"Goodbye, Maria, goodbye."

* * *

Peter's hands were still sweating on the steering wheel as he turned the corner and saw the sign. "Deepdene Nursing Home – where people matter." He had been driving like a demon since hearing from Tracey that Kathleen had gone to see an old lady. The car lurched into the car park and skidded to a halt. His blood ran cold.

There was Kathleen's car, neatly parked in one of the visitors' bays.

"No!" he cried out aloud and leapt from the car, abandoning it where it had stopped.

A gardener pruning a nearby hedge stopped his clipping and looked up as Peter slammed the door.

"Hey, mate. You can't park there. You're blocking those cars in!" he said, but Peter heard none of this.

Instead, his entire focus was finding Kathleen, hoping against hope that it was not too late. Finding her and stopping her from killing an old lady was now his only purpose.

He burst through the main door and quickly located the reception desk.

"Mrs Papa... Papa..." his breath came in short gasps as he struggled to remember the full name.

"Mrs Papadopoulos?" the receptionist had flat eyes and a vacant expression.

"Yes, that's it. Where can I find her?"

"I think she's in 12C... hang on a moment, I'll just check."

The receptionist located the patients' list and ran an index finger down the surname column.

"Gregory, Johannsen, Morrison..." slowly she turned the page over.

"Look, it's important!" there was no mistaking the urgency in Peter's voice.

"Nelson... Palmer... here we are... Papadopoulos... room 12E. Almost got it right, didn't I?"

"12E... which way?"

The woman leaned across the counter and pointed to a corridor on her left.

"Down there. Do you want me to show you the way?"

But Peter had already started running, his shoes fighting for purchase on the highly polished floor as he raced down the long corridor. 1D, 2D, 3D... the numbers didn't seem right, but he kept running hoping they would change. At last a new sequence began... 1E, 2E, 3E.

11E was at the end of the passageway which turned sharply to the right. Inelegantly, he rounded the corner and skidded to a stop against the far wall. Five or six elderly people were milling around outside room 12E and his heart sank as he caught bits of their conversation.

"So sad, poor love."

"At least she's out of it now."

"It happens to all of us, you know."

A couple of the residents looked up at him as he leaned against the wall, bent over with his hands on his knees catching his breath.

'Too late, I was too late. If only she'd waited,' his thoughts were interrupted by a commanding voice from inside the room.

"Come on now, there's nothing here that should interest you, people!"

It was Banks dispersing the small gathering as she moved out into the corridor.

"Back to your rooms now. Move along, come on, let's be going, did you hear what I said? Everyone, please, back to your rooms!"

Peter looked up and caught the Matron's eye.

"Can I help you, young man?" the tone was brusque, almost confrontational.

He was about to reply but the words stopped in his throat as Kathleen came out of the room and stood behind Banks.

"Kath!"

Banks turned to face Kathleen and then back to Peter.

"We're friends," he said.

This appeared to mollify Banks.

"I see. It was one of those things. Ms O'Neill dropped in to see Mrs

Papadopoulos, but sadly she had passed away. By a fortunate coincidence, Mrs Papadopoulos had made her funeral arrangements some time ago with Ms O'Neill, so we can sort things out fairly quickly."

Peter and Kathleen's eyes were locked together, neither spoke.

Banks turned to Kathleen.

"Can I leave the rest to you, Ms O'Neill? The doctor said he'd sign the death certificate when he gets here. I'm sure there will be no need for an autopsy, it's clearly natural causes."

Kathleen nodded and Peter swallowed hard.

"Thank you, Matron. I'll arrange to have someone call to remove the body after the doctor's been."

Kathleen's voice was even and controlled, giving nothing away of her earlier trauma.

"Excellent. We have a large waiting list, you know. Goodbye, Ms O'Neill."

Banks turned on her heel and marched down the corridor leaving Peter and Kathleen alone, the silence between them unbroken, the angst in each other's eyes unchanged.

Peter was the first to speak:

"Kath, why didn't you wait? You promised me you'd wait."

"I couldn't Peter, O'Neill's had promised the old lady we'd help her and this was something I had to do. I'm so sorry for everything, Peter. I didn't mean for Spitz or the other guy to drink the remedy, but I didn't give it to them, I swear, they just took it. I know I'm going to go to jail anyway, so I thought it might as well be for the right reason and not the wrong one. That's why I came here. It was cruel to let the poor lady suffer any longer, she hated the thought of being like that and it was exactly the situation she wanted to avoid, not just for herself, but for her family as well."

"There's going to be an investigation now, you realise that, don't you?" said Peter, who was trying to hold back his tears.

Kathleen moved closer to Peter and put her arms around him, tears running down her face.

"Peter, please try and understand, I had to honour the promise. I knew it would be only a matter of time before Ian Thompson put all the pieces together and knocked on my door. Spitz and his enforcer are dead, aren't they? That's what the call was about?"

Peter nodded and said, "Yes, they're both dead, looking just like Strapp and Cosgrove."

"So it was all for nothing. I was too late anyway," she was crying quietly.

"Too late for what, Kath?" he stood back and stroked her hair.

His heart was breaking.

Kathleen took his hand in hers.

"Peter, let me show you something."

Kathleen led him into the room. An old lady lay on the bed, her long grey hair reaching to her waist. Her face was calm and placid.

"This is Mrs Papadopoulos. She died peacefully in her sleep last night. One of the nurses found her this morning about seven o'clock and called the doctor. He's on his way here now."

Peter turned to Kathleen with a puzzled look on his face.

"So you didn't…"

"No, it was all over by the time I arrived. It's the only time O'Neill's has failed to honour a promise, but I would have gone through with it if I could have. I can deal with death, but unnecessary suffering is the one thing I will never be able to abide. It's been my family's tradition to help ease suffering for one hundred and fifty years and now it's all over and it's my fault. I failed. I kept putting it off and I shouldn't have and, when I finally got up the courage to do it, when I was on my way here, I had the accident with Jock. The old lady didn't die the way she wanted to. We made her a promise and we failed her. Believe me, Peter, that is almost as hard for me to live with as the thought of being taken away from you. Please forgive me. I'm so sorry to have done this to you. You are the last person in the world I ever wanted to hurt."

"Kath, listen to me, there's something you don't know."

She looked into his eyes as he spoke.

"After Spitz and Radic left you, they went to meet James Robertson at the old Harris place at the end of the Bondi Coast Road, by the top of the cliff."

"James Robertson, the funeral director?"

"Yes, and Spitz had a suicide note in the car, a suicide note signed by Robertson, only of course it wasn't really Robertson's signature."

"Peter, please, I don't understand you. What has this got to do with anything?"

"Kath, please listen to what I'm trying to tell you. There's very strong evidence that Spitz and Radic were planning to kill Robertson and make it look like suicide. Your unwitting intervention in their plan undoubtedly saved his life. If they hadn't called on you this morning and drank the mixture you'd prepared for this poor soul," he said, pointing to the old lady, "then undoubtedly Robertson would be dead by now."

He paused, giving her time to take in what he'd said.

"I'm glad they didn't kill Robertson. At least one good thing has come out of all this, but that doesn't really change anything. It won't help me. Spitz took the contract of sale with him with my signature on it. Ian will figure it out and come looking for me, that's a certainty."

Peter grabbed her by the shoulders and held her at arm's length, looking pleadingly into her eyes.

"*Listen* to me, will you? I know that Spitz had the contract, but I found it first!"

"What?"

"Kath, I'm trying to tell you that I found it before Thompson did. It's in my briefcase. He will never know that you saw Spitz and Radic this morning, unless you tell him, because I'm not going to!"

"Oh, Peter. You tampered with the evidence. You did that for me. Oh God, I didn't want to get you involved in all of this."

"I am involved, Kath, because I love you and I know that, whatever I think of what you did, you did it for the most noble of reasons. However misguided I think you are, I know you were motivated by kindness. If I'm honest with myself, a part of me agrees with what you tried to do, especially after seeing what happened to my own mother."

"Do you really mean that, Peter?" she asked. "Because if you do, it makes this bearable. I couldn't tell you about our family secret. I wanted to so many times. I really did, especially when you asked about the plant.

"Now Kath, listen to me. You have to keep your head and trust me. There's a connection with Spitz and Cosgrove. They were seen by a nurse on the balcony at the end of Jock's ward on the night Jock died. They were out there having a smoke."

"Really?"

"Cosgrove was a known drug dealer and, if he was Spitz's supplier, which Thompson now suspects, Cosgrove could have sold him some dodgy pills the night they met on the balcony, which Spitz then shared with Radic. The drugs theory explains three of the bodies at least. So, as long as Thompson doesn't find out that Spitz and his goon paid you a visit this morning, the evidence doesn't point to you at all."

Peter paused to let this part of the explanation sink in, before continuing, "Ian has thought from the start that a new drug was the most likely cause of

Jock's and Cosgrove's deaths. The only thing he couldn't figure out was how Jock got hold of it, but you're not a suspect, Kath. The most likely explanation is that there's another unknown dealer who sold the stuff to Jock as well as to Cosgrove. No one, except you and I, will ever know what really happened. Ian will only be able to surmise what happened, but he'll never know for sure."

"You mean it's over, it's all over?"

"Yes, you're in the clear, Kath, but if you'd gone through with this here, with the old lady, you would have had a lot of explaining to do. Maria died of natural causes, which is the way it is meant to be. It's not for us to intervene."

Peter was watching her carefully. If there was ever a moment when shock could take over, this was certainly it. He didn't have long to wait.

"Peter, oh, Peter…"

Her legs buckled and she began to teeter like a drunk. In a flash, he wrapped a strong arm around her waist, taking all her weight.

"It's alright, I'm here."

\* \* \*

Ian Thompson looked at the flip chart with the boxes, names and interconnecting lines. Now that Spitz and Radic were both dead, the inquiry was firmly going in the direction of drug dealers, especially those connected to Cosgroveand the most likely suspect was Stephen Pickersgill.

When first questioned, Stephen had displayed an uncompromising attitude to the policeman, but his demeanour had quickly changed, when he realised he was a suspect in a murder enquiry. After that, the young thug became far more cooperative, which convinced Thompson that Pickersgill knew a lot more about these deaths than he was letting on.

"So, Stephen, you say that your mate, Cosgrove, only supplied a few bags of weed here and there and only to some of his friends?"

"That's right, just a couple of bags."

"So how come the word on the street is that Cosgrove was working for the Donatello brothers?" Thompson demanded.

The suspect ran a comb through greasy hair which had not seen a shampoo bottle for at least a week, then produced a packet of cigarettes. In a flash, one was in his mouth and about to be lit.

"Not in here!"

Thompson snatched it from him, the command taking the man by surprise and stopping him dead in his tracks. Stephen put the cigarette back in its packet, a defeated look on his face.

Thompson smiled.

"You haven't answered my question, Stephen. Was Cosgrove working for the Donatello brothers?"

"No, mate, no fucking way. Anyway, who told you he was?"

"We all know the Donatellos are into class A drugs in a big way. Your name even came up in connection with their distribution a couple of times."

Thompson bluffed and Stephen was visibly shaken.

"What? I don't know what you're talking about. I don't touch the hard stuff, and I've never sold it neither. Hey, I know I've had a couple of previous for dope, but hard drugs – hell, no, that's not my scene."

Thompson looked unconvinced.

"Really, Stephen? I find that very hard to believe. I know that you and Kevin were mates and he must have talked to you, so until you tell me what you know, you're not going anywhere. I've got plenty of time. Now tell me the truth, was Cosgrove trying out any new stuff?"

"How would I know what he was doing?" replied Stephen defensively.

"New stuff that's stronger and cheaper than crack and can get you high as a kite. If I've heard about it, I'm sure you have."

There had been rumours of a new drug in town, although that's all they were – rumours. Thompson and his team had been unable to gather any hard evidence. However, Cosgrove's name had come up on more than one occasion. Right now he was fishing and he felt he was close to getting a bite.

"I don't know anything about a new fucking drug," Stephen replied forcefully.

Thompson got up from his chair and poured a cup of coffee from a heated glass jug on the coffee machine.

"OK, Stephen, have it your way, but the Donatellos are going to know you were in here. I just might let it slip you were cooperative, in fact *very* cooperative, when it came to supplying information about their distribution network."

The man was on his feet in a flash.

"You can't do that to me, Mr Thompson. If you do that, I'm a marked man. I don't know anything about the Donatellos' business."

The bluff had worked. If Pickersgill knew anything at all, he would now talk.

"If you put word on the street that I'm a grass, I'll end up dead. I could swear on a stack of bibles that nothing happened here today, but the Donatellos don't take chances."

"Well, it's up to you now, Stephen. If you stop lying and tell me what you know, I promise not to spread any dangerous rumours. OK?"

Thompson took a sip of the coffee and looked disinterestedly into the cup, before continuing, "So answer the question, Stephen. Was Cosgrove into anything new?"

"Look, I'll tell you everything I know, but you gotta swear on your mother's life you won't say anything to nobody. Deal?"

Thompson continued to look into the cup.

"Deal?"

Now he was getting somewhere.

"Kevin told me that there was a new pill comin' with a 'high' that would take your head off."

Thompson nodded, but said nothing, waiting instead for Stephen to elaborate.

"That's all I know, Mr Thompson, honest."

The policeman was not impressed and it showed in his tone.

"Who was his supplier? Did he ever mention a man called Spitz?"

"He never mentioned any one like that. I don't know where he got his stuff. That's the God's honest truth. Kevin never talked about his contacts."

"Did he ever try out new stuff himself before he started dealing?"

Stephen shifted uncomfortably in his chair, a reluctance to speak beginning to creep into the conversation.

Thompson however was keen to maintain the pressure.

"Come on, Stephen, Kevin's dead and now three more people he had connections to are dead as well. The stuff is lethal. We've got to get it off the streets. What if your kid brother got his hands on it? How would you feel then? You *have* to give me the name of the supplier."

"I don't know. I've got no idea where those fucking pills came from. All I know is that Kev got some new gear and was goin' to try it out himself. He told everybody that, if it was as good as he was told, it would make him rich as Bondy. It must have been the gear that killed him, because I've never seen him so high. He was bringing me some while I was in the Sydney Memorial to cheer me up. You know what I mean, but he always tried stuff first, so I had to wait. I guess he saved my life."

He looked at the policeman, a tear trickled down his face as he considered how close he had come to death.

"Go on," replied Thompson reassuringly.

"Kev had gone out for a smoke, and, when he came back, he was laughing like a lunatic. Then, all of a sudden, he stopped and his eyes went funny. He dropped right then, with this mad grin on his face. I thought he was muckin' about, but when Kev didn't answer, I started yelling for the nurses and a load of them came rushin' into the room. They were all poundin' on his chest, but it was no good. He was a gonner."

"So did Kevin give you any pills?"

"Yeah."

"What did you do with them?"

"Shit. What would you do with them, if you just saw someone laugh themselves to death? I got shot of them quick, down the dunny. I didn't want any found on me, after what happened to Kev. In fact, I poured all the pills Kev had on him down the bog as well. They were in Kev's shorts, but the nurses never saw them. I took them when the nurses went out of the room to get a gurney."

"So, did Kevin always try the stuff first, before he sold it?"

"Always. Kevin's stuff always gave you a good buzz. He'd never sell it to you, unless he knew it was good gear and tested it for himself. Kevin thought customer satisfaction was really important."

And then as an after thought, he added, "Kevin was a real professional like that. He wouldn't do you."

Thompson grimaced, as another rogue tear appeared on Stephen's face. He tried not to show his disgust and looked away from the young punk. Whilst having this stuff on the streets was bad news, the veteran copper, normally a kind and sympathetic man, wasn't in the slightest bit sorry to hear of Cosgrove's demise. So far, apart from Jock, these pills seemed to have cleared the streets of some pretty unsavoury characters.

"Have you got any idea how many pills Kevin got his hands on?"

"No, he only had a few on him, about half a dozen, in a packet. They were red, like mini-torpedoes. Kev never carried much gear, 'cos he was always being pulled up by the cops. Only took out what he needed to do the biz. I heard his brother got rid of the whole supply, after what happened and no one's going to touch the stuff now."

Thompson hoped that was true.

"OK, Stephen, you've been helpful. Thank you."

"What about the Donatellos?"

"What about them?"

"If they think I've been talking to the law about their business…"

Thompson walked over to the man and patted him on the shoulder:

"Don't worry about that, Stephen, I think this conversation can remain our little secret, don't you? I think we're about done for today. You're free to go."

Stephen needed little encouragement and was at the door in a flash.

"Thanks, Mr Thompson."

By the time the policeman had closed the door behind him, Stephen was halfway down the main corridor and on his way to the street.

Thompson looked again at the flip chart. The information before him fitted the profile of the case. He was a little surprised that Spitz and Radic had taken amphetamines at all, however Cosgrove had the opportunity to supply Spitz with the red torpedoes. Although the evidence was circumstantial, the deaths of Spitz and Radic, in the same manner as Cosgrove, strongly suggested a bad batch of uppers supplied by the latter, was the most likely cause of all three deaths. It didn't explain Jock which had opened up a new line of enquiry. Who was the dealer who supplied Cosgrove and did he also supply the Scotsman?

After speaking to Stephen, he interviewed Kevin's brother, who confirmed the story that the 'red torpedoes' had all been destroyed. Thompson had little choice but to accept their assertions that none of these men knew the name of Cosgrove's supplier. They all swore that the information had gone with Kevin to his grave. Hopefully, there would be no more fatal little red pills popping up, but Thompson was still no closer to finding out the mysterious substance in them, which created such 'a high' and yet which left no discernable trace in any of the bodies.

Peter had also been unable to shed any further light on the matter.

\* \* \*

The bedside clock read three seventeen am. For Peter and Kathleen, it had been the most anxious day either had ever endured. Now, lying together in the quiet of the small hours, sleep was gradually taking its toll.

Peter cupped Kathleen's face in his hand and whispered softly, "When I saw your car in the nursing home car park, I thought I was going to lose you forever."

Kathleen's arm was draped across his chest. She hugged him more tightly.

"If you'd given the drink to the old lady, Thompson would have realised that you were behind the deaths, not Cosgrove. He would have arrested you and then raided the flat and found the plant. That evidence would have put you away for life. I don't think I could have handled that."

He pulled her body tighter against his own, unwilling to let go of what he had come so close to losing.

"No more, Kath, promise me, no more. I couldn't bear it."

"I promise."

Her reply was barely audible as he gently stroked her hair.

"I love you, Kath."

"Mmmm," was her only response, followed by deep rhythmic breathing as she fell into a deep sleep.

"I love you, Kath," he repeated and fought no longer against the heaviness that was forcing his eyes to close.

* * *

The new week brought fresh hope and renewed promise as the sun shone brightly through a cloudless sky. Peter and Kathleen rose together and, after a quiet breakfast, Peter kissed her goodbye and made his way to the laboratory. There was still much to talk through, but it would keep until this evening. Right now, both were content to let themselves be carried along by the current that is the daily routine.

The laboratory was as busy as ever and, for this, Peter was grateful, losing himself in the examination of a cell culture under a microscope, when a tap on his shoulder followed by a cheery "Morning!" announced the arrival of Ian Thompson.

"Hello, Ian, how's everything?"

"Good, Peter, good."

"Really?"

Peter was still anxious about the ongoing investigation in what had come to be known as the 'Dead Happy' case.

"Yes, I managed to pull in some of Cosgrove's cohorts and I think I've got to the bottom of the case of our smiling corpses... a new pill, known as the red torpedo.

"The red what?"

Peter tried his hardest not to look alarmed.

"I interrogated Cosgrove's mates and it seems our violent little gangster was keen on quality control, so he always tested his products himself. Tell you what, meet me after work and I'll tell you the whole story. I've also got something important to tell you and the walls have ears here."

Peter was anxious all day and his nerves completely on edge as he sat down with Thompson at the 'Wallaby's Watering Hole.'

He helped himself to a cold bottle of beer, which Thompson had poured out for him.

"Well," said Peter, apprehensively, "what's this secret news?"

He had been terrified since the morning that Thompson might have uncovered something about Kathleen.

"I'm taking early retirement, my boy, and I wanted you to be the first to know."

"You're retiring?"

Peter's relief was palpable.

"I think that's a great idea, Ian," he responded. "When?"

"At the end of the month, as it happens. This last case with Spitz and Cosgrove has been very taxing. It's been on my mind for ages now. I decided I'd been in the game too long when I started taking it home with me. However I look at it, there are still some things that don't quite fit. I don't know who gave Jock the red torpedoes, though ironically he probably had a kinder end as a result."

Peter was again alarmed, but he needn't have worried.

" What conclusions have you drawn, Ian?"

"You remember the Jacko Sullivan funeral?"

"Who could forget it?" Peter exclaimed.

"I had a chat a couple of days ago with 'My Ways' pyrotechnic expert and he confirmed that Spitz had ordered a couple of devices, just ahead of the Sullivan funeral, ostensibly for fireworks in which to scatter the ashes of a couple of his clients. A check through his books showed no such funerals occurred immediately prior to the Jacko funeral and netiher had any been booked. If Spitz and Radic were still alive I would be charging them both with sabotage and intimidation. Humphries - the funeral director whose hearse was towed into the cemetary - sold up to a property developer about a week ago and moved over to WA. I managed to get hold of him by phone and, once he heard what happened to Spitz and Radic, he told me the whole story. By all accounts, those two were a nasty couple of bastards. I believe that Robertson's only still with us because fate, in the way of some fatal uppers, appear to have found their way to Spitz via Cosgrove."

"Aren't you still looking for Cosgrove's supplier?" Peter asked.

"My enquiries drew a blank. If anybody knows where the drugs originated, they aren't talking, but his mates were so shocked by what happened to their buddy, they swear they ditched the entire batch. With luck, the dealer knows by now what happened and has got rid of the rest. After next week, all this will be somebody else's problem so long as no more grinning bodies turn up."

"Well, Ian, that's quite a case to end on."

"I guess so and now I've decided to do it, I'm quite looking forward to my retirement. After spending so much time with all these funeral directors lately, it occurred to me that I'm not getting any younger and that maybe it was time for me to enjoy myself a bit, so I handed in my notice this morning."

'That's it, it's really over,' thought Peter. 'He and Kathleen were safe.'

He breathed a sigh of relief.

"Well, I guess this calls for a toast," said Peter, raising his beer glass. Relief was mixed with a touch of sadness.

"Cheers, my friend. To a happy retirement. I'm going to miss you, Ian, I really am."

Thompson raised his glass in acknowledgement.

"Cheers, Peter. For what it's worth, I'm going to miss you too."

"Well, Ian, I've got some news too," announced Peter conspiratorially.

The policeman shot him a quizzical look.

"What kind of news?"

"Good news, the best news. Kath and I are getting married."

Thompson could hardly contain himself. He reached across and grabbed Peter by the hand and pumped it vigorously.

"Congratulations, Peter, congratulations!"

"And there's more."

He paused for effect.

"I've been offered a post in Ireland, County Cork. It's a brilliant job, with a lot more money than I'm earning here. I'd be heading up the forensic team at the police headquarters there."

"Peter, that's terrific news. Well done."

"It'll be the most senior position I've held and it will open a lot of doors for me career-wise. We're both pleased about it. Kath's going to sell the business and we're going to give it a go in Ireland. She's got lots of family there and, since her father died, she's pretty well on her own out here, apart from me. I've been thinking about living overseas for ages. To be honest, Ireland had always appealed to me. Who knows, I might even take up drinking Guinness!"

"Well, I don't know about Guinness, but this certainly calls for another round of Tooheys."

He signalled to a passing waitress.

"Another couple of Tooheys, love, ice cold if you please, before this man develops a taste for stout!"

# Epilogue

He could scarcely believe there'd been time to go to work, let alone any kind of relaxation as well. It was a perfect November spring morning. Temperature in the mid twenties, not a cloud in the sky and a gentle breeze coming off the lake.

Ian Thompson had always loved the countryside, with its clean air and tranquility. It was the perfect place to unwind, relax and generally be as one with nature. Thirty six years in the police department – it seemed a lifetime ago.

A crow called lazily in the distance as he checked the fishing line and float. Still nothing, not that it mattered actually, the purpose was not to catch fish if the truth be known. That was incidental to the whole exercise. This was a time for rest and reflection, a kind of healing balm to cover the aches and pains of the last three and a half decades.

The year since he had retired had flown past and, although he missed the camaraderie with his work colleagues, he didn't miss the stress and tension the job brought with it. His mind drifted onto Peter Wilson, the son he wished he'd had. Yes, he missed Peter and the special bond that had grown between them, but he was happy for the lad – happy he had found a lovely girl and also, so it seemed, left the rat race. There was the occasional letter, but nothing in the last few months. He made a mental note to write to them both as he reached for his Thermos flask and poured a cup of tea.

It really was a beautiful morning. A copy of the morning's newspaper lay at his feet and he picked it up and began to idly leaf through it.

A small article on page fourteen caught his attention.

'Ireland – the happiest place in the world to die.'

It went on to describe how an elderly man had died in hospital with a look of utter joy on his face, a phenomenon inexplicable to the medical staff. There was some speculation a miracle had taken place and even eye witness accounts of the Virgin Mary herself appearing at the deceased's bedside immediately prior to his passing. The local Bishop was quoted as saying the church would be conducting a thorough investigation into the alleged sightings of the Blessed Virgin.

An uneasy feeling registered deep in the pit of Ian Thompson's stomach, as his mind leapt back to when he was a young boy and present at his mother's neighbour's funeral. The stone church, the open casket, the grinning body, the black hearse waiting outside, the name on the hearse... O'Neill's?

Quickly, he scanned the article – it appeared to end suddenly, until he read the addendum – continued on page seventeen and there it was, right at the end.

"... the funeral service was conducted by O'Neill's of Co Cork."

The plastic cup of tea rolled out of his hand and onto the ground as he stared blankly at the last sentence... O'Neill's.

Was it possible, had he missed the obvious? Surely not. Suddenly he felt tired, very tired. Grappling with the enormity of what this small article indicated had left him physically drained. The policeman's curiosity had been pricked and his brain involuntarily leapt into investigation mode. He had to remind himself that he had retired.

In any event the thought was so fantastic, he knew no one would take the idea of some kind of sinister plot to end life with a grinning trademark seriously. He could hardly entertain the thought himself, but...

His mind inevitably wandered in that direction. O'Neill was a common name in Ireland and perhaps the funeral director was a different O'Neill and had nothing to do with Kathleen. And yet, deep down inside, he knew this obscure article involved not just Kathleen, but Peter also. There were, he reasoned, only two available courses of action. One – convince his ex-colleagues to reopen the closed files on Spitz, Radic, Strapp and Cosgrove, or two – let sleeping dogs lie.

The float on the fishing line bobbed up and down. He reached for his rod and reeled the line in, at the end of which was a gleaming, fat barramundi, thrashing about, but going nowhere. Slowly, he rose from the camping chair and took the fish in one hand. The wriggling stopped as though somehow the fish had realised it was all over.

Ian Thompson gently removed the hook from inside the fish's mouth and carefully placed the animal back in the water. A few rapid strokes of its fins and the barramundi was gone.

Thompson smiled.

"It wasn't meant to be," he said quietly to the deserted countryside. "It wasn't meant to be."

# County Cork, 2009

It was a bitterly cold November afternoon, the wind whipping up piles of fallen leaves and throwing them against the side of the stone country parish church. A light drizzle had persisted all day and the skies were grey and threatening. Inside the church was at least dry, but the ancient building suffered from numerous drafts and the slate floor did little to create a sense of warmth. The iron radiators barely coped in these temperatures, so perhaps it was no surprise that the small congregation, rather than spreading out, huddled together in a common physical purpose. Over the years, Father Chatten had conducted many Requiem Masses, but the ones which always had a ring of finality to them were small gatherings in weather such as this.

The mass had been said according to the catechism and now it was time for the congregation, if they so chose, to pay their last respects to the deceased.

The priest's voice was clear and strong, reverberating around the stone walls and floor.

"You may now pay your final respects to our dearly departed."

One by one, parts of the congregation rose from their pews and formed an orderly line down the aisle towards the open casket. Seamus Murphy, brother of the deceased, was first. Slowly, he made his way to the open coffin, placed just in front of the altar. Grabbing the handrail to support his ageing legs, he stepped up to the casket and peered over the top.

"Jaaayyysussss!"

His brother, no longer of this earth, smiled back at him, a look of pure joy on his face – dead but happy.

Peter Wilson, chief mourner and part owner of O'Neill's, stood impassively at the rear of the church, a knowing look on his face.

THE END
...or is it?

# About The Authors

*Photo by Harold Neville ARPS*

Warwick was born in Australia and came to the UK for a working holiday in 1974. Within a year he had met Fru, a second generation Greek Cypriot who had just completed a Sociology degree, and they married two years later and had three children. Warwick is currently working in IT and has also worked as an accountant, bulldozer driver, self defence instructor and successful restaurateur.

*Photo by Harold Neville ARPS*

Fru's career has spanned youth work, catering and even some time as a private investigator. The authors had the idea for Dead Happy over a meal, and despite five years of hard toil and creative differences, remain happily married. They hope this is the first of many successful collaborations. A screenplay of the book is currently in development.